James M. Galloway

John Harvey

A Tale of the Twentieth Century

James M. Galloway

John Harvey
A Tale of the Twentieth Century

ISBN/EAN: 9783337023430

Printed in Europe, USA, Canada, Australia, Japan

Cover: Foto ©Andreas Hilbeck / pixelio.de

More available books at **www.hansebooks.com**

JOHN HARVEY

A TALE OF THE TWENTIETH CENTURY

BY

ANON MOORE

CHICAGO
CHARLES H. KERR & COMPANY
1897

DEDICATION.

I dedicate this book to my Wife, who has been my only critic and helper, and whose sympathy and appreciation have been my stimulus in the work.   A. M.

CONTENTS

5

I am the eldest son of the Duke of Dorsetshire, and for many years bore the title of Lord Herbert Maxwell Dudley. I enjoyed superior educational advantages, being sent to the best schools in England and Germany, where I studied with assiduity, and became proficient in all the branches necessary to a liberal education.

On attaining my majority, desiring to see service, I entered the British navy, and held the rank of lieutenant on his majesty's ship Vulcan at the time of her destruction in the harbor of Yokohama, in nineteen hundred and twenty-nine.

I then quitted the navy, and for several years thereafter traveled extensively in various portions of the globe; generally on business connected with the governmental service of Great Britain, but always seeking information about certain problems, in which I was much interested, concerning the advancement of the human race.

I had at one time or another visited the great capitals of Europe, the time-worn and historic cities of Asia, and had picked my way through the motley crowds that throng the narrow streets of China and Japan.

In all these places I had mixed with the highest, the lowest and the middle class of citizens, my object being to observe the various races of mankind in all their developments, and to study philosophically the causes of the poverty and degradation which have always attended them.

In the countries which I visited, various reasons were given for these evils, but none of them were at all satisfactory to me. I had heard the stock phrases of the classes supposed to be most conversant with such subjects—the clergy, with their high moral tone and proffers of a compensatory immortality beyond the grave, blessed promise in which I fully believe; the Malthusian philsopher, with his statistics in regard to population and its proper distribution, and the statesman, with his rules of supply and demand, balance of trade, currency circulation, etc., but none of them, nor all of them together, were able to explain to me why, twenty centuries after the advent of the Prince of Peace, so little had been accomplished to elevate the masses of mankind, and to redeem them from this condition of poverty and want, and from all the burden of anxiety, sin, and woe that invariably accompanies it.

Were the people to hope for comfort and enjoyment only beyond the grave? Was it not possible to make life itself among them something more than a ceaseless treadmill of drudgery to obtain the necessaries and possibly a few of the comforts of existence? Was it not possible to remove from them the constant anxiety lest through some sickness, some error of judgment, or some other calamity their means of obtaining an independent livelihood should be lost?

In my journeyings I had observed that everywhere the members of the human family were, in all matters of business and finance, and even in social relations, in active and continued conflict with each other. I had seen that this strife was not waged for the good of the masses, though some philosophers maintained it was for the ultimate advantage of the race, but that like weaker swimmers on a tempestuous ocean many constantly gave out, and though help was sometimes extended, yet as a rule the exhausted were allowed to perish.

Could not some plan be devised by which this conflict might be avoided, by which the energies displayed in it might be employed in the interests of all, and the pride and supposed honor resulting from individual success be merged in the true pride and honor of caring for the masses, and working together for the advancement of the race?

I had thought a great deal on these subjects, but with no practical results—human ability appeared unable to control human selfishness in dealing with them.

The spring of 1935 found me at Hong Kong and with little to do except to follow my own inclinations. One evening a friend spoke to me of a body called "The Nationality," of which I had heard before as a sort of commune, located in the United States of America, occasioning great anxiety to the government of that nation by reason of its peculiar and socialistic doctrines.

My friend said that this community had been organized less than a quarter of a century previous by John Harvey, a very wealthy man of that country, and that already the unusual character of its principles, the beauty and elegance of its capital, and the comfort and prosperity of its people were attracting great attention. He advised me to visit it and study its peculiar institutions.

This being in accordance with a desire I had long entertained of traveling in the United States, in April I took passage on a steamer for San Francisco, where I arrived early in May.

In this city I heard so much in regard to the Nationality and its capital that, after stopping there only two days, I hurried on by the transcontinental railway to begin my observations within its borders.

JOHN HARVEY:

A Tale of the Twentieth Century.

CHAPTER I.

THE STATUE ON PIKE'S PEAK.

I was told that from the top of Pike's Peak, a great mountain near which I would pass on my way to the capital of the Nationality, I could get the most extensive view to be had of its territory, for if the atmosphere were clear, the outlook to the eastward would be limited only by the possibilities of human vision, the mountain standing so near the plain that nothing intercepted the sight.

On the evening of the fourth of May, 1935, I reached this locality and early on the morning of the fifth ascended the peak by a cog-wheel railway, and stood upon its summit at an elevation of over 14,000 feet above the level of the sea. A heavy fog, or cloud bank, enveloped it and hid the view, but this I was told would be dissipated by the sun's rays within an hour.

The top of the mountain contained an area of about forty acres of level but rock strewn ground, and a small station house, where food and lodging might be procured, was the only building upon it. This stood some distance back from the place on the eastern verge of the mountain, which was shown me as the best locality for obtaining a view of the plains below.

On reaching this point I dismissed the guide, a practice in which I often indulged when desiring to com-

mune uninterruptedly with Nature, and seating myself on
a convenient stone awaited the rising of the fog.

I had recently learned that the Nationality, instead of
being small in territorial extent, as I had previously
thought, embraced a very large area, including the States
of Utah, South Dakota, Nebraska, Kansas, Colorado,
Wyoming, Arizona, New Mexico, and a large part of
Texas; being about one-fourth the size of Europe, and
containing within its borders a population of over ten
million souls.

The plain or level portion of this country a few years
before had been arid land, producing nothing except
short, scanty grass. It had been reclaimed by the construction of a great canal, some hundreds of miles in length,
taken out of the Missouri, one of the great rivers that
traverse the United States.

This work was attributed to John Harvey and had resulted in converting the region into one of remarkable
fertility.

The fog had now begun to lift along the sides of the
mountain, swirling and turning like a live thing in the
calorific influence of the ascending sun. Through its rifts
could occasionally be seen the ragged edges of piles of
granite rocks, and as it let go the mountain's rugged sides,
these were relieved at lower altitudes, by patches of green
pines, and by momentary glimpses of the plain itself. Finally
as the fog broke away entirely and was lifted above me, it
unveiled a view of the plain below, grand in its limitless
extent; beautiful in its verdure, in its variety of coloring,
in its trees, lakes, and ribbon-like streams; and interesting
in the promise of human life, activity, and enterprise, given
by the countless villages and hamlets which could now be
seen on its surface.

The plain touched the very base of the mighty mountain mass on whose summit I sat, and in its high cultivation formed a striking contrast to the rough granite sides of the Peak.

One seemed to be looking from the abode of pristine wildness and Nature into a wonderful garden, vast in extent, and smiling and beautiful in its variety and fertility.

As the mists cleared away, revealing more and more of its surface, I found fresh enjoyment in the contemplation of the region I was about to visit.

The air was pure and clear, the light bright and strong, and there was a newness and exhilaration about the scene such as had never before possessed me in gazing on a landscape.

At the height from which I viewed it, all details blended into the general effect of a great painting, stretched out before me, complete in every part and wonderful in its rich though quiet coloring. The varying shades of green in the fields, grass, and trees; the lighter coloring touched in by the azure tints of numerous lakes and water-courses; the darker shades of newly plowed ground and the shadowy outlines of towns, villages and roadways; all combined to form a most harmonious and enchanting picture; a dream landscape which seemed at any moment ready to dissolve and fade away.

For a long time I gazed upon it, giving myself up to the charm of the situation, imagining the land itself as the abode of an elevated and elevating humanity; as a realization of something, hitherto visionary, exciting feelings of joyous hope and admiration.

At length I recalled my wandering thoughts and began to examine more closely into details.

In the foreground, a large town, or city, embowered in shade, was plainly visible; and in the distance toward the north there seemed another, far greater in extent, with faint domes of colossal size and high structures glistening white in the rising sunlight. I was not sure the latter was real, and taking from my pocket a small map of the locality, which I had procured in the little hamlet at the foot of the mountain, I followed the direction on it and found that what I saw so dimly was an actual city, Neuropolis, the capital city of the Nationality.

I had heard accounts of its beauty from various travelers whom I had met, but had always considered them as tinged with that love of the marvelous so innate in humanity, but now, looking upon this landscape, I felt willing to give credence to any tale, however wonderful, respecting it.

Is it possible, thought I, that this land was, less than a quarter of a century ago, an arid waste? Is it possible that human ingenuity and skill have made it the paradise it seems? Verily if in so short a time my dreams of a dwelling place and a material country have been so fully realized, can I not expect the fulfillment here of other dreams of the enfranchisement of the race?

Was John Harvey the man who first conceived the idea of this transformation? Was it he who had begun this work of converting the wilderness into a land of homes?

He was not entirely a stranger to me. I had known him as performing audacious deeds and possessing wonderful and almost supernatural powers, used, alas! for no such purposes as these, but ruthlessly and cruelly. I had seen the evidence that he was a very rich man, and had been told that he owned a principality, which he had given away.

Could it be possible that I was now looking at it?

The great river coming from the north; had John Harvey made a way for that?

I had heard something of a city he had founded; was it the one I saw in the dim distance? How much or how little of all this was really John Harvey's work?

I had known him only by far different deeds, deeds exciting abhorrence. Doubtless these great works were the products of many minds and many efforts, though not of many years.

Turning as these thoughts passed through my mind and looking around, I saw just behind me, not thirty feet away, the figure of a man, bare-headed and holding a cocked hat in his left hand, his face turned toward me, his eyes shaded from the sun by his uplifted right hand, looking, as I conjectured, directly on me, and I knew him to be John Harvey.

The figure stood still, and when I had recovered from my first sensation of alarm I surveyed it with the utmost attention.

I now saw the eyes were not fixed on me, but were gazing out over the land, with an earnestness and interest such as I had seldom seen depicted on a human face—the whole being, indeed, seemed engaged in the contemplation of the landscape before him. There was an eagerness to observe, a rapt attention, strikingly evident in the eye, the ear, the hand, and the whole attitude.

The body was slightly bent forward, one foot in advance of the other, as if the motion onward had hardly been arrested. The face was noble, kind, and yet very forceful; the nose was large, as was the mouth, the latter firmly compressed; the nostrils wide, the lower jaw strong. The curves of the lips, nose, and brow were graceful, the latter high and full, the eyes dark and piercing, and the figure majestic and commanding.

The feet were cased in boots with whitish tops turned down from near the knee; whitish breeches, or small clothes, covered the lower limbs; a waistcoat of the same color protected the chest, leaving visible shirt front, collar and wristbands of the purest white. A long black overcoat fell below the middle of the leg, and a black tie completed the attire.

The hands were bare, and extremely shapely as were the feet; the face was clean-shaven, and the hair black, sprinkled with gray, but abundant. The left hand held the hat, apparently just removed.

Such was the figure I saw thus unexpectedly; the fog had concealed it as I walked to my place of observation. It was a face and a figure one seldom sees and never forgets, and could belong to none other than to him whom men called John Harvey.

I gazed at this lifelike apparition. Its freshness and vigor were in apt keeping with that of the landscape below. There was not a mark of time's ravages upon it, no corroded line, no blurred or marred feature. In face, in form, in raiment, the man was as complete, as faultless, as if, being yet alive, he had stepped from the train and walked in company with me to the spot where he now stood.

The statue, for such I soon found it to be, was placed upon a low pedestal, or platform rather, of dressed granite about eight feet square, which was covered with the semblance of an altar cloth, made of some strange black material hanging in folds over the sides and ends.

Who placed this imposing memorial on this rocky height, and what was its significance? Was it the work of a few cherished friends, or was it the grateful remembrance of an entire people?

I could not tell, but if John Harvey had really planned, or if his means had made possible the redemption of this land, how appropriately was his statue placed on this lofty pinnacle.

Might not his tempestuous soul occasionally revisit its former abodes and find solace in beholding the happy fruition of these great designs in the peaceful landscape before me. Might it not even now linger near enjoying the emotions which the scene undoubtedly revealed in my face and actions?

I remained some time longer on the summit, now gazing eastward on the landscape ever changing in the shifting light of the sun, and again looking westward on the billows of granite peaks lifting their gray tops skyward, as if a mighty ocean, stirred 'by a mighty storm, had been at some omnipotent fiat suddenly converted into stone.

At lower altitudes, in the intervals among the mountains, lay countless grassy parks, fit dwelling places for peace, quiet and content, and higher up, their sides were clothed by dark masses of sombre pines, and sometimes by a dense undergrowth of smaller trees whose varieties were unknown to me, but which lent color to the scene.

But I looked often and long at the face of the statue, so strong, so earnest, so eager, so sympathetic, gazing out over the land where the man had once dwelt, and from which he was now parted, and I left the spot deeply impressed with the mingled grandeur and pathos of this attempt to insure earthly immortality and remembrance.

I returned to the busy chatel at the base of the mountain, with a feeling of deep interest in this land and all that concerned it.

In the afternoon I continued my journey toward Neuropolis, haunted all the way by the face and figure of the statue of the peak, now left behind me in the awful solitude of the upper air, but still able to overlook the hurrying train as it sped northward toward the capital city.

CHAPTER II.

I reached Neuropolis late in the evening and found lodgings in one of the great hotels of the city.

I had resolved on maintaining an incognito that I might better and more unobtrusively observe and study the institutions of the country, and had prepared for this by procuring letters of introduction and recommendation in the name simply of Mr. Herbert Maxwell, and had so registered and made myself known since landing in America.

A great city, as well as a great country, has many sides, and the stranger desirous of acquiring more than a cursory knowledge of it would better begin with the study of its physical features.

My first days in the capital were accordingly spent in examining its topography and other material characteristics.

It is situated on the eastern side of the great canal before mentioned, about fifty miles from the base of the mountains, and a few miles northward from the summit or crest of the divide between the watersheds of the Arkansas and Platte Rivers.

It is surrounded by a branch of this canal, taken out twenty miles to the northward, running thence eastward and southward, forming in natural depressions several large lakes and emptying into another great branch of the canal known as Lateral B, fifty miles from the point of departure.

The true form of the city proper was a perfect square, but extensive suburbs, to the north and south, gave it somewhat of an oval appearance.

The great freight depots and manufactories for the heavier classes of goods, as well as the plants for furnishing water, electricity, heat and other necessities of the city, were located in the northern suburbs, while the passenger depots and manufactories for the lighter and cleaner classes of goods were situated in the southern. Both suburbs, however, were connected with the great trunk lines of railroad running in all directions from the city. The manufactories and business houses in them, though not lofty, were large and comfortable, and everything around them was kept scrupulously neat and clean.

The employes nearly all lived in the city proper, going to and returning from their labors night and morning in vehicles driven by electricity.

These suburbs, though a part of the city and under the same general government as the rest of it, were divided from it by a boulevard two hundred feet wide, which encompassed it on its four sides. They are not therefore included in the description which I shall now give, with the aid of the accompanying diagram, of the city proper.

A great square, each side facing a cardinal point of the compass and measuring twelve hundred feet in length, formed the center of the city. This contained about thirty acres and was called the Administration Square. An avenue two hundred feet wide, known as the Administration Boulevard, extended around this square. It was divided lengthwise in the center, except where the other boulevards hereafter mentioned entered it, by an ornamental strip ten feet wide, in which grew trees, shrubbery, vines, and flowers of great variety and beauty.

From the outer sides of this Administration Boulevard, eight other boulevards, each two hundred feet wide, extended through the city, connecting with that surrounding it at its outer limits. Four of these ran diagonally from the angles of the Administration Boulevard to

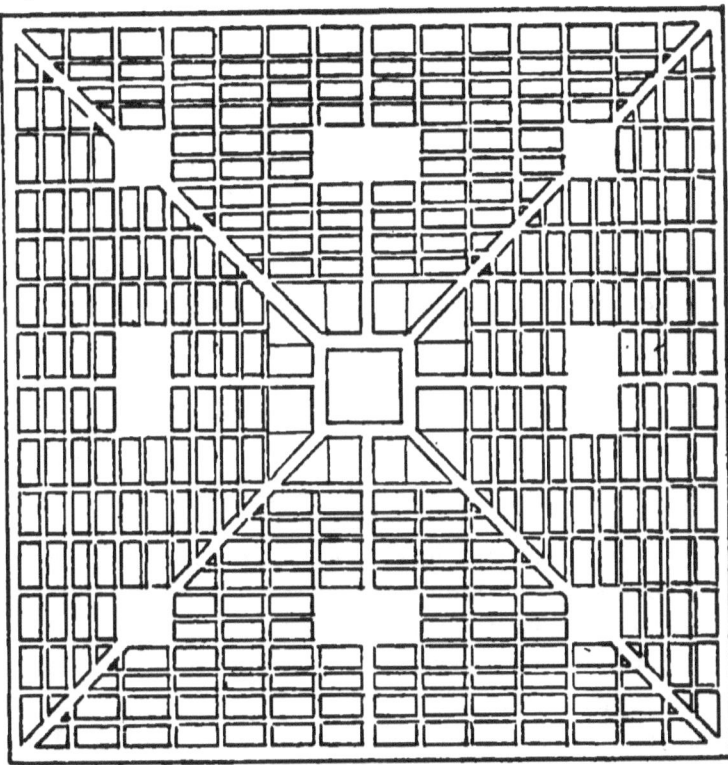

the corresponding angles of the outer boulevard, and were named respectively the Northeast, Northwest, Southwest and Southeast Boulevards. They divided the city into four great cantonments.

Of the others, one began at the center of each side of the Administration Boulevard, and extended at right angles to it, bisecting the cantonment and terminating also in the outer Boulevard, and these four were called

Cardinal Boulevards, and distinguished by the points of the compass to which they ran.

The remainder of the city was traversed by streets one hundred feet wide, which formed blocks seven hundred feet in length and three hundred feet in width, the long sides of the blocks being parallel with the sides of the Administration Boulevard next them.

On each cardinal boulevard, midway through the cantonment it traversed, four blocks were occupied by the public buildings and grounds of the cantonment.

On the diagonal boulevards, at the same distance from the Administration Square, four other blocks were devoted to public parks containing nearly fifteen acres each, and at the intersecting of these boulevards with the outer one were similar parks of double the acreage.

Where blocks were bisected elsewhere by these diagonal boulevards the dwellings faced them, and the parts of the blocks too narrow for building were thrown into parks and set with trees, flowers, grass and shrubbery, and also beautified by fountains and statuary.

In the other residence portions the dwellings faced the streets on the long sides of the blocks, the lots extending to the center of the block.

Such was the general topography of the city—the architectural character of its public buildings and private residences, and the adornments of the grounds about them, all of which had made it celebrated, remain to be described.

In the center of the Administration Square the massive Administration Building, six hundred feet in length and the same in breadth, rose to a height of two hundred and fifty feet, while its great dome towered above it one hundred and fifty feet higher. It was constructed of pure white marble, with pillars of polished granite, and the whole building was adorned with carving and statuary in the simplest and yet most exquisite taste, and was grand in general effect, and beautiful in detail, beyond description.

The buildings facing the Administration Square on the opposite sides of the boulevards were also lofty and imposing, each with its grounds occupying an entire block, but all so planned and arranged as to form with the Administration Building a homogeneous and most attractive center piece of architectural beauty. They were constructed of gray granite, their adornments being of white marble. The two on the north were occupied by the municipal government, those on the east and west by great universities and academies, and those on the south by a theater, and an opera house, each of immense size.

The tiers of blocks immediately outside those on which these structures stood were occupied by other public buildings, such as hotels, auditoriums and schools, universities and theaters of smaller size, and then succeeded the residence portions of the city.

Where the diagonal boulevards cut through the tier of large or double blocks surrounding the Administration Square, eight triangular parks were formed, being extensions of that tier, which were nearly eight hundred feet long on the sides facing the boulevards and six hundred on those facing the streets.

These were given up wholly to adornment, being covered with grass and low shrubbery, with a few tall trees near the acute angles. About three hundred feet from these angles, in each of the parks, a singular structure, extended parallel with the boulevard. In shape this resembled a great vase, rising from an immense foot, with a gradual and graceful sweep first inward and then

outward until at its largest dimensions it was fully two
hundred feet long by fifty feet wide, and at the height of
forty feet its curved and fluted edges overhung its sides
at least fifteen feet and its ends fully twenty-five feet. It
was composed apparently of some metal of the purest
white, and from the summit of its arched upper surface
down to its very edge it was covered with the densest
luxuriance of small trees, fronds of palms, flowers of all
kinds and hues, and moss, and creeping and trailing plants
and vines, of beauty and variety indescribable, which lent
color and shed fragrance all around.

These vases gave wonderful attractiveness to this
portion of the city, and being situated near the entrance
to the great central Administration Square, formed a fit
prelude to the grander beauty of its grounds and buildings.

They were used also as receptacles of water for irrigation, and their tops being arched over and covered
with earth, the vegetation grew luxuriantly on them.

The buildings of the cantonments, grouped around
the blocks, reserved for that purpose on the cardinal
boulevards, comprised houses of worship, public schools,
halls for public assemblies, places of amusement, hotels
and eating-houses, great stores, electric plants, and such
other buildings as were necessary for the wants of the
citizens.

These structures were not composed of as costly
materials, nor were they so great and lofty as the buildings around the Administration Square, but were more in
keeping with the quiet repose of the residence quarters
of which they formed the center. They were, however,
such as would have graced and adorned any European
city. All the streets and boulevards were paved with

asphalt, and all except the Administration Boulevard were beautifully parked, and shaded by trees.

Stone sidewalks were laid throughout the city, varying in width from six feet in the residence districts, to twenty feet on the Administration Boulevard.

Great conduits, in which a man could easily walk upright, were constructed beneath the boulevards, through which the main drains, pipes and sewers extended; on the other streets these were placed under the sidewalks.

All irrigation was performed by means of pipes laid beneath the surface of the ground.

In the residence portions of the city the dwellings were constructed mainly of brick of divers colors, white, ochre and red being prominent, and were generally trimmed with stone.

The lack of ostentatious display among them was a noticeable feature. There were no poor ones; there were no costly ones. There were no unsightly houses, and no palatial abodes; all were comfortable, refined and picturesque in appearance. Each dwelling was set back from the street a distance of not less than thirty feet, and the lot on which it stood was at least forty feet wide; this frontage being devoted to greensward, trees, shrubs, paths and flowers, and there were no division fences.

Harmony in color, architecture and design was wonderfully maintained in the character of all the buildings; no edifice being constructed until its situation and detailed plans were considered and approved by a commission skilled in such work and acquainted with the general scheme for the extension and building up of the city.

Fitness, variety and taste were displayed not in any one particular, or locality, but everywhere; the evident intention being to make no spot in the residence portion of the city conspicuous by unusual expenditure, but the whole a perfect picture.

In all public buildings and improvements the most magnificent erections, the utmost permanence, the costliest materials, often the most elaborate adornments, were employed; in the residence portion adaptibility, beauty, and symmetry of a quieter order reigned supreme.

I thought the city very beautiful, surpassing even the most enthusiastic descriptions given me of it.

Its people seemed contented and happy. I saw no drunkenness, observed no rudeness, heard no bad language among them, and looked upon fewer careworn faces than in any place I had ever visited.

During the day the middle-aged of both sexes monopolized the streets, but in the evening the younger people seemed to possess them. The broad sidewalks and all the parks were full of them; the spacious boulevards were like beehives with the hum of their young voices, and they crowded the theaters, the opera, the libraries, and the lyceums.

CHAPTER III.

The places of amusement in the various cantonments were well arranged and locally well patronized, but the great theater and the opera house on the southern side of the Administration Square were the largest, most commodious, and elegant I had ever seen. In these, performances are often given by the most celebrated European and American actors and vocalists.

Not many days after my arrival in the city, a musical entertainment was advertised for the grand opera house, which I resolved to attend.

The prima donna was one of Europe's most celebrated singers. I had often heard her, with delight, in Continental cities in former years and she was a favorite of mine; in fact, I had had in those years some acquaintance with her.

Desiring to present her with a token of the presence of a friend from abroad and knowing her favorite flowers, rare ones, I determined if possible to procure some of them.

On the afternoon preceding the opera I hunted the city over for these particular flowers and finally discovered a few of them in some beautiful bouquets in the southern cantonment. I purchased one of these and that evening took it with me to the opera, intending on the first fitting opportunity to bestow it surreptitiously upon my former acquaintance, the prima donna, and enjoy her attempts to solve the mystery of the donor.

But fortune seemed unfavorable to my undertaking. On looking at my program I found it stated that, owing to a severe cold and consequent hoarseness, the prima donna would be unable to sing on this the first night of her engagement, and that her place would be filled by Clothilde Beyresen.

My feelings, of course, were those of disappointment, and my first impulse was to leave the house, but it was difficult to do so without attracting observation. Besides, the company was a strong one and much good music might be expected, so I remained.

The performance began and several selections were sung by members of the company; the next one, the program stated, would be rendered by the substitute.

Very unusual interest seemed to be taken in her appearance; the gentlemen straightened themselves in their seats, ladies prepared their opera glasses, and I, familiar with the meaning of such movements, supposed that some well-known amateur, for whose success all felt anxious, was about to attempt the masterpieces of the great prima donna.

I was little prepared for what followed.

From the right wing of the stage entered, alone and unattended, and with all the self-possession, grace, and dignity of the most accomplished leader of the opera, a lady, tall, beautiful, and stately. Her complexion was olive and very clear, such as one sometimes sees in the south of Spain, so pure as to show the red blood in the cheeks and in the lips at the slightest emotion. Her eyes were dark hazel and extremely brilliant, her hair and eyebrows black, the latter beautifully curved, the nose straight, the mouth and chin exquisitely moulded and the figure willowy and graceful.

As she moved across the stage to the footlights an in-

stantaneous clapping of hands and waving of hand-
kerchiefs began in the whole house, and was continued
many seconds after she 'had reached her place, and only
ceased upon her repeated acknowledgments.

Her manner and appearance at once attracted my
undivided attention.

After a slight pause she began to sing. It was Eliza-
beth's Prayer from "Tannhauser."

My wonder and astonishment were at once awakened,
and increased as her performance continued. I leaned
forward and, with a passion almost of entrancement,
caught each pure note as it fell from her lips and filled
the 'house.

I had heard the trained vocalists of Europe, but never
among them all a voice of such compass, purity, and
strength, and such sweetness of tone and delicacy of expression. Then the entire self-possession of the singer,
or rather her utter self-abnegation, was so evident. She
seemed unconscious of 'the effect produced; she made no
effort to produce it. She appeared wrapt and absorbed in
the words and sentiment of the music. She might have
been singing in a drawing-room to a few intimate friends,
so simple and natural was her manner. Indeed, so graceful, so charming, so completely in control of herself and
her hearers was she, that she seemed in a few moments to
have converted the great audience into a circle of such
friends.

She sang the difficult piece throughout in this manner, stood for a moment, apparently hesitating, then
bowed her adieu and disappeared. In an instant the theater resounded with the clapping of hands, the calls for
encore.

After this had continued some little time, she reap-
peared, and sang "Das Veilchen," with the same ease,

grace, and charm, and then again retired and would not respond to a second encore.

The program announced her as reappearing in one other selection only, which was the closing piece of the opera. I thought of my neglected bouquet, and resolved to bestow it upon the gifted singer.

On her re-entry she was greeted with a furor, which showed her to be well known and a favorite.

The piece was Mozart's "Non Paventar." It presented no embarrassments to that peerless voice. There was not a single quavering, or false, or imperfect note; with the same finished style and consummate grace and ease she sang the piece to its conclusion.

Several floral offerings were handed her, costly and elegant, but thinking not of its meagerness, I drew mine from its covering and lightly tossed it on the stage.

The action caught her eye and she lifted it from the floor, shot one swift glance toward myself, whom she evidently recognized as the donor, and hurried from the stage, holding my bouquet in her hand.

A storm of encores succeeded, and the audience, instead of departing, remained seated, though the curtain had descended.

They were not yet satisfied, and in answer to their calls the curtain again rose and the manager came forward on the stage. He announced that Miss Beyresen would sing the national anthem unaccompanied, and the audience and the orchestra were requested to join in the refrain, after which the performance would close.

Perfect silence settled over the theater, and a moment later Miss Beyresen entered. She had changed her costume entirely. The one she now wore was pale orange, with white trimmings. If possible she looked more beau-

tiful than before, and I perceived she was younger than I
had supposed, probably not over twenty-four.

She was received in silence. As she turned and faced
the audience, I saw flowers upon her breast, a few sprays
only, the same ones that had been in my bouquet; the
same wiry stems, with seven blossoms, for I had counted
them casually, the number seemed so small. She had
pulled the bouquet apart evidently, and had chosen these
flowers for some reason known only to herself.

She gave no heed to me, however; never once glancing in my direction. Her eyes swept over the house as
she moved to the footlights; there was a clash of cymbals
and she began the anthem.

Its prelude was an invocation to Deity, imploring
wisdom, guidance, and assistance for the nation; then followed a call to battle, to battle for the right; each stanza
ending with a refrain, an appeal to God to hear the prayer,
to judge the cause, and award the victory.

As with clasped hands and upturned face the singer
raised her voice in pure, sweet notes addressed to heaven,
a reverential feeling like that of solemn worship stole upon
the audience, and they united with subdued voices in the
refrain.

When, however, this concluded, the singer changed
her attitude; her whole being seemed transformed, her
eyes flashed, and as her rich tones filled the house, calling
everyone to conflict, all her strength and action seemed
concentrated in the effort, and an electric thrill of sympathy pervaded the great audience. At the termination of
each stanza they burst into the refrain, and six thousand
voices rang out clear and loud in its response; while upon
the stage the singer stood, graceful in every movement,
an acknowledged leader, her glorious voice rising clear
and strong above the rest.

The anthem continued with varying expression, the audience becoming more and more affected, the singer never hesitating, always self-possessed, graceful, and womanly in the whirlwind of passion which now filled the house.

The last stanza was reached. It expressed triumph in victory won, and a solemn promise of endurance to the end, in which the refrain joined.

There the scene reached its climax. The audience rose to their feet and with eyes uplifted, as were those of their leader, poured out their souls in the final earnest pledge to renewed endeavor and continued trust.

The performance was over, but it left me with a feeling of great interest in the charming singer, which was enhanced by the disposition she had so summarily made of my flowers. I imagined her to be a person of at least national celebrity in the United States.

I inquired about her, and learned to my chagrin that she was a teacher of music in one of the great universities; that although so wonderfully gifted that her name was sufficient at any time to fill the great opera house, yet she did not often sing in public, and that she had acquired the cognomen of "The Princess" by her beauty, her grace, her marvelous voice and other accomplishments.

CHAPTER IV.

Already in my short experience in this city I had observed many unusual and unprecedented business methods.

At the great hotel at which I lodged and a few other places, where special arrangements had been made for the convenience of strangers, money was received in payment for things procured, but except in these I could buy nothing as in other cities. My drafts from abroad were cashed, not at a bank, for there were no banks, but at the treasury department in the Administration Building.

Very soon after my arrival one of the clerks at the hotel explained to me that no such thing as money in the common acceptation of the word was used among the people; that only certain persons entrusted with duties of a public nature were allowed to take it, and all thus received was turned into the general treasury. He advised me to buy a stranger's ticket, which he said would be accepted as current everywhere in the Nationality. I did so and found that each person with whom I had dealings took the ticket and punched the proper amount from it. When the figures on it were all thus used I procured another in a similar way.

I observed also a great difference in character and demeanor between the employes in this and those in other cities. They seemed younger, stronger, and in better health, and were far more affable, courteous, and ac-

33

commodating, though with none of the obsequiousness which frequently characterizes such people in other places. Their intelligence and culture were often of a high order, and I soon found, especially among the younger persons, that the employment in which one was engaged was no safe index to his or her character or attainments.

The causes of these peculiarities I shall not dwell upon here, but will only say that before I had been long in the city I learned that all labor was esteemed honorable; that idleness was considered a disgrace, and that up to a certain age the younger members of the community were required to perform any work assigned them.

While visiting one of the hospitals situated several miles out of the city I had become interested in a young Irishman, comparatively a stranger like myself in this land, who had met with an accident which it was almost certain would in a few days terminate fatally. I went again to see him and remained some time ministering to his mental comfort as best I could. I had left him, and was standing outside his compartment, preparing to return home, when I heard the sound of low, sweet singing, coming from a room in the next ward, but a few steps distant. The words were those of a well-known hymn, and the voice seemed familiar to me, and was full, rich, and most melodious and sympathetic.

I stood quietly listening till the conclusion, when a black-robed Sister of Mercy approached and addressed me thus: "You are a stranger to me, sir, but I know you have been obeying the Lord's command to care for the sick. He whom you have been visiting has told me of your kindness, and he will soon tell it to the Master, who has said that whatsoever service ye do unto such, ye do unto Him."

Looking toward the adjoining room I remarked: "I am not the only visitor you have to-day."

"Ah," she said, "you heard the hymn in yon apartment. There is a woman there who is dying of an incurable disease, and another woman was singing to her. You recognized her voice probably."

"I am a stranger in your city," I replied, "and did not recognize it."

"It is the Princess Clothilde," she said. "God has given her wonderful gifts, and she comes here often to comfort the sick or dying. Such music is a great relief to them; it lifts them above their sufferings."

She went her way, and I remained standing in the background. A moment later the princess came out and I saw her face distinctly, though she did not see me. It was the face of the singer at the opera, and yet it was not the same face; it was more the face of a Saint Cecilia. She remained but a short time talking to some of the attendants, and then passed out, and I did so also, but in a different direction.

I returned to my hotel, and as I stood upon the sidewalk I looked over toward the Administration Building, whose great dome was lit up by the slanting rays of the sun, now fast setting behind the western mountains, and my eye, traveling upward to its summit, rested on an object distinctly visible there which thrilled me.

It was the face and figure of John Harvey, the same face and the same figure, though in a different attitude, that I had seen on the summit of Pike's Peak; clad in the same way, the cocked hat being now on his head. The face was turned toward the east; the attitude was erect and strong; the left hand fell by the side, but the right rested on the pommel of a naked sword set before him,

whose sheen I could distinguish clearly and whose point
was planted firmly on the dome.

I had known John Harvey in life as one who had
wrought swift and terrible destruction among my own
countrymen, and who had levied tribute upon them almost like a freebooter and a pirate, and now, thought I, so
strong is the passion for military success and leadership,
that such acts, coupled with the fact that he once lived
in this land and aided somewhat in the establishment of
this commonwealth, have secured him the honor of a
statue on the very summit of yon noble, grand, and beautiful building.

I looked no longer, but with a feeling almost of dis-
gust entered the hotel and engaged in conversation with
some of its guests with whom I had formed a casual acquaintance. Among these was a gentleman of leisure,
who, having learned that I wished to gain a comprehensive knowledge of the history, laws and labor regulations
of the Nationality, had promised to introduce me to one
of the councilors, or members of parliament, to whom I
could present my letters of recommendation and make
known my wishes in the hope of obtaining the desired
information.

This gentleman now told me that he had spoken to
the Councilor on the subject and that the morrow was
the day set for the formal introduction.

At the time appointed we walked together to the
Administration Building, and on the way my casual friend
informed me the Councilor was Mr. Beyresen. This
statement caused me some astonishment, for the name
was the same as that of the accomplished singer, whom
I had already seen twice, and who had engrossed, especially since the day previous, more of my thoughts than
I cared to acknowledge. My reflections on the matter

were, however, cut short, for a moment later my friend introduced me to Mr. Beyresen, who was a short, stout, active gentleman of about sixty years of age, fatherly and pleasant in manner and ripe in experience of men and affairs. He had been engaged much of his life in various matters connected with the Nationality, in which he had held positions of high control, and was well informed on all subjects relating to it.

I presented my testimonials, which he read with care and then received me with much cordiality. Though my interview with him at this time was not lengthy, yet he was so genial and took so much interest in giving me the information I desired that I soon came to look upon him as a trusted friend, which he in truth proved himself to be, and an intimacy was thus formed which became closer and closer, and lasted during the remainder of his life.

I learned from him the general principles upon which the Nationality was organized, and the chief laws and regulations governing its people. At an early date in our acquaintance I secured from Mr. Beyresen a written statement of these, which I shall present to my readers in the next chapter, leaving minuter details to be explained later, if necessary.

CHAPTER V.

Nearly all governments claim to be organized for the good of their people; their histories, however, show that, to a greater or less extent, they have universally failed to accomplish this object.

These failures have been caused mainly by two great and dominant passions—the love of power, place, and dominion, commonly called ambition, and the love of money and accumulation.

These have led the officers of government, or the people themselves, or both together, to lose sight of the true end or aim of government above stated.

Both these passions have been perverted, but the germ of the first is lofty, and can produce good fruit; that of the latter is base and sordid.

This Nationality, or State, by either of which titles it may be properly designated, contemplates a more definite and individualized object than that of other governments.

It is an organization of the people, for working in co-operation for the equal good of all. It acts through officers and agents chosen, not for political reasons, but for their fitness, skill, and ability in planning, directing and executing that which is necessary to be done to effect its object.

It recognizes the power of the two passions referred to, and aims to change, among its officers and people, the direction of the former, and to utterly destroy the latter.

It fosters the noble ambition to be among the first, wisest and most active in advancing the general happiness and good, and teaches its citizens to encourage such endeavor by bestowing honor, power, and place upon those who display these virtues.

It destroys the passion for money and accumulation by instituting a system which relegates money to its proper function of a mere medium of exchange of values, and interposes insuperable barriers to accumulation.   It does this by adopting the following fundamental principles:

That money, debt, interest and accumulation shall be unknown to the citizen; all moneys received from other states, or their citizens, or in any other way, being turned into the state treasury, and that all business dealings with such other states, or their citizens, shall be conducted solely by the Nationality, or under its prescribed rules and regulations.

That the Nationality, state, or people organized, shall have the absolute title to all property within its borders, and control the same, subject to wise, equitable, and well-known and established rules in regard to its use by the citizen for a limited period, not exceeding his natural life.

By enfranchising its citizens from this one passion for money and accumulation it delivers them from a host of attendant evils, and clears away the debris of former systems of government.

To occupy the ground thus prepared, the Nationality lays the foundation of its own government upon certain other principles consonant with those of justice, which define generally the mutual duties and obligations of the state to the individual citizen, and in turn of the latter to the state, and which are these:

That the Nationality, or state, shall care equally and impartially for all its citizens, supplying them during life with equal opportunities and means for obtaining all that is necessary for their physical, mental, and moral wants, and for gratifying all innocent tastes and amusements.

This duty may be stated more specifically as follows:

It must provide its citizens, required to work, with constant employment; planned and systematically arranged by its skilled officers, and directed so as to produce the best results.

It must see to it that their children be furnished, without individual cost, with all means necessary for the best instruction, physical, mental, and moral, which its resources can command, and that such means are used diligently, individual tastes and aptitudes being reasonably consulted.

It must provide other schools, academies and universities, where other branches can be more specially learned by those willing to pay for such instruction.

It must provide all things necessary for the education, livelihood, advancement, and pleasures of its citizens; those who work, those incapacitated for work, and those past the age of compulsory work.

In return for this care, provision, and assurance for his comfort and safety, each citizen must render to the Nationality, or state, the best labor or service of which he is capable, during such years of life as with the massed labor of its other citizens rendered for an equal time, will enable it to provide thus for all its citizens, and meet any incidental obligations and demands upon it, and lay up sufficient store for unusual contingencies.

As a correlation to the proper discharge of their mutual duties the citizens of the Nationality will, in youth especially, be well instructed; they will be laborious, especially during the years set apart for labor, and at ease afted those years are past, and they will always have occasion to be happy in the assurance afforded them by the state that they are safe, as far as human care can make them so, from business vicissitudes.

Citizenship in the Nationality shall be attained by males at the age of eighteen, and females at the age of fifteen.

To insure an equitable and equal division among its citizens of the joint products of their labor, the Nationality shall provide a medium of exchange to take the place of money, determined in aggregate amount every five years by the estimated average production of the state, and the number of its people, which shall be good only for the year in which it is issued and not transferrable.

On the first days of January, April, July and October of every year, each citizen shall receive a certificate of indebtedness, which shall during the period above mentioned be good, to all intents and purposes, as was money formerly, in payment for anything purchased, or for any service rendered, or in discharge of any due within the borders of the Nationality.

These certificates shall be issued for citizens, and the children of citizens not exceeding four in number in each family, in yearly amount, as follows, the gradation in amount also to be determined every five years.

Children under eight years old.............,..... $150.00
Male child over eight and under eighteen...... 300.00
Female child over eight and under fifteen...... 250.00
Youth, male over eighteen and under twenty-
    one 800.00
Youth, female over fifteen and under eighteen.. 600.00

Man at the age of twenty-one.............. 1,200.00
Woman at the age of eighteen.............. 1,000.00

Provided, however, that parents shall receive the certificates of their children under age, and that guardians and conservators duly appointed shall under the direction of the courts receive and use the certificates of their wards.

The citizen must not be trammeled in the use of his certificate further than that he must provide proper subsistence for himself and family, live morally and peaceably, and perform his labor and service as directed by the laws and regulations of the Nationality.

Such were the general principles, rules and regulations of this body.

Before quitting the subject I will give a short statement of the method of its organization and government.

The whole land is divided into townships, which in the cultivated districts are twelve miles square, and which form the unit of governmental and labor control.

The people live chiefly in towns; located, particularly in the agricultural regions, as nearly in the center of the township as possible. These towns contain from three thousand to six thousand inhabitants, or more, according to the fertility of the soil and the number of persons required for its cultivation, or for other employments. All male citizens, until the age of forty-five, and all female citizens, until the age of forty years, are enrolled as laborers. They work under the direction of officers, chosen yearly by themselves, consisting of a director for every one hundred, a lieutenant for every fifty, and a foreman for every ten laborers; eight hours constituting the work of a day, except in certain kinds of onerous labor, where the hours are less. The men perform all the heavy work, the women being engaged in light employment within doors; those of them who have families caring for them with such assistance as is necessary. Nearly all work is done in co-operation, machinery being made to do its part most advantageously.

Both sexes, from the age of eight until the age of citizenship, are required to attend school. If they have special aptitudes such are developed, and in this period they can also learn trades. If higher, or professional education, be desired they can attend schools until they reach the age of citizenship, their parents paying their expenses, and after becoming citizens, any can pursue their studies, payment being made to the Nationality equal to the amount of the certificate which that body would issue for their service. These payments are of course made by deductions from the certificates of parents or others.

The state has absolute control of the character of labor, and the place at which it is rendered, until the male citizen reaches the age of twenty-four, at which age he may marry. The female citizens may marry at the age of eighteen, and remain with their parents until that time, or until settled in some occupation. After marriage, citizens may expect a permanent home in some locality where they can render to the state the service for which they are best fitted, during the required number of years. All citizens receive certificates during life, provided they perform such labor as they are capable of doing, those incapacitated from any cause being equally provided for.

If any who are capable refuse to work they are admonished, and if they prove incorrigible, are put in a class by themselves, wearing a peculiar uniform, and subjected to severe discipline, their certificates being withheld from them and used for the benefit of their families.

When the years of compulsory service are over, the citizen is at liberty to enjoy himself as he chooses, can

study, travel, or remain at home. Many go to the cities
and live there permanently, enjoying for the remainder
of their lives the comforts, pleasures, and advantages
there afforded, often continuing to serve the public in various capacities.

The higher offices of the Nationality are in many instances filled only by those past this age, and the citizen
who is elected or appointed to such office and accepts its
duties is expected to perform them to the end of his term.

A congressman is elected by the people every two
years in each congressional district of the United States,
and the councilors and representatives from each state
choose United States senators at the time appointed by
law, they themselves not being eligible to such office.

Sixteen townships in the Nationality constitute a
district, controlled by a district executive, elected semi-
annually by its citizens, who also elect every four years
a member of the House of Representatives from among
those who have served honorably a full term, either as
labor directors or as district executives, and have attained the age of thirty years.

The Council, or Upper House, consists of not more
than sixty members; four of whom, at least, shall be from
each state of the United States belonging to the Nationality. It is composed of such persons as have served
honorably twelve years or more as members of either
house, and these are called honorary councilors, and
serve for life or until incapacitated. Any vacancies in
the number, however, can be filled by election in the state
having the least number of representatives in the Council,
from among those who have served one or more terms
as members of either house, and the person so elected
shall hold the office for the term of six years.

The post of councilor, and especially that of honorary

councilor, is regarded as of the highest dignity, and it was this position that my friend Beyresen held.

The Parliament, or joint Houses of Legislature, appoint the chief executive, judges and heads of the various departments, from among those who have served with honor in other places and have attained the age of forty-five years, and these serve until the age of sixty years, unless removed by the appointing power for cause. Those thus appointed have authority to fill all offices in their respective departments not otherwise provided for.

Such was the general scheme of government in the Nationality. There were many minor rules and regulations to which I will not refer, as those I have already mentioned will give my reader sufficient knowledge of the form of government adopted by this unique and happy people.

CHAPTER VI.

CLOTHILDE.

I had been in Neuropolis some weeks and Mr. Beyresen had introduced me to a number of the councilors and finally invited me to his house to spend an evening with his family.

I gladly accepted the invitation, for I felt lonely, and besides desired to see something of the home life of its citizens.

Mr. Beyresen lived in a commodious and very pleasant house situated about a mile from the Administration Building. His family consisted of himself, his wife, a matronly lady; his daughter Anna, a schoolgirl of about fourteen, and an elder daughter, who proved to be no other than the singer, Clothilde. I could hardly restrain an exclamation of surprise when I recognized her. There was also a feeling of satisfaction, for I had been very strangely and unusually attracted on the two previous occasions when I had seen her and had desired to meet her.

And if her self-possession, ease, and grace on the stage had been admirable, in her home they were still more so.

Not a tone, an accent, or a look gave any indication that she had ever seen me, and indeed, I was not assured that she remembered me until some time after, when we had become better acquainted. Even the subject of music was not mentioned, and we all spent the time of my first visit in interchanging thoughts, wise, witty, or frivo-

lous, on various subjects and revealing ourselves to each
other by such means.

The difference in appearance between the two sisters was much greater than is generally found in members of the same family. The younger was fair, with
auburn hair and blue eyes, while the elder was a brunette
of the most distinguished type. I could hardly compare
them further, for the one was as yet unformed, while the
other had enjoyed unusual opportunity for study, culture
and refinement. This was evident in her conversation,
her tone of voice, her every attitude and movement, and
especially in her tact and power of interesting every one
present.

She was certainly not older than twenty-three, or
four, a little above the usual height, and the character of
her bearing and her dark beauty were so attractive, and
her grace and charm of manner so wonderful that I could
readily see how these had given her, even in this great
city, the appellation of princess, by which her father once
or twice playfully addressed her.

From this time onward my visits to Mr. Beyresen's
house were frequent. Mrs. Beyresen was so motherly a
person, Mr. Beyresen was so hospitable and so evidently
desired me to feel at home, and Miss Clothilde was so
kind and entertaining that I soon began to consider that
I was always welcome.

I was invited to dine with the family one evening at
a noted cafe, and we all walked in company to the place.

The little parks along the boulevard were fragrant
and beautiful with flowers, displayed in the soft electric
light which flooded everything, and on up toward the
Administration Square a band was playing.

"The night is perfect and the walk delightful," said

I. "We are attended by both flowers and music. Which do you prefer, Miss Beyresen?"

"You need hardly ask," she answered. "I should dislike to be deprived of either, but music is my delight and my most constant study; it is eternal and divine."

"And you think flowers only earthly?" I inquired.

"I cannot tell," she replied. "I hope there are flowers in heaven, but I am sure there is music. It is like one's soul, unseen, intangible, emotional, and it is a necessity to happiness, almost to existence, I believe."

"It would seem so," I returned. "There are so many harmonious sounds everywhere, each speaking to us in its own peculiar way and they form a great repertoire from which we draw continually and unconsciously."

"But that is not all," said she. "Strains of music I never heard before have come into my mind, or rather floated into my imagination, and kept me company for days. Where did they originate, Mr. Maxwell?"

"I do not know," I answered, "any more than how your thoughts occur. To me the musical composer's mind is more a mystery than to you, who are naturally in affinity with his creative world. I can only say that character, mood, and association have much to do in shaping all expressions of the mind and soul."

"The terms you use are so comprehensive, Mr. Maxwell, that I do not feel particularly enlightened."

"I claim no ability in this direction, Miss Beyresen. The influence of character in musical effort and emotion I cannot estimate. That of mood and association I can trace more easily. The song one's mother sang; the dirge over a friend; the national air of one's country; any music heard on memorable occasions continually recurs whenever anything connected with it stirs memory's silent chambers or even when the soul is in the same mood. I could tell you of an anthem I heard but once, which, with the scene attendant, made so powerful an impression on my mind that I do not think I shall ever forget it. I have been hearing portions of it since we have been walking here together."

She hesitated a moment and then asked: "And pray what was it?"

"You know better than I, for you were the leading spirit of the occasion," I answered. "It may be strange that I should be quietly walking and talking with the inspiring person who sang that anthem, but it is not strange that its words and music should recur to me."

"I believe I know what you mean!" she exclaimed, "and I perceive you are still the same complimentary gentleman who bestowed a bouquet on me that evening. I am really glad to have this opportunity to explain my action to you. I recognized in it certain flowers which I was sure could be found only in our own greenhouse. The plants had been sent me some time previously by a friend from abroad, and my sister had put a few of the blossoms in some bouquets which a neighboring florist had asked her to make for him. I picked the bouquet up therefore and wore the flowers. How you ever found them and came to give them to me I cannot imagine."

"I found them accidentally," I replied. "I happened in at the florist's, saw the flowers which were familiar to me in their native land, and the disposal of them was an involuntary tribute to your rendition of the anthem. I am very glad I had them," I added.

"And so am I," she said, "though your explanation of 'why' you had them might challenge investigation. I was a substitute for another that evening, Mr. Maxwell," she continued, "and I think I could offer a theory more plausible than that you have just given of how they came into your possession. Would you like to hear it?"

"No, thank you," I answered; "your explanations already have destroyed enough illusions. Let me add that I am exceedingly glad there was a substitute that evening."

We entered the cafe together, into a great hall well lighted and beautifully adorned, with small dining-rooms on either side, separated from it by arched openings cased with onyx. In these smaller rooms, which were furnished with all the requisites for comfort and convenience, tables were laid at which parties like our own could sit in comparative privacy, and yet see other guests entering the great hall and crossing it to the main public dining-room.

We took our seats at a table in one of these rooms and ordered our repast. I could not repress my admiration of the cafe and its appointments, and compared it with some that I had seen in Europe. The conversation took a wider range and we were soon talking of foreign countries.

Many years before Mr. and Mrs. Beyresen had spent a short time in Great Britain and on the Continent.

They related some of the incidents of their journey, and Mrs. Beyresen said to me:

"When we were in Liverpool, twenty-five years ago, we became acquainted with a family of your name. The husband was a physician and quite eminent in his profession. There were two daughters and one or two sons in the family. I have wondered if they could have been related to you, Mr. Maxwell?"

"I think not, Mrs. Beyresen," I answered. "My people live in the western portion of England, and though they are often in Liverpool yet none of them ever resided there. Besides, none of my family or relatives were at that time engaged in the practice of medicine."

"Then," said Mrs. Beyresen, "we met another family of Maxwells a little later on, in Scotland, very nice people, travelers like ourselves. They were tenting comfortably at one of the little lochs of which there are so many in that country. The gentleman was in trade, at Aberdeen, I think, and out with his family for recreation. Possibly they were related to you, Mr. Maxwell."

"I think not, Mrs. Beyresen," I replied. "In fact I know they were not. None of my people were at that time engaged in trade at Aberdeen."

"Mr. Maxwell," inquired Anna very earnestly, "what do the people of England do; what did your people do?"

"The people of England do a great many things, Miss Anna. Nearly all my people were farmers and stock-raisers."

"Oh!" said Anna, "I did not think there was room. The island is so small, I am sure it must be crowded. There are only a few counties and they not very large. Let me see if I can remember them." She mentioned the names of all the counties except one which she had forgotten.

"Devonshire," I suggested.

"Oh, yes, thank you, that is in the west, the region you said your people lived in. Was that where you came from?" she inquired.

"It was the county in which I was born, and lived for many years," I replied, feeling a little ill at ease under this questioning.

Miss Clothilde had been listening with an amused smile, which I had noticed. She now interposed:

"Let me make a diversion in your favor, Mr. Maxwell," she said, "before you get hopelessly entangled in a web most innocently woven for you. You are in peril, I believe."

"I am obliged for your interest," I returned, "though I am not aware of any danger. I was simply replying to Miss Anna's inquiries about England and its people."

"Oh, yes," she said, "and to Mamma Beyresen's. Pardon me, but it was the disinterestedness and candor of your answers that led to my proffer of assistance. I did not intend to be officious. But I should like to understand," she continued after a moment's pause, "how you could know, when I am sure you were not over five years of age, that none of your family or relatives were physicians, or none of them were engaged in trade at Aberdeen?"

"If I had such information later in life, or if my family were few in numbers, I might be able to state positively about the matter," I replied.

"Is your family few in numbers, Mr. Maxwell?" she inquired mischievously, "and where, pray, do they market the stock which they raise?"

"I crave your clemency!" I cried. "I cannot answer two questions in one breath. If you call this assistance, Miss Clothilde, forfend me from such."

"I do not call it assistance," she answered laughingly. "I would not be so inexact. I consider it rather as admonition, and if you will take it so, Mr. Maxwell, you need not answer anything."

I tacitly accepted her conditions, and from that time onward no further inquiries were made respecting my home or family.

We soon after left the cafe and returned to the house, where I remained for some time talking with Mr. Beyresen about the Nationality and its affairs, Mrs. Beyresen and Miss Clothilde occasionally making some observation, the latter manifesting a thorough acquaintance with and much interest in the history of that body.

CHAPTER VII.

THE MOUNTAIN AND MINING DISTRICTS.

About the middle of June I made a short journey both for observation and recreation among the mountain regions of the Nationality.

The inhabitants were largely engaged in dairying, fruit and stock raising, and mining.

There were numerous towns and villages situated at irregular intervals, as convenience demanded, and the railroads connecting them generally followed the courses of the streams as a matter of necessity. There were hundreds of quaint hamlets where the locomotive whistle had never been heard, and thousands of beautiful valleys, parks, and camping spots, almost as quiet and undisturbed as they had been for centuries before.

I met many tourists from all portions of the world; for the climate is delightfully cool and refreshing, the sunshine bright, grateful and almost continuous, and the mountain scenery among the grandest and most beautiful on the face of the globe.

The forests, covering a large portion of this region, were preserved with as much care as those in any part of Europe, thousands of acres of young trees being annually planted.

The wild game was carefully protected, extensive areas of country too rough for other uses having been set apart as a refuge for them. The fish in the streams were plentiful, and living in the pure cold water distilled from the melting snows upon the mountains, were among the finest anywhere to be found.

Game could be killed and fish taken only during certain seasons and in limited numbers, and tourists and all others out for such sport were required to take a government officer with them, whose duty it was to see that the laws and regulations in regard to game, and also in regard to forest growth and forest fires, were not violated.

In these regions the Nationality employed very many of its people in mining for coal, iron, lead, copper, and other metals, including gold and silver, which were found in greater abundance here than in any other portion of the globe.

I was much interested in examining into the condition of the mines and miners, thus directly under the control of the government, and spent much of my time among them.

I found that the mines were far freer from danger, better equipped, better timbered, and better lighted, drained, and ventilated than under other systems of ownership in which the largeness of the output and economy in its production were the main objects.

The miners were a most intelligent and sober people, and had as comfortable homes and were as well provided for as any other class of citizens. They worked only six hours in the twenty-four, their places being then filled by others. These short hours were allowed them because of the underground character of their work, and the fact that their health and comfort were considered as of the first importance by the government.

I was surprised to learn that such was their enhanced diligence and such the advantages of extended co-operation and improved methods, that under the management of the Nationality, notwithstanding this reduction in the time of individual labor and the increased expense entailed by sanitary and protective measures, the output of the mines was greater and more profitable than under that of the corporations and owners formerly controlling them.

Certain grievances were charged against the Nationality in connection with the business of mining, the history of which I will endeavor to relate.

Some thirty years previous to the time of which I write, the United States had ceded to the separate states all the lands then belonging to it within their borders, not even excepting those containing precious metals. The business of mining, especially for these metals, had been very profitable, and many corporations and individuals outside the states in which the mines were located had been engaged in it. The states to which these mineral lands were ceded refused to sell them, but rented or leased them for a term of years on a certain royalty.

On the accession of the Nationality the mining lands thus ceded, with all else became its property, and it refused to renew the leases, but as they lapsed worked the mines for the benefit of its own people. Its operations being conducted on a large scale caused the working of the other mines, owned and controlled by the corporations and individuals before mentioned, to become unprofitable.

Many of the latter mines, also, as their owners desired to sell, were bought up by the Nationality with the evident object of controlling the entire output and having but one system of labor, its own, within its borders.

This action extended to and affected mines of all kinds—iron, coal, copper, lead and stone, as well as precious metals.

The proceeding of the Nationality in these respects was tested by suits brought against that body in the United States courts by these corporations and owners, but was decided by the highest tribunals of the land to be perfectly constitutional and legal.

The agitation in regard to these matters had not, however, ceased, being kept up by persons living under the old labor system in other states, and had lately assumed higher ground than before.

It was alleged that the Nationality had gained possession of the principal mines of the country, and controlled the output of the precious metals to its own advantage; that it hoarded them in its vaults, and was able at any time to flood the country with them, and that among its own people they were not used as money.

In regard to these accusations, it was undoubtedly true that the Nationality controlled the amount of the precious metals mined within its borders and dictated the disposition of the same, but not more so than it did that of its other products, it being an essential part of its plan that it should so control all production.

It was undoubtedly true that large quantities of the precious metals were stored away in the vaults of the treasury at Neuropolis, and that they were not used as money among the people of the Nationality.

In fact, the complaints against that body all arose from undeniable differences between its labor system and that of the rest of the Union, and the impossibility of settling them except by the adoption of one system by the whole nation, was evident.

This conviction caused me to turn again with renewed interest to the study of the principles underlying these systems, and to the observation of the condition of the people living under them. Having learned much in the course of my brief visit to the mountains I returned to Neuropolis in the latter part of June, purposing before long to spend some time on the plains, among the more exclusively agricultural communities.

CHAPTER VIII.

I spent many evenings now at Mr. Beyresen's house. It was a great pleasure to me to feel that I had found friends in this strange land, who accepted me for what I was, and not for what I or my family represented.

Mr. Beyresen was much engaged in affairs of state, and I had on these visits opportunities to become better acquainted with Miss Clothilde, who was usually at home.

In addition to her other accomplishments, she was exceedingly well informed on all subjects of literature and art, and seemed to have a knowledge of many of the modern languages.

I obtained my first hint of this one evening when we were talking of the arrangement of books in libraries.

"My adjustment of them," said she, "is very crude. I put the books in English together, the Spanish together, the German together, and the French together. The other languages are massed remorselessly."

"And how many languages, pray, have you in your library?" I inquired.

"Oh, I do not know," she answered. "I have a good many more than I understand, I fear. A large part of my library was left me by a friend, and the books are prized on that account.. Though, indeed, they are all among the best books, and I should be lost without them. Besides these, I have added many of my own choice from

59

time to time during the last twelve years, and I have now quite a good library."

"The last twelve years!" I exclaimed. "You must have begun collecting books at a very early age, Miss Beyresen."

"A woman," she replied, "answers no questions in regard to her age. She is supposed to have youth immortal. I will show you, however, one book presented to me ten years ago, and I assure you, Mr. Maxwell, though I was not then old enough to understand it thoroughly, I could read it as well as either you or I can now."

She brought me a copy of Goethe's works in German, elegantly bound and exquisitely illustrated, a gift worthy of a king. I opened it and turned the leaves. I did not look at the blank leaves where the donor's name might be. She observed this.

"Oh, you may look anywhere in the book. See," she said, pointing to a little golden case set in the leather on the side of the book, and closed by a slide, "the giver's name and presentation note are in that little case."

"If this be a specimen of the books in your library, Miss Beyresen, the collection must be a sight worth seeing. This is a royal gift in its richness of illustration and beauty of finish."

"I am pleased that you like it," she said, "but it is hardly a fair criterion of my books. It is a show-book more than one for general use, and I think possibly the costliest single volume I have."

"If you have more show-books similar to this," said I, looking admiringly at the beautiful illustrations, "I should be very much pleased to see them."

"You told us some time ago you were from Devonshire," she remarked. "I have some engravings of Devonshire scenery, and towns and castles which I can show you."

"I should be glad to see them, if I do not trouble you and if there is time this evening," I answered, a little disconcerted, notwithstanding my curiosity regarding them, at the possible perplexities into which I might be plunged by this quick-witted young lady.

She seemed to notice my hesitation, for she said: "I thought you might be able to tell me something about these places, which would add to my information and be valuable to me in showing the engravings to others. But if you wish to examine them more leisurely I will give them to you as you leave, and you can take them with you."

"By no means," I replied quickly; "the greatest pleasure in looking at your engravings would be foregone if I might not examine them with you. Any information about them I possess will be given you with pleasure. Let us look them over together, please."

She seemed gratified, and brought the book and turned the pages with her own fingers. The engravings were quite numerous, and very fine, evidently the work of the best artists.

I saw familiar places, which, in years gone by, I had frequented, and various events connected with them I remembered distinctly. Miss Beyresen said little, but very evidently enjoyed the interest which she saw I took in them.

Presently my fair entertainer turned a leaf and an unusually fine engraving of Dorsetshire Castle appeared. I was startled at seeing before me an exact representation of a spot associated with my earliest and most cherished recollections.

"This," she said, "is, I believe, the ancestral seat of

the Duke of Dorsetshire. I have heard that it is a famous castle with very beautiful grounds. I suppose you have seen it, Mr. Maxwell?"

I bowed assent, hardly caring to answer audibly, particularly as she was regarding me attentively with her great hazel eyes.

"Then probably you can tell me whether this engraving is an accurate one."

"I hardly understand you," I replied. "It seems to me a very real representation of the place."

"Let us go more into particulars, please," she said. "I think if we do you will understand me better. I have quite a curiosity to know if this engraving really is exact. For instance," she went on, "is that group of high trees represented as standing to the right of the castle truthful; are there such trees there, I mean?"

"I believe there are," I answered. "That is my recollection."

"And do you recall the species of trees?" she asked.

"They are elms, I believe," I replied.

"And the gardens on the left where the ladies and gentlemen stand, are they really there?"

"I believe they are there also," I answered.

"And the rookery, does that exist as represented?"

"There was a rookery at about that place," I answered again, somewhat puzzled at the persistence of my fair interlocutor.

"Well," she continued, "and that high tower, is it really as represented?"

"The tower is undoubtedly there, or was some years ago, when I last saw the place," I replied.

"Now," she said, "that hardly answers my question, Mr. Maxwell. "Do you think the engraving an exact representation of the tower, for instance?"

"I think it is," I replied.

"Look at it again," she said. "Artists are so inaccurate sometimes, and take such liberties with the original, or, rather, depend often on a not very accurate memory for details. Do you see those three windows, one somewhat above the other in a spiral, on the part of the tower shown in the engraving?"

"I do."

"Then look a little to the left. Do you not see another window faintly outlined in the shadow toward the main roof?"

"I believe I do," I said.

"Now, Mr. Maxwell, is there such a window in that tower?"

I was startled. I knew there was no such window, but how on earth could the young lady so promptly challenge its existence?

"There is no such window," I answered positively, thrown a little off my guard.

"I knew it," she said, "because the three spiral windows suggest a stairway, and that window is not only out of place, but would be directly in the way of a stairway. There is a stairway, Mr. Maxwell?"

"Yes," I admitted, "there is a stairway."

"Thank you," she said, "and now one other question. Do you see that figure of a horse on the stables? Is that horse correctly portrayed? Look at its position, Mr. Maxwell. It faces in toward the stables. It should face outwards. It may, however, be a weather-vane, though it is rather large for that, but if it be really a stationary figure I cannot but think the engraver has let his memory deceive him and has placed it wrong."

"It is placed wrong," I answered. "It is not a weather-vane, but a figure in bronze, and does face to-

ward the entrance. How particularly you observe!" I
continued. "Few would have noticed these slight inaccuracies in so fine an engraving."

"Now let me assure you, Mr. Maxwell, I did not call
attention to these inaccuracies for the purpose of exhibiting my small powers of observation, but rather for that
of seeing if they would be verified by your greater knowledge. There is one other point on which I would like to
have your opinion. You see that rustic lookout, or seat,
on the lower branches of the great oak tree in the foreground?"

She was pointing to a seat I myself, as a boy, had
made with the help of the gardener, taking advantage of a
natural curve in one of the large branches of the oak tree.
The gardener and I had made the seat, and I used to occupy it, in company often with a little Spanish maiden
who was visiting at the castle when I was about twelve
years of age. I remembered a fall I once had from it to
the ground, the result of a misstep, and the side of my
left temple still bore a scar which I had then received. I
could, as I looked at the engraving, recall my little companion's shriek of terror as I fell to the ground.

I hesitated and looked at Miss Beyresen, and then
answered: "Yes, I believe I see it."

"Now, Mr. Maxwell," she said, "that seat has puzzled me. The great limb of the tree seems to bend in a
very unnatural way, so as to form a curved back for the
seat. Does it really do so, or is this another defect in my
engraving?"

I glanced at the young lady; there was mischief lurk-
ing in her eye, though her expression otherwise was sweet
and innocent as a summer morning. I could not tell her
about the tree without revealing too great familiarity with
the place, so I replied: "I cannot enlighten you as to that,

Miss Beyresen, but I must be permitted to compliment you on your powers of observation, and to remark that you seem to expect extremely accurate work from the artist. You appear to be very realistic in your demands."

"I have been called idealistic," she demurely answered, "and I liked that expression better."

"Well," I returned, "there has been something about you this evening ideally realistic."

"Thank you," she said; "that is pleasanter."

"And you always suit the scene in this ideally realistic land," I continued, "which is one reason, I suppose, why you are called by the most appropriate name of 'The Princess'."

"I should like you to go on," she said. "I am very much interested and would fain hear more, but from the well-known footfall upon the walk I fear the entrance of Father Beyresen will clip the wings of your fancy in midair, so you would better, Mr. Maxwell, settle down gently before he arrives."

"I beg pardon," I again replied. "I will take your advice; but I have a favor to ask of you before I go. These evenings are so beautiful and I am so English that I think no place is as pleasant as outdoors, with a congenial companion. If your highness would consent to accompany me some evening for a stroll about the avenues and boulevards of this well-kept city I should be very grateful." She hesitated, and I added: "Say to-morrow evening. I understand there is to be an illumination of a unique character in the Administration Square. I believe I can find a quiet place from which we can view it comfortably."

"Thank you, I think I can go," she said. "I should like to go. I generally spend a good deal of time outdoors during summer evenings. Yes, you can depend upon me to-morrow, Mr. Maxwell."

CHAPTER IX.

THE ILLUMINATION.

Half past 7 o'clock the next evening found me at Mr. Beyresen's.

Miss Clothilde was ready for our walk, and when she entered the room I thought I had never seen her looking more animated, charming and graceful.

"Shall we be in the open air all the time, Mr. Maxwell?" she inquired.

"As you desire," I replied, "though I had not supposed anything else, it is such a glorious night."

"Two souls with but a single thought!" she exclaimed. "I have been shut up all day, and the air will be so refreshing. How long shall we be out?"

"I cannot tell that," I answered. "Let us be like children that take no note of time. When you are weary we will turn homeward."

So we sallied forth, and were soon walking arm in arm up the Southeast Avenue leading toward the Administration Square.

It was a beautiful evening in the early part of July, calm, still and languorous. A few white, fleecy clouds drifted across the azure sky, occasionally intercepting the rays of the full moon which shed a changeful light upon all objects, glorifying some and casting others into deep shadow.

Many people were abroad on the avenue like ourselves; others sat under the trees in the little parks, but the avenue was so broad and the parks so many that both seemed but thinly populated. Family groups were out on the lawns in front of their homes enjoying the beauties of the night, often in company with friends and neighbors, and frequently small tables stood near them on which were various light refreshments.

We walked slowly along the avenue, talking of the city and of others in Eastern lands which I had visited, with which I compared it.

"The Oriental glamour and entrancement hang around this scene," I said, "and the mysteries of this land appear to me as fathomless as those of India or Egypt, where every great building and every stupendous work is attributed, in part at least, to some fabled deity or some wonderful and mythologic personage. The same necromancy appears present here to-night as we walk along this noble boulevard toward those majestic public buildings which adorn your city, and so strong a spell does it cast upon my imagination that I could almost expect the genii who created them to rise from behind those mountains and appear visibly to us. Are you ever dominated by such fancies, Miss Clothilde, or do you deem them frivolous?"

"No," she said slowly and reflectively, "I would not wish to be considered as thinking them such; it would not augur well of one's own character. I believe I told you last night that I disclaim living entirely in the realms of the real. I know no one who does live so, and if I did I hardly think I should desire an extended acquaintance. But I hope, Mr. Maxwell, I am not so imaginative as to be too much a dreamer, which I think is one of the faults of the Oriental character. I sometimes look at the clouds, sir, but I look at my feet, too. I like to know where I am going, but I am not oblivious to the songs of the birds and the waters, and the beauty of the flowers and the shadows, and when there is a rainbow I never shut my eyes. I am a mixture, but in what proportions I can't tell, nor would I if I could."

"So we all are," I replied, "and the qualities of our composition are often so varied, and their phases so subtle, that the very finest of them cannot be described at all, for they give out new tones at the touch of every circumstance and incident of life."

"Now, Mr. Maxwell!" she exclaimed, "I had thought to give you some insight into my philosophy, but if you are one of those awful beings, called metaphysicians, who analyze and generalize, and dissect and classify mental phenomena, I am dumb as an oyster."

"No, indeed," I answered, "I am not. Pray continue, for I am sure it will be interesting."

"I do not know about that," she said; "it depends much upon the disposition of the listener. But I will venture to give you my short creed. I think life very mysterious, not in an alarming way, but in a solemn one. We have great responsibilities in regard to it, and though we may enjoy ourselves occasionally, as you and I are doing to-night, yet life should not be all a butterfly existence. I think the best and noblest people have generally been the busiest."

"But the busiest, I have often noticed, are so occupied that they become more or less uncongenial, and sometimes almost repellent to their fellow-beings."

"Then they have not been rightly busy," she replied. "They have been so possessed by work in certain directions that they have forgotten one great duty—to keep themselves in touch with the progress, and in sympathy with the heart of humanity, and to show due regard for the rights and happiness of their fellow beings. That includes a great deal, Mr. Maxwell, a great deal that should never be forgotten: charity, kindliness, cheerfulness and unselfishness. I think every human being owes these to his fellow creatures."

"I agree with you perfectly," I said, "but so many practically ignore them."

"And yet," she continued, "there are no other virtues in whose exercise we can find more pleasure; they react on one's own life and make it enjoyable. It may seem presumptuous, Mr. Maxwell, but I do not believe," she added, "that the old system of government, the one I mean under which you, for instance, have lived, is as conducive to the development of these virtues as the one under which we live here."

"I hope you are right," I answered. "In fact, I think the future happiness of the world depends upon the adoption of some system which cultivates the virtues you have mentioned. The old system does not, I am sure. If you will pardon me, I would like to say one thing more. I have personally experienced these virtues since coming into your city, and I have sometimes thought that the hospitality and kindness so generously shown me might be due in some measure to the influences you suggest, and then again I have wondered whether I had not merely fallen among persons unusually possessed by these qualities. Whatever the cause I have desired the opportunity to express my appreciation and gratitude."

"I hardly know how to answer you, Mr. Maxwell If you wish to resolve your doubts you will have to enlarge your circle of acquaintance. I think I could help you in that if you desired it."

"Many thanks," I answered, "but I pray you let me bask a little longer in the sunshine of the friends I have already found. I want none others just yet."

"Thank you for your courtesy and your kindly expression, Mr. Maxwell," she replied simply.

It was now 8 o'clock, the hour set for beginning the illumination, and as we reached the Administration Boulevard, the entire square, and the surrounding edifices for quite a distance, were suddenly bathed in a flood of silvery light which had been turned upon them.

At a height of about eight hundred feet, above and directly over the great dome of the Administration Building, an immense hemisphere had by some means been suspended. It must have been fully one hundred feet in diameter, and its skyward, or convex surface, was opaque and its outline indistinguishable, while its earthward, or concave one, seemed composed of white glass, and from every portion of it, without cessation or interruption, the light I have mentioned radiated downwards and outwards, a light without heat, steadfast, pure and soft like that of a brililant moon near the earth's surface.

The effect was very beautiful; the white marble of the Administration Building, with its tracings and statuary, came out in full relief, and all the roofs shone like silver in this soft but all-pervading light. It wrapped the sides of the surrounding buildings in its effulgent flood, revealing their noble outlines and gave a new and phantom-like appearance to all objects, great or small, on which it shone.

An exclamation of surprise escaped from Clothilde's lips, and as we hurried along up the East Boulevard under the light of the new orb, her face revealed her delighted wonder.

"Ah, Mr. Maxwell," she exclaimed, "is not this beautiful! I am a thousand times obliged to you for bringing me here."

We stopped near one of the great universities which

faced the eastern side of the Administration Square, and stood for a few moments between it and its adjoining grounds. Great trees cast dark shadows on the street and athwart the walks, while close by us rose the university, a massive building of gray granite. It was many stories high, with numerous porches, nooks and angles on all sides, some of them lighted up by the illumination, others cast in shadow.

The edifice had been closed to general admittance, but many of its porches on the side next the Administration Building were occupied by professors, students and their friends. During the afternoon I had secured the promise of admission to one of the smaller of these high up on the sixth story.

A great concourse of people had already assembled on the square, and many others were constantly arriving.

Clothilde, however, seemed entirely occupied in viewing the illumination, and I stood by her for some minutes enjoying her rapturous enthusiasm. At last I interrupted it and told her of the place I had secured, and in a few moments we were inside the building, and by the aid of a lift reached the sixth story, and were soon on the little portico where, screened by some large pillars and comfortably seated, we could enjoy the scene without discomfort or annoyance.

"I did not think when we started out," said my companion, "that there was such a pleasure in store for us. We seem up here to have been translated into a new world, almost unreal, composed of lights and shadows, an unsubstantial spirit world, beautiful, but vague and dream-like."

The various feelings and emotions of her mind were pictured on her countenance as in a mirror. They added new grace and charm to her appearance, and I did not break the spell by many words.

"Look at the light shining on the golden-ribbed dome of the Administration Building and on its white walls. It seems like a fairy temple, like a new Jerusalem, like a palace of snow, with window panes of ice. There is not a light in any of the windows; they have all been put out that they might not interfere with the effect. And everything is so quiet here, one could imagine we were the only tenants of this solitude. We are not over one hundred feet above the rest of the world, are we?—and yet we are lifted above its ordinary life and thought. What a difference the point of view and the light one uses make in the result."

"They do, indeed," I answered. "There is an undisturbed harmony between the spiritual and material worlds this evening. It is I who am obliged to you for giving it expression."

"Thank you," she replied. "Do you know you have brought me very near the scene of my daily labors? I teach music and languages to young ladies in this very building, on the floor below."

"I knew of your musical but not so much of your linguistic accomplishments," I answered. "Might I inquire what languages you most affect?"

"Oh, I speak in various tongues," she returned, "some pleasant, some not so pleasant."

"I have listened to none but what were very pleasant," I said. "A princess can use no other."

"That shows how superficial your observation has been, or I may as well be plain with you, how little you know of princesses, Mr. Maxwell. You still have hopes? Well, you need not tell me about them. Do you see that broad mirror of silver in the setting of green trees on the plain yonder, and the blue lines running to and from it like cords holding it in place? That is the lake and the canal. See the sailboat skimming over its surface like a white-winged bird? I am acquainted with that lake, Mr. Maxwell, and I have often taken boat rides on it. In fact, some other ladies and I have a boathouse there and go boating frequently. So you have learned of another accomplishment."

"And one, Miss Clothilde, in which fortunately I am somewhat proficient. Could you, or would you, give or accept an invitation to sail together some evening?"

"Yes," she answered, "I think we might have a boat ride some time; I mean a quiet boat ride. I have been out in the larger boats when there was much merriment and laughter and I have enjoyed it, but not so well as in a quieter way, when the water, and the motion, and the small world of the boat, make one happy."

"I hope you will accept an invitation from me," I said, "for some evening this week."

"No," she returned, "please let me choose the time for the boat ride, and I will not make it soon, for the mood in which we are to-night will not bear frequent repetition."

"Well," I answered, "as you wish. But I hope you will let me do the sailing and you can do the singing."

"Yes, I might sing a little, and I may preach to you a little; I can do both, and I like to exercise all my gifts. See that cloud just passing over the face of the moon? Did you ever study cloud effects, Mr. Maxwell? Well, then, let me advise you to do so. We have some of the most beautiful cloud scenery in our skies ever witnessed. Oh, no, not with me! You could not study cloud effects with me. You must be alone. You must observe the size and shape of your cloud, estimate its thickness and

its vaporous contents, note its changes of color and the
way the light falls upon it, and follow it through the sky.
I should only be a divertisement, inimical to real study.

"We ought to be getting home, don't you think so,
Mr. Maxwell? How I have chattered on this stony ledge!
What would the grave professors say could they have
heard me? But we started out to be like children, and
if you have been quietly laughing at me you must remember I have been simply keeping up the character. I have
enjoyed it, though, and to-morrow I shall be as solemn as
a bishop. Now let us go down, please."

We returned slowly toward the house. It was late,
but the illumination still continued with all its former
glory.

We passed by the great vase in the triangular park,
spectrally white in the radiance, and crowned with shrubs
and flowers which gave forth aromatic odors on the night
air, and stopped to pluck a few roses from some bushes
near its base, and then resumed our walk and soon
reached Miss Beyresen's home.

I felt a strange sympathy drawing me to this bright,
lovely and beautiful American girl, who had so uncon-
ventionally accompanied me this evening.

I walked back to my hotel with a feeling of elation,
but once there subjected myself to a rigid and severe
scrutiny.

I realized that I had been interested in the young
lady from the moment I first saw her on the stage. Something, too, told me that the feeling was reciprocated;
there is a telegraphy about such things that cannot be
mistaken.

Was I then a boyish fool? Was I, a high-born Englishman, who had frequented European courts and mingled with wit and beauty in them, to fall helplessly in love

with an American girl of no lineage and no distinction, except such as her voice, manner and beauty had gained for her?

Aye, but there was the mystery. I was not the only one these graces had attracted; the whole city seemed to know her and be proud of her. Everywhere I had heard her called the princess and spoken of with approbation and affection.

Was it nothing to win such a woman—if one could?

There was something very mysterious about this beautiful and gifted girl who was so self-possessed and gracious, who taught music and languages daily, and who owned one book worth at least a hundred pounds, who showed me the costliest engravings of my own home and its surroundings, who could entrance a multitude with the magic of her voice and manner, and chattered fearlessly alone with me high up on a stone balcony, as she had done this night.

I would restrain myself; I would wait and learn about her.

I retired to rest, only to dream of Clothilde Beyresen, original and lovely as ever, sometimes sitting on the stone balcony, sometimes in a boat on the quiet lake, and again clinging to me in a storm-tossed vessel on the ocean's broad expanse.

CHAPTER X.

Two or three days passed before I called again at Mr. Beyresen's. I thought much about Clothilde, however, and learned something more of her history.

She had only lived at home since she was eighteen, having until that age resided in one of the Eastern cities.

She had been received with much favor in Neuropolis, and her appearance on the stage had created a furore which she had put down with great good sense, by declining any marked attention. She seldom sang in public now, but devoted herself assiduously to her work in the university.

She enjoyed walking, riding, boating and other athletic exercises, went a good deal into society, where she was very popular, and was, in short, a high-spirited, good, and wonderfully gifted young lady.

I inquired no further; indeed, so great had become my faith and interest in her that I had felt like a culprit in inquiring at all; I seemed to be unworthily seeking for information in regard to a confiding friend.

When I went again to Mr. Beyresen's I found the family all together and cordial and pleasant as usual. Mrs. Beyresen, however, soon excused herself, having some duties which demanded her attention, and Mr. Beyresen began to talk to me about the controversies between the Nationality and the citizens of other states. He referred to the alleged grievances which I have already stated to the reader, and in addition gave me the history of another difficulty of far graver character.

The United States court of highest appeal, he informed me, had after a long and bitter legal contention rendered final judgment against the Nationality for a sum amounting to more than one hundred million dollars.

This judgment was based on claims against the Nationality, made by a large number of persons, who had been tenants of the company controlling the settlement of the land before the organization of that body.

These persons had rented portions of these lands for a year, or more, but for various causes being considered by the company undesirable tenants, had been refused permission to occupy them any longer.

They had therefore removed to other states. The company was soon after succeeded by the Nationality, of which the tenants remaining became citizens, with certain rights and privileges guaranteed them, chief among which was the support of themselves and their families after a certain age.

The former tenants claimed they had been wronged by the refusal of the company to rent lands to them, and their consequent inability to remain and enjoy the advantages afforded by the new organization, and demanded pecuniary recompense.

Their grievances were fostered and their demands encouraged by astute and cunning men, who saw in them an opportunity of harassing the Nationality and securing gain for themselves.

A corporation of wealthy capitalists was formed in the Eastern states, and in Europe, for the purpose of dealing in these claims, which from time to time purchased them from the original tenants at a merely nominal price.

This corporation, many years before, had brought suit against the Nationality on these demands, maintaining that the latter body succeeded to all liabilities of the first company. They employed eminent counsel, and the officers of the Nationality did likewise.

This suit began in the lower courts of the United States, and was fought step by step up to the highest tribunal, which had just rendered the judgment of which Mr. Beyresen spoke. Continuing the subject, he informed me that the officers of the Nationality did not consider themselves authorized to pay the judgment without submitting the matter to their people, and had applied for a stay of execution to enable them to do so, and the indications were that it would not be granted.

"The rendition of this judgment, however," said he, "means far more than the payment of this amount. It means that the courts of the land are under the control of the Money Power, which always has been and always will be our inveterate foe. It means that all the other issues supposed to have been settled by former decisions will be speedily reopened. The right of the people, or any part of the people, to issue obligatory certificates of indebtedness, which by mutual agreement, shall take the place of money, will be again questioned. Their right, by like agreement, to refrain from using among themselves what currently passes as money in the United States, will again be denied. Our system of state ownership will again be controverted. All these attacks will be made so insidiously and covertly that constant embarrassment will be placed in the way of our progress, peace and happiness.

"The battle between the people and plutocracy has been set for years, and the borders of our Nationality define the line between the contending forces. The power of money is enormous. It is compact and aggressive. It is vigilant, alert, resourceful and unscrupulous. It attracts the brightest and most influential to its side. The people beyond our borders revolt at its debasing rule, but are none the less subjugated by it. It is even now attempting to create divisions among our own people. There are agents of the Money Power in our towns and cities to-day, endeavoring to alienate their affections from this form of government. But they have as yet had no success, I am proud to say; for our people are well satisfied, and true to that government and labor system which has saved them from the evils, and sufferings, and vassalage, which is the lot of their Eastern brethren.

"The battle which is to be fought, Mr. Maxwell, will be a struggle of giants, and will involve more of weal or woe to the American people than any in which they have hitherto engaged. It is a conflict, sir, between systems which are antagonistic, and one or other of them must fall. It seems to me as irrepressible a conflict as that of 1860, and like that, to be about industrial slavery.

"The battlefield hitherto has been the courts; it remains to be seen whether it will hereafter be confined to them. Prior to 1860, our courts were not conducted in the interests of freedom; it will soon be seen how they are controlled to-day.

"But whatever the battlefield, I am sure, Mr. Maxwell, victory will finally be ours. We are united and will wait, if waiting be possible. We shall quickly become stronger. The people, in other states, are daily growing more dissatisfied with their condition. Those nearest us, and who know us best, are with us. The great states of Texas, Arkansas, Missouri and Oklahoma will soon join us and will add largely to our population. Their people have seen the blessings of our system of labor and government and are overwhelmingly in favor of it. We shall soon be so strong that the argument of numbers will be with us. This is what the Money Power fears. This is why it has latterly pushed this controversy, which has been allowed to drag along since the days of John Harvey. Ever since his time it has viewed us with suspicion and distrust."

"Is it not unfortunate," said I, "that the man whom you regard as the founder of the Nationality should have given so much cause for suspicion and distrust, by acts that can scarcely be defended with any show of success in any civilized land?"

Mr. Beyresen looked somewhat surprised, but I continued: "Do you think it wise, sir, in view of a struggle such as you deem approaching, to give so much prominence to the memory and attract so much attention to the deeds of this pioneer of your earlier days? I am an Englishman, not, I trust, without great interest in the social reforms of the age and a newly awakened hope for the success of your form of government, but were I to advocate your cause in England I dare not mention John Harvey's name, for he is there considered as a murderer, a pirate, and a buccaneer. I should assuredly choose some other person among your pioneers as the representative of your principles and government."

Toward the latter portion of my remarks Mr. Beyresen had been seized with a violent fit of coughing which interfered somewhat with them, and caused me to raise my voice rather higher than usual. He rose hurriedly as if still struggling with his bronchial difficulty, and saying, "Excuse me, sir, my daughter will answer you; you need to know John Harvey's history better," left the room, followed at once by Miss Anna, who seemed much concerned at her father's condition.

Somewhat disconcerted by this sudden flight, I looked toward the elder daughter and was still more confused when I saw the change in her appearance and manner.

She had turned and now sat facing me, upright as a statue, her eyes, blazing like coals of fire, fixed full upon me. Her face was pale, but a vivid red spot glowed in each cheek. Her lips were slightly parted, but her white teeth were clinched together, while her small, shapely hands grasped tightly the arms of the easy-chair in which she sat. She seemed struggling to control herself in a passion of almost ungovernable anger, of which I was plainly the object, for her eyes never left mine. It seemed difficult for her to keep her seat or to find voice or words.

To say I was astonished beyond measure, and perplexed and troubled, would be to put it lightly; but I am not of slow perceptions, and comprehended that it was as necessary for me to be still and composed, and await events, as if I faced an angry lioness.

Finally she found voice, low at first and emphatic, but musical, and how bitter and contemptuous!

"I shall not," she said, "accept the task my father has thrown upon me and defend John Harvey's memory. My father knew him as a personal friend and could have done it had he chosen. But I will not sit by and hear an Englishman cast aspersions upon John Harvey's name without suitable reply. Who are you who sit in high and mighty judgment upon the character of a man whose shoe-latchet you are not worthy to untie? What have you, an idler as you are, ever done to enable you even to pass an opinion on the acts of one whose beneficence has blessed ten millions of fellow-beings?

"I will tell you who you are, and what your kind has done, that you may rightly estimate your own importance. You are a descendant of a line of Anglo-Saxons, Danes, and Normans, whose hands were red, constantly red, with the blood of their fellow-men and women; to whom pillage, piracy, robbery, murder, and all crimes, even among their kings and nobles, were everyday occurrences, who, like beasts of prey, ravaged all lands and all seas, and brought distress and woe wherever they went. And what are you now in this twentieth century, when such crimes would meet with condign and merited punishment? Too few to govern the world by the sword, you have erected a golden image of which you are the high priests, and whose worship you recommend to all mankind, and like the Ephesians of old, when your divinity is assailed, when your pockets are touched, you are ready to cry out and vilify and abuse the apostles of freedom; as you yourself, a descendant of such a race, have unjustly and unkindly done to-night. John Harvey and Herbert Maxwell, the philanthropist and the idler, occupy very different spheres. I will choose the former, and my father can dispose of the latter. I will send him to you again," she said scornfully, and she departed.

It is impossible to describe the mortification, suffering, and misery I endured during this tirade, and, though trying to seem composed, I presume I must have shown it. Toward its termination the young lady had arisen and stood near me, gesticulating freely. She was terribly angry, and yet graceful and quick in every movement, and I felt it impossible to turn away or even avoid her look. She was laboring under great excitement, but able to express her sentiments in words as easily as she had on the evening of the illumination. But oh, how different! Then she was the charming comrade and companion; now she was Nemesis herself.

A few minutes later the door opened and Mr. Beyresen entered. He was looking toward the floor, and, rubbing his hands in a hesitating and nervous manner, and seemed as much embarrassed as was I.

I rose to my feet, but he said: "Pray take your seat a few moments, Mr. Maxwell, and let us talk this matter over. I do not know exactly what my daughter has said to you, but I imagine it was nothing pleasant. I do not want to know either," he interrupted, as I was about to make some explanation. "I saw it was coming and I left the room. Excuse me for doing so, but these unfortunate occurrences are better without witnesses. I could not stop it. I might as well have tried to stop a hurricane. My daughter, sir, is a great friend of John Harvey, and you did not understand this."

"My allusion," I replied, "was very unfortunate. But I certainly did not understand either your friendship or your daughter's for that individual, or I should have been more careful. I spoke according to my knowledge of him."

"Your knowledge of him was imperfect or very limited," he answered. "He was a many-sided man; he was a great man, Mr. Maxwell. But we will say no more of him now. Clothilde is a good girl; I cannot make excuses for her. You do not know her provocation, and I must deal justly with you both."

"But what," I exclaimed, "am I to do, Mr. Beyresen? I have visited at your house, and you all, including your elder daughter, have been very friendly with me, and I am distressed. She made it plain to me that it was impossible to meet her on the former footing. She was cruel, Mr. Beyresen, though she may not know it."

"She does know perfectly, Mr. Maxwell," he answered. "She knows all she said. She has a very exact memory."

"Well, will you speak to her, and explain, or get me an opportunity to explain my blunder?" I asked.

"God forbid," said the old gentleman. "You and she must mend this matter. I never shall say a word. I know that Clothilde will think it over, and if she has said too much she will let you know it somehow. She is a girl of fine judgment. I never before saw her so extremely angry. As for me I cannot say a word to her. She chooses her own companions; she does about as she likes, and seldom makes mistakes. She is a royal woman and should be treated as such. Call to see us if you can," he continued; "we wish you to do so. You will either find Clothilde gone, or she will be friendly. If she has been unjust she will repent of it, I know."

And so with a "God bless you" from the old gentleman, who seemed as concerned and as helpless as I was, I left the house.

During the succeeding days I was constantly recurring to the scene of my late discomfiture. I inquired somewhat further into the history of John Harvey, and learned that while he had been guilty of all I had attributed to him, yet he was indeed a many-sided man, and really the founder of the Nationality.

I had several talks with Mr. Beyresen at his office, but he carefully refrained from any allusion to the late unpleasantness, merely saying as I left him, "Come and see us when you can."

But I could not. I had written a note to his daughter, asking her for an opportunity to explain, but beyond a polite acknowledgment of receipt and an expressed doubt as to whether I could explain, the note contained nothing except these words at the end, "Wait a bit," which seemed to me to promise something.

CHAPTER XI.

Very shortly after the events narated in the preceding chapter I made a somewhat prolonged tour throughout the plains, or agricultural portion of the Nationality, my object being to learn all I could about these regions, and to study the character, habits and condition of the people in them, especially so far as they were affected by the peculiar system of government under which they lived.

In these regions it seldom rains, except in the early spring, and not at any time in quantity sufficient to mature crops. During the winter, however, a great amount of snow is deposited upon the sides and tops of the mountains to the westward, where, sheltered in their deep gorges, it melts slowly until the middle of the summer, when the process becomes more rapid. Then the small rivers of the land, few in number and widely separated, all having their sources among the mountains, attain their flood height. These, after reaching the plain, trend in an easterly direction. At no time do they contain water sufficien to fill the wide beds hollowed out ages ago, when indeed they were mighty rivers emptying probably into an inland ocean occupying a large portion of these plains. The water in them, when taken out by artificial channels, was only sufficient to irrigate a narrow fringe of land lying within a few miles of their borders.

The experiments thus made, however, demonstrated that these plains, sloping gently from the mountains to the eastward, were capable of extensive irrigation, and that when irrigated they were very fertile.

About thirty years previous to the time of which I write, a system for watering them had been begun by the construction of the great canal before spoken of, which ran from the north in a southerly direction, along, or near the base of the mountains, for many hundreds of miles. Several large branches, in themselves small rivers, extended from it eastward along the summits of the water sheds of the rivers just mentioned.

From these branches, or laterals, as they were called, numerous smaller canals, or ditches, took the water and distributed it all over the land. During the succeeding years these artificial channels had been extended and multiplied until now the whole constituted the most complete and extensive scheme of irrigation to be found upon the surface of the globe; a great arterial system fully as essential to the nurture and development of these regions as that of the human body is to human life.

The railroads were a feature that at once attracted my attention. As has been before stated the unit of division of the land was the township, twelve miles square. Near the center of each of these a village had been built, in which all of its inhabitants lived, and these villages were connected by railroads running north, south, east and west, generally in direct lines from one to another, until they finally merged in great trunk roads communicating with the metropolis and the larger cities of the Nationality, and with the other portions of the United States. The system resembled the meshes of a great net, stretched regularly and carefully over the land, with occasional stronger cords crossing it in other directions leading to larger knots and ganglions, and its convenience and completeness for all purposes of transportation could hardly be estimated. The propulsive force employed was electricity, which was generated at, and distributed from, numerous places in the mountains and on the plains, where abundant water power, or great beds of coal, made its production easy and inexpensive. The possibilities of this strange agency had been wonderfully realized in this land and in my journey through it, recalling my imagination of the genii of the east, I saw them typified in this mysterious force, which was performing in every home, in every workshop, and in the open fields, rapidly and successfully, a great part of the hard labor which had formerly been accomplished only by long continued human toil.

Everything was so unusual, so ethereal, and so beautiful, that my brightest fancies of an ideal land were realized. The railway and the public road for vehicles generally accompanying it, were bordered on each side by tall trees, trimmed so as not to obstruct the view, which was ever changing and far-reaching and most delightful. Broad meadows and pastures, and extensive orchards and groves of trees, clothed the earth with varying shades of green. Acres of maize tossed their long leaves, and waved their tasseled plumage in the gentle breeze; and great fields of golden grain yet unreaped gave richness of coloring to the scene, while distant lakes added their ethereal blue to idealize and lighten it.

Every portion of the land showed intelligent attention and loving care. No fences, nor unsightly objects of any character marred it. All noxious growth and things inimical to thorough cultivation, or offensive to the senses or repellent to ascetic tastes, had been removed. Wherever for any reason the soil was unfit for cultivation it had been set in trees, and at the angles where the townships joined each other, forests had been planted four miles square, in which were deer, elk, grouse, quail and other game, all carefully protected and preserved. These forests gave wonderful variety and interest to the landscape, and exercised a very beneficial influence on the climatology of the country, and afforded places for quiet recreation and enjoyment.

In the distance, villages and towns dotted here and there upon the landscape, succeeded one another, connected by the ever present railroads that bore the produce of the land upon their steel net work to its more populous cities and to foreign countries.

As I gazed from the car windows on these scenes of rural beauty and life and activity, I realized the perfection which Nature can attain when assisted and directed in her work by the intelligence of man, and wondered how it had been possible for this people in so short a time to so thoroughly awaken her dormant energies.

As we approached the villages, the wide-spreading fields and pastures were superseded by lesser areas devoted to orchards, small fruits and gardens. When we reached them, the quiet grace, comfort and adornment of their dwellings, embowered in shade and surrounded by well-kept lawns and walks, and the artistic beauty of their public grounds and buildings, so unexpected in places so remote from cities, continually astonished me.

I stopped at several of these villages and district towns and spent some time in gaining an acquaintance with the practical workings of this new governmental and labor system.

The department chiefs at Neuropolis, it appeared, made yearly estimates of the kinds and quantities of the various products required for home consumption and for sale. They were thoroughly acquainted with the capabilities of each district for certain purposes, and their directions to the district officers in respect to labor and the nature of production were governed by this knowledge. The latter controlled the execution of these orders, and divided the work judiciously among their townships. The labor directors, each in charge of a certain portion of the land, or a certain department of labor, arranged it and saw that it was properly done.

All products of farm, mine, forest and stream were taken to public yards, or warehouses, and properly weighed, measured, or numbered, and the surplus products intended for sale were shipped to Neuropolis, and of the remainder, a sufficient portion was retained for home consumption, while the rest was kept in the district warehouses for use in other portions of the Nationality. All cereals requiring further preparation were sent to large mills located at certain points, and all animals intended for slaughter were conveyed to other places, where such operations were conducted on a scale of great magnitude and with the closest economy.

In each village a thorough system of accounts was maintained, and in the district towns accounts were kept with each village, with other districts and with Neuropolis, and in the latter place with all the districts, and with the outside world.

From the books in the various departments of state could be obtained a complete history of the character and value of the products of every township of the Nationality, from its first organization down to the present time, the disposal made of them, and everything regarding them. Any failure in production was at once noted and its causes carefully ascertained and, if possible, removed.

Thus a comprehensive system of intelligent and eminently successful labor and production was maintained; continually improving in thoroughness and effectiveness, because the best brain and skill of the land were enlisted in its service. The hours of labor were not long, and those engaged in it at a distance from their homes employed the railroads in conveyance to and from their work, and every facility for its easy, prompt, and complete performance was afforded them.

Co-operation and equality were the keynotes of the system. The people worked together happily and contentedly under the direction of their own elective officers, who labored with them and were in turn governed, as to general objects, methods and results, by established rules, and subject to still higher officers. Labor was made honorable; the way to office and preferment lay in doing good and effective work, and planning and directing for the general welfare.

Education formed a separate department, employing the best minds in perfecting its methods and advancing its interests. The public schools, especially, were zealously protected, and carefully supported. In each village ample accommodations were provided for free instruction up to academic grades, and other public schools of more special character, where trades were taught, were located in the district towns. In the larger cities and in Neuropolis, as has been stated, still greater schools existed, where the pupil could be educated in any branches or professions.

The stores were managed singularly, samples only being shown with prices marked, the goods being just as represented. When ordered they were paid for, and if the order was for something not in stock, it was selected, often from a catalogue, and sent for promptly. The prices were much lower than in other countries, and no effort was made to sell goods, the quantity sold being a matter of indifference to all except the purchaser. A

general manager, three or four clerks and as many delivery men and roustabouts, were all the persons employed in the conduct of a business that under other systems would have required several times this number.

Ample time remained to the people for recreation,
for social diversion, or for enjoyment in the family circle.
Public libraries and reading-rooms, theaters, parks and
similar resorts were always open to them, and were constantly filled by those seeking instruction, or amusement.

Houses of worship were among the most prominent
buildings in all the villages and towns. They were erected
and owned by the state. The churches were sustained,
however, by the voluntary contributions of the members.
The people, not overwearied in mind, or body, by the
cares and labors of the week, filled these temples every
Sabbath, and learned those lessons which inculcate a
higher than mere human responsibility, and observed the
day as one dedicated to God's service, and not to mere
mental and physical recuperation.

Crime was scant. The establishment of government
ownership, the disuse of money, and abolishment of private accumulation, had blotted from the calendar all
crimes connected with the love of gain. The manufacture and sale of intoxicants as a beverage ceased, as a
consequence of the former action, and wrought nearly
as much diminution in crime, and only that arising from
the ordinary and unstimulated passions of mankind remained, and was rendered far less frequent by assured
employment and the removal of the insidious temptations
of poverty and want.

The loyalty of the people to their government and
land seemed most intense, and as I journeyed through it
and saw its richness, its beauty, its peacefulness, its at-

tractiveness, and promise of present and future comfort, guaranteed by governmental authority, I felt they had just cause for pride and patriotism. Under other systems, livelihood and comfort and advantages were sought after for years, unremittingly, unintelligently, painfully and often unsuccessfully. Man fought man in an unceasing struggle and crime was a constant and necessary concomitant. Men failed in honest endeavor, and with their families suffered, and many sinned.

The Nationality said to its citizens: "The People collectively offer to you and each of you the opportunity to work, during reasonable hours, intelligently and with the best appliances. You shall not fail if we can help it. You have our assurance of success in providing for yourselves and your families. If you are sick, or otherwise incapacitated for labor, you still have that assurance, not as a charity, but as a matter of right."

As a consequence men worked better, more buoyantly and cheerfully than elsewhere. They looked freer and more independent. They lived in more comfort, had more time for study, and were more intelligent and capable than elsewhere.

Fully as much might be said of the women. They were strong, and bright, and happy, and many of them were of high culture and refinement. I could tell now whence came the bright, healthy and intelligent men and women I had seen in the metropolis. They came from pleasant and refined homes and families in these towns and villages, replete with the strength derived from pure air and proper exercise, and animated by the integrity and happiness obtained by earnest endeavor for honest objects.

After spending much time in these rural regions I proceeded on my way, by rail, to visit Sterling, one of the large manufacturing cities located on the South Platte River, intending from thence to return to Neuropolis, stopping on my road to examine the celebrated bridge, or aqueduct, which carries the waters of the great canal over the bed of that river.

We passed through an agricultural country much the same as that I have already described, until we approached within thirty miles of the river, when the extent of forest became greater.

Wide-spreading sand dunes had formerly rendered this section of country barren, and these forests had been planted to protect it from further innovation, and to reclaim it. This had been done so successfully that but little evidence of the shifting nature of the soil remained, and in the intervals among the forests herds of cattle as fine as I had ever seen were now grazing.

When we arrived within view of the river the singularity of its appearance attracted my attention. It was crossed, at distances of from two to three miles apart, by dams from twenty to forty feet in height, which made a succession of terraced lakes, or sheets of water. From these, canals were carried out upon the banks for irrigating the lands adjoining, and the water power furnished by these dams was used for various purposes.

Late in the evening we reached Sterling, situated in the valley of the South Platte and containing nearly fifty thousand inhabitants. Being quite fatigued, I retired to rest soon after my arrival. When I awoke next morning it was late, and after breakfast I set out to visit some of the great manufactories of the place, consisting of flouring mills, glass and brick works, and potteries for producing terra cotta, tile, and other articles from clay.

A trunk railway ran to and from this city, and a massive dam thrown across the river formed a large lake,

and furnished power for the greatest flouring mills I had
ever seen. I was shown through them and was much
interested in the statistics of their annual production,
which was so great that I remember entering into a
mental calculation of how many people their output would
feed, and it was several millions. A large part of the flour
and other products were, however, exported by way of
the Gulf of Mexico to South America and Europe.

In the manufacture of brick and tile, and other articles formed from clay, over three thousand persons were
employed, and a great quantity and variety of such articles
were produced.

In the afternoon I visited several of the glass works,
and was very much surprised at their magnitude, and the
beauty of their products. For delicacy of design, coloring and finish, I never saw the superior of the articles of
glass manufactured in this city. They comprised nearly
every description of such ware known, and from this
point shipments of these articles were made all over the
world. Over four thousand persons were engaged in this
industry; the most approved methods and machinery were
used, and many of the new processes and inventions orig-
inated, I was told, among the workmen.

I returned to the hotel toward evening, and found a
middle-aged lady, the wife of the manager, in the clerk's
office. I inquired of her concerning the great aqueduct
conveying the water of the canal over the Platte River,
and she informed me it was only about forty miles distant from Sterling, and that the railroad crossed the river
on a bridge but a little distance below it. We talked together for some time, and she asked me if I had been at
the opera house the preceding evening. I replied in the
negative, and inquired if any special entertainment had
been given.

"Yes," she answered, "the princess sang there last night. There was a large audience, and you missed a fine performance, which is to be regretted, for she does not often sing in public."

"The Princess Clothilde, from Neuropolis?" I exclaimed .

"Yes," she returned. "Do you know her and have you heard her sing?"

"I have met the princess," I said. "Please tell me when she came, and if she is still here."   .

"She arrived two days ago. There were several ladies in the party, and they all left last night for Neuropolis."

I was much disturbed. I had heard nothing the evening before of this performance. I had gone lazily to sleep, when the person I most desired to see was in the same town, and in full view at the opera house.

I cared nothing now for further inspection of the city, the view of the bridge, or anything else; I only wished to be again in Neuropolis. There might be a letter, or a message; anyway, I should see her father and learn about her.

I bought my ticket and at 11 o'clock that night took the train for that city, where I awoke next morning.

There was no message for me, and Mr. Beyresen had left the capital some days before for the southern portion of the Nationality, but was expected to return soon.

CHAPTER XII.

Shortly after my return I met several of the councilors with whom I was acquainted.

From conversation with them I learned that the parliament of which they were members had been in session during my absence, and I was satisfied that the political situation in the United States was very grave.

These gentlemen understood that I was in sympathy with them, and I communicated to them a resolution I had formed of visiting some of the Eastern cities and learning the condition of the people there and their feeling toward the Nationality. They advised me to postpone this journey for some weeks, until matters had assumed more definite shape, and to this I consented.

A few days later Mr. Beyresen returned, and I went to see him. He informed me that his daughter had spoken to him of our difference, and intimated that she would be willing to meet me any time I might appoint. Though I considered myself far less blameworthy in the affair than she appeared to think me, yet my wish to see her was so great that I waived all scruples and set the next evening for my call.

I reached the door with no definite plan of action, and was ushered into the well-known sitting-room and told that Miss Beyresen would see me in a few moments. Mechanically I picked up a book which proved to be her volume of engravings, and opened it at the view of Dorsetshire Castle and its surroundings. As my eyes and thoughts were thus engaged and before I was aware of her approach, Miss Clothilde entered the room.

"Good evening, Mr. Maxwell," she said. "I see you have the book of engravings."

She did not offer her hand, but was perfectly easy and unembarassed.

"I hope," returned I, "I am doing no harm. I found it on the table and almost unconsciously opened it."

"You need make no excuse," she said pleasantly, "in regard to that or anything else. My father informs me you have been absent for some time traveling over the country. Doubtless you will have some interesting things to tell us."

"I have been away," I replied. "I have been studying your country and am gradually becoming acquainted with the customs and manners of its people. When I have acquired proper knowledge of these, and also of the likes and dislikes of my auditors, I shall possibly be able to express opinions which may meet with approbation. Till then, I have learned to be very cautious. So pray do not expect me to enter much into detail about my journey."

She hesitated for a moment and then said slowly: "I do not suppose, Mr. Maxwell, you imagine such vigilance as you indicate at all required of you by any one. But I tell you plainly you will have to use care when you speak of those endeared to an entire people. Do you not understand that yet?"

"I admit this," I replied, "that opinions vary greatly in regard to the character of such persons as you refer to, and I acknowledge also that one should be very careful in expressing his own opinions, even among friends, or in a small assemblage, lest there be some one present with different views who might feel aggrieved by such expression. And if I, at any time, by lack of such care, have wounded anyone I beg pardon for it."

She looked toward the floor, and I saw the color rise in her cheek. At last she said: "But the opinion itself remains unchanged."

"Opinion with me," I answered, "is a matter of evidence. I have evidence, personal evidence, on which to base the one in question. In fact, I hope you will excuse personal reference, for we cannot well get along without it—I met John Harvey once in the China Seas. If you care to hear the story I will tell it to you, as briefly and plainly as I can."

"Anything that relates to John Harvey is of interest to me, Mr. Maxwell," she returned.

"Well, then," I replied, "I will try to tell you the story. In 1929, six years ago, I was one of the lieutenants on his majesty's ship of war, Vulcan, an armored line of battle ship, built in the very best modern manner. She lay at that time in the harbor of Yokohama, and was the flagship of Admiral Berne, who had command in Japanese waters.

"There were in the port, also, two other British war vessels, the Hecla and the Alert, smaller but yet very formidable ships, belonging to the squadron under Admiral Berne's command. The Vulcan mustered five hundred men all told, the Hecla about three hundred, and the Alert two hundred and fifty. As part of her armament the flagship carried on each side, port and starboard, a twelve-inch gun mounted in a revolving turret, throwing a projectile weighing over one thousand pounds.

"My place was in the starboard turret in command of one of these heavy guns. I will not weary you with details, but a few other points in the situation must be mentioned.

"Owing to difficulties about the Nicaraguan canal, the relations between the United States and Great Britain were, at the time, greatly strained and war was known to be imminent. A large number of American merchant vessels lay in the harbor, awaiting results, unwilling to put to sea for fear of capture by British cruisers. Two French warships were also at anchor in the harbor. Such was the condition of affairs the latter part of August nineteen hundred and twenty-nine.

"One day, about that time, we witnessed in that harbor one of the strangest and most beautiful sights ever beheld on any waters. I wish you could have seen it, Miss Beyresen; it is difficult to describe.

"Moving down the waters of the Bay came a white vessel, not of the color made by paint, but a pure white, exquisitely modeled, and graceful in every movement. She was a good-sized craft, about three hundred and twenty-five feet long, and sixty-five feet beam, and seemed to be made of one piece of some strange white metal. The curves of her sides and bow, and the flutings on her upper works were beautiful, and all wrought in the same material. She was wonderfully clean, no smudge appearing anywhere. Her figurehead was a queenly woman, and the name, Albatross, was distinctly visible, inlaid in black letters below it.

"Her deck was occupied by ladies and gentlemen, attired gaily. She carried the flag of the United States, and came to anchorage near the shore, within a quarter of a mile of where the French warships lay, and somewhat farther from us.

"In a short time white boats manned by sailors in blue jackets and white trousers, and filled with her pas-

sengers, put off from her for the shore. During the succeeding days such communication, back and forth, was
constantly kept up, and we learned that the strange vessel was a pleasure boat, built and owned by John Harvey,
an American gentleman, of immense wealth, obtained
from a great mine in that country, and that she was said
to be constructed of a peculiar metal found in the mine.
The latter statement we regarded as mythical, but the
former was corroborated by letters and telegrams received from various other points where the vessel had
stopped and remained days and weeks.

"The French Admiral paid his respects by a visit to
the Albatross, and a little later Admiral Berne did the
same. Both were received by Mr. Harvey in person and
conducted through portions of the vessel, but Admiral
Berne was not entirely pleased with his reception. All
the officers, on their return, expressed surprise at the
wealth expended in building and fitting out the ship, and
I, who saw her later, may say that millions must have
been used in this way. The magnificence of her decora-
tions was indescribable. Silver was common, and gold
plentiful, everywhere. I will not dwell on this, however,
but hasten to tell what followed.

"The political situation between the United States
and England became daily more threatening, but those
on the Albatross seemed to be engaged in pleasure merely, and to take no thought in regard to such matters.

"About ten days after his arrival, John Harvey gave
a grand ball to which the French Admiral and his officers
were invited, but the English were unnoticed. What I
did on that occasion cannot be defended.

"I determined to attend that ball. I had been intimate with some of the French officers, and they proposed
to take me as one of their number, and did so,

"I obtained leave of absence over night, and none of our officers knew where I had been. I saw what I could of the American vessel. The salon and dining-room, which were among the places to which we had access, were simply magnificent.

"I have never beheld their equal. I saw John Harvey and talked with him and drank some wine with him. He was a tall, dark, fine-looking man; the statue on Pike's Peak is exactly like him; I recognized it in a moment.

"All the ladies and gentlemen were very kind and agreeable, and I had a pleasant time.

"Next day after the ball I returned on board the Vulcan. There was a change of feeling toward the Albatross. Old sailors, who somehow always reflect the secret opinions of their officers, said that if war were declared the American vessel would soon entertain a different party on her decks. Officers also spoke slightingly of the ship.

"Search-lights are constantly kept burning at night on men-of-war in harbor, and orders were given to turn the light frequently toward the American vessels, so that none of them could leave the harbor unseen. Shortly after, war was actually declared, and secret orders came to seize any American vessel that attempted to leave the harbor, especially the Albatross.

"Admiral Berne informed the captains of the American vessels that they would not be permitted to leave. The Hecla was ordered out two miles toward the entrance of the harbor, and the Alert still farther out, to intercept any that should attempt to do so. On the Vulcan we had orders to fire across the bows of any such vessel, and to bring her to.

"I heard from the French officers that the Albatross intended to depart. It seemed to me a duty to inform those on board her that if they did so they would be fired on.

"I wrote a letter in a disguised hand informing John Harvey, and again obtaining permission to go ashore, and putting on a Japanese costume, I hired a native boatman to take me out to the Albatross. I did not dare go on board, but, rowing around the vessel in search of some one to take the letter, approached an open porthole."

"And I suppose," interrupted Miss Beyresen, "you found some lorn Dulcinea to receive your message?"

"I found," continued I, "a young lady sitting there whom I had met at the ball, and who promised to deliver my letter. Your supposition was not far from correct. Might I inquire how you came to make it?"

"Oh," she answered, "there is a fitness and a proper sequence in these matters. Given a young lieutenant, and the young lady is sure to appear in the story. I have been looking for her for some time. But please go on, Mr. Maxwell," she continued, "and excuse my rather rude interruption. Indeed I could not help it," she said plaintively.

"I will try to pick up my story," I replied, not a little disconcerted. "I returned to the Vulcan, and the next morning dawned. When the light grew strong enough to see it was noticed that a change had come over the Albatross. All her upper works had disappeared, and her deck was unbroken. At her stern a round turret, about fourteen feet high, of the same material as the vessel, had arisen in the night. Her ports were closed entirely, and even her small boats had been stowed away somewhere. She bore no flag, and was slowly moving nearly a mile away from us, though not in the direction of the outlet of the harbor. Word was sent to the Admiral, who at once came on deck. He watched her for a few moments and then said: 'I think she means to go out. If she puts her bow seaward, and moves in that direction, fire a shot athwart her and await orders. Call the men quickly to action.'

"This was done, and the Hecla and the Alert were signaled that the vessel was coming out, and to prepare to stop her.

"The Albatross drifted on a short distance, when she halted, and ran up the stars and stripes. A moment later —it was about half past 8 o'clock—she swung lazily around, quartering us, with her bow pointed seaward, and moved rapidly forward, as the Admiral had predicted. A twelve-pound gun in our secondary battery boomed over the water, and its shot crossed about forty feet in advance of her bow.

"All in the starboard turret who could, myself among the number, were watching intently. The Albatross checked her speed. I saw her turret revolving; I heard a midshipman call out, 'To your gun; she is going to fire!' A line of red, blue and green lightning shot from her to us. I heard a horrible grinding crash in the fore part of the Vulcan; the entire front of her deck seemed to lift bodily, and then fall back. That shot killed one hundred men and wounded one hundred more, many of whom afterward died. Admiral Berne, who was in the larboard turret, ordered all the guns to open fire on her. I discharged my twelve-inch rifle. The shot struck the side of the Albatross, and, glancing off, was buried in the sea. That from the larboard rifle also glanced and, flying into the town, killed several Japanese. The Hecla, about two miles distant, opened fire. The Albatross moved calmly outward toward the open water. The Hecla and Alert hastened inward to encounter her, all the vessels firing at her.

"We had turned to follow her, and our larboard battery opened on her. Suddenly she squared her head a little toward the shore, and a moment later a flash of colored lightning from her struck the Hecla, now over a mile distant. Her upper decks flew into the air, a great chasm, partly under water, appeared in her bow, the sea rushed in, and in a moment the fore part of the vessel plunged beneath its surface, throwing the hind part in the air, and then all disappeared. Not a soul was saved.

"We ceased firing, but just as the order was given another awful flash came from the turret of the Albatross toward us. There was a horrid convulsion near me. I was knocked senseless by the explosion, and when I recovered found the twelve-inch gun dismounted, the bodies of two men crushed to death beneath it, and myself deserted by the others who had sprung into the sea. The larboard turret against which the bolt had been directed, with Admiral Berne and all within it, was swept into the sea.

"The vessel was a charnel-house, and drifted, an unmanageable wreck, upon the waters. The Albatross was moving toward the entrance of the harbor, swiftly pursuing the Alert, which fled before her. As I looked, the former yawed a little, and again the ominous flash shot toward the Alert, but the bolt went over her. A moment after she flashed another with better aim, for the Union Jack went down, and the Alert at once surrendered. A half hour later the Albatross returned, followed by the Alert in charge of a prize crew. Soon after an American merchant vessel brought the Vulcan to anchorage near the Albatross, which seemed entirely undamaged by the shot which had struck her.

"The work of removing the English dead and wounded to the shore was at once begun by the remaining crew and officers, assisted by the British consul; and a few hours later the wrecks of the Vulcan and Alert, towed by American vessels, by John Harvey's orders, he leading in the Albatross, were taken to the mouth of the harbor and sunk bow foremost in shallow water, and a notice posted on them that no British war vessel should enter for four days thereafter, on pain of being similarly treated.

"That evening the passengers, whom the American consul had sheltered during the fight, returned to the Albatross, and the next morning she bore her customary appearance. Her turret was gone; her upper works were restored; her boats were in their davits, and her many ports were open.

"In that struggle fully six hundred lives were lost. The news was at once telegraphed to England, and created great distress, alarm, and consternation.

"This was war, cruel, bloody war. But this, though all I witnessed, was not all. Four days later the Albatross left the harbor, and three weeks after entered a Spanish port on the Bay of Biscay, from whence John Harvey telegraphed the English government of his arrival, and demanded a ransom of fifty million pounds in gold for Liverpool, and the same sum for London, to be paid to his account in this Spanish port, otherwise on September 25th he would begin the destruction of these cities. In earnest of his ability to do this, if the ransom were not paid, he would fire an empty shell over the former city, and wait till 1 o'clock, when a steady fire of destruction would begin.

"The English filled the channel with all their available ironclads to protect these cities, and on September 24th an awful sea battle occurred, in which so terrible were his unknown thunderbolts and so invulnerable was his own vessel, that John Harvey sunk or crippled ten

English warships in four hours, and the futility of further resistance was demonstrated.

"On September 25th the amount was paid, in golden vessels, in bars, and in other ways, and John Harvey took his passengers on board again, and with a chartered ship in company started for America.

"The war between England and the United States was quickly ended and peace concluded. I understand John Harvey and his vessel soon after went down in the Atlantic, and his terrible engine of destruction and all his secrets and his treasure perished with him.

"In my country, Miss Beyresen, the ignorant and some not so ignorant, call him a wizard, and I have heard he is so regarded by many in the eastern portion of your own land.

"You have listened very patiently to this long story, which contains the evidence on which I based my opinion of John Harvey's character. I have, however, heard many things about him that show me he had other, and even philanthropic traits. He seems to have done much for this land, but he certainly inflicted a heavy blow on mine."

"I hardly know what to say to your story, Mr. Maxwell," said she. "It is a terrible history, of terrible destruction, brought on by arbitrary rashness. I have heard that Admiral Berne wrote to John Harvey that if he attempted to leave the harbor he would blow him out of the water. He thought that easily done; the event proved his mistake; it did not justify his design. But let us say no more about this fearful business, Mr. Maxwell. Let us forget it if we can."

"I cannot forget it, Miss Beyresen," I answered. "Scenes such as those I have described are never forgotten. If, however, you so desire, I shall not again allude to them."

'I think," she replied, "that would be the wiser course. It is not pleasant to have a stain upon one's idols pointed out. Let us speak of something else," she continued. "I suppose I may ask you now if you enjoyed your journey."

"I did," I answered rather coldly, "only I missed your opera at Sterling. I was in the city that night, but did not know of your performance. I sincerely hope I may have another opportunity."

"Thank you, Mr. Maxwell," she replied. "I am glad to know you still approve my singing."

After a little further conversation I took my leave. She invited me to return, and said that all would be glad to see me. But I was far from satisfied with my visit. I never received such scathing denunciation from any person as from Miss Beyresen on the occasion of our talk about John Harvey, and I thought it wholly undeserved. She listened oddly to my narration of the reasons for my opinion of him. She was interested, but evidently unconcerned. The truth of the story she never questioned, indeed she intimated she had heard it before. But it did not move her. She passed it by as readily as if it were one of Shakspeare's stories of fictitious bloodshed, and simply declined to discuss it.

I was sadly disappointed in her conduct and resolved to talk mostly with her father on my future visits, for I considered him a kindly hearted, sensible, well-balanced man.

CHAPTER XIII.

As the reader is doubtless aware from what has been before said, my object in visiting the United States had been mainly to study economic and social problems, and to ascertain how far these had been wisely solved by the governmental regulations of the country. If he think I have digressed from my original purpose he must remember that I am narrating incidents that actually befell me in this land, as well as what I learned concerning these important questions.

For a long series of years after its establishment the government of the United States had been considered the freest and the best in existence, and this had been understood to mean the most advanced in its treatment of these problems.

From what I had already seen and heard, however, I was forced to certain conclusions which I will now state.

There could be no doubt, that no matter what had been its former condition, the general government had fallen to an alarming extent under the debasing influence of the Money Power. There could be no doubt, that in the general desire among the officers of the government to win the favor of that Power, and share in its mercenary rewards, the interests of the people were neglected and their liberties endangered.

There could be no doubt that that Power was permitted to manipulate and control the labor and business systems of the country, outside the Nationality, to its own advantage, and that it was the bitter enemy of any radical change in them.

There could also be no doubt that a struggle of some character was approaching between the two systems of labor and government; that existing in the Nationality and that in the rest of the United States, which would only be terminated by the virtual destruction of one of them.

In such a conflict my own course, however unimportant it might be to others, was yet matter of conscience to myself. The principles upon which the Nationalistic system was founded seemed admirably adapted for securing, and protecting, that equality in opportunity of obtaining comfort, enjoyment and advancement, which is the right of every citizen, and of enforcing the fraternal obligations which each owes to his fellow man, and I had resolved that if on further examination I was satisfied that they were really the most efficient means for such ends, then with heart and hand, with soul and strength, in triumph or defeat I would be with the Nationality.

It was the middle of August and the parliament was in secret session. Many strangers, men of mark and prominence, were in the city, chiefly from the neighboring states of Texas, Missouri, Arkansas and Oklahoma. In these states at the last election the question of becoming part of the Nationality had been made an issue, and been affirmatively decided by the election of officers and members of the legislatures supposed to be in favor of it, and unless bribery or other improper means were resorted to there was little doubt that on the meeting of the state legislatures in December formal steps would be taken to consummate such a union. The chief opposition to the measure came from the great city of St. Louis, where wealth had accumulated and many interests centered, which the opponents of the change asserted would be jeopardized by it.

The representative men of these states, now in Neuropolis, were, I learned, there for the purpose of discussing these matters with the members of the parliament, and perfecting plans for presentation to their respective legislatures.

The intended affiliation had already become matter of discussion in the public prints, and the intense opposition shown by most of the leading eastern journals to such a measure, and the bitterness and partisan character of many of their utterances, plainly the result of their being subsidized by the Money Power, seemed not only likely to further the result which they deprecated, but also to aid the cause of the Nationality in other states.

The minds of the people throughout the entire Union, earnestly engaged in trying to effect a solution of the great social problems so sternly thrust by necessity upon them, had arrived at that point where empty denunciation and vindictive diatribes only induced them to study more closely the real merits of that which provoked such unreasonable opposition, and caused them to regard the latter with suspicion.

The attitude assumed by the Nationality also had great effect. It had taken no active steps in proselytism. Though its senators and representatives in the National Congress were able men, who had already worsted their antagonists in many debates, and though its leaders were shrewd and zealous in its cause, yet they had not solicited other states to join it, and in fact would not counsel alliance with any unless upon a sound and equitable basis.

The numerous charges made against it had been an-

swered, not so much by verbal argument, as by the attention shown to its legitimate business of providing for
the welfare of its citizens. This position won for the Nationality respect among the masses, and enhanced in the
minds of the people of the surrounding states the privilege of being admitted to its system and form of government.

Mr. Beyresen was much engaged in his parliament-
ary labors, but I met him several times at his own house,
and had quite lengthy conversations with him in regard
to the subjects just mentioned. It was plain that he ap-
prehended serious trouble with the authorities of the
United States, and thought it would not be long deferred.

I called one afternoon; it was the 17th of August—
I remember the date well. He and I had a very earnest
talk about the affairs of the Nationality and particularly
in regard to its defensive resources. These Mr. Beyresen
declared were greatly underestimated.

"I have little fear," said he in concluding his remarks, "of the result of a conflict, but I am very anxious
that this matter should be settled peaceably. Our people
are patriotic, well disciplined, and accustomed to united
action, and already constitute an army, organized for labor, which it would be easy to convert into one for defense. Our supplies of food and all necessaries are abund-
antly sufficient to maintain it, for we yearly export great
quantities of these to other portions of the United States
and to foreign countries."

It was about 6 o'clock in the evening and I rose to
depart. Mr. Beyresen said he would go with me as far as
the Administration Building, where he desired to procure
some papers. He excused himself for a few minutes, and
when he returned was accompanied by his daughter
Clothilde, of whom I had seen but little lately.

She spoke to me pleasantly, saying: "Papa tells me you and he are going to the Administration Building, and I would like the walk if you have no objection, Mr. Maxwell."

On this point I hastened to reassure her, and we started together, Miss Beyresen laughing and talking gaily, and soon reached the building. She and I stopped in the hallway near the door of the treasury department, while her father went on to procure his papers.

After awaiting his return for some time she said: "We are not likely to see papa again soon if he becomes engaged in his office. I may be left to entertain you, Mr. Maxwell."

"Which you will do most charmingly, no doubt," I answered.

"Ah, you put me on my mettle, do you?" she exclaimed. "Then, sir, I can show you a sight such as you have never beheld before, unless possibly in the Bank of England. You must promise to keep it secret, though."

I answered that I would, but requested her not to compromise herself in showing me anything.

"Oh, I have the right," she replied confidently, "and will trust you if you will follow me."

"I will!" I exclaimed, "anywhere you lead."

She turned toward the treasurer's office, and at a sign from her I waited at the outer door while she went in. I heard a portion of the conversation between her and one of the officials, an elderly gentleman.

Miss Beyresen asked him for her keys and he seemed to hesitate. I heard her say to him: "Your memory, I fear, is at fault. The order was plain, 'at any time.'"

He gave her the keys at once, and, I supposed, asked her if he should send some one with her, for she answered, "No, I want no one; I will return within an hour."

She came out, and, motioning me to follow her, went quickly down a narrow corridor, turned an angle and waited for me to come up. She stood before an iron door to which she fitted a key, and with my assistance opened it. She pressed a button and an electric light sprang up; we closed the door behind us and she led the way down a narrow passage and stopped before the strong door of what seemed a vault, which fastened with a combination lock. She turned the handle of the latter part way round, and said to me:

"Please push up the little lever above the door; it will disconnect a burglar alarm and we can open it without molestation. What I wish to show you lies within."

I did so, and she unlocked the door, and with our united strength we opened it. A vestibule extended at right angles to this door, and in its inner wall were two other iron doors. One of these she opened with another key, and again pressing a button, a second electric light sprang up and disclosed a large vault into which we entered. It seemed about ten feet wide and probably twenty feet long, though its farther end was but dimly visible. Its sides were shelved for about half their length, and the shelves were crowded with small canvas bags, and in places with great piles of golden coin. About midway down the vault a large table was stationed, which was covered by what seemed to be golden vessels of all kinds.

Miss Beyresen had preceded me, and now stood some distance within. On entering I stumbled over a box of singular appearance placed upon the floor. It was cubical in form and about six inches in dimensions, with a ring attached to its upper side. It was of a glossy black color, with a purplish tinge on all surfaces exposed, and the ring was of the same hue. The light was reflected from its polished sides as from a mirror,

"What is this?" I asked. "I hope I have not injured it."

"Lift it, please, and see," was her quick rejoinder.

I tried to raise the ring which lay on its side that I might lift the box by it, but failed. Though only of quarter-inch metal and hardly three inches in outer diameter, it was immensely heavy. Using both hands I finally accomplished this, but was unable to lift the box from the floor, Miss Beyresen standing by and watching my futile efforts. I could not even turn it over or around. "It is fastened to the stone floor!" I exclaimed much chagrined.

"Let it alone, please," said she. "I did not know it was here. Let me show you these," and she pointed to the golden coin upon the shelves, which I had not yet observed.

The pieces seemed of familiar size and appearance, and I picked up and examined a number of them. They were all English sovereigns of somewhat remote date. Turning to another shelf laden with canvas bags, I asked:

"Are those, too, filled with gold?"

She bowed her head.

"May I open them?"

She again made a gesture of assent. I proceeded to open one. It was full of English gold pieces of a date of several years back. I opened another from a different shelf, and still found English gold pieces. She was watching me intently, and, I thought, a little maliciously. Her eyes glistened and she showed the whiteness of her teeth. I turned to still another shelf and, opening another bag, found English gold coins of about the same date.

"You are surprised," she said, "and you think some one has robbed the English Treasury. If you imagine a share of it belongs to you, take it; there will be plenty left."

Her tone nettled me. "It is not mine," I answered, "and I am not so scarce of gold that I needs must steal it."

"Well, look around you," she continued, "and see if you can find anything that is yours. Gold coin is hard to identify. Search this table if you will. Possibly among this ware you may find something you can recognize, something that belonged to some of your English friends."

She moved aside with a lofty air to give me room, and I, determined to know the full truth, took her at her word, and began to search the table. A moment later, my eye fell upon a large goblet of pure gold. I lifted it in my hands and turning it bottom side up, read the inscription and the name, "The Duchess of Dorsetshire."

I set the goblet down hastily and springing forward, caught Clothilde, who retreated as far as she could, in a firm grasp by the arms. She was speechless, but looked steadily in my face, and I was completely tongue-tied. We stood thus for a moment, when she found voice:

"Let me go, Mr. Maxwell! Unloose me this moment! How dare you do this!"

She spoke not loudly, but angrily, and made no struggle.

"Let go my arms," she said. "I should have known better than to show an Englishman so much gold."

"I will not let you go until you tell me whence came this treasure, and that cup."

"Take the cup; take anything; take two cups," she said, mockingly, "but release my arms. This conduct is inexcusable. Have you lost your mind?"

"Clothilde," I exclaimed, "are you witch or woman?"

"Unloose me, sir," she gasped. "If I only were a

man, and somewhere near your equal in strength! Release me."

I did so at once. She moved toward the table.

"Let me see if I can find the cause of this attack," she said. She raised the cup, looked it over and set it down.

"This conduct, sir," she continued, facing me determinedly, "requires explanation."

"You shall have it," I replied, "but there must be mutual explanation. This is no time nor place for it."

"Your attack was so unwarranted," she said, looking me firmly in the eye, "so thoroughly English."

"Do you think so?" I replied.

"I do think so," she returned, "and I trust you will remember your promised explanation. I will stay here no longer with you," she added.

"As you wish," I answered.

She led the way out, extinguished the lights, and we locked the several doors and regained the corridor. She held the keys up in her hand. "Wait till I return these," she said briefly. She was back in a few moments, and we went together to the entrance of the Administration Building. It was already dark outside. "Where do you go now?" I asked doubtfully.

"Home," she answered.

"Shall I accompany you?"

"Of course," she said. "I will have a little plain talk with you on the way."

She took my arm and we reached the street.

"Are you subject to such attacks?" she asked. "If so, it must be extremely unpleasant for any strangers unacquainted with your peculiarity who may happen to be with you."

"Would you not better be quiet?" I asked.

"I think not," she answered. "I am desirous of having this scene explained as soon as possible."

"You shall have an explanation when we reach a suitable place, your home," I replied. "But as I said before, the explanation must be mutual."

We walked pretty rapidly, and she said nothing for quite a distance.

"Your attack was so unexpected, Mr. Maxwell," she began again, " that I had no opportunity to defend myself. I am something of an athlete, but I was rendered completely powerless by your procedure. Oh! why did you act so? You must have been mad," she continued, in a slightly louder voice.

"I entreat you to be quiet," I returned. "People on the street will think we are quarreling."

"I would not give much for your chances, if they did," she replied. "In such an event I could scarcely protect you from injury, and if I made myself known, and called for help, all your strength would avail you nothing. I am a princess in my own land, Mr. Maxwell, and you are only an Englishman."

I knew not what to make of this strange girl. She did not seem at all alarmed. She talked in a quiet, determined tone, only once, I thought I heard something like a sob. She looked me full in the face occasionally when talking, and she kept her usual easy hold on my arm, and said bitter things.

We reached the house and she asked me in. We entered the sitting room; her sister Anna was there.

"Anna," she said, "will you entertain Mr. Maxwell a few moments?" and she passed into an adjoining apartment.

Mr. Beyresen came in. "You are just in time for dinner," said he. "Come right out. We are dining en famile to-day, and are nearly through; Mrs. Beyresen will attend you; I, myself, must be moving; Clothilde will be in directly. Come on at once."

I could not refuse, and though caring little to eat, I took my place and a few moments later Clothilde took hers near me. Mrs. Beyresen did the honors. Clothilde acted much as usual. She answered inquiries about our walk, spoke to me occasionally, and seemed entirely self-possessed and natural. I had much difficulty to refrain from smiling at several of her witty sallies. I ate little, for I felt confused, puzzled, and tired. We returned to the sitting-room, mother, daughter, and myself. No opportunity for giving or receiving any explanation was afforded me, and though every courtesy was extended, I felt and no doubt looked distrait. I did not remain long, not more than half an hour after dinner.

When I signified my intention of departure, Mrs. Beyresen said most innocently: "I think we should have some music, Clothilde; can you not sing something for us before Mr. Maxwell goes?"

"You dear old mother," Clothilde answered. "I don't think Mr. Maxwell cares for singing. He looks tired and distressed. His walk and company seem to have been too much for him. Let me redeem myself before you go," she said to me, and she actually brought me a glass of sherbet, and I had to take it from her hand and swallow its contents.

Contrary to her usual custom she went with me to the door, and her clear, cool voice saying: "Come back and see us soon, Mr. Maxwell," I remember distinctly.

But I did not go back soon. I concluded to wait awhile, or go only in the afternoon when Mr. Beyresen might be at home, or at any rate when Miss Beyresen would be in her schoolroom.

A British peer, I thought, had some rights which even an American princess should respect.

In the meantime, I was bound by my promise to her, to say nothing of our late adventure. I awaited enlightenment on many points, but I did not know when or where it would come. There seemed but one source, however, and that was Miss Beyresen herself. She could give it at her pleasure; I determined not to ask her for it.

For a week I ceased entirely going to Mr. Beyresen's. The head of the house was occupied constantly during the day, for the parliament of which he was a member was in session. Of their proceedings I knew little. They separated generally when they left their hall and never, even among themselves, appeared to talk outside of what had occurred within.

I met Mr. Beyresen occasionally. He was very friendly, and was anxious that I should meet the councilors and other public men of the Nationality, to whom he invariably introduced me when occasion presented. About the occurrence between Miss Clothilde and myself at the Treasury he said nothing.

I knew not what to think about that young lady's action. I was satisfied that I had been shown a portion of John Harvey's booty, in fact the cup I had examined was, as the reader may have surmised, one contributed by my mother to the indemnity levied by that individual. I had supposed this treasure lost in the depths of the Atlantic, but this was evidently a mistake. From my late experiences I was forced to the conclusion that Clothilde Beyresen was more intimately acquainted with the secrets, and had much more influence in the affairs of the Nationality than I had imagined. Her conduct was utterly incomprehensible. Why should she have disclosed the existence and the hiding-place of this booty to me? It seemed a dangerous caprice to indulge in, and yet that she should have power, at will, to obtain access to so great and so singular a treasure, was proof conclusive of far greater importance and standing among its custodians than I had supposed she possessed.

During the week succeeding I neither saw nor heard of her, but soon after I received the following note by a messenger:

"August twenty-ninth, 1935.

"Dear Mr. Maxwell:

"I remember you expressed regret at missing an operatic performance in the town of Sterling not long since, and also a hope that you might have the opportunity some time to hear another.

"I am vain enough to desire an appreciative auditor like yourself, and therefore take the liberty of enclosing a ticket for such a performance to-morrow night at the South Boulevard theater.

"I am a little nervous over the affair, which will be a very select one. I wish you were an opera singer, or something, and could assist me.

"Your friend

"CLOTHILDE BEYRESEN."

Enclosed was a ticket of admission to one of the best seats in the house. I was astonished at the entire ignoring of all that had recently taken place. But I hastened to acknowledge the receipt of the note, and thank the sender for the courtesy.

I attended the performance, taking a seat in another part of the house, however, not the one designated on the ticket. On her entrance, I saw Miss Clothilde glance toward my unoccupied place, and then look over the theater, but she did not discover me, for I sat far back, concealed by some pillars.

A large number of members of parliament and the elite of the city were present, and the house, which seated about eight thousand people, was filled to its utmost capacity.

Miss Beyresen was elegantly dressed and looked royally beautiful, and the power and sweetness of her voice were amazing.

There were no dramatic effects, as on the previous occasion, but she was repeatedly encored, and was plainly the favorite and chief attraction of the opera.

The following evening I called at Mr. Beyresen's house to see her, and her reception was very cordial.

"I knew you would come," she said, "to tell me how you liked the opera."

I again expressed my thanks for the invitation.

"But you did not take the seat the ticket called for."

"No, I did not; I am, however, as thoroughly obliged as if I had occupied it."

"Possibly you did not like the seat."

"Possibly," said I; "I did not try it."

"You were in another part of the theater," she declared.

"Did you see me?" I asked.

"No, I did not, though I tried to discover you. You had hidden yourself effectually."

"Are you really sure I was there?" I returned. "I might have been prevented from attending, you know."

"Your presence was shown by that!" she exclaimed, and she handed me the cancelled ticket.

We had quite a long and pleasant conversation, and not the slightest reference was made to the occurrences of our visit to the Treasury vault.

She seemed much interested in a short account I gave of some incidents of my late journey, and informed me that she and some friends were making up a party to go by rail to the aqueduct bridge I had missed seeing, and asked me to go with them. This invitation I readily accepted, and with the understanding that we should meet again on that occasion, we parted.

CHAPTER XIV.

The party made up for the visit to the aqueduct was composed of eight persons.

Miss Ashley, one of these, was the daughter of a celebrated physician of the city. She was a blonde, and her coloring was as perfect as a picture. Her golden hair, blue eyes, finely chiseled features, and symmetrical figure, presented an ensemble of beauty seldom seen. She was quiet and rather reserved, but had very decided opinions on many important questions, which she expressed in a low, sweet, musical voice, without hesitation or obscurity.

Accompanying her was Mr. John Francis King, a talented writer on one of the great evening papers, whom I had met and learned to like on previous occasions.

There was also a Miss Myra Erickson, daughter of one of the councilors, a bright, vivacious young lady, and a Mr. Bradbury, a civil engineer of much information and ability; a Miss Ruth Brastow, an especial friend and fellow teacher of Miss Clothilde, and a Mr. Ernest Fosdyke, one of the officers of the treasury department, and Miss Beyresen and myself.

At an early hour we met at the station house, where an electric car was placed at our disposal. It was light, commodious and elegantly appointed and furnished, and supplied with its own electric motive power. It ran on schedule time, being one of a succession of such cars, passing regularly over the road, at intervals of not more than fifteen minutes. Its smooth, noiseless, almost imperceptible motion made observation and conversation easy; and we looked out now on the side of the car to the east, viewing the trim, highly-cultivated landscape, and then again on the side to the west, where the solemn mountains and their attendant hills rose in long ranges beyond us.

"What impressions have our mountains made upon you, Mr. Maxwell?" inquired Miss Brastow, who had noticed me gazing toward them. "I understand you have lately been traveling among them."

"Yes, Mr. Maxwell, give us your impressions, please!" exclaimed Miss Erickson, "and then let us each in turn give his or hers. I will act as prompter and general referee, and call upon you. Proceed, Mr. Maxwell, and open the ball, and the rest of you prepare to keep it going."

"The air of sedateness and antiquity which the mountains give to the scene appears to me their most striking characteristic," I said. "Without them the landscape picture which you people have created, might look too modern and too artificial. The mountains represent the age and conservatism of Nature; they disdain the bright robes and civilized trappings in which the rest of the land rejoices; and lift bald heads to the blue sky, and toss the scanty locks of vegetation that cling around them freely to the wind and storm, of which they have no fear. They are like strong, vigorous old men, viewing the sports of their children of the plains, with gravity and forbearance; careful guardians defending them from the tempest, the heat and the cold, keeping watch and ward over the liberties and destinies of the land, and never nurture slaves but always freemen. They partition the earth into dwelling places for the nations, and set barriers between them which only the civilized and skillful can overcome. The mountains have a strong influence on the mental and physical qualities of men; and I think it a great blessing to any nation to abide under the ministrations of such snow-clad peaks as those we see yonder, which, like white stoled priests, continually present their orisons in those lonely regions where, remote from little scenes of art, great Nature has for ages dwelt in awful solitude."

"We are very much obliged, Mr. Maxwell," said Miss Erickson, "though it does seem to me I have heard something like that concluding passage before. Now, Miss Ashley, it is your turn."

"My thought," said she, quietly, "was somewhat different from Mr. Maxwell's, though induced by the same idea of protection and watchful care. I am reminded of the passage of Holy Writ which says, 'As the mountains are round about Jerusalem, so the Lord is round about His people from henceforth, even forever.' I never travel among the mountains, nor view them from the plain, without this thought recurring to me and investing them with peculiar interest."

"Now, Miss Beyresen; no, I will ask Mr. King first, and see what he says," said Miss Erickson; "if this solemn strain continues we may want the princess to sing a psalm for her part. Tell us, please, Mr. Editor, what you think about the mountains. Be breezy and picturesque, like your subject, sir."

"Editors," responded Mr. King, "are peculiar beings, and much misunderstood. When asked to give their opinions on a subject that has as many practical sides as this, they have little use for poetic exaggeration. They simply speak the truth as they see it; they cannot do otherwise, and those who listen have to be content. Mountains have been much too fantastically considered. They have been personified, apostrophized and even deified; to

such an extent has the imagination been allowed to mislead the reason in regard to them. Not, however, by the
profession I have to-day the honor to represent, among
whom truthfulness is never sacrificed on the altar of fancy.
We recognize in them a wise provision for modifying climate and receiving and preserving precipitation; we see
in them a habitat provided for various untamed denizens
of air, forest and stream; we regard them as places for
enjoyment, revivification and rejuvenation. We love to
visit them; not, however, to imagine them peopled by
nymphs, naiads, and dryads; but to rest and gain strength
on their umbrageous sides; and to study the nature and
habits of these wild tenants of air, land and water. Sensible people spend their leisure time among the mountains,
not out on the hot plains toward which we are journeying.
Oh, for a tent, a gun, and a fishing rod, and a day amid
their cool shadows!"

"Now, Mr. King!" exclaimed Miss Erickson, "you
must stop; you are worse than a failure; you are casting
reflections upon this party. I will call on the princess to
rebuke you. Miss Clothilde, come to our rescue."

"This journey," said the latter, promptly, "was not
planned to please lazy or weak people; it is made for the
purpose of viewing one of the great achievements of modern times; one of the wonders of the world. Mr. Bradbury tells me there were seven of them years ago; and we
are now going to see the eighth. Mr. Maxwell, and several of you, including Mr. King, who claims to be so
practical, have been talking of mountains. It is always
so, I am told, with some people; they sigh for what is not
at hand."

"Now, Mr. Fosdyke," said Miss Erickson, "it is your
turn." But Mr. Fosdyke declared that he had no fresh
ideas to communicate on the subject, and Mr. Bradbury,

who was next called for, was out on the rear platform, looking at the great canal, along whose eastern bank we were traveling rapidly.

Miss Brastow thought the mountains were always impressive, and most so in winter, particularly after a snowstorm; and Miss Erickson, who gave her opinion last, had just finished saying that their bare peaks reminded her of beggars who had worn their clothing through at elbows, knees and toes, when the descent into the valley of the Platte began, and we distributed ourselves along the side of the car to obtain the first view of the great aqueduct.

In a few moments we reached the railroad bridge, located about one mile below it. This bridge, though long, was in no place over fifty feet above the bed of the river, while the aqueduct being on a level with the river banks, was carried over at a height of fully one hundred feet. The approach and departure of the canal to and from the river were made by a series of cuts and fills through the rough country lying on each side.

Owing to the sandy nature of the bed of the South Platte, peculiar means had been employed for obtaining a firm foundation. The sand extended to a depth of fifteen or twenty feet, and was permeated by water slowly seeping through it and forming quite a subterranean river. This sand was enclosed by a framework of posts driven vertically to the bottom, against which planks were laid, and the whole mass was then concreted by a churning process into a solid wall from the rock foundation below to the surface. Successive strips of twenty or thirty feet in width were thus cemented.

As the work progressed across the bed of the river, a great volume of water, shut off from its former passage, forced its way through the yet uncemented sand.

A canal was constructed on one side of the river, cutting through the cemented wall and continuing down the stream, climbing its banks gradually, and the water thus accumulated was used for irrigation, and when not required for that purpose was discharged into the river again.

The process of cementing was continued until an unbroken belt over four hundred feet wide, and a mile long, and of great strength and weight, was formed across the river bed. This was fastened at each end to five great parallel walls of granite, which presented a solid side view and were built into the hills or banks for quite a long distance. The walls were each twenty feet thick and arched over longitudinally by four great arches, with a span of seventy-five feet each, forming at the top a foundation for the bottom of the canal three hundred and eighty feet wide. This was made smooth and level by cement, and the outside walls being continued up fifteen feet higher, with a thickness of only ten feet, however, formed sides for the aqueduct and gave room for a broad walk on top.

These walls carried the aqueduct down to the river valley, or bed proper, a mile in width, which, as I have just mentioned, was crossed by the cemented foundation. On the latter, a granite casing eight feet thick was laid, bound together by metallic bands and also cemented, extending over its whole surface.

Hollow pillars of steel, cased with a singular white metal, which will be hereafter more fully described, rested on the granite, and carried the aqueduct in a nearly straight line across the valley. These pillars were set eighty feet apart; in eleven parallel rows forty feet distant from each other, the pillars alternating in the different rows. The inner ones rested on the foundation itself, but the outer were placed on bases of granite about eight feet square. They were four feet in diameter at the bottom, tapering gracefully toward their capitals, and nearly one hundred feet in height. They were fluted, and with their tasteful entablatures were very beautiful.

A frieze, twenty-five feet broad, fifteen feet of which, being ten feet in thickness, extended upward and formed sides for the aqueduct and gave room on top for a continuation of the walk across it, and ten feet of which extended below, and hid the metal network which supported its bed, ran from one outer pillar to another, and bound them together.

This frieze, also cased with the white metal, was moulded in various ornamental traceries, and was very beautiful.

The pillars, nearly eight hundred in number, were bound together near the top by arches of steel, hidden by the frieze; and a network of the same metal, also hidden from view, supported the bottom or bed of the aqueduct, which, as well as its sides, and the walk across it, was plated with the white metal.

The railroad bridge which crossed below was set on granite abutments, eighty feet apart, connected by arches. These were capped by a frieze of the white metal curving upward, as did the arches, effectually concealing them and holding all in a firm embrace. These arches supported the foundation for the roadbed, over eighty feet in width.

The railroad bridge was very beautiful, but was dwarfed by the wondrous beauty of the aqueduct, which from a drawing, or any account given of it, could only be faintly imagined.

The metal was so pure and soft in color, and its curves aud mouldings so full of grace and elegance, that it attracted phenomenal attention; and probably will continue to do so to the end of time, for the white metal, at least, seems indestructible.

It was with great interest and admiration that I, the only one of our party who had never before seen it, viewed this beautiful structure from the window as the car moved over the railroad bridge.

After crossing the river we left the car and followed a broad paved walk, which ran through a large and tastefully ornamented park toward the aqueduct. A branch of this walk extended to the granite foundation and supporting pillars of that structure; but the main walk led to the side of the wall, where the top of the aqueduct was reached by a long flight of stone steps. We ascended these, and stood on the walk on its summit, which was protected by a low railing. We went out on this some distance toward the center of the aqueduct. The whole scene was most remarkable. A great river of pure, clear water, in quiet, though rapid movement, seemed carried on a bed of marble over the tops of the hills below and over the valley. We hung in mid-air, our only attachments to earth appearing to be the long converging lines of white foot walks, narrowing to a thread at either end, and the broader band of silvery water sparkling in the sunlight, which might be broken in a moment and from this great height converted into an angry devastating cataract.

Upon two of us at least, Miss Beyresen and myself, the sight had a strange and sympathetic effect. While the others laughed and talked, and declared their intention of crossing over upon the foot walk after lunch, we looked together in silent, almost reverent, contemplation now down the long-reaching valley of the river, and then at the restless, quick-moving water; my mind filled with the magnitude of this great undertaking and the

beautiful and enduring manner of its execution, and hers
mutely coresponsive, and by some undefinable correlation, silently assisting my reflections instead of interrupt-
ing them by noisy speech. By and by we two were left
alone, the others having gone on out some distance farther.

"It is a wonderful structure!" I exclaimed, finally
rousing myself to speak. "It must have cost millions and
consumed years in the building. It will last for ages to
come."

"Yes," she said, "and for all that time it will carry
water, pure, refreshing water, to a hundred lakes and to
millions of thirsty acres. It was constructed for no mercenary or warlike purposes, the ends for which money is
usually squandered; it is a provision for the health, livelihood and comfort of all the people."

"It was a grand conception and a glorious accomplishment," I returned, "and I honor the brain that origi-
nated it and the skill that directed its execution. Who
did it, Miss Beyresen, the Nationality?"

"No," she said, slowly, "my friend John Harvey."

I started, and looked at the girl. There were tears in
her voice and they stood also plainly visible in her eyes;
she was evidently very deeply moved.

"Let us retrace our steps," I said; "we can see it
much better from the park. After lunch, while the rest
take their trip across, you and I, if you will, can stroll
around and get other views of the structure and examine
it more closely."

We started back, lingering here and there over some
point of observation, or special interest, with all of which
she appeared well acquainted, and finally reached the park
only a short time before the rest arrived.

We were very enthusiastic on the subject of the aqueduct bridge, and while some of the party prepared the repast the others sat looking at the structure, so graceful and seemingly so light and airy, stretching like a white phantom across the wide expanse of the valley high up against the blue sky line, and yet really so strong, so material and so useful, conveying water, the most precious of all fluids, in a constant stream for the use of human beings dependent upon it.

After luncheon the rest of the party again ascended the steps, and Miss Clothilde and myself set out for our stroll, taking the branch walk leading under the aqueduct. As we approached it, its massive strength and stability grew upon me; and the whiteness and purity of color of its many pillars reminded me of but one other object, the Albatross, which six years before I had seen enter the busy harbor of Yokohama.

The white metal used in both was unmistakably the same; and the grace and elegance of the bridge recalled vividly like traits of the vessel. Then my mind reverted to the revelation made to me in the vault, of the existence of a portion at least of the stolen treasure, and Miss Clothilde's intimate connection with it. I glanced at her as she walked by my side. I could hardly imagine the graceful, dignified personage I saw there as the same being whose angry utterances on that and a previous occasion I so well remembered.

On these subjects I could not question her. There was an air of majesty about her that effectually precluded such interrogatory. She was distinctly individual, and like all such characters, whatever disturbed that individuality was promptly challenged as offensive.

She was pensive to-day, not in her usual high spirits, and talked but little, and evidently with some effort; her mind seemingly engaged on other subjects, but she was more royally beautiful than ever, and this mood had for me a fresh charm. Her tall, willowy, perfect figure, the full Greek contour of her face, with its clear olive tint, and the brilliancy of her large hazel eyes, subdued by the grave character of her thoughts, and shaded by their long black lashes, which vied in color with the purple blackness of her hair, all gave her a full rich and regal aspect which commanded the utmost respect, and which her vigorous step and high-bred bearing enhanced in every particular.

And yet she had confided the secret of this treasure to me, a stranger. She had done that which must inevitably, if known, have compromised herself, not only with the authorities of the Nationality, but with those of other countries, and for what purpose I could not tell.

Was this remembrance sobering her thoughts and changing her manner to-day? I looked attentively at her again. No, there was no apprehension, no doubt expressed in her countenance, though it was graver than usual, with a trace of sadness in it.

We reached the foundation and passed beneath the structure, and were soon lost among the massive white pillars which supported it, whose phantom lengths were very material to the touch. We crossed on its northern end to the center, and stopped and began to look about more leisurely.

In all directions stood the white pillars, extending in rows southward for a long distance, and on either side, for two hundred feet, surmounted at a dizzy height by the arches and the great superstructure which formed the bottom of the aqueduct.

"What other creation can this resemble?" I said, uncertainly.

"It reminds me always," said Miss Clothilde, "of the

interior of a great cathedral, only freer and grander than any cathedral I ever saw. On breezy days the wind thrums against the metal network overhead and one could imagine an organ hidden somewhere, possibly within those walls," and she pointed to the granite side walls near by. Moving up toward them we found a seat.

"Can you tell me, Miss Clothilde," I said, "of what material these pillars are made, and where it was obtained?"

"They are of steel," she answered, "and are only covered by the white metal. This plating, or covering, however, is some inches thick, and adds very greatly to the strength of the pillars. I cannot tell you what the white metal is, Mr. Maxwell. It was only produced in one place in the world, and the supply has been exhausted for some years. What I know in regard to it I have learned chiefly from a little manuscript book. I have thought I should like to loan you this little book, if you care to read it," she continued, "for it gives much information on these subjects. It is very precious, Mr. Maxwell, and few people have seen it. It is the only book of the kind in existence and has never been out of my possession. Only the old men of our Nationality know I have it; and its contents, though merely descriptive, are not to be spoken of publicly; especially now, when there are those who are scheming to injure our land. But you can see it, and read it, if you wish; for I am sure you will not reveal the fact of its existence, nor any of its contents."

She hesitated and added, "I have shown and told you other things, Mr. Maxwell, which would injure my country and myself were they revealed, but I can trust you."

"I respect your confidence, as I have always respected it," I answered, "and I would very much like to read the book. And," I added, "I wish to say to you most solemnly that I will never abuse your trust, nor reveal anything about the book, or about the other matters of which you have spoken, or even ask questions of yourself about them which I think you would not wish to answer."

"Oh, thank you, Mr. Maxwell," she said, warmly, "that assurance is so kind and noble of you; I did not need it, but it is very grateful. When we reach home I shall be pleased to give you the manuscript, and if you have a se· cure place in which to keep it, you can take it to your room. It is, indeed, a very, very precious book to me, though it is only a history of the Bilboa mines, of which you have probably heard something, and of this canal, and of the founding of this Nationality. I would like you to come often though, and tell me what you have read, and your thoughts about it," she added.

"I will, gladly," I answered, "and I am more obliged than I can tell you, Miss Beyresen, for your kindness."

We returned to the park in a happier mood, where we met the others, and about five o'clock started for Neuropolis, bidding adieu to the great aqueduct whose life-giving waters followed us as we sped homeward to the great city.

On our way back, Mr. King and I sat for some time together, and I mentioned my contemplated journey east, and remarked that I supposed social conditions there were much the same as in European countries, and that I could hardly expect to find as happy a people as in the Nationality.

"No," he replied, thoughtfully, "you will not. You will see class distinctions, based mainly on wealth, such as could not exist here, for there money and accumulation are the actuating motives, and unlock the doors to success, enjoyment and power."

"And all this," I asked, "has been abolished in the

Nationality? I cannot yet understand your doctrine of equality in the rewards of labor, when its character and efficiency are so different."

"One educated as I suppose you have been can hardly understand it," he replied. "Had we time it might be worth while to consider whether there is so great a difference between workers in the results of their honest productive labor, and also whether the world's estimate of the value of labor is founded on equity, or is largely artificial. The equality, too, which you mention is only in the material rewards of labor, and it has been often averred that the really good work of the world is not done for such rewards. These thoughts are only suggestive; they can be followed out, though, Mr. Maxwell, until it will be found that the course most in accordance with natural justice and best calculated to prevent a recurrence of the terrible evils of the system prevailing throughout other portions of the civilized world, in fact, the only one to obviate these curses, is the course which we have adopted. The principle is, that this equality shall exist among the members of the classes into which the community is justly divided. This classification we have made to rest upon age, and the assuming the responsibility of heads of families. Whether it is the best division, is a question separate and apart from that of the principle. There was a time when an increase in the amount given for subsistence, to begin when the years of compulsory labor were over, was advocated on the ground that then the citizen had more leisure, and should be given more means with which to enjoy it. To adopt such a plan would not have controverted the principle, but many citizens are of great service to us after that age, and had this increase been made their minds might have been too much devoted to pleasure. The sustenance now allotted to each citizen is sufficient for all purposes, and the productive capacity of the Nationality is becoming so great that the amount will likely soon be increased, or the years of compulsory labor shortened; an alternative to be decided upon after wise consideration."

"Do you find," I asked, "that your people work as well under your system as the old?"

"Better, much better," he replied, "they work peacefully, intelligently and in proper channels, being directed by skillful officers, and the results would astonish you. It would be very interesting to you, I have no doubt, Mr. Maxwell, to spend some time looking over the statistics of production in the Nationality. Such a research would answer your questions conclusively."

I thanked Mr. King for his suggestion, and, as I desired to examine every phase of the labor question that I might arrive at settled convictions concerning it, afterward availed myself of it, and found his statements to be fully substantiated by my examination.

Shortly after this conversation we reached Neuropolis, where I dined with Mr. Beyresen and his family at the cafe, and on my departure from his house Miss Clothilde gave me a small package which I took with me.

CHAPTER XV.

On opening the package I found a leathern-bound manuscript volume of about one hundred pages, evidently some years old, and written in a bold, free hand. It read as follows:

"The great Bilboa mines were discovered June 18th, 1901, by John Harvey, then about thirty years of age, a mineralogist and metallurgist of considerable repute.

"They were situated in one of the great parks in the mountain portion of the State of Colorado.

"He found gold in certain black sand and fragments of rock of the same material, appearing at intervals for quite a distance, just where the eastern edge of the park was cut by the first of a long succession of granite ridges extending northerly and southerly. He satisfied himself that this material followed the granite, and that a vast quantity of it, probably in a molten state, had been poured out of some great fissure, or fissures, into the park itself, and had been covered to greater or lesser depth in after years by an alluvial deposit.

"He also satisfied himself that this sand and rock contained from twenty to forty dollars' worth of gold to the ton, and could be readily smelted by ordinary methods, and was likely to prove amenable to chlorination processes, in which he himself was an expert.

"Mr. Harvey therefore took proper steps at once to procure title to these lands, then considered wholly valueless, unless for pasture. The South Platte River, on its course eastward, cuts the granite ridge near the point where the discovery was made, and is followed by a railroad running from this park to the great plains outside the mountains.

"By the middle of July he had purchased a strip of land two miles broad, extending about three miles northward along the ridge from the point where the river divides it.

"On the twentieth of that month work was begun by sinking a shaft, one thousand feet northward from the river, close to the granite wall, and on August second the first shipment was made, being about fifty tons of ore, from which a return of twenty-five hundred dollars was received.

"Drifting was then begun at a depth of seventy-five feet in this shaft, along the vein close to the granite which formed the eastern wall rock, and five other shafts were started at various points northward. From fifty to seventy-five tons of ore were shipped daily from the first shaft, from which an income of about three thousand dollars was received.

"By September first the new shafts were down a distance of seventy-five feet, and ore similar in character and value to that discovered in the first had been found in all of them. At a depth of two hundred feet in the first shaft, which was designated as No. 1, the western wall rock was reached, and the fissure from whence the gold-bearing lava had issued was discovered, being eight feet wide, its walls tending to close together toward the south, but maintaining its full width to the northward. At this date about two hundred tons of ore were shipped daily to the smelters on the plains, and about eight thousand dollars were received for the same.

"In the meantime, however, during the months of

July and August, Mr. Harvey had been making experiments in reducing the ore by his own peculiar methods, with some surprising results.

"A small furnace, capable of holding about four tons, had been erected and filled with crushed ore, which at an intense heat was subjected to the operation of certain gases, chiefly chlorine.

"When the aperture for withdrawing the gold was opened, the first discharge into the mould placed for receiving it consisted of a very small quantity, not more than two spoonfuls of a singular substance, in color ebon black, with a purplish tinge, and the gold was allowed to flow out on the top of this.

"On taking the deposit from the mould, it was found that this substance formed a thin coating on the bottom of the gold, like a paper on the bottom of a baked cake, from which, however, it was easily detached. It resisted all attempts to spring, or bend it, and retained on all sides its singular, glossy, purplish black color; and was an exact impression of the mould in which it had been cast. Its weight also was very great. The yield of gold by the new process was quite satisfactory, and the mould being small the gold was run into it several successive times, but no more of the black substance was obtained.

"The slag was then removed from the furnace and dumped, when another singular result was observed. The portion first run off, and which had been most thoroughly exposed to the action of the gases, on becoming cold, was, in large sections, pure white—whiter than the whitest paint could make it. Places were observed where dark lines ran through it, as if some other substance, black as charcoal, had been fused and suddenly cooled in it. The parts of the slag less exposed to the action of the gases remained dark-gray in color.

"The white portions were without crack, or flaw, and resisted all attempts to break them. No impression could be made upon them by repeated blows from the heaviest sledge hammers; they seemed quite elastic, and when struck emitted a distinct metallic sound.

"These results gave Mr. Harvey occasion for much study and many experiments. He observed that the white slag had all the characteristics of a new metal. He began his investigations with the purest specimen he could find, and desiring to separate it from the remainder of the mass, attempted to cut it with a finely tempered saw, running with great rapidity. The saw bit slowly into the white substance, until when about half way through it encountered one of the dark lines mentioned, and the teeth flew from it like corn from the cob in a shelling machine.

"Another saw was procured, a cut made at right angles to the first, and a large piece of pure white metal obtained. By this cutting the dark line was laid bare in its length, and proved to be a spicula of the black substance, not thicker, nor much longer than an ordinary needle; it was not bent, nor marred, nor in any way affected by the action of the saw. Throughout its entire mass the piece thus obtained was of the purest white. In weight it was scarcely two-thirds that of iron, and its texture was close and firm. It was again subjected to the action of heat, and at a temperature much higher than that required to soften iron became malleable and ductile, and at a still higher temperature fused and could be readily molded into any shape.

"A portion was run into small bars, and while still ductile one of these was drawn into wire which, when cold, resisted bending with great pertinacity, but when properly heated could be bent readily, and then retained its acquired form with the same obstinacy. When heated the bars could be welded together or beaten into shape like iron or steel; but when cold nothing could be done with them except with saw or lathe, and that only with the best tempered tools.

"Such were the principal characteristics observed by Mr. Harvey in his experiments with this white substance. He was satisfied that he had discovered a new and probably very valuable metal, lighter than iron, and at the proper heat fully as malleable and ductile, and of far greater strength and durability. On this latter account he named the substance, Robur.

"Two subjects of inquiry now presented themselves to him, the first being the best manner of separating this metal, which seemed to exist in such great quantities in his mines, from the gold, and from all impurities, especially the refractory black substance which attended it, and the second, as a prudent man looking after his own interests, to ascertain whether any bodies of similar ore existed in the vicinity.

"Mr. Harvey spent much time in examining all the country adjacent for other deposits, but without success, and it is now well known that no further discoveries were made, and that the Bilboa mines were the only ones that ever produced the famous metals whose story is here to be related.

"Toward the answer to the first inquiry, Mr. Harvey's active mind was given with a fervor difficult for one uninterested to understand. He was shipping daily a very large amount of ore, the most valuable part of which, being irrecoverable and unrecognized by the method of smelting employed, was cast away as worthless. There was a possibility that its existence might be discovered by those from whom he wished most sedulously to guard it. Being, however, without means except those arising from his shipments, and necessarily at great expense in conducting and extending his operations, he resolved to continue, but not to increase them, until such time as his own processes could be perfected and his own works built.

"He called to his aid at once all those within his reach possessing valuable knowledge, either scientific or experimental, on the subject of metallurgy, and such of them as he found capable were converted into valuable friends and allies.

"In a short time his processes were so perfected that a mass of robur entirely pure could be obtained from the small furnace.

"Mr. Harvey, and his scientific friends, then began a series of researches and examinations into all matters pertaining to the production and applications of the gases, forms of furnaces, materials for same, interior surfaces and their relative efficiency.

"Toward the close of September plans were adopted that gave satisfaction as promising the best results, and immediately Mr. Harvey began the erection of eight large, continuous smelting furnaces, crushers, buildings, tramways and all the necessary concomitants of a great smelting industry."

It would only weary the reader to follow the minute description given in Miss Beyresen's book, so I omit it, and proceed with the more interesting portion relating to the first practical test of the new process.

"On the 28th of November, the charging of the two trial furnaces, of the capacity of twenty tons of ore each, was commenced, the fires having been started in them some time previously. The night following, and the next day, were periods of great anxiety to all concerned in the operations.

"By 8 o'clock on the morning of the 29th, a considerable downslide of the crushed ore in the chimneys indicated that the process of melting was well begun in the lower levels, and the furnaces were again filled up.

"At 10 o'clock the view holes of the receptacles for gold in the lower part of the furnaces being opened, it was found that quite a quantity of that metal had already percolated into them. The gas blast was then put into operation to ensure the complete reduction of the ore by chemical action.

"Owing to the newness of the furnaces, it was determined to allow an unusually long time to elapse before opening them, and to permit only one-half of the contents to escape, retaining the remainder an additional half day. Thereafter, every twelve hours, ten tons would be discharged from each furnace, and the gas being continuously used would be brought into intimate contact with every portion of the molten mass.

"At noon of November 29th all preparations had been made for the first discharge. Sufficient molds for running the metal into pigs of convenient size had been formed in the sand spread in front of the furnaces, and channels constructed to properly direct its flow.

"A heavy trough, asbestos lined, connected them with the vents, and Mr. Harvey, his aides and his workmen, stood by watching every movement, anxious to determine as soon as possible the success of the operation.

"After the ten tons, or thereabouts, of the white metal had been taken from each of the furnaces the gold vent would be opened, and the product run into small iron molds capable of holding from one to five pounds each. From the amount of gold thus obtained the yield per ton could hardly be determined, the quantity of melted ore from which it came being uncertain, but after a number of runs had been made it could be accurately stated.

"The interest, however, as far as Mr. Harvey and his friends were concerned, centered mainly in the strange white metal, their great anxiety being to obtain it pure and free from the intractable, unworkable black substance.

"As soon as the pigs were cooled their color would show the completeness of the operation, for if there were no evidence of the existence of the black substance on the outside of them there was little likelihood of its lodgment within.

"A few of the workmen had seen the operation in the small furnace, and the singularity of the slag then produced had attracted their attention, but this had all been carefully stored away, and they had no idea that it was a metal and could be made useful.

"The moment had come to open the two furnaces; the moment for action. At each stood a workman, with sharpened bar in hand, ready on the word to break down the barrier of baked clay which closed the vents.

" 'Strike,' said Mr. Harvey, and the workmen struck repeated blows, and opened a way which the molten metal soon cleared. As the clay was broken a beam like a searchlight shot across the building from the openings, and the white metal poured forth unapproachable in its glory. It was not the brightness of the golden sun, but rather that of the silver moon, intensified ten thousand times; the pure white liquid mass flowed along, not coruscating, but with brilliant white light that lit up all the space around it. It glided rapidly down the iron troughs and along the sandy channels, transforming the latter into glassy ones by its intense heat, and into the open molds, without noise or undue haste.

"One by one they were filled, and the tide turned toward others until all were reached, and then the signal was given to close the vents. The men seized other long iron bars, at one end of which hung on a pivot thick triangular sheets of iron. These they thrust into the apertures of the furnaces, the iron sheets entering horizontally. When once in they drew them forward vertically, bringing their flat surfaces against the inner wall of the furnaces. The flow was stopped till the red hot plates should have burned through, but other men plastered cakes of clay with other irons against the plates till they filled the orifice, and it baked and hardened like rock and the vents were closed completely.

"Meanwhile the stream of white metal thus cut off disappeared within the molds and was rapidly cooling there as the heat emitted from them evinced."

CHAPTER XVI.

THE TALK.

I had read thus far in the manuscript on the day following that on which I had received it, and in the evening called at Mr. Beyresen's and found Mr. King and Miss Ashley there.

They were all talking of our excursion and of the architecture and beauty of the aqueduct bridge. Mr. King told me there were several other aqueducts on the course of the canal, notably one over the North Platte River, constructed of the same material and much the same in style as that we had seen, and another of greater length at the crossing of the Arkansas River; but that this latter, being built only of iron and steel, lacked the impressive beauty given to the two former by the peculiar character of the white metal.

My late journey through portions of the Nationality was referred to, and I remarked that in all my travels I had never seen a land so universally well kept and cared for, in regard not merely to practical, but also to esthetic effects.

"I had supposed, Mr. Maxwell," said Miss Ashley, "that the very finest esthetic effects were found in the great parks and grounds of the nobility and the financial kings of your own land."

"That may be true," I replied, "but those are private grounds, and are examples of what can be done by lavish expenditure and the employment of the best skill. They are not representative of the general taste of the country, and are often in striking contrast with that portion of it immediately surrounding them. The English rural scenery is the result of centuries of care and cultivation, and though famous for its general quiet beauty and taste, is frequently marred by barren wastes and neglected, or abandoned fields and dwellings, and poverty and misery and other offensive and saddening sights often present themselves there.

"But in my recent travels through this land of yours it all seemed a garden, every portion of which had been a subject of thought, and care, and treated so as to bring out its best natural resources, and there was none of the squalor, poverty, and wretchedness which one meets in European and other countries.

"How you have secured such happy results and in so short a time is to me an enigma, made more difficult of solution from the fact that it has been the work of a people who receive no other reward for their labors than that of a comfortable and assured livelihood."

"You are quite complimentary in your remarks, Mr. Maxwell, and it seems very proper for us to try to relieve your perplexities," said Miss Clothilde. "They occur to nearly every stranger visiting us. Their explanation is simple, and is found in the difference between our people and others, which is very marked, but is generally overlooked.

"During your observations," she continued, "did it never dawn upon you that we are a wiser, better kind of people than those whom you have hitherto known, gifted with more energy, and higher faculties for learning, and knowing, and doing, and enjoying?"

"No," I answered dubiously, amidst a general smile, "such an idea had not occurred to me so plainly as you present it, nor, I must say, am I now prepared to admit the proposition in all its disinterestedness."

"Then," said she, "I will have to demonstrate it to you, Mr. Maxwell. I have had to do so with others similarly circumstanced, so that it inconveniences me very little. You admitted that the ability and taste necessary for adorning and beautifying landscapes existed, and was readily procured by those possessing pecuniary means. The services of persons who could add utility to taste and beauty could also be procured for a suitable remuneration, could they not?"

"Yes," I answered, "that is granted."

"Now, Mr. Maxwell, if such persons were employed, not in beautifying and adorning a few parks the property of a select class, but in utilizing the whole land, and at the same time rendering it grateful to all esthetic tastes, would not the result be something such as you have seen in your late travels?"

"Yes," I replied, "but the marvel is how quickly and how well it has been done."

"Suppose," she continued, "that the people living in the land cultivated esthetic as well as utilitarian tastes, so that under the direction of such skilled leaders they created only pleasant and beautiful things. Suppose each citizen considered it a personal duty to remove every obnoxious or offensive object, how long do you think it would take to change the country into such an one as you seem to have found it?"

"I suppose not so very long," I replied.

"That," said she, "is exactly the spirit, the feeling, our people have, and the land you have seen is its practical result."

"But," I said, "how is it that your people are so full of this spirit, and so ready to labor for such ends? How

is it that ability and skill are willing to devote themselves
to such unremunerated work? I have not found it so elsewhere."

"I have already told you!" she exclaimed triumph-
antly, "and though you would not admit it, you have in-
advertently confessed it. We are a superior kind of people. I won't ask you to say so. I won't tell you how we
became such, which is what you now seem desirous of
knowing; but our works, the very surest test, plainly
show that my statement is entirely correct."

"I am obliged for your frankness," I said laughing,
"and shall not deny your superiority. Meanwhile the
enigma is unsolved, and in a land of light I remain in
darkness."

Mr. King, who during this rencontre between Miss
Clothilde and myself had been gravely musing, now
turned to me and remarked: "It is almost as difficult to
answer your questions fully, Mr. Maxwell, as it is to explain how one shoot grows into a tall, graceful tree, while
another withers and dies; so many circumstances of time
and place determine the result.

"As a people we have undoubtedly been favored in all
these circumstances. Our soil was new and unobstructed
by the noxious growths of prejudice and custom that en-
cumber so many older fields. Then, too, our people during their colonization period were under the sagacious
and wise control of those who had fully thought out, and
understood the scheme of our present government, and
were quick to perceive danger and powerful enough to
evade it, or to remove at once any poisonous growth that
sprang up in our midst. Our entire civilization was modeled on a different basis from that of any other state, and
yet on one for which humanity had been so hungrily
longing, and toward which it had been so constantly

tending, that men were ready to receive and embrace this civilization warmly, and endeavor very earnestly to make it successful.

"So wisely were our institutions molded and directed and so propitious were the times, that their spirit took possession of our people in one generation to a far greater extent than might have been expected, and the results have thus far been what you have seen among us.

"We are yet only in our infancy," he continued, "but the essential principles upon which our government is founded have made us already a people very differently constituted and organized from others, if not a superior people, as the princess has affirmed.

"Our leaders hold views in regard to human capability and duty very different from those entertained in most communities, and the masses of our people put these principles, to a certain extent at least, into constant practice. In the future we hope, by their more perfect application, and by the same zealous care over them that has been exercised in the past, to produce far greater results for the benefit of humanity than have yet been obtained."

Mr. King stopped, but we all begged him to continue, and I asked him to give us an exposition of these principles.

"If you will not consider me wearisome," he said, after a little pause, "I will give you as concise and clear a verbal statement as I can, of the points in which the spirit of our government differs from that of others.

"In other governments, money, and credit its representative, is the main, basal principle. It may not have been so at first, but it becomes so in the end. Money controls everything, and its fortunate possessor can procure all the accessories for ease and enjoyment, and has in it a most powerful aid in the race constantly in progress for honor, power, or advancement among his fellows.

"In such governments the relationship of the citizen to other citizens is determined almost entirely by contract; the masses, who have but little money, being dependent upon those possessing it, and contracting their services to them for it, and are consequently very greatly dominated and controlled by this latter class.

"The status of the people is essentially a servile one, often so in name even, as with the slave, serf or servant, always so in fact. The system exalts those owning or controlling money, property, or credit, and puts them in the position of masters of the earth and all that is therein, while the rest of mankind are merely their creatures.

"The acquisition of money, or private property, by any means becomes the main object of the aspiring citizen, and selfishness, chicanery, fraud and corruption are among the legitimate fruits of the system.

"Its pleasures, too, are transitory and low in degree, and the highest moral types it can claim are those exhibiting fidelity and faithfulness to employers, or justice and equity toward others, as defined and regulated by its axioms.

"In our government the fundamental principle is life, and the aim is to afford the highest opportunity for its universal enjoyment and improvement.

"This gives relative value to everything else, and the united efforts of all are directed to securing for each and all, the means for such enjoyment and development.

"The relationship of the citizen to other citizens is that of brotherhood and fellowship, as co-workers in this lofty undertaking. His individual status is determined by his efficiency in this work, as judged by his fellows. Headship, honor and advancement are given to those most earnest in promoting the good of all, or most skillful in devising means, or executing the work necessary to attain it.

"Love of fellow-men forms the chief bond, and universal joy, peace, contentment and happiness are its legitimate fruits. Society becomes one great family, working in harmony for a common end, and each enjoying to the extent of his wish and ability all good and desirable things.

"This is a short general presentation of the differences between our government and others, and also of the ideal existing among us. We cannot hasten its full fruition except by educating the people up to it; it is a growth, an evolution, rather than a revolution. We cannot force it on mankind; our system is the last of all to employ force, unless it be in self-defense; it must be extended and perfected by instructed human volition alone."

He stopped and I remarked: "The principles you have mentioned are not new, and are of the most advanced character, but the chief difficulty has hitherto been in inducing mankind to adopt and live by them. My observation has been too hasty and superficial for me to form an intelligent opinion as to whether your people will do this with more success than others. I can see they have made great progress in material matters, but this is only a step in the right direction."

"I know it," said Mr. King, "but material happiness is very necessary to successful endeavor in other directions. I do not mean the false happiness derived from luxury, but the contentment arising from proper provision for the future, gained by cheerful industry. But I would like to hear the opinions of the ladies on these subjects, and I will ask the princess to give us hers."

"As you may imagine," responded she, "after what

I have just said about our people, which was not all in jest, I have great faith in them and in their leaders, and I can see they have already accomplished much. The evidence of this may be mainly material, as Mr. Maxwell inclines to think, but there is a satisfaction and delight among our people in what they have already done that attaches them strongly to our institutions, and spurs them on to further progress.

"Our system, too, furnishes many safeguards against the evils which have destroyed other governments.

"Excessive luxury could hardly exist where all share equally; slavery, industrial or otherwise, could not occur where there were no masters, and the moral, social and mental qualities must improve when a great part of the cares and worries of life are removed, when employment is furnished to all, and industrious habits cherished, and at the same time sufficient leisure and opportunity are given for this higher cultivation.

"And we do furnish opportunities, Mr. Maxwell, and they are improved by our people.

"Our schools are better, and more universally attended than in any other country; our reading-rooms, our libraries and our lyceums are well filled everywhere, and the churches are well supported. Besides, ours is a land of homes which we protect as they are protected nowhere else, and they are happy homes, with happy people in them, for I have been among them and I know.

"I am not apprehensive for the future of our people; there is the best spirit among them, and it is constantly growing. I look on the bright side; I am optimistic, not pessimistic. And now," she concluded, "we all want to hear from Miss Ashley, for she has thought much on this subject, and has probably higher views in regard to it than have yet been stated. Won't you please give them to us?" she added. "It will lift us up a little."

"I do not know whether I can clearly," Miss Ashley said, and after a moment she continued: "I think all honest endeavor in any department of human exertion and knowledge is, if not advancement in the right road, at least a means for discovering it.

"I do not think we can all expect to take an equally important part in the forward movement. There must always be the spiritual, and the more material among us. The main thing is that all work together, and be in earnest in proceeding onward. There is a great difference in the functions of the several accessories of a coach in motion over a road. The wheels perform certain duties, the brakes certain others, the driver still others, yet all are necessary to and connected with the coach's progress, and move forward simultaneously with it. There must be thinkers and doers, directors and directed; I suppose a great part of humanity will always have to be directed. The important thing in regard to them is that they have such knowledge of the end in view, and such earnestness in attaining it that they may be willing to be guided. But I think a far greater responsibility, one that cannot be overestimated, rests upon those who have to do the directing. They must know far more, and be unselfish, patient, capable, conscientious men and women. They must be more than this—they must be Christian men and women."

She paused, but Clothilde said: "Go on, dear; give us your whole thought; it will help us all.'

Miss Ashley continued with some hesitation: "If we expect to advance to the highest plane we must be as a nation, and in all our relations with one another, as nearly as possible conformable to the rules which our Creator, God, has established, and that means in conformity with his will. He says: 'The kingdom of God cometh with righteousness, and righteousness exalteth a nation.' I think there the whole matter is stated, and so long as our people and rulers observe righteousness I have no fear for their progress, or happiness."

There was silence for a few seconds, and then I asked: "Regarding your people in the light of what you have just said, Miss Ashley, are you encouraged?"

She replied: "Sometimes I am, and then again I doubt. I see very great diminution of crime, but this may be caused by the removal of temptation, and I see, too, a great and growing respect for the rights of others, and a wonderful increase in brotherly kindness and charity among us. But the righteousness of which I speak lies far deeper, and must not be mistaken for mere morality. I hope we are advancing in this higher life, but our community has existed so short a time that the results in this direction are not as evident as they have been in others."

"Do you think, Miss Ashley," said I, "that the kingdom of God will ever come literally on this earth?"

"I can only say," she answered, "that I know not why it should be impossible. I think it will come whenever mankind are connected in unity by a spiritual bond into one great brotherhood, and all to God, who is acknowledged as its supreme head and director. I think, then, the Lord might visibly rule over us. But this is only my opinion and but little weight should be given it."

"Well," said Miss Clothilde, "I believe we are all growing and will keep on growing. I think I am wiser and better than I was a few years ago, and I expect to be still more so a few years hence. In fact, I believe I am better than I was an hour ago, and I think we have been benefited by this little talk."

Thus the conversation closed, and we all soon took our leave.

CHAPTER XVII.

I resumed the reading of the manuscript Miss Clothilde had given me, which continued as follows:

"Mr. Harvey and his men now proceeded to that part of the furnace where the opening of the receptacle for precious metals was located.

"The bottom of the furnace was concave, and this receptacle was situated under its lowest part, allowing the precious metals to run into it by numerous small apertures. It was not large, and was shaped somewhat like an inverted cone, at the lowest part of which the discharge vent began. This, sloping gently, pierced the walls of the furnace; and could be opened and closed at two places, separately, or simultaneously, as might be desired; one situated by the receptacle, the other outside the walls of the furnace. A trough-like conduit, being a continuation of the vent, extended a short distance out over an iron stand, upon which proper moulds were placed to receive the gold.

"The smallest of these moulds, in inner measurement three inches long, one inch wide and one inch deep and designed to hold one pound of gold only, was placed beneath the end of this trough, and Mr. Harvey with his own hand opened the two slides about one-third of their extent.

"For a second, or so, there was no result, and then a purplish light beamed from the outer orifice of the vent, the precursor of the singular substance that followed.

"There appeared at the partially open orifice, and flowed through it slowly, a procession of matter, tenaciously adhering together, emitting much heat, and a haze of purplish light that extended upward several feet and bathed the faces of those bending over it.

"The substance moved slowly along the conduit, and fell in a continuous rope, or cord, into the mould to whose contour it immediately adjusted itself. It was not a stream; it was not sufficiently liquid for that, but rather presented the appearance of a beautiful dark purple bar moving through the conduit and dropping into the mould. Its particles, strongly attached or bound together, were agitated by a motion from bottom to top hard to describe, but which lasted only for a moment; the substance soon assuming a perfectly tranquil appearance.

"When nine or ten inches of its length had appeared, a pale orange light, supplanting the purple, showed the approach of the gold; and as the yellow stream made its appearance, Mr. Harvey closed the outer orifice for the moment that it might not mingle with the preceding substance.

"The black metal, for such it evidently was, had been so little in quantity that it had only filled the small mould to the depth of half an inch. A workman attempted with his gloved hand to shove aside the mould to make way for another to receive the gold, but it did not yield and, to his astonishment, so heavy was it, it required the united efforts of both hands to accomplish his object.

"A large mould was then placed in position and the vent again opened, when the molten gold poured forth in a glorious stream, until exhausted. In value it was about six hundred dollars, and in weight about two pounds. Mr. Harvey was fully satisfied with this portion of the operation.

"Like results attended the tapping of the other receptacle, and he awaited the cooling of the white metal to be fully assured of the success attending the whole process.

"A few hours elapsed, fresh preparations were made for the midnight run, and the gold having solidified, was turned out from the moulds, that it might be duly weighed, tested and the proper records of the results made, and it be placed in the vaults prepared for its safe keeping. This was soon done, and the weight and value of the gold from each furnace was found to be nearly the same as before stated.

"Mr. Harvey then ordered the two moulds containing the black metal to be brought out. Its great weight caused the first astonishment. The quantity which had been taken from each furnace was small, but the weight was comparatively enormous. To add to the astonishment, the substance on being turned over for emptying in the usual manner, obstinately refused to leave the moulds. All ordinary means employed for this purpose having failed, Mr. Harvey ordered them to be broken. This was done, and the bars freed, except from several pieces which still remained attached to them.

"The workmen laid the bars upon their edges, and attempted to remove the pieces by hammering upon them, but only succeeded by shattering them completely.

"The bars were of surpassing beauty. On all sides, even those in contact with the moulds, they had a glossy smoothness, like that of newly-run pitch.

"The rough handling, and the repeated blows, had not at all marred them, which was matter of still further astonishment. Every angle of the mould had been most minutely followed and was imprinted on the substance.

"The bars, each weighed about ten pounds, fully

twenty times the weight of a similar piece of gold. Mr. Harvey realized that he had discovered the heaviest known substance on the globe, and certainly another metal.

"He had already made many experiments with the thin plate obtained from the small furnace. It had resisted all attempts to cut, break, or bend it, or to alter its shape in any particular. Saws, files, and chisels made no impression on it, and did not even dim the lustre of its surface, which was like that of a mirror. Ordinary heat seemed to have little effect upon it; it was almost a non-conductor. Though the plate was very thin, one surface of it could be exposed to the flame of a powerful blow-pipe for ten minutes and the hand applied to the other surface without discomfort.

"On being removed from the flame it soon cooled, retaining all its original lustre. It seemed an anomaly in nature, inelastic, irresponsive, indestructible; setting at defiance all known methods. Mr. Harvey had the newly-run bars of this metal removed to his laboratory, and spent much of the remainder of the day examining them. They were identical in substance with the plate formerly obtained. He viewed them carefully through a microscope. On the sides and bottom several minute projections, much smaller than a pinhead, with a little neck, caught his eye. Their surface was as smoothly polished and glossy as any part of the bars. A thought occurred to him. He sent for the broken pieces of the moulds and examined them also, and found in them several small imperfections, probably occasioned by minute air holes. Comparing these with the globules on the bars, he saw they corresponded. He was profoundly astonished.

"Was this, then, the secret of the attachment of the moulds to the bars; had the tiny necks of these few small globules withstood the shock of heavy hammers without a scar, or blemish?

"He spent some time scrutinizing them, and then, like the practical man he was, gave orders that in future the black metal should be most carefully saved, and run into polished moulds of gun metal.

"About 9 a. m. of the day following, the workmen, armed with great tongs and other tools, dragged forth the pigs of white metal, now well cooled, from their sandy beds, while Mr. Harvey intently observed the operation. As each pig was drawn forth a few smart blows of a hammer shook off the adhering sand, and it lay in its pure whiteness, no trace of the black substance, or any discoloration being visible.

"The pigs, three hundred and twenty in number, and weighing about one hundred pounds each, were piled in one end of the room, while as many more, the result of the midnight run, lay cooling in their sandy beds, and about two and a half pounds of gold, and two small bars of the black metal, represented the more precious yield.

"Mr. Harvey calculated that the ore had yielded a trifle over forty dollars to the ton in gold, and a quantity of robur equal to four-fifths of the ore smelted, an estimate afterwards found to be correct.

"Entirely satisfied, he ordered the other six furnaces to be forthwith charged, and returned to his office.

"From that day no further shipments of crude ore were made from the Bilboa mines, it all being smelted on the spot."

It is unnecessary for me to give my readers the details as set forth in the manuscript, of John Harvey's operations during the next two years. They were voluminous, showing the constant enlargement of his works, and their increased production in gold and robur. For the general

reader it will be sufficient to state the changes made at
Bilboa, and the condition of the mines, and their production, at the end of the year 1903.

At that time a city had been built on a high plateau
owned by Mr. Harvey, which contained fully fifty thousand inhabitants, and was supplied with all things necessary for their comfort and convenience.

The average daily production of Mr. Harvey's works
was sixty thousand dollars in gold, and twelve hundred
tons of robur, which brought a gross price of one hundred
and twenty-five dollars per ton. The greater part of the
latter metal, however, was stored away for future use.

His vaults contained about four hundred tons of
black metal, nearly all in the form of the small bars in
which it came from the furnaces, not a particle having left
his possession.

From his mines and works he derived an average
daily income of one hundred and sixty thousand dollars,
and an additional revenue from rents and other sources.

He employed about six thousand men, whose daily
pay roll amounted to twenty-four thousand dollars, and
the other expenses of conducting his works were about
the same sum.

He had, therefore, a net daily income of one hundred
and ten thousand dollars. During the last two years his
receipts had been large, his operations having been rapidly extended after the discoveries recounted in the manuscript.

In that time he had spent about ten million dollars in
the purchase of lands and the building of the city to which
I have referred. Thirty-five million dollars in gold, then
the only money metal of the world, remained in his treasure vaults.

The mines had been worked largely by open or surface cuts made along the line of the original fissure. The ore had not increased materially in richness, though there were changes in its character as narrated in the manuscript, to which I will now return for further description. It read as follows:

"The open cut along the fissure extended for a distance of six thousand feet, or as far as ore was found, beginning about five hundred feet south of the original, or No. 1, shaft. From this initial point to a distance of over fifteen hundred feet to the northward, the ore had been removed to a depth of two hundred feet, or down to the true fissure, which was eight feet wide. For the remainder of the six thousand feet the ore in the cut had been taken out only about one hundred feet in depth.

"On the fifteen hundred feet connected with shaft No. 1, the ore had held its value well in gold, until it reached the bottom of the cut. Then it had failed rapidly, and at that depth scarcely yielded ten dollars per ton.

• "At the south end the fissure was filled entirely with an impure limestone, which sloped at a small angle to the northward so that at two hundred feet in depth the ore body to the south of shaft No. 1 was little over four hundred feet in length, instead of five hundred, as it was originally.

"The forty-five hundred feet to the north held its full value in gold.

"Four other shafts had been sunk upon the vein; No. 2 being about fifteen hundred feet north of No. 1, and nearly one thousand feet deep, and Nos. 3, 4 and 5, located to the north at varying distances apart, which were sunk to depths of from two hundred to four hundred feet.

"They showed no signs of diminution in gold production, and in all of them the amount of robur yielded remained about the same.

"On the failure of the gold production in and about shaft No. 1 Mr. Harvey had ordered work discontinued in the cut, but pushed the sinking of the shaft itself.

"At a depth of one thousand feet a level had been run northward a distance of eight hundred feet, but throughout its entire length the continuous ore body was barren of gold, except a small number of shot-like globules found in various places.

"It had also been observed that in the shaft and level the ore body seemed softer than in the other shafts, and was permeated, or honeycombed, by small holes or tubes, in which the shot-like gold had been found.

"On the 8th day of January, 1904, the ore in shaft No. 1 ceased, at a depth of one thousand three hundred and forty-seven feet, and the impure limestone before mentioned came in in its place from the south at a small angle.

"Unlike the limestone on the southern slope, however, of which it was undoubtedly a continuation, it was completely honeycombed by small vertical holes. Only a blast, or two, had been made when it was found to be full of free gold, mostly in globules from the size of bird shot to buck shot, with occasional short cylinders of the same diameter, completely filling the holes. This occurred across the entire bottom of the shaft, which was about eight feet square, and the gold deposit apparently extended along the fissure north and south.

"The find was immediately reported to Mr. Harvey, and he descended the shaft. It was decided to sink the latter as rapidly as possible through the limestone as far as the gold extended, and afterwards remove the ore to the northward and southward by stoping.

"The gold-laden limestone was carefully hoisted in canvas bags to the surface. Four shifts of miners, working only six hours each, were employed constantly, and these were cautioned against giving out any information in regard to the find. They worked for two days, reaching a depth of twenty-four feet in the limestone, and no diminution in the quantity of gold was perceptible.

"On the third day, however, it began diminishing very rapidly, and by evening the limestone became hard and compact, and without pores. The bottom of the find was evidently reached.

"Work was continued some distance farther, but all trace of gold was lost. Preparations had been made for drifting and stoping out the gold-laden limestone along the line of the fissure, and this was immediately begun.

"In both directions it was at first found fully as rich as in the shaft, but continued so in the drift to the south at the bottom of the shaft, for a distance of fifty feet only, when the limestone which had been lying almost horizontal, took an upward slope at a very acute angle, and soon became hard and compact, and the gold ceased.

"In the level to the north the limestone continued, rich as before, for a distance of about eighty feet from the shaft, and then the gold ceased, but the rock, though very hard, was completely honeycombed, as in the one thousand-foot level.

"Work in the drift was stopped, and the limestone within the boundaries above indicated was stoped out as rapidly as possible.

"By the 25th of January all the gold-bearing limestone had been removed and the superincumbent fissure matter shored up by pillars. The deposit had also been smelted and the result was amazing, for, from that small area, about one hundred and forty feet long by thirty-five feet deep and eight feet wide, twenty-five million dollars in gold had been taken, and so quietly that none but those employed knew of its existence.

"Various opinions were entertained as to what might be expected from the matter to the north of the pocket, or deposit, thus removed. It continued in a honeycombed wall on down into the fissure, and it was supposed that somewhere below, the gold formerly contained in the now barren matter above it had found lodgment, as had that just worked out.

"The sudden cessation of the gold, however, seemed unaccountable on this hypothesis alone. In appearance the limestone exactly resembled that from which the gold had been taken, yet it contained none.

"After a thorough discussion of the matter with his chief engineer, Mr. Harvey concluded to run a drift from the bottom of the shaft into this limestone to see how far it continued barren. The drift was run for a distance of one hundred feet horizontally, but the rock continued barren.

"Mr. Harvey then ordered that a vertical shaft should be sunk at the north end of the one hundred-foot drift.

"This was begun on the 10th day of February, and on the 12th the workmen declared that the limestone beneath them was hollow, as evidenced by the sound of the blows on their drills.

"Blasting was discontinued, and resort had to chisels and other tools to cut out the rock.

"On the afternoon of the 15th, the shaft being sunk twelve feet below the bottom of the drift, a workman suddenly felt resistance to a blow cease, and saw his chisel fall to its head through the hole, about two feet deep.

"Proper tackle was at once rigged up for supporting the men, and the cutting out of the limestone was resumed with increased vigor. About midnight it had been cut through to within six inches, and unmistakable evidences of a cavity were manifest.

"At 1 o'clock a. m. the rock had been pierced at short distances around the entire square of the shaft, and two workmen only were left suspended in slings to break it away by means of heavy hammers.

"From the tunnel Mr. Bond, the trusted engineer, and Mr. Harvey watched the proceedings. No impure air had been observed coming from the cavity, but three workmen stood ready to hoist their fellows, if necessary, by tackle and pulleys attached to the slings.

"A few blows detached the mass, and the entire bottom of the shaft fell with a crash into the cavity below. A few more blows cleared the ragged edges of the opening and the workmen ascended to the tunnel. Some seconds later, when the dust occasioned by the fall had cleared away, a light was lowered down the shaft, and the floor or bottom of the cavity was revealed at no great distance below, and Mr. Harvey and Mr. Bond peering down, saw amid the wreck and debris the yellow sheen of gold.

"They prepared to descend; an electric light with many long coils of wire attached was fastened to a sling; the lamp hanging a few feet below it, and a light pick and a signal cord were also provided.

"They took their places and were lowered cautiously until the end of the shaft was reached. Slowly the electric light passed into the cavern, irradiating it; and slowly the two men followed until they also had passed through.

"An involuntary exclamation burst from their lips, and both almost closed their eyes until the floor was reached. The wealth of all the Indies seemed beneath their feet, and piled around them. They were in an irregular cavern, extending along the fissure north and south from them.

"The floor from three to six feet wide, and parts of the walls, which varied from six to fifteen feet in height, were covered with gold. The white light of the electric lamp shone yellow with the reflection, and the heads of the two men grew dizzy at the sight of this vast accumulation of the metal for which men had worked, and toiled, and died, since time began.

"Mr. Harvey first recovered, and released himself from the sling. Without a word he unfastened the electric light with its wire coils and gave it to Mr. Bond, and, taking the pick in his own hand, led the way; and the two men, excitement depicted on every feature, began their exploration toward the northward.

"The cavern bore in this direction uninterruptedly a distance of nearly one hundred and twenty feet, when further progress was barred by a partition of granite rising from the floor. A narrow aperture, however, was found, through which Mr. Bond passed holding the light, and Mr. Harvey came after. The cavern still followed the trend of the fissure northward.

"Everywhere its floor, which, however, was narrower than the ceiling or top, was covered with gold, and other areas or patches of gold occupied places on its sides; and wherever there was a shelf, it was covered with gold. The metal seemed to have fallen into the cavern from above, in a liquid, or molten state, and to have attached itself wherever it could find lodgment.

"Slowly the now dazed explorers picked their way; sometimes stooping, again walking upright, as the head room was lower or higher; sometimes passing through narrow lanes, until over four hundred feet more had been traversed.

"At this point the fissure merged into a solid granite wall in which no aperture could be found.

"They had reached the northern boundary of the cavity, at a little over six hundred feet from their point of entrance, and throughout the whole distance gold had been found in abundance everywhere.

"No fissure existed in the bottom, and all the gold seemed to have come from the ore above, filtered through the limestone rock into the long pocket, or cavern, now revealed.

"Silently the two men retraced their steps, stopping occasionally to strike a few blows with the sharp pick through the gold covering on the floor to ascertain its thickness and the nature of the rock beneath. This as well as the walls on either side they found to be granite, and the gold was from one-fourth to three and even four inches thick.

"The light of their lamp shone up the shaft, informing the miners overhead of their safe return, and they proceeded on southward. The same generous deposit of gold continued, but the cavern began to narrow, and at a little over eighty feet the granite walls came together, and its southern boundary was reached.

"The two men paused, and conversed in regard to the find, and the future.

" 'The possession of this great treasure fills me with awe,' said Mr. Harvey. 'You know my ideas, Bond, in regard to what men call wealth; that its possessor rightfully holds it to be employed for the comfort and happiness of others as well as his own. I have tried to use what has already been given me in this manner; to make men better and life brighter and more beautiful for them. This new discovery puts fresh labors on me, and on you, and on all of us. I have great schemes, Bond, for the welfare of humanity, that have as yet been only dreams; but this vast treasure promises so much aid in their accomplishment that, as I stand here, they seem already realities. I want to discuss them thoroughly with you and others, whose assistance we must call in if we make them facts. In the meantime we must bring this treasure to the surface and convert it into money that will buy for us material, labor, skill, and experience, as we require them, and we shall require them soon, I think.'

"It was then settled between them that the discovery should be kept secret for the present, and that the entrance to the cavern should be sealed up by an iron door, at the departure of the drift from the main shaft. They returned quietly and were hoisted up by the workmen.

" 'It is a long, narrow, tortuous cavity,' said Mr. Harvey to the miners, 'and needs further exploration, which is not safe until the ore and limestone above are taken care of. We shall have to shut it up and, I think, work the ore down from the top.'

"These words were in accordance with what was afterwards done, and aided in concealing the great discovery, and none of the miners imagined that gold had been found.

"On the 5th day of March, 1904, Messrs. Harvey and Bond, with seven miners, went down the main shaft. These miners were the first of three relays of seven men each, who were to work in shifts of eight hours in taking out the ore in the cavern. Forty men in all had been chosen; some to hoist the ore; some to convey it along a covered way to the walled court of the laboratory, and others to smelt it and store the precious metal in the great treasure vaults. All these operations were to be carefully concealed, and these men were required to devote themselves entirely to this work till completed, and to remain till then inside the laboratory grounds, where the smelting would take place, and were solemnly sworn to the utmost secrecy. All apparatus for lighting the shaft, tunnel, and cavern, was ready to be put in place by the miners. No eyes but those of Messrs. Harvey and Bond had as yet beheld the cavern; and it may be added no eyes but theirs, and those of the twenty-one miners, ever beheld it till shorn of all its golden glory and richness.

"Some time was spent in the tunnel, in getting the hoisting apparatus and that for ventilation and light in order; but about 3 o'clock p. m., Mr. Harvey and Mr. Bond descended, a light having been lowered first. Then two of the miners followed. They were stricken dumb with amazement at the wealth which surrounded them, but were put immediately at work receiving the tools and supplies lowered from the tunnel by the other workmen.

"At 5 o'clock two more miners, skilled in electric arrangement, were lowered. They also were bewildered, but in charge of Mr. Bond immediately began the putting in place of the wires and lamps for the electric lighting of the cavern; while the other two, under direction of Mr. Harvey, completed the rest of the preliminary work and received the remaining stores. By half-past six o'clock this was all done; the electric current was turned on, and the remaining three men came down the shaft.

"The other two relays of seven men each had also been summoned, and a few moments later the twenty-one miners and Mr. Harvey and Mr. Bond stood in a group in the cavern.

"Mr. Harvey addressed them as follows:

" 'There are many astonishing things to be seen here, my men. After we have partaken of food, a half hour will be allowed in which you may examine the cavern. I will then speak briefly to you all, assembled here, of my wishes and intentions; and then to work, to work, at such work as the world never saw.'

"The repast finished, for half an hour, singly and in groups, the workmen explored the inmost recesses of the cavern, and discussed the wondrous wealth therein contained. They were again called together by Mr. Harvey, and, standing around him, were thus impressively addressed:

" 'My men and fellow-workers, in the last half hour you have seen one of the most wonderful sights that it has ever fallen to the lot of man to behold. Neither Mr. Bond nor myself has much conception of the wealth contained in the great cavity on whose floor we stand.

" 'Since the world began men have used gold, because of its scarcity and adaptability for the purpose, as a standard by which to gauge the value, and to purchase all other things produced, owned, or consumed among them.

" 'This long-continued use has so inwrought in the mind the idea of its great value that I see astonishment and excitement in your faces at this spectacle. Had this cavern contained like quantities of iron, lead or copper, no such emotions would have been aroused; and yet any one of these metals in itself is worth far more to mankind than gold. The fictitious value which men have given it, alone makes it worth a thousand times more than a like amount of any of these metals, but might easily be disturbed were great quantities of it found.

" 'I desire that this discovery should be kept secret. I am but the custodian of this treasure, and must use it at the valuation the world puts upon it, not for my own benefit alone, but for that of mankind.

" 'I have tried to make what has already been given me a blessing to myself and to my countrymen; I hope to make this discovery a means of still greater good to a still greater number.

" 'I have plans for this purpose which I cannot disclose, and which it will take years to mature, for time and thought are required for their completion.

" 'Were it known that this addition had been thus made to what men call my wealth, a hundred hindrances would be placed in my way by others desirous of gain. The eyes of greedy and unscrupulous men would be turned on me, and their subtle brain and energy would be used to secure a portion of this fortune, and to thwart and hinder my plans, which if carried out will be a great and permanent blessing to you, to me, and to posterity.

" 'You can aid me in the furthering of these designs by concealing this discovery from the knowledge of all persons, even from your wives and children, until I have matured and perfected them; until I give you leave to speak.

" 'You are picked men, chosen from six thousand, for your intelligence, your reticence, and your loyalty to me.

" 'You are all middle-aged men, men of families, and in addition to the oaths of loyalty and secrecy you have already taken, I charge you to lisp not, breathe not, the fact of this discovery to any one; to hide it and all I may have spoken, in your hearts; nay, even to discourage curiosity by your commonplace and disparaging remarks about it.

" 'Do this until I give you leave to speak, and then you may tell the story of how you stood this night in the depths of the Bilboa mines and looked on that wondrous store of gold that in after years so changed the land. Then you may claim to have been my acknowledged fellow-workers in labors vast and grand, and fraught with untold benefit to the human race. Then, when you go abroad, men will turn and look upon you and say: "There goes one of the twenty-three, who alone saw the great riches of the Bilboa mines."

" 'In return I promise each and every one of you that you shall be my especial care, through life, at death, and your children after you; only requiring that you keep your oaths in truth and verity.

" 'This, also, I shall promise, on similar conditions, to the nineteen men above, engaged in another part of this great work.

" 'All this I confirm by my oath as you have by yours. Woe to the man recreant to these vows; upon him be visited the vengeance of man and of God.'

"He ceased his address, which was delivered and received with great solemnity, and after giving minute directions for the prosecution of the work, returned with Mr. Bond, and the unemployed miners, to the surface.

"Until the 10th day of May, 1904, work was continued in the cavity thus found. On that day its entire contents had been removed and smelted, and the gold produced, or its equivalent in coin, deposited in Mr. Harvey's treasure vaults, and it reached the enormous sum of one hundred and forty million dollars.

"Altogether he had in them two hundred million dollars, of which about seventy-five million was in bars, the remainder being in coin.

"The unminted gold had been sold in Europe and in various places in the United States; yet in so quiet a way that no rumors of the recent discovery had been set afloat."

CHAPTER XVIII.

Thus the manuscript described the finding of this great treasure, talk of which I had heard in my boyhood. The story had even now the air of a romance, yet within the last few days I had seen a structure largely composed of the white metal taken from the very mines of which I had been reading.

I soon called again to see Miss Clothilde. I found her alone, and informed her of the progress I had made in perusing the book and the interest it excited in my mind.

"I have read far enough," I said, "to understand that John Harvey considered himself as merely holding this treasure in trust, but not far enough to know how he did in fact use it."

"That," she replied, "will appear later. But," and she hesitated a moment, "it would be interesting to imagine what we ourselves would do with such a vast sum if we possessed it. Suppose that you, for instance, Mr. Maxwell, found yourself in absolute control of millions, not accumulated by the schemes and labors of a lifetime, but suddenly thrust upon you; what do you think you would do with them?"

"Frankly I cannot tell, Miss Clothilde," I answered, with some embarrassment at the unusual question.

"Nay," she said, noticing this, "I did not intend my inquiry to be either impertinent or idly curious; but I have an earnest desire that you should compare John

Harvey's disposition of his wealth with that which others make of theirs, and judge his character accordingly."

"Great wealth," I replied, "has usually been employed by its possesors in comprehensive schemes for securing control of production, or the profits of its distribution."

"And for what objects, Mr. Maxwell?" she asked.

"Mainly, I regret to say, for self-aggrandizement or self-gratification. There have been exceptional cases, but these have been the general objects."

"They certainly are not very high ones!" she exclaimed.

"No," I again answered, "they might be called potent, but assuredly not high motives. Miss Ashley, the other evening, spoke of what are truly high ones, and I believe with her that before we can have full recognition of the rights of man we must be christianized."

"I believe so too," she replied, "but that statement is often used either as an excuse for the wilful ignoring of those rights, or for doing nothing to secure them. An awakened christianity, practicing the principles which glorify it, is what we need.

"All over the land," she continued, "thousands throng the churches. I have read that in the times when slavery was a recognized institution both masters and slaves were church-goers; yet the former never acknowledged the rights of the latter, and excused this neglect by the alleged unfitness of the slaves to exercise those rights, and were zealous in promulgating among them that emotional christianity which tended to reconcile them to vassalage and make them more conscientious and faithful servants. There is an immense amount of this same teaching in churches to-day, and it has no practical result for the benefit of the people, Mr. Maxwell."

"I agree with you," I said. "I have heard it often. The leaders, in the church as well as elsewhere, should be men who love justice, deal honestly, and speak the truth fearlessly and constantly. There are many such men, but they are overborne by the system under which they live."

"I have little patience," said she, "with half way measures, or such leaders. Let them change the system. Let them have the bravery and the manhood to do it. It was done in the days of slavery, and later another kind of serfdom was prohibited in this land of ours, largely by the efforts of one clear-sighted man.

"I think the difficulty is principally with the leaders. They have not been in earnest; they have not been ready to adopt proper means to emancipate the race; they do everything by old rules.

"Frequently self-glorification is the main object. Societies for the advancement of nearly all phases of man's condition meet in convention, indulge in self-laudation, pass resolutions, collect money, and adjourn without taking such steps as earnest business men endeavoring to effect the same ends would at once employ. And then again, Mr. Maxwell, how many of such reforms get down to the roots of the evils they aim to remove? You see no drunkenness in the Nationality, but this is not so much because of laws against the sale of intoxicants as that we have abolished the causes, poverty, hopelessness, and enforced idleness, which led men to use stimulants. Had we been fetter bound by an old system we could not have laid the ax at the root of the tree of evil, but would have kept on lopping off branches while others were continually growing out.

"All our successes have been attained, and will continue to be attained, only in the line of thorough and intelligent removal of the causes of evil. The masses of mankind will be rapidly converted—only when Chris-, tians exhibit the results of their profession by extending justice and brotherly kindness, not charity and alms, to their fellow men."

She had grown very earnest and animated in her remarks, which were a new revelation of the vigor of her thought.

"I am glad, Miss Clothilde," I said, "that you have spoken so freely. I have thought long on these subjects, and am beginning to see my way clearly, and have obtained much light from you and your friends."

She accompanied me to the door and asked me to return soon, and I walked home more than ever charmed with her loveliness and manifest intelligence.

Next day I resumed the reading of the manuscript which continued as follows:

"Almost simultaneously with the discovery of this great treasure, Mr. Harvey began preparing to carry out the schemes to which he had alluded in his address to the workmen and in his talk with Mr. Bond.

"He desired to secure a vast body of arid land now lying waste and valueless, and to build great canals for irrigating and a network of railroads for traversing it, and finally to settle a colony upon it, organized on novel and humanitarian principles.

"He called to his aid eminent lawyers, skillful engineers, and a few well-known philanthropists, to whom alone he revealed his final purpose. These persons were all sworn to secrecy, and a brotherhood was thus formed, which was lifelong in its duration and far-reaching in its effects.

"Many millions of acres of arid, and semi-arid land, lie within the boundaries of the states of South Dakota,

Wyoming, Nebraska, Colorado, Kansas, Arizona, New Mexico, Texas, and Oklahoma. These lands form for the most part great plains, broken in some places, but generally level, or gently rolling, with an equable fall from the mountains to the east, very favorable for irrigation.

"At intervals of a hundred miles, or so, apart, they are traversed by small streams, hardly worthy of being dignified by the name of rivers, which have, however, in bygone times had an important part in fertilizing and shaping this land.

"There was but little or no rainfall in this region, and but little water. A native growth of scant grass covered it, and it had been given up almost entirely to pasturage.

"A few years before, the government of the United States had donated to the individual states all the lands belonging to it, within their respective borders.

"The states in which these arid lands were situated were but thinly settled and were poor and in debt, and to add to their distresses, a great monetary panic, or revulsion, had occurred which lasted many years.

"This was caused largely by the peculiar monetary system of the United States and Europe, which rendered it possible for a few financial kings to control the supply of money and manipulate it as they pleased. For years these persons dictated legislation in regard to it, furtively increasing its value, and decreasing that of labor and all commodities.

"Finally the relations between money and other property were so distorted that all values were unsettled, the mass of small money owners became frightened, and this revulsion occurred throughout the civilized world with unprecedented suddenness, and industry was paralyzed.

"In the United States a comparatively undeveloped and debtor nation, the effect was to double and treble every one's liabilities, and for some time men stood aghast, completely overcome by the calamity that had fallen upon them like a bolt from heaven, uncertain to what to attribute it, and entirely at a loss how to remedy the disaster.

"The inevitable results were pauperism and distress among the people, and bankruptcy and failure of credit among the states, especially those before mentioned.

"In this dilemma the project of selling these arid lands had been broached. It was thought that some persons, or company, could be found willing to buy them, and thus enable these states to replenish their treasuries without burdening their struggling people.

"The project found favor with their citizens, and their legislatures passed laws, nearly uniform, authorizing the issuance of scrip which would be received in payment for the public lands.

"These laws provided for their classification into arid, semi-arid, irrigable, pasture, timber and mineral bearing lands, and fixed prices upon them, and commissioners were already at work, inspecting and enumerating them under these heads.

"Any amount of this scrip could be bought and located anywhere, by any person or company at the fixed price per acre, on any land thus classified, and all land thus bought and located was exempt from taxation for ten years. Such were the general provisions of these laws.

"On the 1st of June of the year 1904, parties of skilled engineers and topographers were sent out by Mr. Harvey with orders to make close and accurate surveys of these lands, showing their elevations and depressions, the nature of their soils, and giving all information necessary to a thorough knowledge of them.

"From the Missouri River in South Dakota, to the Arkansas River in Colorado, and from thence down into Texas, other parties of engineers were busy locating the line of a great canal along and near the base of the mountains.

"This region was thinly settled, and it was supposed by the inhabitants that the engineering work upon the great plains was done at the instance of companies who, contemplated extensive purchases of land for cattle raising, and designed building a line of railway.

"By the end of November Mr. Harvey's engineering department had in their possession a complete topographical description of all this arid region, and had also established on the ground the line of the contemplated canal and railway.

"A summary of the report of the engineering department will, however, best explain the work thus planned, which was afterward completed as therein set forth.

"This report says:

"'The problem presented to your engineers was a mighty one, being no less than to determine the feasibility of reclaiming by irrigation a great body of arid and semi-arid lands extending from the 104th, or 105th, to the 98th degree of longitude; said lands being in portions of the states of South Dakota, Wyoming, Nebraska, Kansas, Colorado, New Mexico, Arizona, Texas and Oklahoma.

"'This could only be done by the construction of a great irrigating canal extending northerly and southerly in main direction through this region, with several great lateral canals from it; the main canal to be taken out from the Missouri River, that being the only stream capable of furnishing an adequate supply of water for the purpose.

" 'The necessity of veiling the scheme until its feasibility and the exact line of the canal could be determined, and the lands to be watered from it could be cheaply secured, was also impressed upon your engineers, and they are happy to say that this was accomplished, for a great line of railroad running northerly and southerly and connected with, or capable of being continued to, some point on the Gulf Coast possessing a convenient harbor, was another and a very necessary part of the plan, and furnished an adequate excuse to the public for the extensive surveys made.

" 'It was found, after running various lines, that the mouth of the canal must be thrown much farther to the eastward on the Missouri River than had been at first supposed, and that no part of Wyoming could be included in the present scheme.

" 'It was also found that the amount of land originally contemplated to be watered was so great as to make the scheme almost impracticable, and it is therefore advised that the canal be primarily extended only as far as the Arkansas River.

" 'It is recommended, however, that it be made of such size as to furnish abundance of water for the irrigation of all lands under it, so as to be capable of extension south of the Arkansas River as soon as these lands shall be thoroughly saturated, and the water courses running through them, of which the Niobrara, the White, the Platte and its confluents are the principal, begin to swell, when the amount of water requisite to be furnished from the canal for the irrigation of these lands can be very materially diminished.

" 'To make this plainer, your engineers estimate the amount of water necessary to be carried in the main canal during the irrigating season of five months, for irrigating thirty million acres of land during the first year after the construction of the canal, to be such a quantity as would cover the land one foot in depth if spread upon it; but that owing to causes above mentioned, in succeeding years, probably as soon as in the third year of irrigation, only one-half as much water need be used from the canal for the same purpose.

" 'Your engineers mention thirty million acres of land, as that is the amount they expect to irrigate directly from the canal they have decided to recommend for construction.

" 'There are, however, on the line of the canal many reservoirs of great capacity which can be filled at other times than during the months of May, June, July, August and September, the season for irrigation.

" 'The quantity which can be stored in them has been carefully estimated by your engineers, and is found to be amply sufficient for the irrigation of twenty-seven million more acres of land, and they would therefore recommend the purchase of fifty-seven million acres of land as hereinafter more fully described, to be watered from the canal and its reservoirs.

" 'For many reasons besides that of assistance in constructing the canal, it is desirable that the railroad should follow the course of the former, and it is recommended that throughout its entire length it be a double track line.

" 'Your engineers have located the northern terminus of the railroad at a point on the Northern Pacific Road in Dakota, about fifty miles northeast of the Missouri River, near the town of Bessieres.

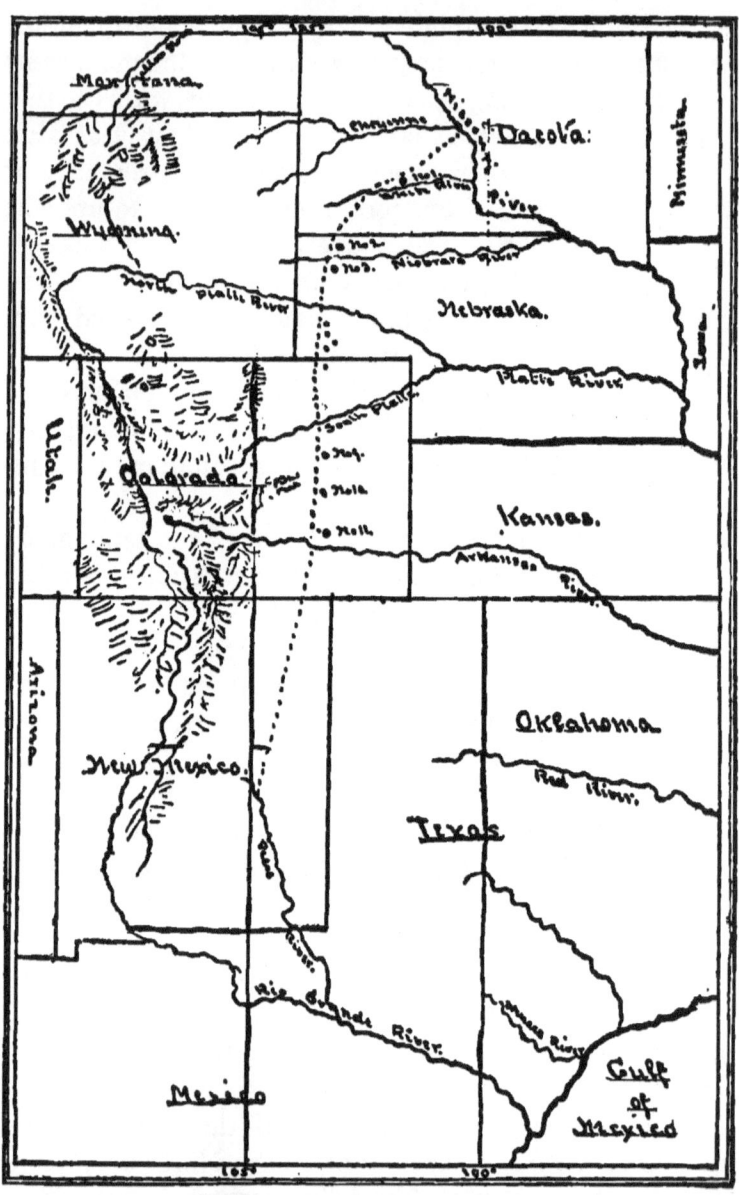

MAP OF THE IRRIGATING CANAL.

" 'It will cross the Missouri River by a bridge at, or near, the head gate of the canal, and follow the eastern bank of the latter to the Arkansas River, and proceed thence as shown on the accompanying map of the entire region, through New Mexico and Texas to its southern terminus at Corpus Christi, on the Gulf of Mexico.

" 'The head gate of the canal will be located on the Missouri, just south of where the Cheyenne River enters it, the rocky walls through which the Missouri there passes ensuring solidity and permanence.

" 'At the head gate the canal will be six hundred feet wide, and continue this width for about three miles. It will then widen until, at the distance of two miles farther, it will attain its full width of nine hundred feet. This whole distance of five miles will be cut through solid rock. The canal will then run, with the width last above mentioned, and with an average depth of fifteen feet, which depth it will maintain throughout its entire course, about seventy-five miles, in a south-easterly direction, when occurs the first great reservoir, marked No. 1, covering twenty-thousand acres, which can be filled to an average depth of one hundred feet, and is capable of storing water for the use of nearly all the five million acres of semi-arid land in South Dakota.

" 'It will continue the same course seventy-five miles farther, and cross the southern boundary line of South Dakota about thirty-five miles from the southwest corner of the state, and continuing the same general direction for a distance of fifty miles through the northwest corner of the state of Nebraska toward its western boundary, will cut past the head of the Niobrara River.

" 'Two great reservoirs, Nos. 2 and 3, are met with in this fifty miles, the smaller located about ten miles south of the northern boundary line of the state of Nebraska, containing twenty-five thousand acres, with an average depth of sixty feet, in which can be stored nearly enough water for the three million acres of semi-arid land lying north of the Niobrara in Nebraska, the other lying just south of the Niobrara River containing nearly fifty thousand acres, with an average depth of eighty feet, capable of holding sufficient water to irrigate about six millions of the twenty million acres of arid land lying north of the Platte River, and west of the 98th degree of longitude, in Nebraska.

"'For this whole distance of two hundred miles, except the first five miles, the course of the canal lies through an arable country, though much broken, and no great fills, nor any considerable amount of rock work is met with.

"'Turning nearly due south, at a distance of about thirty miles from the western boundary of the state of Nebraska, the canal will pass through an easy country, until it approaches the valley of the North Platte River, which is generally from one to two miles wide, but at the point chosen for crossing is narrowed to a distance of three-fourths of a mile, rocky bluffs rising to the level of the canal on either side. Prior to reaching this valley, however, and about ten miles south of reservoir No. 3, a great lateral, A, will be taken out of the canal, and flow eastward along the dividing line between the water sheds of the Niobrara and the Platte Rivers. It will run in that direction nearly three hundred miles, and is intended to water the remaining fourteen million acres of land unwatered by reservoir No. 3, and lying on those water sheds.

"'Up to the debouchment of this lateral, the canal will maintain its full width of nine hundred feet; after that point, however, it will be reduced to six hundred.

" 'The valley of the North Platte River will be crossed by an aqueduct four hundred feet in width, and the canal now six hundred feet wide will pursue about the same course as before, to the northern boundary line of the state of Colorado, a distance of fifty miles farther.

" 'The country, however, is much rougher, and no less than five reservoir sites, numbered 4, 5, 6, 7, 8, are found, of various sizes, ranging from three thousand to ten thousand acres, and capable of storing sufficient water to irrigate all the land lying under the canal between the north and south branches of the Platte, estimated at four million acres.

" 'The canal will enter the state of Colorado about one hundred miles west of its eastern boundary line, and pass through an easy country in a direction a little west of south for a distance of fifty miles, until it reaches the valley of the South Platte River about forty miles south-west of the town of Sterling, and in longitude 104½ degrees west.

" 'This valley will be crossed also by an aqueduct of the same width as that over the North Platte, but much longer. After crossing, but little difficulty is met with in the work; the great plain between the Platte, and the Arkansas Rivers, stretching from the 105th to the 98th degree of longitude and constituting parts of the states of Colorado, Nebraska and Kansas, lying for the most part very level.

" 'The canal will pursue a southerly course for a distance of seventy miles, till a little southeast of the city of Denver, when reservoir No. 9 is met with, containing fifteen thousand acres.

" 'It will leave the city of Denver about thirty miles to the westward, and run southward a short distance, then trend to the east fifteen miles to gain the summit

of the divide between the waters of the Platte and Arkansas Rivers.

" 'At the point where the summit is reached another
great lateral, B, will carry a large part of the water of
the canal eastward for three hundred miles, along the
top of this divide, for the purpose of watering the lands
between these two rivers.

" 'The terminus of this lateral might be called the
present terminus of the canal itself.

" 'The canal, however, only fifty feet wide, will bend
back westward, after crossing the divide, and run southward, meeting another reservoir, No. 10, of about fifteen
thousand acres, west of the city of Colorado Springs,
and running thence on to within twenty miles of the Arkansas River, and about fifty miles east of Pueblo will
terminate in a great reservoir, No. 11, of thirty thousand
acres, capable of storing water for the irrigation of three
million acres of land.

" 'When the canal is extended across the Arkansas
this portion can be widened to the proper size.

" 'The entire length of the canal thus marked on
the ground by your engineers will be four hundred and
ninety miles from its mouth to its termination in reservoir No. 11.

" 'The course marked on the map indicates how it
may hereafter be carried across the Arkansas River, and
through New Mexico to the heads of the Pecos and Rio
Grande Rivers, whose beds might be used as channels
for conveying water for the irrigation of the semi-arid
lands lying in that state, in Texas, and in Oklahoma.

" 'Your engineers have considered that the canal
should have a constant flow of water through its entire
length during the whole year, the amount to be regulated
by the head gates.

" 'They have made the following summary of lands capable of being irrigated either directly, or indirectly, therefrom, stating from whence the water for irrigating the same can be taken:

" 'In South Dakota (semi-arid)—
To be watered from reservoir No. 1 and from the White and Niobrara Rivers, increased in flow.......... 5,000,000

" 'In Nebraska (north of the Niobrara River, semi-arid)—
To be watered from reservoir No. 2............. 3,000,000

" 'In Nebraska (north of the Platte, arid)—
To be watered from reservoir No. 3 and the Platte River 6,000,000
To be watered from canal. ... 14,000,000

" 'In Nebraska (between the North and South Platte Rivers, arid)—
To be watered from reservoirs Nos. 4, 5, 6, 7, 8 and the Platte River..... 2,500,000

" 'In Colorado............... 1,500,000

" 'In Nebraska (south of the Platte River, arid)—
To be watered from the Platte River............ 1,000,000
To be watered from the canal. 4,000,000

" 'In Colorado (between the Platte and Arkansas Rivers, arid)—
To be watered from reservoirs Nos. 9, 10 and 11........ 5,000,000

To be watered from the
   canal   3,000,000
" 'In Kansas (arid)—
   To be watered from the Arkansas River............ 3,000,000
   To be watered from the
   canal   9,000,000
                        _____ _____
                        27,000,000 30,000,000

"This report of the engineers was accompanied by a great mass of details, estimates and drawings, unnecessary to give here.

"A report on the lands above described, giving exact topographical surveys, and all particulars in regard to them was also submitted.

"In December, 1904, and in January of the year succeeding, the reports of the commissioners for classification of lands in the several states having been returned and accepted by the proper officers, all the states before mentioned offered their scrip for sale, which was at once taken by John Harvey, and his agents, in the name of a company formed for the purpose of concealing the identity of his operations, and was located on the lands above mentioned, and on large tracts in Texas, Arizona and New Mexico, as well as upon all the coal, iron and other mineral lands offered.

"After paying thirty millions of dollars for the lands thus bought, and expending five million more in the erection of a great iron and steel plant on the Arkansas River in Colorado, Mr. Harvey in January, 1905, had remaining in his treasure vaults nearly two hundred and ten million dollars, and was prepared to begin work on the railroad and canal and the improvement of his land on a scale of magnitude never before known in the world."

CHAPTER XIX.

THE ENTERTAINMENT.

Miss Beyresen and I had been invited to an entertainment at the residence of General Knox, one of the councilors, in honor of his daughter, Mrs. Hamilton, now the wife of a member of congress from the state of New York.

I had a desire to learn how such affairs were managed among this people in relation to pecuniary outlay, and asked Miss Clothilde about the arrangements.

"There will be music," said she, "and possibly cards for those who wish to play; the rooms will be adorned with flowers, and refreshments of some nature will undoubtedly be served, and, indeed, everything will be much the same as you have seen on similar occasions in a dozen cities in—well, in China—for that I believe is the place you last came from.

"There will not likely be the abundance, or the variety of delicacies with which Europeans and Americans farther east load their tables, and, excuse me, befuddle their brains.

"I might stop here, Mr. Maxwell, and not risk shocking your prejudices, but my characteristic candor impels me to explain, what I have no doubt you are curious to know, how the expenses of such entertainments are borne amongst us.

"You see that little figure 50c, in the scroll at the top of my invitation. It is erased from yours, for you are not supposed to be acquainted with the cabalistic lore of this

land. It means that the guests are each expected to contribute that amount to such expenses as I have mentioned. They bring their allowance tickets with them,
and deposit them in a box at the door, and that sum is
deducted from them, and they are quietly returned to
their owners.

"If a dinner party were given, it might cost each person, possibly a dollar. The whole matter is arranged in
this simple way. If one does not wish to go, the invitation can be declined. We have public festivities, which
the state conducts on a far more lavish scale, but our private parties are not expected to be occasions for ostentation."

On thinking the matter over I was satisfied that all
repellent feelings about this plan were, indeed, the result
of mere prejudice, and that probably no other could be
devised more effectual in preventing the evils of competi-
tive extravagance so often displayed in the social world
on such occasions.

Miss Clothilde and I arrived about eight o'clock, and
I met a number of distinguished persons, some of whom
I will now present to the reader.

Our host, General Knox, was six feet four inches in
height, perfectly proportioned, and of great strength and
vigor. He was in the prime of life, about fifty years of
age, and was evidently a man of much acquaintance and
experience with men and affairs.

His daughter, Mrs. Hamilton, was a society woman
of culture and discernment, exhibiting many of her father's best traits, very handsome, and of fine physique.

General Canly, whom I had not before seen, was
about the same age as General Knox, tall, rather slender,
but muscular, dark-complexioned, and with a countenance expressing clear insight, careful examination, decis-

ion, prompt execution, and indomitable courage and resolution. Great respect and consideration were shown
him by all present, and by none more than our host himself, and I soon learned that he was one of the most prominent men of the Nationality. He was accompanied by
his daughter, a young lady of twenty-two or twenty-three
years of age. Though not beautiful, she was regular in
feature, tall, willowy and graceful in figure, very cultured,
and an apt conversationalist; in fact, I never met any one
who could more perfectly and easily command the appropriate word to express the exact shade of thought in
her mind.

Doctor Ashley and his wife were present, and also
Miss Ashley, to whom the reader has been previously introduced.

Among the young men were a few of the literati of
the city: Leon de Sutor, a gifted author, earnest, fiery
and high-spirited, well known in the literary world by several volumes of poems he had published; John Francis
King, who has been introduced before; and Herbert
Jones, whose works on Political Economy and Races of
Men were just coming into notice.

My friends, Mr. Bradbury and Miss Erickson, were
also present, the latter as breezy and lively as ever.

Altogether there were not more than one hundred
persons in this assemblage, and they were so congenial,
and so evidently met for mutual enjoyment, that it was
impossible for even a comparative stranger like myself to
feel otherwise than as if surrounded by friends.

Some of the ladies and gentlemen were highly cultivated musicians, and others belonged to Thespian societies in the city, and we were entertained by them with
music and various character renditions that were most
artistic and interesting.

The utmost cordiality and good-fellowship prevailed, and there was none of that fashionable rivalry in outward display so often exhibited elsewhere on such occasions.

It was a republican assemblage, where no one had precedence except that gained by superiority in intelligence, wit, cultivation and manners; and this was accorded without jealousy and maintained without pride, or exclusiveness.

Very shortly after our arrival Miss Clothilde left me talking with Miss Ashley and some others, and though I saw her frequently afterward, I had little conversation with her.

Nothing surprised me more than the way in which she was received. Every one appeared to know and honor her, and she was addressed as the Princess, quite as frequently as Miss Beyresen. She wore the title as if to the manor born, and her attitude and bearing were of the most queenly and royal character. Her tall, graceful figure, her shapely head crowned with abundant black hair, her clear brown cheeks slightly tinged with color, and her dark hazel eyes made her conspicuous amid the company, and the frank, honest expression of her countenance, with her winning words and ways, belied the thought that at first arose in my mind, that she was merely playing the part of princess.

She moved among the assemblage with quiet dignity and most unaffected grace, with a pleasant word for every one and a bright sparkle in her dark eye for an especial friend. In the course of the evening I think she spoke to nearly every person in the room. I saw her saying something pleasant to De Sutor, for his face kindled with appreciation, and I could not help observing that others were following her movements with looks of admiration.

The evening passed by, and I made the acquaintance of many members of the company whom, in after years, I came to know more thoroughly.

Shortly before the party broke up, I met General Canly, and we began talking about England and other European countries, and particularly their military power. I discovered that the General was of French birth, and had served as' an officer in the armies of his native country. I afterwards learned that he had won his title in the bloody battles of the Franco-German struggle of 1918, and at its close had become a citizen of the Nationality. He informed me that he still kept up his military studies, "For unfortunately," said he, "the happy time has not yet come when nations may beat the sword into the plowshare and the spear into the pruning-hook and enlightened arbitration take the place of war. We have present here to-night," he continued, "three persons who have served in European armies, yourself, General Knox and myself. The General and I were on opposite sides, he being in command of the cavalry in a German army corps. He is a remarkable man, noted for his skill, personal bravery, strength and endurance, and many wonderful stories are told of his heroism. He also still keeps up a thorough acquaintance with military matters, and though since 1920 he has lived peacefully in the Nationality, yet, if occasion should demand, he is able and willing to do good service in behalf of his adopted country."

Shortly after this conversation the party broke up and Miss Clothilde and I were soon on our way home.

"I hope, Mr. Maxwell, you have enjoyed yourself this evening, despite the republican simplicity of our entertainment," she said.

"It could hardly be styled republican," I answered, "when royalty herself was present. My grievance is that

among the multitude of her subjects she hardly noticed
me at all. Many of them I grant have held longer allegiance, but none are more truly loyal; except for that I
did enjoy the evening."

"Mr. Maxwell," she returned, "I don't think you
have any cause for complaint; the chevalier attendant
has the post of honor. Besides, you did not render homage with much assiduity. I was sufficiently interested to
observe your actions, and you consoled yourself most
readily. You had a charming companion in Miss Ashley, and I do not believe you thought once of me while
you talked with her. In fáct, a few more such passages,
and your loyalty might very reasonably be questioned."

"I crave permission to explain," I replied. "My loyalty was never more intense than to-night. For a good
while past I have had before me the image of the most
royally beautiful and charming woman I have ever met,
and to-night I saw her hold her court amongst republi-
cans as if to the purple born. I hope your highness will
not misconstrue my sincere though silent homage."

Hardly," she answered, quickly, "if it be measured
by your pretty speeches. But I require more than words,
sir. I want to speak to you to-night about another matter. I am commissioned to invite you to a boating party.
Miss Ashley, myself, and a number of other ladies give
the party; that is, we furnish the boats and their equip-
ment; the gentlemen are expected to provide carriages
and lend their escort. You can call for either of the two
persons I have mentioned; only please let me know
which, as the time is short, and there are some preparations to make."

"Truly," said I, with mock hesitation, "this is a most
perplexing situation. Miss Ashley has been very kind
to me this evening."

"I know it," said Clothilde, "and I am glad you remember it so well, Mr. Maxwell. Am I to consider the matter settled?"

"No, not just yet. Is it probable there will be another boating party soon?" I inquired.

"No, there will not be," she said, decidedly. "Your loyalty is not even what I thought it was; I was merely trying it. I will dispose of you at once for that unnecessary remark. Mr. King has already arranged to call for Miss Ashley; you will have no choice; you will have to go with me."

"Most willingly, most cheerfully," I replied, "you could not have a more happy captive."

We had reached the house, and I arranged to call for her on the afternoon of the boat ride, and returned home thinking of the opportunity the anticipated excursion might give me to tell Clothilde, what I had long since admitted to my own heart, that I loved her.

CHAPTER XX.

I resumed the reading of the manuscript, which described very fully the building of the great canal and its laterals; the construction of the villages and railways, and the colonization of a large part of the land Mr. Harvey had purchased.

I omit much of this description, giving only those parts which are likely to prove interesting to the general reader, and just enough of the other matter to enable him to follow the chronological sequence of events, and to convey an adequate idea of the undertaking, and the success attending it.

The more curious or scientific may gain further information from the manuscript itself, and the charts and other data connected with it, which are now being prepared for publication.

"In the month of March, 1905, Mr. Harvey began constructive operations.

"The railway from Bilboa to Denver had been extended westerly, so as to strike the course of the proposed canal near the site of reservoir No. 9. Early in that month one thousand men were employed in building the railway northward from this reservoir. At the point on the Union Pacific where the canal would cross the South Platte as many more men were similarly engaged, and five hundred others were employed in constructing a temporary bridge over the river.

"In Nebraska, on the main line of the Union Pacific,

two thousand men were building northward toward the North Platte, and others were erecting a temporary bridge over that river.

"From the terminus on the Northern Pacific Railroad seven hundred men were building southward to the head of the canal on the Missouri River, and materials were being prepared for a railroad bridge at the latter point.

"Work progressed at a rapid rate, and by the end of September a continuous line of double track railway, crossing the Platte Rivers on the temporary bridges mentioned, extended from Reservoir No. 9 along the east bank of the proposed canal to the Missouri River at the point where the head gates were to be put in, and thence northeasterly to a junction with the Northern Pacific Railway.

"A great electric plant had been constructed near the crossing of the Missouri, and another and still greater, was being erected on the Cheyenne River, and the railway bridge over the Missouri was nearly completed.

"During the succeeding five months a double-track road was built along and following the course of lateral A.

"The winter of 1905 and 1906 was a time of wonderful activity in Bilboa and at the steel and iron works on the Arkansas; an enormous amount of material being produced at these places for the aqueducts, railroads, and other buildings and improvements contemplated.

"Great quantities of cement made of cheap, but durable material, discovered near Bilboa, were also manufactured, being the same water cement now so extensively used and known as Bilboa cement.

"On the 15th of April, 1906, one thousand men began construction on the first five miles of the canal. For this distance its route lay entirely through granite rock.

The head gates were to be set back four hundred feet
from the mouth of the canal, and a wall two hundred feet
thick left between the river and the point to which the cut
was made, not to be broken down till the head gates and
the waste gates should have been put in place.

"A cut, seventy-five feet deep at the head gate and
six hundred feet wide, was to be made to reach the bottom grade of the canal, and this cut continued, averaging
fifty feet deep, for three miles farther, when it gradually
diminished in depth to about thirty feet at the end of the
fourth mile, and at the end of the fifth the rock disappeared and the canal debouched into an alluvial country,
with full width of nine hundred feet, having been gradually widened in its passage through the last two miles.

"Peculiar saws of varying sizes were used to cut the
granite. They were made of the black metal; cast in an
accurate mould, the teeth very sharply angled and about
an inch long, the sides notched and cross cut like those
of a rasp, or file, to clear away any binding rock or other
substance.

"The largest of these saws was forty feet long, one-
fourth inch thick, ten inches broad in the center, and six
inches broad at the ends, and weighed six thousand four
hundred pounds. The method of operating it was as follows: Forty feet from the free and open end of the cut a
hole was drilled in the granite in the exact direction which
the saw was to follow. The latter was then carefully set
and stayed upon the granite; an electric power was applied at the free end, the saw being drawn outwards about
two-thirds its length and driven inwards to the exact center of the drill hole at every stroke. The operation of
these saws was very rapid and effective, often sinking a
distance of three feet in the granite in a quarter hour, and
cutting it out in large blocks of such sizes and weights as

could be loaded on cars for transportation and use elsewhere.

"About one hundred saws of various sizes were employed in manner similar to that described, and were used whenever rock work was encountered in the building of the canal, and when it was completed, and they were carefully collected for storage at Bilboa, none of them were affected by the severe test to which they had been exposed, so indestructible was this singular metal.

"In constructing the canal through the alluvial plain, two hundred and forty machines, also of peculiar character, were employed, which proved so successful that they were afterwards used in making many of the laterals and smaller canals and ditches. These machines were, in fact, giant plows made of robur, or white metal, each cutting out a furrow five feet wide and three feet deep. The earth was cast by the plow upon an attendant traveler, which conveyed it out on the bank, or wherever needed.

"Each plow, with the end of the traveler attached, was drawn by a wire rope, about eight hundred feet long, which was taken up on a large wheel, or drum, the machinery turning the drum, and operating the traveler, being moved by electricity.

"The traveler followed the plow, running upon rails placed at proper distances, and could be lengthened, or shortened, at will, and used at varying angles, and discharged the earth continuously at any point where wanted on the bank, or on cars, if required to be transported to a distance, or to the rear, if making a fill.

"When the plow reached the end of the furrow, near the large drum, the power was applied to a small drum fastened where the furrow had begun, generally eight hundred feet distant, and a smaller rope, winding up on this drum, dragged plow, traveler and larger rope to the

point of beginning to renew the operation. The drums
at both ends could be easily reset when required by the
progress of the work.

"In excavating the canal the plows were usually
worked in gangs of four, the large drums of two such
gangs being set back to back, and their frames bound together as well as to posts; the return wheels of one gang
being set eight hundred feet up, and of the other, eight
hundred feet down the course of the canal. Every thirty
minutes these two gangs of plows could excavate a strip
of the canal twenty feet broad, sixteen hundred feet long,
and three feet deep.

"The ridge in the center, on which the larger drums
stood, was cut out as the latter were moved, and carried
off by an extra traveler.

"In alluvial soil, eight of these plows completed,
every fifteen days, the excavation of a portion of the canal
about sixteen hundred feet long, and of a breadth of nine
hundred, and a depth of fifteen feet; and in that time all of
the machines excavated about nine miles in length.

"Succeeding these, a number of other machines were
used for thoroughly rolling and compressing the earth
on the bottom and sloping sides of the canal; the last of
which was a roller sixty feet long, cased with black metal,
and weighing fully one hundred and fifty tons. After
this came an apparatus for thoroughly spraying the earth
in the canal with Bilboa cement, and then light rollers
slightly heated were used, until its bed and sides were
thoroughly compacted and cemented.

"It may be stated here that on all the reservoirs the
work of leveling, compacting and cementing was as thoroughly done as on the canal itself. The construction progressed during the summer of 1906, over ten thousand
men being constantly employed upon it.

"Mr. Harvey's plan contemplated the division of all his land into townships, each twelve miles square.

"As far as practicable, the lateral canals were constructed east and west, north and south, along these township lines, leaving the interior and smaller ditches to be made by the settlers themselves under the direction of the engineers.

"At the center of each township he designed erecting a village of neat, convenient and attractive homes; furnished with light, water, heat and electricity; containing also schools, churches, libraries, public halls and other buildings.

"These villages were to be connected by lines of electric railway running through them north and south, and east and west, as nearly as practicable, on which the citizens could be carried to and from their places of labor within the township, and passengers and freight could be conveyed from one village to another, or to the larger cities which should be built later, at suitable points, as the settlement progressed.

"During this summer of 1906, the preparing of the sublaterals for the irrigation of the eight million acres of semi-arid land lying north of the Niobrara, and to be watered from that stream, and reservoirs Nos. 1 and 2, was carried far toward completion; and many houses were erected in such villages in that region, and great quantities of building material were stored at convenient points for the erection of others during the winter.

"The system of railways alluded to was also well completed in this district by the fall of 1906.

"By the end of November of that year, reservoirs No. 1 and 2, and one hundred and forty miles of the main canal, had been finished, and the great head gates put in, and only the two hundred feet of rockwork remained as

a barrier to the admission of the water. These great
works had cost thus far ninety million dollars, and it is
needless to say had attracted great attention throughout
the United States, and excited much comment in the
public press.

"In the month of September, Mr. Harvey organized
a Bureau of Immigration, and in the name of a company
published his plan for leasing, year by year, beginning
April 1, 1907, the eight million acres of land in the region
above mentioned. This plan was briefly as follows:

"First—A family to consist of a man, his wife, his
children under age, and his own, or wife's, sisters, not to
exceed in all five persons.

"Second—No member of a family, and no unmarried
man, to exceed the age of thirty.

"Third—All to be healthy, somewhat used to physical labor, and to be of good moral character.

"Fourth—All males over the age of eighteen, and all
females over fifteen to be able to read and write.

"Fifth—Each male head of a family, and each unmarried man over eighteen years of age, to pay to the
company an entrance fee of three hundred dollars.

"On or before April 1st, 1907, each family to be furnished with a proper, convenient, and comfortable home.

"All power needed, except manual power, all tools,
implements, seeds, etc., to be furnished by the company
free of charge.

"Other supplies to be furnished from the village
storehouse of the company at cost to the colonists and
charged, if necessary; but no family account to aggregate
over three hundred dollars, and that of no unmarried man
over two hundred dollars, per year, and ratably for parts
of year.

"All children over the age of six; males up to eighteen and females up to fifteen, to attend public schools.

"Every male and female above school age to work as directed eight hours per day; the women, however, at home, or in the villages; work to be done diligently, intelligently, and cheerfully.

"Labor to be directed by captains chosen by every fifty laborers, approved, however, and liable to be dismissed from office by the company, or its agents, and these captains to share in the labor.

"All products to be reported at and taken to the village storehouse; the storekeeper, being the agent of the company, to keep account of all products received, and of those sold.

"On January 1st of each year, accounts to be closed, one-half of the proceeds, or equivalent for that proportion of those sold, to be given to the company; the other half to be credited to heads of families, or unmarried men before described; their balances to be paid them March 1st ensuing, or earlier, if they desire to leave the colony. The company to guarantee a fixed scale of prices on products unsold.

"On March 1st all products to be sold, or turned over to the company at such prices, and every colonist to receive his balance.

"On February 1st, those desiring to lease for another year must notify the company, and if their services and conduct have been satisfactory, may renew their leases, no further fee being required; the entrance fee already paid to be the property of the con.pany.

"The great sums disbursed by Mr. Harvey had furnished many poor men with means for becoming members of the colony; and farther east the hardships of the times induced many others to join it; and no sooner was Mr. Harvey's scheme made known than numerous applications for membership were received by his Bureau of Immigration.

"By February 1st, 1907, the number necessary to people the eight million acres, on the scale which Mr. Harvey at first adopted of receiving one family, or one unmarried man, for each one hundred and sixty acres of land, had been accepted; and by April 1st of that year fifty thousand persons had paid their entrance fees, and been located in villages, and were prepared to engage in agricultural and other pursuits.

"Of these, about twenty thousand were men of family and represented probably eighty thousand persons. The remaining thirty thousand were unmarried men, who generally boarded and lodged with the families."

In order to avoid the repetition in the manuscript, I will simply state that this scheme of colonization was eminently successful, and was carried out by Mr. Harvey on all the lands under his canal until the time when he made the complete change in the manner of holding title to them.

It may be well, also, to add that the work of building railroads, laterals, villages and additional houses was continued by him without cessation until that time.

The colonists generally worked well, and were contented and happy. Some who were lazy and indolent, and some who were vicious, were refused a renewal of lease, and quite a number of these made claims against the company for a return of their entrance fees, and for damages, but in no case were these claims allowed.

"In April, 1907, the canal had been completed a little beyond Reservoir 2; the wall of rock two hundred feet thick at its head had been removed; and the water was now surging against the head gates.

"The 20th day of April had been set as the time for

opening the latter, and permitting the water to flow through the canal into the reservoirs, so that it could be available for the irrigation of the land already settled.

"On that day a large concourse of personages, engineers, statisticians, electricians and eminent public men, proceeded by special train to the head of the canal to view the new, strange, and unexampled spectacle of the turning at once of a mighty river into an untried channel.

"Sublime confidence in the perfection of work was never more fully displayed than by Mr. Harvey and his engineers on that day.   .

"Orders had been given to the electricians and others to be ready at ten o'clock a. m., to raise all the head gates simultaneously to a height of two feet, and to increase that height as directed.

"Competent men were stationed at intervals of three miles to ride that distance as the current proceeded, and to watch the movement of the water, and report the same by telephone to the little station at the head gate.

"As the hour approached, expectancy attained almost breathless interest among those assembled there.

"Shortly before 10 o'clock, the waste ways, three miles farther down the canal were opened, that the first volume of the water might pass through them.

"Promptly at the moment, with the solemn invocation, 'In the Name of God,' the chief electrician touched his button, and the ponderous robur head gates, ten in number, each weighing over one hundred tons, rose slowly in their grooved channels to the prescribed distance. and a mighty current of clear, pure water, six hundred feet wide, swept under them and down the rocky bed of the canal at a velocity of fully eight miles per hour; picking up the debris of rocks, sand, wood and even spikes and iron bars, and carrying it all rapidly toward the waste ways.

"Thirty minutes later, the water was reported to be pouring over them and again into the river by the channel cut for it. For half an hour it was allowed thus to spend its strength, and then the secondary head gates were raised, those of the waste ways shut, and the flood passed down the gradually widening canal bed.

"Until 12 o'clock the engineers and spectators watched the passage of the water through the head gates, receiving constant dispatches as to its progress and the condition of the canal, all of which were very satisfactory.

"At that hour the head gates were opened to a height of four feet, and the advance of the stream being reported over twelve miles distant, the spectators boarded the train to follow it. At 2 p. m. the party overtook the advance of the water, then at a distance of twenty miles from the head of the canal.

"It was moving satisfactorily five miles per hour; and after keeping pace with it till 4 p. m., the party went on to Reservoir No. 1, where accommodations for the night had been prepared.

"By 4 o'clock next morning the water was rapidly pouring into this reservoir, and orders were given to raise the head gates gradually to a height of eight feet, and this was in the succeeding week increased to twelve feet; the water flowing at this height at a rate of about six miles per hour.

"By the 20th of May, Reservoir No. 1 was filled and the water was then sent on down the channel of the canal to Reservoir No. 2, which was filled by June 10th, and very shortly after, water was running in all the laterals and sublaterals dependent on these two reservoirs.

"By the 1st of January, 1908, the main canal had been completed a distance of sixty miles farther and was now nearing the valley of the North Platte River. For the last ten miles of its course, however, it had only been six hundred feet wide, the great lateral A running eastward, three hundred feet wide at its head, having been taken out of it, and with a large part of its sublaterals fully finished.

"A great reservoir, No. 3, one of the largest on the entire route, with its system of conduits, was also finished and water was flowing into it. This reservoir, it will be remembered, was estimated to be capable of watering six million acres of the arid land between the Niobrara and the Platte Rivers; the remaining fourteen million acres being watered from the lateral A. The capacity of the reservoir and lateral was found to be sufficient for this purpose, and the construction of about one hundred villages on this twenty million acres had been begun, and the land thrown open for settlement.

"The aqueducts across the North and South Platte Rivers were also in course of completion.

"The expenses of construction this year had been enormous, reaching a sum of over one hundred and fifty million dollars. Mr. Harvey's share of the crop of 1907, amounting to thirty million dollars, was held by him for seeding purposes and for the supply of the settlers already peopling the twenty million acres now ready for occupation.

"By April 1st, 1908, one hundred thousand families and unmarried men occupied these lands, and from their entrance fees thirty million dollars was obtained to help meet the expenditures of the year.

"The total cost of the canal, and the system of irrigation attending it, was so far about one hundred and ninety million dollars. This sum, especially when the cost of the land itself and numerous other items are added to it, seems enormous.

"Mr. Harvey had, however, remaining in his coffers, at the date above mentioned, forty million dollars, and in his storehouses supplies sufficient to meet all demands upon him.

"During the year 1908 work was continued with great activity on the canal; the aqueduct across the North Platte, and Reservoirs Nos. 4, 5, 6, 7 and 8 were completed by the 1st of June, and a month later the aqueduct across the South Platte River was finished.

"The construction was pushed rapidly southward, and by the end of this year the summit of the divide between the Platte and the Arkansas Rivers was reached, being a distance of two hundred and five miles from where the work was taken up at the beginning of the year, and a total distance of four hundred and forty miles from the mouth of the canal.

"At this point, lateral B, three hundred feet wide at its mouth, was begun and carried along the divide about two hundred miles eastward.

"A double-track railway from Reservoir No. 9 to the Arkansas, and another following the course of this lateral, and the permanent crossings over the North and South Platte Rivers, had also been completed.

"All the land lying between these two rivers, being four million acres, and all that lying under lateral "B," as far as constructed, amounting to about fifteen million acres, was thrown open for settlement and ready for occupancy by January 1st, 1909.

"About one hundred and thirty thousand heads of families and unmarried men, representing over two hundred and seventy-five thousand persons, settled on these lands; their fees for entrance amounting to about forty million dollars. The one-half of the crop of 1908 belonging to Mr. Harvey, part of which was sold and the balance retained for seed and for supplying the wants of the newly-arrived colonists, amounted in value to ninety million dollars.

"The expenses of the year, although not so great as those of the preceding one, had been fully one hundred million dollars, and Mr. Harvey found about the same sum remaining in his coffers as at the beginning of 1908.

"During the year 1909 the line of railway was pushed rapidly southward toward Corpus Christi; and the traffic on the main line through the country already settled being too great for the road, another trunk line was constructed from a point on the Platte River near the Missouri, thence following the former stream and the South Platte westerly to the crossing of the railroad bridge over the latter, and thence along the eastern bank of the canal to Reservoir No. 9.

"Near this reservoir great warehouses were built in what is now a suburb of the city of Neuropolis, and plans were made for the building of the city itself.

"The canal was continued southward as contemplated in the report of the engineers through Reservoir No. 10, and terminated in Reservoir No. 11, and the great lateral "B" was completed.

"The remainder of the land, that lying between lateral "B" and the Arkansas River, amounting to nearly fourteen million acres, was ready for occupancy, and was leased by January 1st, 1910.

"The expenses of Mr. Harvey in 1909 were heavy, amounting to over one hundred million dollars; but his revenues were large.

"From colonists' fees he received nearly eighteen

million dollars, and from sales of his half the crop of 1909 about sixty million dollars more. At the end of that year Mr. Harvey had a balance of fully forty million dollars in his coffers; and if the crop of 1910 proved to be good his income from his share of it, and from his mines, could hardly be less than two hundred million dollars.

"There were now more than one million inhabitants in the irrigated portion of the arid region purchased by Mr. Harvey, living in peace, comfort and contentment; and the permanency of the enterprise was assured.

"From the very beginning of his colonization operations, Mr. Harvey had the founding of the Nationality in view, and, in fact, then communicated his purpose to a few of his most trusted assistants.

"In January, 1910, he submitted to the district officers a plan for changing the colony into the Nationality."

This plan contemplated:

First—The formal adoption by the new government of the general principles hereinbefore stated as given me by Mr. Beyresen.

Second—The equitable abolition of money as a medium of exchange among its citizens, and certain regulations in regard to the election, qualifications, authority and duties of its officers.

Third—Definite rules and regulations in regard to citizenship.

Fourth—The building of a great and beautiful city as a capital, where those desiring a liberal education could obtain it, and where those past the years of labor could live if they so wished.

Fifth—The sale by Mr. Harvey to the Nationality of the fifty-seven millions acres of land now owned by him, and the canals, railroads, villages and other improvements upon them.

"In reference to item third, concerning citizenship, Mr. Harvey's plan contemplated that at the time of its adoption all the members of the colony who would con-form to the principles of the Nationality should at once become citizens thereof, and their children also as they arrived at proper age.

"In regard to the admission of other persons it pre-scribed the following general rules: That no person shall become a citizen unless he takes up residence within the Nationality, or is a citizen of some state of the Union a majority of whose people seek admission, or already be-long to that body.

"That no person except as immediately hereinafter provided shall become a citizen of the Nationality unless he, and his family if he have one, conform to rules Nos. 1, 2, 3 and 4, prescribed originally for the admission of tenants, and unless he owns land, or its equivalent in other desirable property, to the value of sixteen hundred dollars, which said land and all other property owned by said person, or his family, shall be conveyed to the Na-tionality.

"That whenever any large body of persons, compris-ing a majority of the citizens of any state of the Union, shall through the legislatures of their states, or by peti-tion, seek admission to citizenship in the Nationality, they may be admitted upon such terms and conditions in regard to qualifications and possession of property as may be determined by a two-third vote of the parliament of the Nationality. Provided, however, that the ques-tion of their admission on such terms and conditions be first submitted to a vote and be approved by a majority of the then existing citizens of the Nationality.

"In regard to the fourth item, Mr. Harvey desired that the site he had already chosen, and the plans he had prepared for the building of the city should be accepted, and also that the new government should, for the period of five years after its organization, set apart from its revenues one hundred million dollars annually, and he himself would contribute fifty million dollars annually, to be expended in carrying out these plans.

"In regard to the fifth item, upon the acceptance of his propositions, and the organization of the Nationality in acordance therewith, he agreed to sell to that body all the fifty-seven million acres of land within its limits, and all property thereon, for the sum of one billion dollars, to be paid in five equal, annual installments, without interest, the first to be made one year after the completion of the organization. He reserved, however, the right to extend the canal and use the same, in manner as originally contemplated, for carrying water for the irrigation of the other lands remaining to him, and also the right to sit in parliament, in person or by proxy, and vote as any other member during the term of his natural life, to be notified of all its meetings, and to have power to cast five-twelfths of the votes of that body for the period of ten years after the organization of the Nationality.

"Mr. Harvey requested the district officers to submit this plan of organization to the colonists for their action before the time of the annual renting of the lands, and, leaving the matter in their care, sailed for Europe in January, 1910.

"His propositions were formally accepted by the colonists very soon after, and were ratified by Mr. Harvey by cablegram, and the colony was thus merged into the Nationality.

"In June, 1910, Mr. Harvey married a sister of King Alphonso of Spain, a lady whose beauty and accomplishments were known and acknowledged throughout

Europe, and with whom he had become acquainted on a previous visit.

"In September of the same year he returned to America with his wife, and they resided in his own home in Bilboa, where in October of the succeeding year she gave birth to a child.

"In the fall of 1914, owing to failing health, she returned to Spain, Mr. Harvey visiting her very frequently, and being there at the time of her death, which took place in 1917.

"During these years Mr. Harvey had been busily engaged in extending the great canal to water the lands he had remaining, and settling colonies upon them on the same principles as those adopted by the Nationality, with a view to an ultimate union with it.

"In the year 1917 the states of Nebraska and South Dakota, by formal action of their legislatures and at the earnest desire of their people, applied for admission and were received into the Nationality, retaining only enough of the semblance of their former government to enable them to maintain their position as independent states of the Union, and in 1918 the states of New Mexico, Kansas and Colorado, in all of which there had been a fierce fight made against the proposition, did the same. The history of this movement is interesting.

"The process was one of gradual accretion to the Nationality at the expense of the state governments, from the inception of the former to the end of the latter. Individual by individual, county by county, joined that body, until in self-protection those left clamored for the change.

"In 1919 the state of Arizona, in which another system of irrigation existed, and the states of Utah and Wyoming were received into the Nationality. None of them have ever regretted the change; all of them have prospered beyond comparison with any former period.

"The capital city of this entire region remained at Neuropolis, which in 1919 was already a beautiful and favored city.

"Great public buildings had been erected, and habitations and other structures were constantly added as they were required by the rapidly increasing population.

"In other portions of the land the same work was carried on, for new houses were continually needed, especially in the older and more thoroughly cultivated regions.

"In 1917 the nature of the mines at Bilboa began to change. The quantity of gold and of the two strange metals diminishing, a superior quality of iron ore taking their places.

"Mr. Harvey had never parted with any of the black metal, and but little of the robur had left the Nationality. In 1919 the output of gold and these two metals ceased entirely, and thereafter the mines produced iron only.

"Mr. Harvey, despite his great expenditures, was yet possessed of enormous wealth. His vaults contained millions, which were now constantly increasing.

"These riches, however, he declared it to be his intention to leave, with all his other possessions, to the Nationality, or for its use, his only thought, especially since the death of his wife, being for its extension and success.

"In the year 1925, satisfied that its affairs were in wise hands and that its permanency was assured, Mr. Harvey determined to carry out his intention of bestowing upon it all his landed possessions, and of spending some years abroad visiting other countries, and studying mankind and its condition throughout the globe.

"For this latter purpose he began the building of a

vessel, which should be at once a means of conveyance and a home for himself and his friends. It was unique in character and construction, and was built, adorned and furnished without regard to cost. It was not of great size, being only calculated to carry forty passengers, but it was undoubtedly the most elegant, graceful and beautiful, and at the same time the strongest and most powerful vessel ever put afloat.

"Its method of propulsion, and many of its peculiarities, were kept secret. It was generally understood, however, that its motive power was electricity, generated in the ordinary way, but augmented many-fold by the action of the sea water on thousands of wires which surrounded and were inlaid in the hull of the vessel below its water line, forming an immense magnet from whose ends the current was taken up, and used, or stored, as required.

"The vessel was constructed of robur, or white metal, its plates being cast at Bilboa and put together, or rather welded together by electricity at the dock yards in Corpus Christi, where it was launched in the spring of 1927.

"She made a final trial trip in the adjoining waters in April, 1928, and in May of that year John Harvey and his friends embarked on her, bound for Europe and other portions of the globe.

"Before his departure Mr. Harvey conveyed all his landed and other estate to the Nationality, reserving only his cash in hand and the two metals he had so strangely discovered. The former and the black metal he deposited for safe-keeping in the vaults of the Nationality in Neuropolis, but the robur was kept in great storehouses at Bilboa.

"He left all these treasures in the care of friends, who also had in their custody a will made in case of acci-

dent, and who were instructed to forward to him such
sums as he might require in foreign lands, though it was
generally supposed that he took with him on his vessel a
very large amount in gold."

Thus ended the manuscript, rather abruptly it must
be confessed. Its perusal had given me a different idea
of the character of John Harvey. If it were a true history, and I had no doubt of it, then he was really one
of the world's great men; one of its heroes and benefac-
tors, possessed of comprehensive intellect, wonderful sagacity and the most earnest philanthropy.

He had used these great gifts for the founding of
a common wealth on principles of true brotherhood, and
had done more than any other mere man to rescue humanity from the mercenary spirit and degradation which
has possessed it in all ages.

CHAPTER XXI.

THE BOAT RIDE.

It was about 4 o'clock of a beautiful September afternoon when I reached Mr. Beyresen's to take Miss Clothilde for the boat ride. She was dressed simply, but from the coiffure of her hair to the very tip of her small shoe everything about her was in the most perfect taste. Her face wore an expression of unusual thoughtfulness, but when she saw some flowers I had brought this gave way to a look of pleased animation.

"You and I," she said, "owe our acquaintance to a bunch of flowers."

"I hope," I rejoined, "to nothing so trivial. I like to believe that it was something far higher, that it was indeed predetermined."

"Perhaps it was due to Papa Beyresen," she returned.

"No," I answered, "he had no idea of the favor he was doing me when he invited me to his house; nor had I, for that matter, for I did not expect to meet you there. I did expect to meet you somewhere."

"Since when?" she asked.

"From the time I first saw you," I said, "since the evening of the opera."

"It would have been rather strange," she replied hurriedly, "if two persons like you and me had lived so long in this city, and had not met. Let us accept results, which to-day are very pleasant, and stop imagining causes. I think we shall have a pleasant time, for the party is made up of congenial spirits. You have met nearly all of them, I think, Mr. Maxwell."

"And yet," I answered, "I cannot be said to know them as you and they know each other. I am the stranger, but I can enjoy the getting acquainted. So I have a pleasure all my own."

"Do you feel like a stranger among us, Mr. Maxwell?" she inquired.

"Not often," I replied, "not as I have in many other parts of the world I have visited, and not nearly as much as I supposed I should. I have never felt so with Mr. and Mrs. Beyresen, nor with you, Miss Clothilde. It may appear odd, but it seemed the first time I saw you as if we had met before, possibly in some previous existence."

"Probably you were reminded of some other person by some accidental resemblance. Such things often happen," she said.

"They do," I replied, "but I cannot fix it in your case. I have tried, but it seems impossible."

"You may recall it hereafter," she returned, "or you may lose the feeling. I have had such hallucinations myself, and I am not prone to fancies. I hear you are going East; might I ask how soon?"

"In a very few weeks," I answered. "I want to know more of the condition of your Eastern people."

"You may learn something of that from Mrs. Hamilton; she is pretty well acquainted with their situation, and was giving me a rather doleful account of it lately. If you go East, however, you can judge much better. Do you intend writing a book when you return to England, Mr. Maxwell?" she inquired demurely.

"I have more material than many who do," I answered mischievously.

"Much of which you could not use," she replied, scrutinizing me narrowly.

"That is my present feeling about it," I returned.

"One cannot tell what one will think some years hence. I could write some stirring chapters, entitling them, 'The Princess,' for instance."

"I am not afraid of your doing that, without permission," she said after a moment's pause.

"Well," I answered, "I do hope your highness will remember this evening that some attention is due to incipient authors."

"I will look after you, Mr. Maxwell," she returned. "I may meet you in a third state of existence, you know, and then it would be pleasant to recall kindnesses bestowed in this."

"Thank you," I replied. "I bespeak remembrance in all stages."

It was after 5 o'clock when we started down the lake. A gentle breeze filled the sails, and for some time we all sat near the bow watching the panorama before us.

The lake was about ten miles long by four or five broad, and its waters were clear and pure.

Its southern shore was covered with a forest of well-grown trees and its western banks nearest the city were occupied by gardens and orchards, and all the agricultural life concomitant to its proximity to the capital. A large township village stood about midway of the northern boundary, along which hurrying trains were seen passing back and forth; busy messengers between the country and the great city, whose imposing public buildings were massed spectrally above the sea of green which swept around the peaceful homes of its citizens.

Beyond, still farther to the west, towered the colossal peaks of the continental range, whose great snow fields, lifted to the sky, etherealized their summits, and crowned them kings and princes of the land.

"This," said Mrs. Hamilton, "is as fair a scene as I

ever looked upon. Yon jewel of a city has a perfect setting, in a bed of emerald, beneath a vault of the purest
turquoise. You people of Neuropolis should be content;
you live in one of the fairest and most delightful spots in
the world."

"We are content," said Mr. Herbert Jones, "as those
who have made a good day's journey; but not satisfied
as those who have reached its end. We are progressing,
I think, rationally, Mrs. Hamilton."

"Ah," said she, "ideas about progression are so deceptive. We, in the Eastern states, thought we had made
much progress, but now it seems as though we had been
deluded. There is to-day more uncertainty, inquietude,
and far more suffering among our people than ever before. We have constant agitation, distrust, and much
bitterness between classes."

"Bitter feelings are to be deplored," said Mr. Jones,
"but the agitation is a hopeful sign. It shows that stag-
nation has not overtaken you; that the spirit has not been
crushed out of your people; that you may yet find the road
to true progress."

"What is true progress, Mr. Jones?" inquired Mrs.
Hamilton.

"Many answers have been given to that question,"
replied he. "Pride has induced nearly every nation to
put forward some special trait, or achievement, as evidence of its superiority."

"Yes," said Mrs. Hamilton, "we Eastern people used
to boast of our enterprise and wealth as sure signs of
our progress, but it is pretty well understood now that
such indications are fallacious."

"They always will be," responded Mr. Jones. "True
national progress must be evidenced by far loftier attainments than those you mention."

"If you will give us your idea of what such progress is, Mr. Jones, we shall be much obliged," said Miss Clothilde.

"I should say it consists in increasing enlightenment of the national conscience, broadening reasoning powers, and sturdy physical development among the citizens; all in active operation in the affairs of the nation, the first shaping its course in accordance with strict rules of natural justice and right, the second planning and directing wisely and successfully, and the third conferring ability to perform. There may be as many differences and degrees in these attainments among the people of the nation, as there are in the proficiencies of the individual soldiers comprising an army, but there must be the same unity of action, the same spirit of self-sacrifice, and the same esprit de corps. A people so governed and directed can truthfully be called great in national character, and if the qualities I have mentioned be increasing, are on the true road in national advancement."

"But how can we ensure this result? how are we to acquire these high qualities?" interrogated Mrs. Hamilton.

"Ah" said he, "that has been the problem of the ages, always confronting mankind, and yet until modern times but dimly recognized by them. It was long, Mrs. Hamilton, in the history of the race, before we had formulated this problem in the clear and unequivocal terms in which you and I, and thousands of other inquiring citizens, have it before us to-day, and the distinctness with which it is now stated augurs everything for its speedy solution. How can we best develop among our people an enlightened and ever-growing conscience and reason, that shall direct and guide them in all national and private affairs; and how can we preserve in their

highest condition those independent, manly, physical
powers which are so essential to the well-being of the
race? What has the state done, and what can it be made
to do, to secure these results? What has the old system
of civilization, of ownership, of distribution, of education
accomplished, and what can be hoped from it in the future?
What incentives does it offer, and what opportunities does it afford for the cultivation of these qualities?
Such are the questions which men are asking now with
an earnestness born of a conviction that governments
and systems, and motives and opportunity, can be better
arranged to ensure the true happiness, and advancement,
and enfranchisement of mankind."

"But how would you answer them; what would you
do to develop the virtues of which you speak?" asked
Mrs. Hamilton.

"First of all," said Mr. Jones, "I would employ direct methods, instead of the indirect ones heretofore
used. The ends to be attained must be acknowledged,
and governments and systems of civilization must be organized in such forms and on such principles as will best
and quickest secure them. Humanity has been moving
hitherto like a bewildered and befogged mob, without
purpose or proper regulation; it must now be officered
and disciplined like an efficient army to perform a definite work.

"Drill, exertion, exercise of any faculty, moral,
mental, or physical, are the most potent factors in its development. How can growth in the high qualities we
have spoken of be promoted by a system of government
and of civilization which appeals to self-interest as its
strongest incentive, and permits its citizens, actuated by
that morbidly developed passion, under the forms of law
and the code of morals it has adopted, to lie, steal, cheat,

enslave, and to break every commandment of God, and violate every moral obligation of man to man? "The teachings of the Church alone have tended to cultivate broad principles of justice, humanity and duty, and her influence has been inestimable. Like the gentle rain, descending from the same source whence she claims her inspiration, her doctrines have permeated the earth, and where the soil was good have brought forth fruits of brotherly kindness and charity which have kept the world from famine.

"But the spirit of this age demands a government and a civilization which, instead of sowing thorns and thistles in that soil, shall aid in mellowing and fertilizing it, and shall assist in the cultivation of such fruitage."

"You would not have the Church control the government?" inquired I.

"By no means," answered Mr. Jones, "but I would have the State advance to a higher plane, upon which I think it can now safely stand; one near the still higher plane occupied by the Church. I would have it modeled upon and ready to enforce by precept and example those eternal principles of justice and morality which are taught by the Church. I would so organize it that its appeal should be made largely to the higher and nobler qualities of its citizens; that so it would exercise and develop those qualities among them. Its concern as now would be chiefly about the moral, social and temporal condition of its citizens, the Church being occupied more exclusively with their spiritual necessities, but Church and State should work together for the cause of human advancement in all these directions. This is what the founders of our Nationality have tried to do, with such measure of success as we all have seen, and in further answering your question, Mrs. Hamilton, I can do no more than to point to it as the most illustrious example, now existing, of a civilization organized to develop among the people the virtues of which we have been speaking."

"I should like to hear from Miss Ashley," said I, "in regard to the position which Church and State should occupy in these matters."

"I would not call it Church, but Christianity," said she. "I agree with Mr. Herbert Jones that each has its sphere in which it should work unitedly with the other for the purposes he has defined. These spheres, it seems to me, should be separate only because of the temporary inability of those in the lower to live up to the standards of the higher. They should be like classes in one school, taught by the same great master. He would not use one set of principles for one grade of his pupils, and others contradictory thereof for another.

"The great commandment, 'Thou shalt love the Lord thy God with all thy heart, and with all thy soul, and with all thy mind and with all thy strength,' and 'Thou shalt love thy neighbor as thyself,' to my mind presents the principles on which the State should be organized and by which both Church and State should be governed. The recognition and practice of these principles among the masses are the signposts by which I discern the true road to national advancement, and the people's progress on it."

"Alas," said Mrs. Hamilton, "judged by such standards I fear the condition of the people in our Eastern states would be considered very serious. There doesn't seem to be much growth in love toward one's neighbor, the love seems to be all kept for one's self. We exercise a certain kind of charity toward the poor, oftener, however, to still conscience and get rid of unpleasant importunity than to obey the commandment. We punish the criminal deterrently without much considering the causes which led to the commission of the offense. We are, I fear, far from the progressive road which has been outlined this evening."

"At least," said Clothilde, "you seem to recognize the deficiencies of your system and that is a hopeful condition."

"I do not think," replied Mrs. Hamilton, "that any considerable portion of the class in which I move do even that. They are the people possessing wealth, and living lives of luxury and ease, and the condition of what we call the lower classes is seldom brought home to them in its real character. You must remember that not many years ago I, too, was an inhabitant of your land, and therefore observe the differences between it, and that where I now dwell, more closely than those born and reared there. I often think the rich really try to ignore the existence of these evils as much as possible."

"But," said Clothilde, "is not the dominant class among you aware of the threatening character of social conditions, the changes liable to occur, and the necessity of directing them wisely?"

"They are," said Mrs. Hamilton, "to a certain extent, but they seem asleep to the gravity of the situation, and unwilling to make any radical change which would disturb their present luxurious slumbers. The really intelligent, the leaders among us, fully appreciate the antagonisms which your people and your system have so largely aided in engendering, but instead of dispelling these by remedial measures, are striving to unify our people in opposition to you and your principles. It is needless to say that I have no sympathy with this spirit."

"If it ever find expression in force," said Mr. King, "it will be met most determinedly. The roar of the breakers on the Eastern seaboard in a wild storm would be a meet comparison to the mighty surge of humanity which will occur should such a course be adopted. Thank God we are awake, and thank God, the masses of your people are not entirely deceived."

"I hope, I sincerely hope, for the sake of my father, my family, my friends and all others, that this trouble will be soon and amicably settled," said Mrs. Hamilton.

"I hope for the sake of humanity that it may be rightly settled," said Clothilde. "It may cost something, all great achievements have, as Mr. Jones would tell you, but I have no fear of the result for us and great hope of the future for you. Our people are intelligent, their patriotism knows no bounds, and their leaders are wise and governed by no mercenary motives. Do I exaggerate, Mr. Maxwell?" she inquired, turning to me.

"I think not," I answered. "I have seen something of your country, and I would like to say one word. In the homes of a people may be found the surest index of their condition, their loyalty and their future. (Impoverish them and you crush manhood and womanhood, and destroy freedom and happiness and hope.) This is a land of cheerful happy homes, and a people who are not slaves, but sprung from a free ancestry. Their earnest conscientiousness, their manifest intelligence, their strong physique and free movement are to me a guarantee of their ability to protect their habitations, their families and their country."

Our conversation was brought to a close by the appearance of Miss Erickson, who informed us that while we had been talking, she and some of the others had prepared lunch in what they called the dining-room, being the after part of the boat, which they had ingeniously curtained off with a sail.

By the time this repast was over we had reached the eastern limit of the lake, where it had been the intention to land, but as it was now after 7 o'clock, and several of the party desired a moonlight ride in some of the smaller boats, it was decided to return.

Our craft was therefore put about and we started back, skirting the southern shores of the lake, tacking sometimes into the increasing shadows of the forest, sometimes into the bright water lit up by the slanting rays of the fast setting sun.

That luminary had now disappeared below the western mountains, but from behind them wrought a miracle of transient glory.

Great banks of clouds, riven and divided and of many shapes, formed a canvas on which he cast a wealth of changing coloring never seen but in such clear, pure air, and in such high altitudes as these. The clouds lay motionless and extended half way round the horizon, emblazoned in crimson, gold, and green, royal in purple, delicate in blue and gray and smoke, every tint changing and shifting in constant variety as the sun, greatest of painters, with his myriad pointed brush, filled with purest color, limned them at his pleasure, making the last hours of the dying day glorious by his art.

In various moods we sat and watched his work, while he pictured the heavens with wonders such as Revelation speaks of in describing the celestial city.

When we reached the boat house from which we had started, his light had faded, only its faint reflection tinged the western sky, and the soft rays of the silvery moon, ascending in the east, shone upon the waters.

Mrs. Hamilton, Mr. Jones, and several of the others remained upon the larger boat now moored to the landing, but the rest of us made haste to procure smaller boats in which to spend an additional hour or so upon the water.

These were fitted with comfortable seats, and shawls and wraps were ready at hand. Each boat carried at its masthead an electric light of a different color from the others. Miss Clothilde and I selected one constructed of the white metal, about fifteen feet long and four feet wide, carrying a lateen sail. The mast was festooned with ever-greens and flowers, among which I recognized some of those I had brought.

"You are a good sailor, I presume," said she, falling back somewhat into the bantering air she frequently adopted with me, "and you can take the helm and command the craft, while I will be passenger. You can set the rudder by raising the tiller and dropping it into that little slot, and the sail will not give us much trouble, there being so little wind. Your passenger also will give as little trouble as possible, and, if you like, will favor you from time to time with such serious thoughts on life, and reflections and moralizings on kindred subjects, as occur to her, such as she thinks will be for your future good."

"If my passenger will be kind enough to take a seat beside me where I can see her she will oblige me very much," I returned.

She did so without further words and we started, the last boat, with a silver light at our masthead, shining down dimly on us and out upon the water.

The others were fast scattering, but the moonlight irradiating the scene made the white hulls and sails of the little flotilla very plainly visible, looking like great birds with snowy plumage flitting over the water.

I spoke of this to Clothilde, and she replied: "I have seen such a sight as this a number of times, but I always enjoy it. There is something ethereal about it.

The dancing, unsubstantial water, the shadowy boats upon it, and the white clouds overhead, through which the moon seems to cleave her way in placid, quiet content; the warm air, and the light breeze cause me to feel as if I were in wonderland, and almost to doubt whether there is the evil and suffering in the world, of which we were speaking a little while ago."

"You can understand, Miss Clothilde," I replied, "that while there must be the spirit to appreciate and the disposition to enjoy, yet the surroundings do make a wonderful difference in the world in which we live."

"Well," she said, "my world has generally been a happy one. Not always, though, but, indeed, I could not wish for uninterrupted happiness. There have to be variations in life. There are storms and there are nights like these. The first fit one for enjoying the other.) Don't you think so?" she said, turing her face to me.

"I do," I answered, "and, besides, we know each other after storms often better than ever before. We learn who are worthy friends, who are false. The lightning purifies the air."

She was silent a little while, and sat looking out on the water, her clear profile cut charmingly against the white sail near us. She spoke again slowly and in measured tones without turning her head, almost soliloquizing as I often knew her to do in addressing me.

"I believe," she said, "I am better for the trials that have visited me. There may be others coming whose effect I cannot foresee, but I will not anticipate them, not on a night as peaceful as this. You eulogized our people highly this evening, Mr. Maxwell. Was it an outburst of compliment or was it a conviction?"

"It was not the first," I answered, "for in talking on such vital subjects with my friends I should be careful not to mislead, nor to be misled by momentary impulses, or the desire to speak pleasant things. It was an opinion that I do not think will ever change."

"Are your opinions unchangeable; no, I did not mean that—are your opinions easily or quickly formed?" she said.

"In most matters," I replied, "my opinions are not quickly formed and, though not unchangeable, they are not fickle. A just equality has ever been one of my dreams. I think I have found it well exemplified among your people, an opinion I did not express to-day, but which I take pleasure in confessing to you now, if you value it."

"I do, indeed," she said quickly, "but I did not mean to draw you out upon such a subject; I only wanted to know if what you said to-day was well considered.

"Do you intend remaining long in the East?" she inquired.

"About a month," I answered, "and then I shall return to Neuropolis; I am too much interested in this city and some of its inhabitants to think of quitting it just yet."

"And these grand old mountains, Mr. Maxwell," she said hastily. "You must not leave us till you have traveled more among them. They are the glory of our land; the peers of the Swiss Alps, or your Scotch hills; you should spend a whole summer among them—it would repay you grandly."

"Perhaps I shall," I said; "I am not thinking at all of leaving you yet; indeed, I may take up my abode here."

"You!" she exclaimed; "I can hardly believe it. You, an Englishman! Are you sincere, or are you jesting?"

"Heaven forbid that I should be insincere with you

above all others," I answered. "I state nothing more than what is possible; what I have thought of, if events favor me."

"May the omens prove propitious," she cried gaily; "may we be so fortunate as to have an educated, talented and accomplished Englishman, in your own person, cast in his lot among us."

"May I be pardoned," I inquired, entirely disregarding her interruption, "if I refer to just one topic in the conversation on the boat this afternoon?"

"Certainly," she said; "pray, what was it?"

"In regard to home," I answered, "and to its great importance. I think you will agree with me that a person without a home is destitute of one of the sweetest of life's precious things.) I mean that, and I ought to know, for I have been a rover and have had no home."

"I do not think you sincere now," she said quickly. "You have a home in England. You are simply away from home temporarily."

"Well, I have dreamed of another," I continued, "and it was mine, not my father's. It was an audacious dream. There was the vision of a face and a figure that have been with me constantly for the last few months; a face and a figure I can never forget, they are so dear to me, and they seemed to abide in the home of which I have dreamed and made its light and its sunshine."

"Oh, Mr. Maxwell!" she said rising, "stop your story long enough to look at the red light from Mr. King's boat. See its glow on the sail, and the water and on the two people in the boat. I am going to try if I can make them hear me," and she rose and moved quickly to the mast.

I gave the rudder a little turn to swing the boat around in another direction and fastened the tiller as she had told me, and in a moment was by her side.

She was very pale and held to the mast, apparently to sustain herself.

"Clothilde," I said, "you must hear me out. Yours is the face and yours is the form I have seen in my dreams, and I want you, for I love you as man seldom loves woman; I want you for my own, for my wife."

I put my arm about her and continued: "You are the one woman on earth for me, dear, and have been since the first moment I saw you, and I have been longing to tell you so for months. Have you no word for me, Clothilde, or must I wait for my answer?"

She was very pale as she turned her face to me, and hesitated for words. "Oh, Mr., what shall I call you, Mr. Herbert, I am so sorry you said this for I cannot—I cannot. I tried to stop you, but you would not. I cannot be your wife, or the wife of any one."

"Then there is no one else?" I asked eagerly.

"There is no one else," she said, "but I cannot be your wife."

I felt her tremble on my arm.

"I think," she said, "you had better let me go."

I did so at once. "I do not frighten you?" I asked.

"Oh, no," she said, "you do not. I trust you and I know you to be true, but I cannot be your wife."

"Then," I said, "I will not give you up, Clothilde. Let us go back to the seat." We returned to it and sat down.

"There are many mysteries about you, Clothilde," I continued. "I have wondered at them. Once a long time ago I thought to ask about them, but could make no progress. It seemed to me, even then, like asking questions about my own. I ceased and made this resolution; I will ask no one, not even herself. She will tell me if she wishes; I will trust my Love."

"And I cannot tell you much now," she answered. "I am of the blood royal, sir," she said, looking me earnestly and steadily in the face.

"I know not what you mean," I said, "but if you were a being from another world, as I have sometimes almost thought, as I marveled at your beauty and grace, I would not give you up, Clothilde, unless you were plighted to another, and then I should depart, for I would not vex you, loving you so dearly."

"And in return for all this," she replied, drawing a little nearer, "I can only say a very selfish thing. Though there be no obstacle as men count obstacles, I cannot promise what you wish, but I cannot afford to lose you, Mr. Herbert Maxwell."

She stopped, apparently at a loss for words.

"Truly, Clothilde," I said, "you dispose of me right royally."

"You are not offended with me, are you?" she asked.

"By no means," I replied; "I could not be."

"Well, then," she said, "believe I have done the best I could, and that you and I are only a little nearer for this scene, and none will be the wiser."

"But I may ask you again, dear," said I, "if I think you have come to know me better?"

"You may," she answered, "but I know you better than you think, Mr. Herbert. Let us sit together in the boat, and watch the lights and shadows on the water, and the clouds which I remember once telling you you would have to study alone, and look up at the moon, which has been wondering at us for some time back, and especially at you, who seem to think all that is necessary to your happiness is the love of one lone woman."

"And I, I am only afraid, Clothilde, that you have wings, and will fly away and leave me."

"Well, you may imagine the wings, if you please," she said. "I am not aware of them, and I have no intention of deserting as true and constant a friend as you have proved yourself to be to me."

We remained on the water a half hour longer, and then I took her home, and she bade me good-night, and I returned to my lodgings, thinking of her and the womanliness and tact she had displayed, and more ardently in love with her than ever.

CHAPTER XXII.

On the 20th of September an incident occurred pre-
cipitating the struggle which had long been imminent between the two systems of labor in existence in the United
States.

Some time previous to that date the courts had refused the stay of execution applied for by the Nationality,
and the creditor corporation had at once proceeded to
levy upon and sell no less than ten townships, containing
an aggregate of nearly one million acres, with all the
buildings, railroads and other property in, or upon, them,
and also an interest in the great canal to supply water for
irrigation. The entire property thus sold was bought in
by the creditor corporation.

These townships were adjacent to each other, and
were situated in the state of Nebraska, not far from its
eastern border.

A writ had finally been put in the hands of the United
States marshals, commanding them to deliver possession
of these ten townships to those who had bought them.

Nearly fifty thousand persons inhabited them, and
attempts had been made to induce them to become tenants of the purchasers, but in vain; they refused to pay
even a nominal rent, or to sign any obligation therefor.

On the day mentioned an effort was made to evict
some of these tenants, and induct others who would be
loyal to their landlords. Five hundred United States marshals, sworn in for the purpose, accompanied by a large

number of other persons to take the place of the dispos-
sessed tenants, arrived by special train in one of these
township villages.

They demanded possession of its dwellings, its lands,
and all other property of the township.

It is not likely that the contrivers of the plot supposed that the marshals would be successful in their undertaking. They probably only intended to provoke a
disturbance that would give ground for further action.
The scene which followed can be better imagined than
described. Emboldened by their numbers, and the fact
that the men of the community were nearly all at work in
the fields, the officers proceeded at once to force entrance
and take possession of stores and other buildings. They
also inducted their creatures into some of the dwellings,
while their former occupants assembled on the streets,
and hurriedly sent word to the men in the fields of what
had occurred. These alarmed the surrounding townships,
and returned at once to their village, where, under the orders of their labor leaders, they remained quietly in a
body, while the marshals pursued their work.

By 12 o'clock train load after train load of determined men began to arrive in quick succession from other villages, and the marshals and their creatures found themselves surrounded.

They would gladly have retreated, but their means of
conveyance were now in possession of the citizens, who
intermingled with them and, by a preconcerted movement, disarmed them.

They were commanded to replace all the goods they
had seized, and restore the village at once to its former
condition, and those who refused to aid in so doing were
thrust into the water of a large and muddy canal; not
once only, but until they were willing to do as required.

Over two hundred of the marshals, and a large number of those accompanying them were thus treated, but no other indignity was offered.

About 3 o'clock p. m., they were compelled, wet, muddy, and hungry, to board their train, which, preceded and followed by others filled with citizens, quickly carried them back to the Missouri, where, with many threats as to the consequences if they returned again on such an errand, they were sent across that river beyond the borders of the Nationality.

This occurrence created great excitement throughout the Union, and its consequences were everywhere discussed.

The general government, with a self-willed and determined Executive at its head, and the Nationality whose existence and perpetuity were threatened, were brought into direct opposition to each other, and their action was awaited with great anxiety.

The evening of this occurrence I went to see Clothilde, and found her much excited over it, and we talked long and earnestly about it. I had brought with me the manuscript of John Harvey, and returned it to her, and we talked of that also.

"What do you think of his philanthropy?" she inquired, eagerly. "What do you think of his plans for the amelioration of the condition of mankind?"

"I have the highest appreciation of them," I replied. "The true philanthropist is he who shows mankind the way to help themselves.) John Harvey did that in founding this Nationality. I see a great people made better and happier by his work, and those who knew him personally, revering and cherishing his memory. His name is indissolubly connected with this people, and though the quality of his actions cannot be affected, yet the estimate

placed upon them by future generations will be very
greatly influenced by their success or failure. His name
may stand on a parity with those of Washington and Lincoln.")

"I think," said Clothilde, "that he foresaw this struggle on which we are now entering, and I think, too, he
saw its triumphant ending. The Nationality cannot be
overthrown by force; its people are numerous, loyal and
well officered, and its cause appeals to every one but
the selfishly rich. If you stay among us you may, indeed,
be able to write a book, not about me, though, but about
the Nationality."

"I am going to stay," I answered, "and I hope to do
far better work than that. I am no idle dreamer; I have
long wished for a chance to aid humanity. I see it approaching, and I shall not be found wanting, Clothilde."

"I know it," she said, "I was only referring to our
former conversation in a sort of sorrowful fun."

I bade her adieu, promising to come as often as I
could, and bring her word of any event of importance.

I had, indeed, fully determined to offer my services
to the Nationality in the struggle impending between it
and the Money Power.

Though all my education and class interests were in
favor of the latter, yet my conscience, my regard for the
rights of humanity, and my love of justice, truth and
right, drew me to the other side. That the authorities of
the Nationality expected such a conflict was evident. All
trains entering its territory were subjected to strict sur-
veillance, and its labor leaders were under orders to hold
their men ready to repel any attempted invasion, whether
of marshals or soldiery.

That the Nationality was supplied with the most

approved weapons to arm its citizens I was well satisfied.

In the latter part of August four or five vessels from Europe had arrived at Corpus Christi, and since that time every train from that port had been more or less loaded with their cargoes; a portion of which was conveyed to the mountain towns and another portion discharged at an immense warehouse in the southern part of Neuropolis.

I had seen some of these stores, and my eye, accustomed to viewing munitions of war, had caught the familiar sight of thousands of rifle and ammunition boxes.

The leaders of the Nationalistic party in the Congress of the United States, were men of very great ability and force. In the Senate, John Paul, the senior member from the state of Colorado, commanded universal respect and high consideration for his integrity, unblemished character, clear intellect and dignified, calm, and moderate demeanor.

In the House of Representatives, Philip Oram, a member from the state of Kansas, held a much similar position. Oram, however, who was younger than Paul, was eloquent, demonstrative and aggressive. The two statesmen were firm friends and acted in unison, the elder exercising much influence over the younger.

Shortly after the difficulty with the marshals, they had announced their intention of paying a flying visit to Neuropolis, desiring to meet other Nationalistic leaders there, and to confer with them on the critical situation.

The evening of their arrival, a public reception was given them in the largest academy of music in the city.

The great assembly room was decorated in the most artistic manner, with evergreens, banks of flowers, and rare tropical plants, and was resplendent with light and coloring.

On a raised dais at the stage end of the room sat the councilors and other dignitaries of the Nationality, and in front of this the two members of Congress stood, receiving the salutations of the many hundreds of their constituents who passed before them; while a large and brilliant company of those immediately acquainted with them collected in front, awaiting the time when the more formal reception should be over.

At an early hour in the evening I had been presented by General Knox, and was talking with Miss Ashley at a little distance from the dais, when I saw Miss Clothilde approaching it on the arm of General Canly, followed immediately by Miss Canly and Mr. Beyresen; behind them came Mrs. Beyresen, accompanied by a gentleman whom I afterwards learned was St. John, a man well known . throughout the entire Nationality for his daring, determination, and utter contempt for opposition, or criticism, traits which his countenance and bearing manifested.

I was startled at the appearance of Clothilde Beyresen. She was richly dressed, wearing as ornaments, diamond bracelets and necklace, while a circlet of frosted silver set with diamonds encompassed her head and shone above her raven black hair. Her tall figure was the embodiment of the fabled grace and beauty of Diana, and she bore herself with the most courtly dignity, ease, and self-possession.

She and General Canly spent some moments conversing with the Congressmen; and then the two, with Mr. Beyresen, ascended the dais, where to my surprise Clothilde remained, occupying a seat apparently reserved for her.

Some time after the formal reception was over, I saw her engaged in earnest conversation with Senator Paul. They walked slowly past an avenue in which I stood, to-

ward the east end of the room. They had not at first observed me, but after turning to come back evidently did
so, for they halted, and she soon left the Senator, who at
once came toward me.

He was a man past fifty years of age, tall and dignified in appearance, with an intellectual face, a keen, ob-
servant eye, and a pleasant, musical voice.

He addressed me, saying, "You are Mr. Maxwell, I
believe. I do not remember your name from the formal
introduction, but my friend the princess has just been
speaking of you. I understand you are a visitor here and
a native of Great Britain."

"I am," I replied, "and have been so much interested
in your fair city, and prosperous land, that my visit has
been quite prolonged."

"Then we may hope," said he, "you have met nothing among us to offend the conservatism so marked in
English character. Our institutions in this Nationality
are very different from yours, and though time has not
proven their qualities of endurance, yet we consider them
founded on principles capable of development into a higher and nobler form of government than any yet known.
Are you interested in these subjects, Mr. Maxwell? Pardon me, I have heard you are," he said, fixing his dark
eye on me.

"I am, indeed," I answered, "and have given much
thought to them. Lately I have been studying the history
of John Harvey in connection with this land, and have
now a very different opinion of him from that which, in
common with most Englishmen, I hitherto entertained."

"Ah, I know," said the Senator, with evident feeling.
"You refer to that awful catastrophe of a few years back,
in which John Harvey was the principal actor. It embit-
tered his whole after life, Mr. Maxwell, and caused his

premature death, which occurred in little more than a year after that incident. And yet, Mr. Maxwell, you cannot judge the character of men such as he by isolated acts. John Harvey, too, had provocation; no one can deny that the firing on him in Japanese waters was a gross violation of the laws of nations, and of all rules of war. That incident cost England less blood and even less treasure than many other conflicts in which she had been engaged, but the terrible destructiveness of the missiles John Harvey used gave prominence to his act.

"He offended the Money Power mortally, not only in your country, but in his own. The government of the United States was then as now in the hands of that Power, and he found himself virtually expatriated. He returned home a victor, laden with spoils, only to find that the ruling power considered itself assailed, and that his government was ready to lift its hand against him unless his treasure and his secret of warfare were put at its disposal. Seeing that his act was about to be used to his own destruction he left the port of New York one night, and, as is supposed, scuttled his vessel and sank her beneath the waves of the stormy Atlantic."

"Did you know John Harvey, Senator?" I asked.

"Yes," he replied, "he and I were trusted friends. I knew him well, and, Mr. Maxwell, no man has lived on the face of the globe for the last century who was his peer. Socially he was genial, companionable and attractive; intellectually he was broad, comprehensive, and quick. His foresight was almost prophetic, and his knowledge of men, and his ability to deal with them, wonderful. He could be most fascinating when he wished. There was a charm and magnetic attraction in his very presence. This was much broken and marred after the incident to which I have alluded. But he who saw John Harvey before

that, and conversed a half hour with him, could never forget him. (Would to God he were alive to-day! I cannot
refer to him, Mr. Maxwell," the Senator added, "even
now without emotion. Some other time we may talk further of him. I want to know about yourself."

"There is little to know of me," I said. "I am an Englishman, who, in 1929, was an officer on board his majesty's ship Vulcan, which fired the shot at John Harvey's
vessel, the Albatross, and precipitated the tragedy to
which you referred. At that time I formed a hasty and
immature judgment of your great fellow countryman,
which has been dispelled by an insight into the magnificent provision he has made for distressed humanity. I
have studied your people and your institutions, and am
convinced, as an Englishman can only be convinced, after
mature consideration, that the hope of the world's future
lies in them. I am ready and waiting the opportunity of
offering to your Nationality the services of my hand and
sword in the struggle which now seems imminent. I have
been an officer in the artillery in both land and naval service, and have an extensive and accurate acquaintance
with all the details of modern gunnery. If I can be of use
I desire to enlist with you. I wish to do so as soon as possible, for I intend starting next week on a visit to the principal cities of the East." I then informed the Senator of
my name and rank, and asked his good offices in further-
ance of the wish I had expressed. He deliberated a few
moments, and then said: "There is one person here to
whom, if it be your purpose to join us, I would like to present you at once; I refer to Mr. Philip Oram; if agreeable
to you, we will have a short talk with him on the subject."

We soon found Mr. Oram, and Senator Paul, after a
little private conversation with him, introduced me, and
stated my intentions.

Mr. Oram was very cordial, and assured me of the pleasure it gave him to know that I was about to cast in my lot with the Nationality. An appointment was made to meet the two gentlemen the following afternoon at the office of Mr. Beyresen, in the Administration Building, and we separated.

It was now past midnight, and the hall was fast becoming deserted. As I strolled down one of its aisles I came upon Clothilde Beyresen, apparently making her way to the cloak room.

"Ah!" she exclaimed, "Mr. Maxwell, I have not seen you to-night, except at a distance."

"It is not too late, is it, for a turn in the conservatory with me?" I asked.

"Oh, no," she replied, and we took the shortest way to that place.

"I ought to have a more brilliant escort," she continued. "You should have worn your uniform, sir; it is a night for display."

"The uniform and trappings of an English lieutenant would be but poor plumes in an assemblage like this," I replied.

"Could you do no better than that, my lord?" she returned. "I should like to have seen you once with all your insignia of power and place, and you could have worn them so well to-night."

"I do not understand your highness," I said.

"O, prince of deceit!" she exclaimed, "thy name is Herbert Maxwell, thy father a simple farmer, thy dwelling a cottage, thy rank a lieutenant. Lo, and behold, in our republican court stalks in disguise an English peer, Lord Herbert Maxwell Dudley, without choosing to honor our presence with his real name and orders. Is that your title, sir?" she asked.

For a moment I was bewildered. "I crave your pardon, Princess," I said. "That is my name which seems to be known to you. I hope it offends you not; it has been considered honorable."

"It is," she answered, "then why conceal it, my lord?"

"You would have known it to-morrow," I replied. "I have just told Senator Paul and Philip Oram. I am not sure," I added, "you did not know it yesterday."

We turned down a path in the conservatory. "Will you answer me one question, Clothilde?" I asked. "Had I told you my full name that evening in the boat would it have made any difference?"

"It would not," she said, simply.

"I am glad of that, dear," I replied.

"I knew your title then," she said, "as certainly as I know it now. Still I thought you should have begun your story by telling me who you were."

"But," I asked, eagerly, "would your answer have been any different?"

"It could not have been, Mr. Herbert," she said, slowly.

"But I will hope some day to change it," I replied. "Who is with you here?"

"Papa and mamma Beyresen," she answered.

"Might I assume their place and take you home?"

"I think you may," she said. "Let us find them and I will see. The process will be simple, and I hope its republican directness will commend it."

We found Mr. and Mrs. Beyresen evidently searching for Clothilde. "Mamma," said she, "Mr. Maxwell wishes to take me home."

"Indeed," said Mrs. Beyresen, "I hope some one will do it, for we have been trying for the last half hour."

We entered the carriage, and drove slowly home. Clothilde was full of animation.

"What shall I style you, anyway?" she said. "I have been calling you Mr. Herbert; I think I shall continue to do so."

"And you; what shall I call you?" I asked.

"Oh! I have assumed no disguises."

"What, are you not called the princess?" I inquired.

"And am I not of the blood royal, sir?"

"You cannot disturb me by any such claim," I said. "I have been calling you Clothilde, and shall continue to do so till forbidden."

We soon arrived at Mr. Beyresen's house, and I took my departure more than ever mystified. That Clothilde was not indifferent to me was evident. In her manner with others she was the princess, dignified and gracious; with me she was the woman, frank, outspoken and sometimes strangely confidential. That she took pleasure in my visits and my company she did not conceal. Indeed, had the former ceased, I was satisfied she would have asked the reason, so unconventional was she with me, and yet with others she was not so. I saw around her men of character and worth, who would have prized the companionship with which I was honored, but who were not admitted to it. If she were not mine, at least she belonged to none other.

On the succeeding day I met Senator Paul, Philip Oram and several others at Mr. Beyresen's office, and, after a long conversation, it was arranged that on the next day I, accompanied by Senator Paul, should meet the councilors in session and give and receive such assurances as should be deemed necessary.

I will not dwell upon the formal proceedings of the meeting with the councilors. Their session was held in a grand and noble hall in the eastern portion of the Administration Building, and nearly fifty of them were present, with many of whom I had some acquaintance.

Quite a number of questions were asked me in an informal manner, and then the presiding officer called the body to order and by unanimous vote my offer of services was accepted. An impressive oath of secrecy in regard to all affairs of the Nationality was administered, and the ceremony was over.

It was tacitly understood that I should go East as originally contemplated, and that on my return I should make a formal report to the councilors, and be assigned to other duties.

Senator Paul, in a short speech, counseled the greatest prudence and moderation in all public affairs, expressions, and displays. At its conclusion the Senator and I left the hall and he bade me farewell, expressing an earnest desire to see me when I arrived at Washington.

To one person alone I ardently desired to reveal the results of this meeting, but my oath and all considerations of honor forbade me. It is needless to say that this person was the one foremost in my thoughts, Clothilde Beyresen. And yet I was not sure but that she was already cognizant of all that had occurred, so intimate seemed her connection with the Nationality, and so strange the confidence reposed in her.

She had never offered a word of explanation of the mysteries surrounding her, and though I had avowed myself her lover, she set barriers between us in regard to them which I could not surmount. I could only wait, and this I resolved to do patiently, working meanwhile zealously in what was now a joint labor with her, the real interests of humanity.

CHAPTER XXIII.

THE EAST.

A few days after the events narrated in the last chapter I left Neuropolis for my eastern journey. The evening previous to my departure, I called at Mr. Beyresen's house, and he gave me letters of introduction to some of his friends in Chicago and New York.

I said good-by to the others, and asked Clothilde if she would go for a short walk, and in a few moments we were out together on the boulevard.

"I wanted a little talk with you," I began. "I have a wish that fills my heart and yet has no promise of attainment. I am leaving behind me the one dearest to me in all the world, and she has given me no promise of acceptance. Can you not answer me to-night, Clothilde, so that I may send back messages of love to you as mine own?"

She was silent for a moment and then, as I looked down at her, she replied: "I cannot now, Mr. Herbert. I can only say that you are a very near friend. I cannot say what you wish. Neither you nor I know what the book of fate holds for us."

"I hope it holds better things than appear," I answered.

"Well," she said, "I hope so, too, but let us wait till it reveals itself. It cannot be long, for events are crowding. Let us both be true to friendship. You will not be long gone?" she inquired.

"About a month," I replied. "May I write you often and hope for prompt answers, Clothilde?"

"You may," she said; "I shall have much leisure time, and there will be no pleasanter way of employing it."

"You are not very comforting, Clothilde, and you could be so comforting."

"Judge leniently," she answered, and I thought I saw tears in her eyes, though there was a smile on her face.

"We have had our talk," she continued; "let us go home, please," and we went slowly, arm in arm, and I bade her good-by at the door.

I returned to my room, and the following morning left Neuropolis for the East.

In the course of my tour I visited many parts of the country, and will give in a condensed form my observations of the general condition of its inhabitants, and then pass on to narrate various incidents which occurred.

(The entire business of the Eastern states was under the control of a few giant corporations and trusts, which dictated the manner in which it was conducted, and reaped the profits arising from it.)

They were the survivors of a multitude of such companies, which years before had competed fiercely for ascendency in the markets of the land, and fought each other in the courts and legislatures of the nation, by means legitimate, or otherwise, until all but the more powerful and unscrupulous had perished. These divided the field amongst themselves, and now seldom trespassed on one another's territory; their respective rights being regulated by a board of arbitration which they had established; and all made common cause against any transgressor of their rules, or invader of their respective limits. The essential object of these great trusts, or corporations, was the amassing of enormous wealth for those owning and controlling them; and being devoid of the moral characteristics and responsibilities of individuals, the means they employed to attain this object were often most iniquitous in character and pernicious in effect.

They were restrained only by the regulations of their own board of arbitration, and the laws passed by the various state legislatures as interpreted by the courts. Both legislatures and courts, moreover, had long since been corrupted by, and rendered subservient to them.

The men controlling these trusts and corporations were the real rulers and princes of the land. They had far greater power and used it more absolutely than any of the nobility of Europe; since they virtually controlled the government, the manufactures, the commerce, and the money of the country.

The great landed proprietors of the United States, who now owned nearly all its soil and leased it to tenants, occupied more the position of the nobility in England than any other class I met, having a certain community of interest with their tenantry.

Unlike the English nobility, however, they had no distinct political power, and were unable to oppose successfully the aggressions of the great trusts and corporations, which, being able to fix the mercantile value of all that they produced, continually hampered and embarrassed them in their efforts to improve the condition of their lands and tenantry.

Between these two classes there were antagonisms which manifested themselves in occasional struggles, that generally resulted in the tightening of the cords by which those controlling the trade, commerce, and money of the country held the other bound; and it was now believed by many that ere long the landed interests would also be entirely owned by these trusts and corporations.

In all other respects competition had been dethroned
by mutual agreement; class distinctions based mainly on
wealth had been instituted; and the land and its riches appropriated as conquered territory by persons so few in
number, and so unified in interest, that the usual divisions and dissensions among the victors, which give hope
to the vanquished, did not occur.

The following extracts from a letter, written to Mr.
Beyresen after I had been absent several weeks, will show
from another point of view my estimate of the condition
of the country and the people.

"Colossal establishments control every department
of manufactures and business. They use the latest and
the best machinery; but its introduction has increased
rather than lessened the amount of toil necessary for human existence, having simply rendered the employe more
thoroughly a slave by making the employer more independent of him.

"They pay as little as possible for labor, exacting
long hours of work from their employes, whom they regard as little better than the cogs in the wheels of their
machinery; the only persons remunerated sufficiently to
enable them to live in comfort being those connected
with the management of their business, and the skilled
workmen, without whom it must suffer.

"They limit their productions to an amount, and sell
them at a price, fixed by the managers of similar establishments all over the country; such as will afford the
best possible return to their owners.

"They set values for raw material so low, that extensive capital, and the closest attention, are necessary
for its production on a scale promising even a small
profit.

"The effect has been very marked among all classes

formerly engaged in such pursuits, especially in the agrarian regions.

"The independent middle class of fifty years ago, who owned their own farms and lived upon them, are nearly all gone, having been destroyed by these new conditions; and their homes have been merged in the possessions of the great landed proprietor, who counts his acres by the thousands or millions, and engages in agriculture, or stock raising, or kindred pursuits, on a scale of great magnitude. Those who were once the owners of the soil now occupy the position of hired laborers, living generally in ill-constructed and unhealthy dwellings; poorly clothed, poorly fed, and poorly educated.

"The destruction of competition throughout the land has been most thorough, but unfortunately entirely in the interests, not of the masses as among your people, my friend, but of the few.

"The owners of these great establishments, corporations, and trusts, and the great landed proprietors, form a select class, who build palatial houses in city and country, own their own pleasure vessels at sea, and their own special trains on land, in which they travel like princes, and enjoy life in luxury, ease and comfort.

"They boast, at home and abroad, of the wealth, the enterprise and the advancement of their country, and point to their own successes as the evidence of its immeasurable superiority over all others.

"It is unnecessary to tell you how empty, vain and frivolous this self-glorification appears to me, for I have looked already beneath the surface, and have seen upon what human suffering, want, and injustice all this colossal fabric rests.)

"The class next to this aristocratic one consists of their employes and dependents. It is impossible to describe the various degrees of prosperity and contentment amongst them; ranging from comfort to destitution, from placid submission to the existing state of things as the only one possible, down to the deep murmur of the illy-paid and illy-fed multitude, that can be heard in its sullen monotone all over the land, like the voice of an angry ocean; but in the attitude of dependency all can be classed together.

"The evolution of organized control in the interest of the few came gradually; and for years the hardships it brought were, and are, even yet by many of the people, attributed to causes other than the true ones; the existence and peculiar characteristics of your Nationality being those generally adduced.

"I need not enumerate the grievances alleged against it, for you are well acquainted with them, but I find the ruling class, who are its inveterate enemies, continually charging it with all the distresses which have fallen on the people. Their allegations, however, are not now so universally accepted as they were formerly by the shrewd and intelligent middle class, who have begun to think and judge for themselves. I find many among them who look to the ultimate adoption of your system as the only means of escape from the evils surrounding them.

"Amid the host of reformers of all kinds, however, who exist in every community, and the conflict of opinions among them, there has as yet been no ability manifested to devise ways, or means, or to ensure unity of action, for breaking the shackles so strangely riveted upon this people.

"There is another and lower class, probably fully as great in strength as the middle class, which must be wisely directed, or, like a blind Samson, it may, in the midst of popular disturbance, pull down, in sheer desperation, the pillars of the entire fabric of civilization.

"I refer to the unemployed, who are a mighty army in the land, and who are being constantly recruited by misfortune, despair, incapacity and other causes, and for whom no one cares, and who, therefore, care for no one.)

"They live as they can, in dilapidated dwelling houses or crowded tenements, by beggary, by crime, by occasional work; and seem to have no hope in this world, and often no care for the next. They are the dangerous class, who, in event of opportunity, strike unreasoningly in revenge for wrong; and are as likely to be engaged in destruction as upbuilding, or in manacling their fellow creatures as in unloosing their fetters."

The first city which I visited on my journey was Chicago, the emporium of the great northwestern states, and I must mention a singular incident which befell me there.

A few nights after my arrival, while passing along one of the streets, I saw, a short distance before me, a man walking rapidly in the direction in which I was proceeding. His strong figure and firm and peculiar step seemed somewhat familiar, and in a few moments I was satisfied that it was St. John. Wishing to speak with him I followed. He turned a corner abruptly, and disappeared within a door which closed behind him. An instant later I reached it, and on my statement that I wished to see Mr. St. John, who had just entered, I was admitted. The room, which was the antechamber to a larger hall, was filled by men plainly of the working class, but of evident character and intelligence. Many of them went at once into the larger room, giving some kind of a pass word, and others who lingered longer looked suspiciously at me. I saw that I had intruded upon a meeting of some secret order, and attempted to pass out of the door into the street, but was refused egress, with the statement that I would be required to account for my presence.

There was only one thing to be done, and I requested the men to give my name to Mr. St. John, and ask him to please come out to see me. This he did in a few moments, and recognized me, and I informed him of the unfortunate blunder I had made. He looked much concerned, and his manner was stern and reserved. He took me aside and impressed upon me in no very gentle terms the requirement of absolute secrecy in regard to my meeting with him, and the circumstances attending it; adding that he had no doubt my sentiments of honor would cause me to accede to his request. Without more ceremony, or delay, he instructed those in charge of the outer door to allow me to depart, which I did at once, wondering at the presence of this man in Chicago.

I arrived in New York City on the tenth day of October, 1935, and found letters from Clothilde and Mr. Beyresen awaiting me.

I answered them soon after, and will give some extracts from the one sent Clothilde:

"This is a city second only to London in population. Many of its inhabitants live in palaces, surrounded by magnificence; a still larger number in genteel poverty, and a host in penury and absolute want.

"Thousands tramp the streets without employment, kept from audacious crime by the iron hand of the law alone, which becomes more and more rigid as the years go by.

"I have seen poverty in European cities, but there the government feeds and clothes the needy as a matter of right and public safety; while here no such policy has been adopted; and no one cares systematically for the unemployed or their families. Their existence is considered a disgrace to themselves, and to the community in which they live.

"All my ideas in regard to riches and poverty have changed since I have seen the Nationality. I do not think I could be content to live in opulence, knowing my neighbor to be in want, and yet under the old system, if I spent all I had in charity I could relieve but a tithe of the suffering, and might myself be speedily in want. It is the system that is wrong; not so much the people. I have been asked many questions about your land, all of which I have answered as fully as I could; but I find it almost impossible to explain to any one here how life can be of much account without some opportunity of money getting.

"Possibly if you talked to them their ideas might be changed, for I am so late a convert that the fault may be mine own.

"Speculators and adventurers of all kinds, and promoters of schemes of all natures; the shrewdest, keenest, most daring and unscrupulous men anywhere to be found, flock here; all intent on getting money. Their sagacity and boldness are wonderful, and their manipulations of the money and stock markets of the country are often successfully managed, but their gain means ruin to thousands of others.

"Though I belong, as you now know, to the leisure class, I have not been accustomed to seeing riches obtained by avowed chicanery, and legalized robbery. Though such methods may be employed in England, I have never been brought in contact with them, and wherever used they must be condemned.

"The more I learn of the country to the east of you and of the system under which its people live, the more am I in love with your own happy land, and the more am

I impressed with the idea that you have very largely solved the problem of the ages of which Mr. Jones spoke on the momentous occasion of our boat ride.

"I am becoming disgusted with the world's estimate of people. The nearer one values men and women for what they really are in themselves, the nearer he gets to the estimate which their Creator places upon them. I do not mean that they should be judged by what they have done, for the opportunity to do may not have been afforded them; neither by what their ancestors have done, for their acts belong to themselves, and their children can only claim respect by being worthy scions of a worthy race.

"I do not undervalue good blood; I have seen what it can do and endure; and in the presence of danger I would rather trust to the good blood of England, or France, which has character to support, than to meaner strains coming from the same nations. But, after all, we must finally look to the man himself. Has he the composition of a churl or a hero; is he noble or ignoble?) I am sure you have decided views on these subjects, and if you will communicate them to me I shall be glad to receive them. Write me, please, another of your cheery letters, bright and breezy as your skies and full of the aroma of your mountains, and I will bless the unconscious postman who delivers it."

I had an object in referring to class distinctions in this letter. I knew that if I connected myself with the Nationality, my residence must be permanently within its borders, and my rank among the English nobility would be virtually forfeited. I had fully made up my mind to this before proposing to Clothilde, and had desired to make her acquainted with my intention. During the next few weeks she and I exchanged letters, in which the sub-

ject was incidentally mentioned, and we came to a tacit
but clear understanding about it.

The manner in which I was received in New York
confirmed my decision. My name and title appeared to
be the sesame which opened the doors of its most exclu-
sive clubs and its richest and most aristocratic society. I
was asked to dinners and entertainments so numerous
that to attend a tithe of them would have completely frus-
trated the object of my visit. I accepted several such in-
vitations, and declined many, and found invariably that
my regrets were received with much disappointment and
chagrin. This experience was oppressive to me. These
people only wished to court, fete, and lionize me that they
might associate my title with themselves. Time was
when I would not have inquired into their motives so
misanthropically; now I did, and it was a humiliation.
Thereafter I persistently refused all attention tendered
from such motives, and occupied myself sedulously in
gaining information about the condition of the Eastern
people, and the attitude they were likely to assume toward the Nationality

Some of the rich business men of the city, who were
in frequent and intimate communication with the President, assured me that he had not as yet decided what
course to pursue in the controversy, and the majority of
them thought him too slow in action. With one hundred thousand regular troops at his command, they declared he should at once have taken possession of the disputed townships, and asserted the supremacy of the law
by delivering them to the parties who had bought them
and were their rightful owners.

On my intimating that the matter might possibly be
too important to be thus summarily dealt with, I was met
by a legal argument to which, as it was based on the prin-

ciples of their system, I could not reply. This was usually supplemented by the statement that the Nationality was inimical to all the other interests of the country, and could not endure.

Very few of them had any doubt of the final result of a conflict. They considered the Nationality as a body founded on absurd principles, by John Harvey, whom they designated as an unscrupulous demagogue, who had failed in an attempt at dictatorship, and they declared that it would quickly fall to pieces if attacked.

Among the great lawyers and politicians of the metropolis, I found more division of feeling. Many of the former questioned the correctness of the decision of the courts, but none of them saw any other course than its enforcement. Those in these professions were better informed as to the principles and resources of the Nationality than the business men, but considered its system opposed to that of the rest of the country; and as chimerical; and thought that in time its inherent weakness would cause its failure; but confessed that if a lengthy struggle should occur there was great danger, in the present condition of affairs, that a socialistic revolution would sweep over the land.

The opinions of the clergy were as various as their positions. Some of them who ministered to rich congregations prayed openly that the heresy of attempting to evade the ancient fiat, that in the sweat of his brow man must earn his daily bread, might be forever eradicated; and others, the pastors of less wealthy churches, said little, but admitted that if the principles of the Nationality could be carried out, the burdens on the people would be lightened.

I found nearly all of the middle class anxious for some beneficial change; and many of them well acquaint-

ed with the principles of the Nationality and deprecating
any invasion of its territory.

The third class here, as in other places, was ready
for any change, no matter what; ready at any moment to
join an army of subjugation, or to break forth in riot
against civic authority at home.

When I had concluded my inquiries, I must confess
I was sick at heart. After nineteen hundred years of civilization, was one of the most important questions ever
given man to decide, in which the future of his race was
so greatly concerned, to be determined with so little consideration and so largely by prejudice.

In the labor organizations, alone, did hope remain.
They knit together the men of the middle and lower
classes, the bone and sinew of the land. It was a period
of constant though secret agitation among them; meetings of their leaders had been held in all the large cities,
and one was now in progress in New York. I had seen
on the streets of that city the powerful figure of St. John,
and I could divine now the character of his mission here,
and that of the assembly I had so unwittingly entered in
Chicago.

But of the exact position of the labor organizations on
these matters every one seemed ignorant; and it was generally supposed that they were discordant and diverse in
opinion among themselves. One name, however, was
always mentioned with respect and regard by their members, and that was the name of Philip Oram. Among
bankers, brokers and others of that class, John Paul was
credited with being the most able leader of the Nationality; but among the people Philip Oram's utterances and
opinions seemed to have the greatest influence.

It was evident that these two men; the one an eminent Senator, the other an eloquent, magnetic Congress-

man, would be the leaders on the Nationalistic side in any conflict; and that the words of the latter, especially, would have great weight with the masses of the people.

On the afternoon of the 20th of October, came by telegram, a proclamation from the President, that day issued in Washington, exciting universal attention and causing breathless surprise, even in this city, used to stirring and sensational events.

It recited in resonant words the resistance offered to the execution of the laws of the United States in certain townships in the State of Nebraska, on the 20th day of September, 1935; and declared that the civil authorities of that state, though requested so to do, were unable, or unwilling, to suppress this insurrection; that these townships were now occupied by large bodies of men, ready by force and arms to obstruct the execution of the laws of the United States, and the judgment of its courts; and that the President commanded all such persons to disperse, and cease their unlawful acts against the peace and dignity of the United States, and all others upholding them to desist, within the period of thirty days from and after the issuing of the proclamation; otherwise he would see to it that the laws and decrees of the courts were obeyey; and that the entire power of the government would, if necessary, be used to compel such obedience.

This proclamation was posted on the bulletin boards of the city, and immense crowds assembled around them and the offices of the great dailies, to gain all available information. The attitude of these papers is shown by the following head-lines, which I preserved:

"The Laws Must Be Executed and the Judgment of the Courts Respected;" "The President Takes a Decided Stand in Favor of Law and Order;" "The President Will Meet Force by Force;" "A Struggle Between Law

and Order, and Mob Rule and Anarchy Imminent;"
"Shall the Courts Be Obeyed? The President Says They
Shall," etc.

That evening I mingled with the crowds upon the
streets, and observed that they were composed very
largely of the idle and lower class of the people. The
working men on their way home did not pause long to
read the bulletins, or linger with the multitude, and manifested no enthusiasm or approval.

On the day following, I visited several clubs where I
was pretty well acquainted, and give some of the sentiments expressed there by other classes of citizens.

"He could do nothing less," said a prominent business man, referring to the President; "either we have a
government, or we have none, and we shall teach these
Western states that we have one."

"The President is right legally," said an eminent
lawyer. "The next question is, will the states compris-
ing the Nationality have the patriotism to see it, and submit?"

"I am glad this question is to be settled once for all
time," said a speculator. "This socialism has been an
incubus on business for the last fifteen years, and the
sooner it is ended the better."

"The matter is brought to a focus now," said a rich
banker, "and we shall see whether the ten million fanatics
rule the nation, or its ninety million freemen."

Thus they talked, but I failed to find that the President had any of the support that springs from the mighty
heart of a sympathetic and patriotic people, which considered its life, or its cherished institutions threatened.
Self-interest seemed the mainspring of all the approval
expressed, and I left New York for Washington a few
days later, feeling that when the President became aware

of the true nature of his support, he might hesitate in using force.

I then knew little of the character of the Executive, of the power of the moneyed classes, and the great advantage they possessed in the logical legality of their proceedings.

I was unacquainted with the respect shown by all Americans for law, even when the spirit was dead and the form only existed; and I was to discover later, how powerful self-interest could be in urging even good men to extreme action.

On these matters I found John Paul, Philip Oram, and other leaders of the Nationality much better posted than myself. They understood well the magnitude of the task of showing to their fellow countrymen the justice of their cause, and the injustice of the proceeding against them.

Congress was in session in Washington, and politicians filled every hall, and hourly discussed the situation. There was a sense of expectancy in the air. The President was universally considered a very determined man, and the proclamation was issued, it was said, after full discussion by, and with the unanimous approval of his cabinet. It was understood that he commanded sufficient strength in Congress to secure all necessary appropriations, and that neither men nor money would be wanting to aid him in the course he had adopted.

I met my friends and acquaintances, and among them Senator Paul, and learned that Philip Oram was daily expected to arrive from Neuropolis. The former introduced me to a number of Congressmen, advising me, however, not to appear at present as a partisan in the controversy. He also wished me to visit the President, and mentioned Mr. Hamilton, with whose wife, now in Washington, he knew I had some acquaintance, as a very good person to present me.

The next day I called upon Mrs. Hamilton and renewed the acquaintance so pleasantly begun in Neuropolis. She had been informed of my true name and title, and accused me of masquerading. Mr. Hamilton soon came in and conversed quite at length on various topics. He was very guarded in what he said in reference to the controversy with the Nationality, being, as I had been informed, of the party of the President.

He was not, however, a thorough advocate of the policy of force; though he said it was very difficult to see why the laws and decisions of the courts ought not to have the same effect in the state of Nebraska as in the state of New York, and that it would be hard to make the citizens of the latter state believe that there should be any difference. This, he said, was the ground the President took, and it was very strong ground on which to stand before the American people.

On my expressing a wish to meet the President, he at once offered his services, informing me that he had an appointment with him, and would request permission to introduce me the next day. After some further talk, I departed, and in the morning a message from Mr. Hamilton informed me that the President would receive us at 4 o'clock p. m.

A little before that hour we reached the executive mansion, and were soon ushered into the presence of the chief magistrate. The President of the United States was a large, corpulent man, of full habit, about forty-eight years of age, evidently of great self-confidence, of much ability, and fully impressed with a sense of the dignity and importance of his office. He spoke slowly and distinctly, often pausing to determine upon the proper word to give force to his utterances, which were oracularly de-livered. He had, I understood, risen by rapid gradations from obscurity to his present position, and commanded his party by an assumption of superior wisdom, how well founded I could not tell. But he had in the main been successful in his political battles, and had always been re-garded as a victorious leader, possessing great sagacity, foresight and political acumen.

While this prestige had suffered some diminution from the continued monetary and business distresses then prevalent, yet he was still considered by most of his party as the foremost man of the times in ability, honesty and patriotism.

He was the man to have friends and also to make en-emies; I could see that in the short period of my inter-view. He questioned me about many things relative to England, China, and India; and especially the colonial sys-tem of Great Britain; and volunteered much information as to the relations of the government of the United States, and the individual states, and the constitutional limits of each, and stated that these had in the past been overstep-ped and disregarded; a fact which he deplored, but attrib-uted to the circumstances of the times, and the short-sightedness of those engaged in the conduct of affairs.

Though nothing was said of the existing troubles with the Nationality, yet I could divine that he had these in view in many of the remarks he made. I could also see that he undertook their settlement with that cool, phleg-matical temperament, which, when once determined, can seldom be shaken by anything less than overwhelming defeat. I left his presence convinced that from him the Nationality could expect nothing, and would meet a strong will bent on absolute submission.

I spent the ensuing evening at home, having taken a

severe cold which kept me confined to my room for two days, a circumstance which I regretted very much at the time, for discussions had already begun in Congress, on the matters in controversy between the Nationality and the government.

I afterward found I was really little the loser, since during this time only the preliminary skirmishing between the captains and lieutenants of the respective parties occurred, and I was so fortunate as to hear finally the speeches of their great leaders.

During my enforced seclusion, I received from Clothilde Beyresen a letter descriptive of what was occurring in the Nationality, a portion of which I quote for the information of the reader.

After some remarks upon the President's proclamation, she described its effect upon popular feeling thus: "Every one is aroused to the full appreciation of the danger, and apparently ready to meet it. It strikes at the homes of our citizens, and has all the force of a personal attack, as well as one upon our country.

"The tension is very great and finds relief all over our land in public meetings, drills and songs of a patriotic character. I see how a peaceful nation, as well as a peaceful individual, can be suddenly changed into a war-like one.

"I must say that I disapprove of much of the feeling exhibited, especially as it borders often upon the vindictive. However, the lioness who finds a stranger in her lair, does not tear him to pieces in a remorseful manner, but I fancy she growls with satisfaction as she does it. God save us from this feeling, and from all other evil ones, and deliver us from our troubles. This has been my constant prayer to Him."

CHAPTER XXIV.

PROCEEDINGS IN CONGRESS.

As soon as I had recovered from my indisposition I attended one or other of the houses of congress daily and listened to the debates going on in them. The speeches were very earnest, for the feeling had already become intense.

In the senate, owing possibly to the more dignified habits, smaller number and greater age of its members, this was more repressed than in the house, but even there manifestations of a partisan character frequently occurred.

The chief leader of the Administration in the senate was Mr. Edmundson, of New York state, a man of much forensic ability and acumen. He had spoken briefly at the opening of the debate, and had given notice that he desired to be heard again on the second day of November.

It was understood that his speech would be a review of the causes which had led to the unhappy imbroglio with the states of the Nationality, and an appeal for the preservation of law and order at all hazards. It was expected that Senator Paul, of Colorado, would reply, and would indicate the course the Nationality would pursue.

I was present in the consular gallery and heard these speeches and will give a brief resume of them.

Mr. Edmundson said: "Among the well-known and

approved principles of law, none is better established than the duty of all persons, natural or artificial, to pay all debts found to be just and legal by the courts of the land. On refusal so to pay, a sequestration and sale of sufficient of the property of the debtor to satisfy the judgment invariably follow. This universal sequence had occurred in the controversy carried on in the courts between the body called the Nationality and certain other parties.

"Upon the sequestration and sale of its property the Nationality refused to deliver it to the purchaser, and accordingly the court issued a writ of possession.

"The officers of the law, charged with the execution of this writ, had, however, been met by organized and determined resistance of so formidable a character they were unable to overcome it. An appeal for aid was therefore made to the executive arm, in which reposes the collective strength of the government.

"The President of the United States, the Executive of the nation, has now issued his proclamation commanding all persons so resisting, hindering, or obstructing the execution of the mandates of the court, or in any way aiding or abetting in such resistance, hindrance, or obstruction, to desist from so doing within the period of thirty days.

"The proclamation is a note of warning that, if such . unlawful interference continue, other and decided action will follow. The President has done his duty; he has taken the first step, in accordance with his oath of office, in seeing to it that the laws be executed.

"Obligations no less plain devolve upon the legislative branch of the government; co-ordinate as it is with the Executive it must assist him in the performance of this task by giving him its moral and material aid; responsible as it for the enactment of laws for the protection of the lives, liberty, property, peace and happiness of all its citizens, it must inquire into whatever threatens to jeopardize any of these, and by proper legislation restrain, or remove it.

"That member of the legislative branch of the government who hesitates to support the President, or to inquire into the causes of this resistance to the enforcement of the laws, must be called recreant to his duty and to the trust reposed in him by the people.

"What material aid the President may require does not yet appear, and is matter for later determination, but we should without delay ascertain the causes of this organized resistance."

Mr. Edmundson then entered upon a lengthy discussion of the history, principles, and aims of the Nationality, in the course of which he extolled the magnanimity of the general government in giving to the eight states composing that organization all the land, mineral and agricultural, it possessed within their borders.

He said: "This land is the common heritage and property of all Americans, and was given that it might be freely occupied and used by all citizens who wish so to do.

"It contains nearly every known mineral, and the greatest deposits of gold and silver on the North American continent, designed to fill and swell the veins and arteries of the trade and commerce of the entire nation, and the entire world.

"The gift was munificent, and was intended to be used in accordance with the precedent and the well-known rules and regulations then so far adopted by all civilized states. But unfortunately, it has fallen into the possession of an oligarchy who fence it round with such peculiar regulations, and so manipulate and control the occupancy and use of the land that the intention of the gift has been perverted, and it is practically beneficial only to themselves.

"This organization aims to control the labor, dispose of the products, and decide the destinies of all those dwelling within its limits. Free men hesitate to submit to such dictation, no matter how great the allurements held out to them.

"But the evil has not ceased here. The management of this gift by this oligarchy is further marked by anti-republican principles, and by dangerous practices.

"Owning the source of supply, it controls the output of the money metals of the nation, and hoards, or spends them at pleasure, causing redundancy or scarcity as it wishes, creating an element of continual uncertainty, in the media of exchange.

"It goes further; it gathers together and controls the surplus products of a great territory; those of the field, the quarry, and the loom, and those of the mine and the mill and disposes of them also at its pleasure, thus disturbing prices, and shaping them to its advantage, having power almost to create a famine or a feast in the land. It is thus a constant menace to the monetary and industrial world.

"It has erected great cities, adorning them with princely buildings, attractive to. the imagination, but filled largely with an idle population.

"In politics the attitudes and methods of this organization have been specially reprehensible. It has swallowed up eight states of the Union, and created a capital, rivaling that of the general government in extent and greatness, and organized another government therein, whose legislative and administrative bodies really dictate whom these states should send as their representatives to the congress of the United States.

"It preserves only enough of the form of state organization to comply with the laws of the general government, while it violates them in spirit in every respect.

"It has recently made overtures to certain other states, with intent to swallow them up also, and acquire the Mississippi and Missouri Rivers as its eastern boundary line.

"And, finally, this oligarchical Nationality, not content with these departures and deviations from republican government, and its other aggressions, after a long and arduous contest in the courts of the land, waged primarily with a number of its discontented and aggrieved citizens, and conducted on its side by the best skilled jurists it could employ, refuses to abide by the decisions of these courts and, as is now generally understood, sanctions open resistance to the authority of the United States."

Mr. Edmundson called upon the senators of the eight Nationalistic states to declare if his assertions were not true, and also to purge themselves of all sympathy with such treasonable practices.

He proceeded at considerable length to animadvert upon the peculiar characteristics of the Nationality, predicting its early collapse, and appealed to its citizens to renew their loyalty to the United States, and to frown on such incendiary principles.

He repeatedly accused the Nationality of being itself the primary cause of the distresses of the times, of the uncertainty of business and the want of confidence manifested by capitalists and investors, and ended with an appeal for firmness and union in dealing with these disturbances, so that they might be settled on a lasting basis.

He had hardly taken his seat when Senator Paul arose, and addressed the senate as follows:

"Mr. President, the officers of a great vessel, the habitation and the only means of safety of hundreds of human beings, in the midst of one of those devastating storms which sometimes sweep the seas, have great responsibilities cast upon them, by which doubtless they are often appalled, but which nevertheless they must meet.

"As a member of this body, responsible for the lives, safety and happiness of one hundred millions of human beings threatened with unknown dangers by the clouds of dissension and civil strife now impending over us, I cannot but be likewise solicitous in addressing my fellow senators and my fellow countrymen, lest any unwise word, any unwarranted assumption, any false premise of mine, should misguide reason, should pervert judgment, and thus tend to ultimate disaster.

"No less as a trusted representative of the body called the Nationality, whose people, ten millions in number, have this day been assailed, and been charged with permitting themselves to be governed by an oligarchical despotism, am I solicitous lest by any weakness of mine, by any word of anger uttered by me in reply to this attack upon a people whom I love, their cause, which I believe to be the cause of humanity, should be discredited before the eyes of the other ninety millions of their fellow countrymen, or the way which they have chosen, which I as firmly believe to be the only way to that equality of condition, and that honesty of intention and honesty of deed, which mankind have for ages sought, should be obstructed, or obscured.

"I will therefore strive, in what I shall now say, to be actuated by motives of the purest patriotism; but at the same time shall abate none of that fearlessness which as a public duty strips falsehood of the thin covering of plausibility which it so often assumes when it desires to masquerade in the guise of truth.

"There are differences between the ten million people whom I and my colleagues represent, and their brethren in the other states, and before going further I shall attempt to classify these differences by their causes.

"Differences of opinion, differences of management, differences of ways of life, often exist among intelligent and liberty and humanity loving people. As such persons are really striving for the same ends, their differences are not irreconcilable, for they are not in regard to results, but in regard to methods.

"There is, however, another class of differences of which I cannot speak so hopefully. These may be termed selfish, or specious differences. Their creators and promoters always try to hide their character under various disguises of which the most common, when they relate to political matters, are those of patriotism and philanthropy. These differences, being selfish in aim, and false in the attitude they assume, are irreconcilable with pure motives and honest actions.

"Between the people of the Nationality and the great mass of their brethren in the other states the differences which exist to-day, are, I believe, of the first class wholly, being mainly in respect to methods, and have been created largely by education and environment. Both are actuated by one common aim and feeling—the relief and elevation of humanity, the love of freedom and the hatred of tyranny and wrong. In time of famine, fire, flood or pestilence the people of either section, if untrammeled, would hasten to relieve the other's wants, and in time of war would sink all differences and fight side by side, making common cause against their country's foes.

"But the differences between the people of the Nationality, and the class to which the gentleman who has just spoken belongs, are, I fear, utterly irreconcilable.

"Of the two hundred and fifty multi-millionaires, the class to which the gentleman belongs, the class which to-day own nearly three-quarters of the entire property of the nation, not one person possesses a foot of land or any other kind of property in the Nationality. Between that class and it there exists an irrepressible conflict created and maintained on the part of the former by self-interest, on that of the latter by an instinct of self-preservation.

"The Nationality has set a barrier to private acquisition, such as the Almighty has established against the restless ocean, and graven upon the escarpment of its coasts, 'Thus far may'st thou come, but no farther.'

"Like the chafed and angry sea, this devouring class to-day beat the shores with high-swelling waves and fill the air with the strident notes of windy tempests, that they may increase the fury of the waters, and break down the defenses, and force an entrance into the sheltered land.)

"The education and the environment of the people of the Nationality have for years been quite different from those of their brethren of the Eastern states, and I venture to say they can discriminate more closely, and more accurately, between the cause of humanity in general, and the cause of the millionaire.

"The main points of difference between their system and others may be stated as existing in the economic fields of ownership, production and use, and in the political one of form and character of government.

"The ownership of the property of the Nationality inheres in the people, and is joint but indivisible. .

"Production is obtained by the labor of all capable of labor, in the arena for which the individual is best fitted, and can be most effectively employed, its amount being measured by what is found necessary to provide comfortably for all during life, the term of the directed labor of the individual being regulated by the time necessary to secure that amount.

"Equality in the means of subsistence, and liberty in the manner of enjoying it, are obtained by the issuance to each citizen of a like amount of a media of exchange, ample in quantity, with which anything produced or bought by the Nationality can be purchased. This currency, however, has such power only during the year in which it is issued, and the use, only, of commodities of a permanent character can be acquired.

"The principles of the Nationality in regard to ownership, production and use, which have been tried for twenty years, and not found wanting, may then be thus briefly summed up: State ownership, co-operation of the able in directed labor for a term of years sufficient for the securing of a comfortable support for themselves, and the unable, and equality in sustenance for all in the present, and the highest assurance of its continuance during life.

"Is this system slavery? I ask the toiling millions in the factories, in the mills, and in the workshops of other states who labor long hours for a scanty support, with no assurance for the future.

"I ask the other millions who have no means and no employment, who would welcome the most menial service to earn daily bread for themselves and their families.

"I ask those who know, which is practical slavery, and it is not necessary to wait for their reply.

"Does this system impose new burdens on the productive classes in providing for the unable?

"I ask, do not these classes in other states assume far greater burdens, in the support, not only of the decrepit and the unfortunate, but also of the millionaire, the speculator, and the great swarm of other idlers who are such from inclination, from education, from habit, or from necessity, and again it is not necessary to wait for a reply.

"Is it a chimera?

"Does the gentleman who has just spoken, or his class, so charge?

"According to his statement we produce too much; we obstruct the market.

"He has referred to monetary affairs. In regard to them the principles of the Nationality are simple. It uses no money except in dealing with other peoples who live under a system employing it.

"All moneys received by citizens are turned into the coffers of the state, to be used in such dealings. The learned exposition in regard to money and kindred subjects with which the gentleman who has just spoken has favored us, and with which gentlemen of his class so often favor us, with which in fact our time and attention as law-makers is so largely occupied in these halls, is of no interest to the ten million citizens of the Nationality. If the distinguished gentleman who preceded me would think worth while to speak to my people about honor gained by duty well performed, about intelligence increased by leisure time well spent, about pure motives and honest actions in the public service, they would appreciate his efforts; but if he lectured upon money, banks, bills, bonds and notes, subjects which his class love so well, his audience might consider their time ill-spent.

"If in addition he described to them his princely mansion on the Hudson, if he told them of his many acres and his many millions, and of his many liveried servants, the private fortune and bedizened flunkies of a public man, they might strangely think his story evidence that the gentleman had not always lived justly toward his fellowmen.

"In form the government of the Nationality is not much different from those of the other states. A representative house chosen by the people, and an upper house composed of those who have served with credit in the other, constitute the legislature. The members of this legislature discuss mainly, not politics, but business interests; not punishment for crime, for crime is light; not protection of property, for there is no individual property, but the common weal, how to best assure the interests, material, mental and spiritual, of the people. Bribery and corruption find no place among them, for the vehicle of corruption is wanting. Once in two years they elect their representatives to these halls of congress. They do it, quietly and peacefully at least, if the wisdom of their choice is not always apparent. They do it, honestly at least, and if they be ever actuated by favoritism, it is not for me to deny it. They do it, I will venture to say, according to the principles of justice, and good citizenship, and the dictates of their own conscience.

"This the gentleman who has just spoken has denied, and he has dared to call upon us, the chosen representatives of this people, to answer if his statements be not correct, and to purge ourselves from certain fictions of his own disordered brain.

"His temerity receives from me this answer: That I do not believe his statements to be true, but that I do consider them of that mischievous character which assumes the garb of truth to entrap the unwary multitude, and which steals the livery of legality in which to serve injustice.

"I will say further, and I am glad to be able to say it, that the political methods employed by the gentleman and his class are not the methods in use among the people I have the honor to represent.

"I will say, that so far as I am acquainted with the political history of the gentleman, this is true from the inception of his career down to his late stormy election at Albany, made possible only by the strong influences which he and his class know so well how to employ.

"I will say that in my opinion the gentleman has willfully or ignorantly misstated the question now before the American people, and has failed to estimate its momentous importance; that he has talked of a paltry debt when two great labor systems are on trial before them, and speaks of money owing to a syndicate of designing capitalists, when the lives, liberty and happiness of millions of his fellow men are in jeopardy.

"His statements require more careful digest in his own brain before they will receive further attention from me.

"I turn from him and his class, whom I believe to be in irreconcilable conflict with me and mine, to my other fellow senators, and to that great mass of my fellow countrymen, who, differing from us only by reason of education and environment, seek honestly the same great end, the good of humanity, and ask in conclusion, which of these two systems best promotes comfort, happiness, intelligence and usefulness among mankind?

"This should be the chief inquiry, and I address myself to it.

"I tell you, fellow senators and fellow countrymen,

that while in other states, men, women and children are
starving, in the Nationality all live in comfort; while in
other states, care for the present and anxiety for the future furrow the brow and silver the hair prematurely,
these burdens are rolled from the shoulders of the people
of the Nationality; while in other states toil incessant,
even to old age, gives little time or opportunity for the
cultivation of the mind, among the people of the Nationality the short hours of labor during active life, and the
cessation of compulsory service before decrepitude has
laid its heavy hand upon men, give abundant time, and
the pleasant rural cities, with their libraries, academies,
schools and churches, afford abundant opportunity for
the cultivation of the mind and higher nature.

"Even that queenly city, complained of as the abode
of an idle population, is one of the most potent factors in
cultivating and disseminating those true opinions in regard to human rights and human wrongs which are so
welcome to the people and so hated by tyrants.

"If these things be true, and they are susceptible of
proof, why assume that the system that made them possible in the Nationality cannot make them possible elsewhere? Why assume that its aims and its efforts at extension are anti-republican?

"The scope of true republicanism is not limited by
definitions, precedents and arbitrary rules and regulations.

"All that concerns the safety, the good, the happiness of humanity is germinal within it. Its growth must
be coterminous with that of the human soul. It must
know no bounds save those imposed by wisdom, moderation and intelligence; the elements of the soil in which
it thrives. Why, then, assume that this system, which for
twenty years has blessed the Nationality, is not a new de-

velopment in the progress of humanity, a mighty upward movement in the science of government, a higher
vantage ground from which to unfurl the banner of freedom, equality and fraternity?

"Why assume that it is to be handicapped, throttled,
or destroyed?

"Is this statesmanship?   Why attempt armed entry
into the territory of the Nationality to plant there a colony unfriendly to its system and inimical to its interests?
Is this the best way that can be devised to settle a difference with ten millions of freemen?

"I will not permit myself to think of the consequences of such an attempt, but I lift my warning voice
against it.

"In concluding I refer the President and his ad-
visers to a story in an ancient Book, in whose perusal they
may find much profit.

"It is a tale of the olden time, when the charge was
brought that certain men had filled a Jewish city with
their doctrine, and stirred up sedition within it; of a time
when these men were brought by the captains and the
officers before the council, and there claimed the high right
to obey God rather than men, and when the violent sought
to slay them.   There then stood up in that council a
doctor of the law, a fearless man, and I think a wiser
man than many of the present doctors, and he said: 'Ye
men of Israel, take heed what ye intend to do touching
these men, and let them alone, for if this work be of men
it will come to naught, but if it be of God ye cannot overthrow it, lest haply ye be found to fight against God.' "

These speeches were listened to with great attention,
and were characterized as sound or unsound, as patriotic
or factional, largely as they accorded with the individual
views of their critics.

Both were published throughout the country, and while in the senate few members were influenced permanently by the speech of John Paul, yet among the thinking and discriminating class in Washington it had a great effect, and would undoubtedly have still greater in other portions of the United States.

I wrote to Mr. Beyresen and also to Clothilde, describing the scenes which I witnessed, and received in return letters from them giving accounts of proceedings in the Nationality.

From these I was satisfied that steps were being taken to oppose a most determined resistance to any attempt at coercion.

The letters were guarded in language, but gave me information of frequent and enthusiastic meetings among the people, and of constant drills ordered and controlled by the directors of labor.

I recognized that the country was fast getting into that condition when any unfortunate movement, any injudicious act, might precipitate a collision which good men universally would deplore.

I learned from various sources that all shipments of bread stuffs, meats and other provisions from the Nationality to the Eastern states had ceased, and that these were being stored up to meet the exigencies of the times and the possible wants of their own people. As an immense amount of such goods was yearly exported, the prices of all these commodities had already been enhanced, and the Nationality seemed, indeed, in the language of Mr. Edmundson, to be able almost to create a famine.

The government had, a month since, quietly sent orders to the navy yards on the Mississippi and to several individual firms in the large cities on the great streams

tributary to that river, to fit out with as much dispatch
and secrecy as possible, a fleet of gunboats, able to navi-
gate and control these waters.

Its army, numbering about one hundred thousand
men, had been massed as far as practicable in such position as would enable them to concentrate with rapidity
on the borders of the Nationality near the disputed townships, and the officers could be seen daily parading the
streets of Washington, and gave them quite a warlike
appearance.

No one among my correspondents seemed more
deeply to deplore the condition of affairs than did Clothilde Beyresen. Her letters, while breathing the most
patriotic spirit, were filled with reflections on the awful
character of war, and the suffering and bloodshed attendant upon it. It seemed to me strange that so young a
girl, living in so peaceful a community, should be so fully
alive to the miseries which would necessarily attend such
strife. Her letters to me now were frequent, and had
changed in character.

She appeared often to be solicitous for my safety
and anxious for my return. This she did not attempt to
conceal and I knew not whether to regard it as evidence
of mere friendly interest, or something more pleasing to
myself.

CHAPTER XXV.

It was now the 10th of November, and some time had elapsed since the delivery of the speeches from which I have quoted.

Other debates had followed in both houses of Congress, but approach to a settlement of the controversy seemed as remote as ever. Speeches had been made on both sides of the question in the House of Representatives, where a much more equal division of opinion existed than in the Senate.

Some time previous it had been announced that on the 11th of November Philip Oram would address the House, and my desire to hear him had induced me to defer my return to Neuropolis till after that date.

On the morning of the 11th, some hours before the time of the meeting, the great Hall of Representatives began to fill, and by noon it was densely packed with a most unusual audience.

A large number of ladies were in attendance; the diplomatic and consular representatives were in their places; but all the rest of the house, its galleries, aisles, and every available space, was occupied by men, hardhanded and rugged-featured, strong and sturdy in figure, and resolute in appearance; who, though comfortably and neatly clothed, were very unlike the daintily clad audience that filled the hall on other occasions when a great and stirring speech was expected.

As I looked over the assemblage, I saw at once that
the city of Washington had never furnished this audience,
and on inquiry found that the labor unions all over the
land had sent their leaders and select men to hear the
great orator, who had been taunted in this very place
with being their adviser, and even their chief.

The name of Oram, often repeated among this multitude and the fact that some days previous, threats had
been made that he would not be allowed to proceed were
his language considered incendiary, led me to the belief
that he stood under the aegis of a power that would tol-
erate no such interruption, and which was so mighty
that it would finally prove a most potent factor in deciding
the controversy.

When Philip Oram rose to speak, no applause, or
sound of welcome, broke from the lips of any of these
men, who probably for the first time dominated in this
hall; but they all listened with breathless attention to his
every word.

He said: "Mr. Speaker: I believe God to be the
Creator of the universe and the Ruler over the affairs of
men. I believe He governs by certain laws, very universal in their application, and which, therefore, can be discovered.

"In the formation of the globe both science and Revelation teach us that distinct successive steps marked the
ascending scale by which the Supreme Architect oper-
ated, from the time when the earth was without form and
void and darkness brooded upon the face of the waters,
until that moment when, carpeted in perennial green,
adorned with banks of flowers reflected in the silvery
sheen of pure sun-kissed waters, and curtained by light,
fleecy clouds, it was prepared a fit home for the human
race.

"We are informed that this wonderful creation, and all this beauty, adornment, and preparation were not fashioned at once by the fiat of omnipotence; but that for age after age God was content to see creation after creation, type after type, suited to ever-varying conditions, and governed by laws adapted to them, begin, culminate, and end, until in the progress of time the earth was ready for man.

"Then our race came into existence, and being endowed with reasoning faculties, seems in many things to have been left to work out its own destiny.

"The great law of ascending cycles was not altered; but its operation was modified by the fact that mankind possessed minds and souls to be exercised, trained and developed, by dealing with the problems surrounding them.

"Principal among these were those economic questions which relate to the possession, ownership, and use of the heritage God had given us. These being at the very basis of all civilization, and the parents of all social and political questions, have formed fruitful subjects of discussion, agreement, and disagreement in all ages. '

"Let me refer briefly to the varying methods of dealing with these problems from their inception down to the present time.

"It has been said that in a state of nature every man had a right to the ownership and use of whatever he produced, or brought into his possession.

"That state, however, and the rights thus defined never existed. The moment a second human being came into the world, other rights began, having their foundation, not in the organization of society, but in the nobler law of moral obligation.

"Man then became in large measure his brother's

keeper, and though, like Cain, he disavowed the responsibility, yet by so doing he has shared through his long
succeeding history much the same divinely appointed
punishment.

"In the early ages, as society became more fully organized, other claims, more artificial in character, were
put forth for the ownership and use of a part of its production.

"The ruling power, or the government, claimed a
portion for the maintenance of the officers necessary for
discharging its duties; and very soon this claim, equitable
in itself, was perverted by these officers into the appro-
priation of unequal and unjust proportions for their own
benefit.

"Then speedily other exactions followed.

"The powerful demanded tribute and obtained it by
force; the shrewd, the cunning, the designing, and a host
of others acquired by the use of their respective arts an
unequal and unjust share; and being the lawmakers, established a quasi legal character for their aggressions.

"Mankind soon became divided into two great
classes: Those who by honest toil and effort contributed
to production, and those whose energies were directed
to obtaining possession, or control, of that production.

"The latter class, though numerically the smaller, by
their superior organization, their systematic efforts, and
their control of legislation, so degraded labor that the
tiller of the soil, and the tender of flocks and herds,
were for a long time designated as villeins and serfs, and
sold with the land; and during that time it was considered
disgraceful to be engaged in such occupations.

"As the era of force, however, became somewhat
spent, the laborers, from among whom the bone, brain
and sinew of the land have always been recruited; despite

the indignities, disadvantages and miseries heaped upon and surrounding them, became more numerous and more prosperous.

"Then cunning, intrigue, and statecraft began in earnest the work of despoliation. Designing men fomented division among the laboring classes; they contrived a thousand inventions to maintain superiority; they instituted aristocracy; they established standing armies; they increased taxation, and passed iniquitous laws; they perverted money from its legitimate use as a mere measure of value, and made it interest bearing; they created a system of bonds, notes, bills, and other evidences of indebtedness, also interest bearing, and payable in money. As they grew more daring and skillful, they manipulated this money so that it became scarcer, and the indebtedness more difficult to discharge.

"Thus increasingly the members of the unproductive class of mankind gained control of all property; the drones obtained possession of the hive of industry; and to-day a few nonproducers regulate the media of exchange, and fix the price of all production.

"The nineteenth century was distinguished for its wonderful discoveries and inventions. Great bodies of coal, oil and gas, and immense deposits of valuable metals, were found in the earth's bosom; and better and cheaper methods of utilizing these were devised. The agencies of steam and electricity were developed, and the power of machinery was wonderfully increased.

"These inventions and discoveries furnished means adequate to perform the work, supply the wants, and mitigate the toil of millions of the human race.

"But no such happy results were accomplished. They were seized upon by the controlling class, and employed for their particular advantage. They became in the hands of that class means to make them more autocratic.

A horde of applicants clamored for work, to whom they could dictate terms. They required still longer hours of labor for still smaller pay; and an increased production, whose profits stored up in the vaults of the rich, begat the community of millionaires who now possess the land, while distress and want, like gaunt spectres, stalk amid its shadows.

"Meanwhile this system has been so buttressed by various so-called axioms, that have from time to time been sapiently enunciated by its apostles, and its enormities have been so concealed by the murky atmosphere of countless volumes of jurisprudence enacted to regulate it, that not until lately have the people begun to question the absolute truth of the former, or the infallible wisdom of the latter.

"They have been told that the rights of owners in property are sacred as defined by the courts, and that beyond their judgment no one might inquire how that property was obtained.

"They have been told that our credit, national and individual, must be maintained inviolate, and that debts incurred by either nation, or individual, must be paid in the currency of the land, no matter how much that currency be reduced in quantity, or debt-paying power, and no matter how the debts were contracted.

"They have been told that their share in the advantages arising from the discovery of new material and forces in nature, and the invention of improved machinery, is to be found in reduced prices of goods, despite the fact that their decreased wages leave them scant money with which to make purchases.

"They have been told that the demand for labor, and its supply, regulate its price infallibly by natural law.

"They have been told that capital is stored up labor,

ignoring the fact that it has been largely created by legislation and accumulated interest.

'They have been told that under the present system
humanity has made all its advancement; they have been
told this is the best system human ingenuity can devise.

They have been told these half truths, solemnly and
oracularly; by men who knew their falsity, but were interested in upholding them as truth, and by others who
were themselves deceived and thought them to be true.

"The people have been told these things, and for
long years they have believed, or tried to believe them.

"Mankind, however, have grown in moral and mental perception.

"Sophistries gilded with truth, and false statements
cast in its epigrammatic mould, have no longer the old
acceptance among them. They no longer adopt the conclusions of others unchallenged; they now think for
themselves.

"Two hundred and fifty persons to-day possess almost the entire property of the nation, and dictate its
laws and control its production. In their madness and
their lust of greed they have alienated from themselves
all classes of society, and engendered an instinct of self-
preservation in the whole body politic.

"The people are now ready to act, and, thank God,
patriotic leaders are at hand; men of strong will, stout
hearts, and iron hands, yea, such as stand within this hall
to-day.

"Thanks be to Him, that another of His divinely or-
dained cycles of human progression has begun, in which
the brotherhood of man is to be recognized; and in which
the earth is to be delivered over from the possession of
the few, and used for the benefit of all.

"To-day, fellow Representatives, two great labor

systems, founded on opposite principles confront each other, claiming this broad land,

"The one I have already described. It is hoary with age, overgrown with parasites and surrounded with effete and baneful traditions, rules and regulations.

"Its logic has been individual competition, and the extinction of the weak, the helpless, and the unfortunate.

"Experience proves that a civilization founded upon a violation of moral rights can only be ephemeral in existence, and unsatisfactory in results.

"To understand the other system, the one on which the civilization of my own people is founded, we must return again to the fundamental principle that the earth is the Lord's, given to mankind for their use under certain moral and equitable laws regarding that use, the violation of which ensures the failure of any civilization, as certainly as their observance will secure the perpetuity of another.

"We must return again to the moment when mutual rights in ownership, possession and use, sprang up between different members of the human family; to the moment when man came to the adjustment of these rights with his fellow man.

"In order to understand these rights clearly, without entanglement in the network of intricacies and sophistries which the old system has woven around them, I will resort to a simple illustration.

"Ten men landed on an island in midocean, having with them seeds and necessary implements for the planting and tilling of the earth. One was hopelessly a cripple, one was old and feeble and unable to work, the rest varied in degrees of strength. The island contained one hundred acres of arable land, and the able-bodied men each cultivated a portion of this soil; some with abundant return, others with scanty success, and two with none at all.

"What, then, were their moral rights in the distribution of the production? What was the measure to be used? Was it success in their respective fields of labor? Was it even the individual amount of that labor?

"I trow not. I believe that in the minds of intelligent and unprejudiced judges it would be considered that all, the successful and the unsuccessful, the cripple and the old and feeble, should share equally.

"I will go a step further and suppose that one man was morose and refused to work. Should he then be allowed to starve?

"Again I trow not. (He should have, not an equal share, but sufficient to sustain life, and by this difference and by the example and the moral force of the others should be compelled to be industrious.)

"I desire thus to illustrate the fundamental principles violated in the very beginning of the old system, and upon which the new rests.

"They may be thus expressed: (that all exerting their capabilities for production, with those incapable, must share equally in the result, and that those able but willfully refusing to exert their capabilities must be compelled to do so by such means as may be found most advisable, but must be supported in life.

{"These are the principles for which the civilized world, crowded to-day like the supposed island, hungers. These are the principles which recognize the right of any individual to demand of society a place to work according to his ability, and a share of the joint production equal to any other. These are the principles which insist upon the right of the helpless and feeble also to an equal share in that production; the principles which acknowledge the duty of society to preserve the idle from starvation and to enforce industrious habits upon them.)

"These principles must be expounded intelligently, carried into practice carefully and guarded by such regulations as are necessary to prevent them from being perverted by designing and cunning men. They must be extended wisely, lest the new system founded upon them be shipwrecked by collision with the debris and derelicts of the old.

"These principles of equality are recognized in my own land as extending into the mental, moral and spiritual worlds, as far as opportunity is concerned; the results depending on unseen and hidden forces, being individual and often not fully known.

"To ensure the continuation of this equality, private ownership must cease, and society, or the state, must hold all property in trust for the people. Debt and its evidences, interest, individual accumulation by descent, grant, purchase, or in any other way must cease, and all the machinery of the old system concerning it must be abandoned.

"Society, or the State, must control labor and production, and unite its citizens in a common effort to obtain the best possible livelihood for all, and to furnish equal opportunities for higher improvement.

"The great storehouses of Nature, her mighty energies, and the wondrous capabilities of machinery, must be used to full advantage, but to lessen the toil of the masses, not to increase and perpetuate it.

It must be understood that the happiness and the growth of mankind toward the full stature of manhood, not mere material riches; that mental, moral and spiritual advancement, not mere sensual pleasures, are to be the worthy objects of the ambition of the future.) Such is the high ideal of the new system, such are the principles upon which it is based.

"Certain objections have been made to it, many of which are too trivial for notice, and all of which come with poor grace from the advocates of the old system fraught with so many and such glaring wrongs. A few of the more plausible of these I will, however, briefly notice.

"It is alleged that in the new system enormous responsibility is cast upon the government in ordering and regulating labor, and distributing its proceeds.

"I answer that the responsibility of doing this always has devolved upon, and to a certain extent been accepted by government, and that under the old system it has been most imperfectly performed. Under that system government delegates this duty to individuals, and consumes its time and wastes its energies in making, remaking and amending laws to control them in its performance, and in defining the transgressions thereof, while the injured suffer, or die. Instead of employing these individuals as its agents to accomplish this work it allows them to do it for themselves, surrounded by temptations, and inanely strives to prescribe punishment sufficient to prevent the yielding to them. In plain words, Gentlemen, government under the old system, by machinery and means as illogical, cumbrous and unfitted for the purpose as could be imagined, attempts to do the very work which it is alleged it could not perform untrammeled.

"Ah! Gentlemen of this House, a decade hence, you and I, if here, will under the new system perform our work in a very different spirit and in a very different manner from that of to-day. Instead of being occupied mainly in providing for the protection of property and the rights of its individual owners, we shall be busy in estimating the production necessary for the maintenance of the people, and in determining where the various items composing it can best be grown, or manufactured, and in issuing the proper orders therefor.

"Instead of spending our time in defining a long list of criminal offenses, we shall, when the love of money, the great temptation to crime, is removed, be employed in perfecting the means for distributing this production equally, and in devising ways for that improvement of the masses socially, morally and mentally, made possible by the shortening of their hours of toil for material things. And instead of being ourselves engrossed in political schemes, embarrassed by the solicitation of corporations, lobbied by interested parties, and tempted by a thousand allurements, nearly all presented by the Money Power, we shall be aided by the counsels of the wisest of the land; we shall be actuated by true patriotism and love of humanity, and be able to perform our duties independently, and as the best interests of the nation demand.

"God grant, that in the future the members of this House may be delivered from the snares, intrigues, and pitfalls that have so long beset them, and may be true to themselves, true to the interests of the people, and true to the principles which conserve them.\

"It has been alleged that under the new system a uniform and monotonous level of human action will occur, caused by the removal of the great incentive to enterprise, the love of reward and hope of accumulation. I have stated the objection in the form in which it is generally put forward and which is as usual deceptive and erroneous. It is so because the only incentive to action, removed by the new system, is not the love of reward, but the love of material possessions in excess of the material possessions of others.

"Few will have the hardihood to assert that this latter motive is worthy. Who will deny that the love of riches is miserly, or that the procuring of honor, or preferment by their use is other than a mere subornation, to be punished by the State and frowned upon by every good citizen?

"The real object of the masses of mankind in striving for accumulation is to secure that certainty of provision for themselves and families which the possession of money, or property, assumes to give.

"Under the new system the first mentioned motive is destroyed, and the latter is attained with more certainty, and by juster means. Under its operation the performance of duty is the source of honor and preferment, and the latter cannot be bought and sold. Under that system all the higher ambitions, love of country, love of humanity, love of approbation, love of good conscience, are made incentives to the proper performance of duty.

"With the stimulation of these high motives for exertion no dead plane of uniformity, no listless idleness, are possible, but like a pure elixir of life, these motives will cause the blood of the body politic to circulate more rapidly, and stir all its members to renewed activity.

"It has been alleged that under the new system of equal material compensation, and of directed labor, mankind will finally become dependent, nerveless workers.

"I have no such fear. Under that system, if for some years labor is directed will it be the less efficient?

"The manner in which it is now performed under the old system negatives such assumption.

"Will it be less forceful, less energetic, if directed for

the common weal, than if by and for the benefit of a few men as at present?

"The allegation shows but little knowledge of the character and wants of humanity.

"In fact, mankind love employment, if it be made honorable and pleasant, if it be intelligently directed and be not excessive.

'Has any one the right to assume that service, probably of a much higher character than that rendered at present, will not be voluntarily continued under the new system long after the years of compulsory labor have ceased?

"Are material wants the only wants? Are mankind always to be mere drudges? Is there to be no time for intellectual, moral and spiritual education among the masses? Has any one ground for the assumption that if the time and opportunity are given, these higher faculties will not be correspondingly developed?

"Aristotle, Euclid, Galileo, Newton, Shakspeare, Franklin, Edison, Lincoln, all sprang from the common people, out of the fogs and cloud banks of the old system, and their worthy successors will come from the same source under the bright sunlight of the new.

"It is useless to pursue these objections further; they have no foundation.

"Fellow members of this House, I do not for a moment imagine that this new system can attain full fruition at once.

"It must have time to mature; thoughtful men must regulate the methods of its progression; kind hands must tend it; wisdom and experience must decide upon many questions of fitness and expediency.

"Its fundamental principles, however, must remain unchanged. In the land wherein I dwell, ten million freemen live in peace, plenty and security under its protection.

"They have redeemed that land from primitive wildness and made it to blossom as the rose.

"In the beginning, however, they were obliged to expel certain unworthy members, and cunning and crafty men are now endeavoring by taking advantage of that action to destroy the very foundation of the civilization of my land.

"This cannot be done; I repeat it—this cannot be done. A million freemen on the plains and among the mountains of that land say that this cannot be done, and other millions in your own states join them in the fiat.

"These two system must be fairly judged upon their merits. Constitutional amendment, and legislative enactment must provide legal ways by which the people of this Union, or any portion of it, may adopt the new system if they choose.

"The nature of these provisions remains yet undetermined, and this affords field for the display of true statesmanship among us.

"God grant us wisdom to devise these means, patriotism to adopt them, and high prudence to carry them into effect. /

"The mutterings of selfish ambition and the threats of the partisans of the Money Power are heard distinctly throughout the land. I am told that he who temporarily controls the government of this nation, regards the point in issue as simply the collection of a debt. I am told that the army is massed near the borders of the land in which I dwell, and the navy yards on the Mississippi are busy. What means this display of force? Does he who commands it think for a moment that the men who redeemed that land, that the men who love it, that the men who would die for it, will permit its invasion?

"Already to meet the exigencies threatened by this action the rich products of that land are withheld from the market, and the people of other states suffer. Already the treasure of that land is withdrawn for a similar purpose, and the autocrat, Gold, is in mourning.

"When the flimsy mask that veils the designs of the Money Power is rended asunder, what will then be disclosed? I prophesy that it will be some scheme for the perpetuation of that power by defrauding the people of choice. It may be invasion with the intent to overthrow and destroy the new system. If so, the attempt will be futile. It may be that the eyes of disunion will at last flash out from under the mask. If so, the tramp of a million men will at once be heard in the land where I dwell, marching to join the millions of the other states to close those eyes forever in the sleep of death.

"This battle will be fought out in this Union. It will be fought out fairly. It will be fought upon the merits of the two systems, the people themselves being the judges.

"I have no doubt of the result. I have no doubt that the new cycle will move forward no matter who strive to obstruct it—

> "The new age stands as yet,
>   Half built against the sky,
> Open to every threat
>   Of storms that clamor by;
> Scaffolding veils the walls,
> And dim dust floats and falls,
> But moving to and fro,
>   Their task the builders ply."

"Fellow members of this House, upon our action rests largely the manner of the termination of this controversy.

"I have indicated the means necessary to discharge our responsibility aright. They are not found in threats and warlike demonstrations, but in recognition of the rights of the people, and honest preparation for their conservation.

"If the present be a time to turn deaf ears to the groans of the masses; if it be a moment to prepare stronger shackles for them, then indeed your countenance may be given to the measures already taken; but if it be a time for the breaking of fetters, for the unloosing of the prisoner, for the ransoming of the people, then you must act in opposition to them. God give to this people and to you and to me, also, wisdom to see the right, and strength, and resolution to do the right."

This speech was listened to with great attention by the Representatives and the audience. At its conclusion the House adjourned for the day, and Philip Oram, hastening from the hall, was at once surrounded by a large number of the laboring men who had filled it, and who were desirous of taking him by the hand.

I watched them with interest, for I saw that these men were deeply moved. Nearly every one of them uttered some ejaculation of praise, or thanks, sometimes to the speaker, sometimes to God.

I saw members of the House watching the scene and evidently considering its meaning.

One idea seemed to have been impressed upon the audience, that the Nationality was far more determined and unified in resistance than had been supposed.

In the daily press, and among the leading politicians, and the citizens of Washington, the speech met with but scant approval, and was generally spoken of as dangerous and revolutionary in its tendencies.

Various measures were suggested to meet the dilemma. Some considered that the standing army should be very largely increased, and that the bill for that purpose now before congress should be passed at once; others thought that laws prohibiting revolutionary utterances and publications should be enacted.

In none of these remedies, however, could I see any hope of relief for the distressed people.

CHAPTER XXVI.

The 12th of November I left Washington to return to Neuropolis, and on the evening of the 13th reached Cincinnati, a city situated on the Ohio River, and containing several hundred thousand inhabitants.

Here an encampment of twenty-five thousand United States troops, infantry and cavalry, ready for marching orders, showed the intentions of the government. Six gunboats were also anchored in the Ohio River. The arrival of these troops and vessels within the last twenty days had caused much excitement among the people, and made them realize the possibility of war.

Public sentiment here was much divided; the richer classes endorsing the President's course, and many of the less wealthy openly protesting against it. Recruiting for the army was going forward rapidly, as many thousands of persons were out of employment.

On the 15th I reached St. Louis, a great city in the state of Missouri. An encampment containing thirty thousand United States troops occupied the eastern bank of the Mississippi River, nearly opposite to it. It had been originally intended that these troops should pitch their tents within the state of Missouri, just outside St. Louis, but upon the remonstrance of both municipal and state authorities they had been halted on the spot where they now were. Eight gunboats lay in the river just below the city.

I discovered among the richer classes in St. Louis a

feeling quite different from that in places farther east. The precipitate action of the government was very generally condemned; the presence of the troops and the gunboats was resented as a menace, and the people generally regarded the Nationality in a very friendly way, and were what the government authorities would have called revolutionary in feeling. The city was quiet and orderly, and less suffering existed and fewer persons were out of employment than in any other I had visited. Many of its most intelligent public men were in favor of joining the Nationality.

On the evening of the 18th of November I left St. Louis and proceeded by rail toward Neuropolis, and, crossing the boundary line of Nebraska on the morning of the 19th was once more in the territory of the Nationality, not far from the disputed townships.

I observed that the personnel of the passengers was carefully scrutinized, though without ostentation, by certain officials who passed through the train.

As we went onward I was more than ever charmed by the thrift, industry, contentment and happiness evident throughout the land. About sixty miles inland from the Missouri a city of white tents suddenly broke upon my vision. Around it stretched fields and villages and all the insignia of peace and plenty, and to me its presence seemed incongruous, and showed plainly how easily this scene of quiet and content could be transformed into one of strife and carnage.

I quitted the train here and waited upon the officers commanding the troops, presenting credentials furnished me by the authorities at Neuropolis, and learned that this encampment of forty thousand men and a smaller one on the Missouri, near the head of the great canal, had been made very shortly after my departure from the Nationality. I spent several hours at this place, and found that those thus suddenly called from their usual avocations had already attained much proficiency in military drill and movement. The officers informed me that the able-bodied population throughout the Nationality were busily engaged in similar preparation with a zeal and unanimity that left no doubt of their patriotism.

I resumed my journey in the evening, and when I awoke on the morning of the 20th we were nearing the city of Neuropolis. The great dome of the Administration Building could be already seen, lifting its white, shadowy form into the morning sunlight. Farther away in the dim distance the solemn mountains tossed their everlasting billows skyward, the great Continental range in the center, white with snow fields presaging the advent of winter. Trains were speeding in and out, and all the adjuncts of the city became constantly more numerous.

My thoughts involuntarily turned from the stern topics of the times, with which for the last few weeks they had been almost constantly engaged, to the lovely view around me and the picture of prosperity and security here presented. In all this land there was no man, woman, or child without means of livelihood and a comfortable home.

Sheltered amid groves of trees, whose fading glories proclaimed the presence of the autumn, were numberless villages, around which spread wide acres of productive lands, owned by the community and cultivated for the good of all.

In these homes there might be sickness and death, but there was no want of material comforts; there might be sorrowful partings, but there was no apprehension of future hardships and deprivations to loved ones. In those fields and their products, in those groves and their shade, all had an equal proprietorship. No great magnate, but the people themselves owned them. The majesty of this thought engrossed me; the possibilities of this system, the impossibility of its overthrow, the wonderful patriotism it evolved, the camps I had seen, the earnest men I had talked with, all filled my mind, and to compare these results with those of the old system seemed like pitting the work of intelligent manhood against the incomplete attempts of children, or the idle efforts of insanity.

We were nearing the city, and as I looked once more toward the great dome which surmounted its proud Administration Building my eye caught the stern figure of John Harvey on its summit, plainly discernible, in black coat and white nether garments, resting upon the naked sword, set point downward before him, gazing far out to the eastward.

With a feeling of self-condemnation I thought of how ready I had been to malign the character of this man, the originator and founder of this system.

Soon the clear waters of the lake, reflecting with roseate glow the light of the rising sun, recalled the boat ride upon it, and the image of Clothilde, never long apsent from my mind.

I thought of her, beautiful, proud, and reserved, so strangely circumstanced in this land; of her persistent and unexplained refusal of my suit, and yet her constant and apparently unwavering trust in me. I thought of my meeting with her, and my heart bounded with joy in the prospect of seeing her again, and the hope that she might now understand me better and give me a more lover-like greeting.

We reached Neuropolis and my hand was grasped

warmly by Councilor Beyresen, who had come to meet me. We proceeded at once to his house, where he said all were expecting me.

I was cordially received by Mrs. Beyresen and her younger daughter, and a few minutes later Clothilde came into the room. She was very earnest in her manner, and though less demonstrative than I could have wished, was evidently glad to see me.

I remained for several hours, and gave them as full an account as I could of the impressions I had received while abroad.

I was told that the Parliament was in session, and had some time previous called a meeting of all the labor directors of the Nationality, which would convene at Neuropolis on the morrow.

About 10 o'clock of the morning of the 21st I met with a committee of the Parliament, and communicated to them the knowledge I had gained abroad in regard to the condition of the people of the other states, and their feeling toward the Nationality.

It was evident the gravity of the situation was fully understood by the committee, and I learned that the meeting of the labor directors was called to complete the organization of their forces, and to ensure perfect harmony, and rapid and effective movement and action in case of any emergency. In the afternoon their first session was held in the Administration Building, and nearly eight thousand of them were in attendance, and it was expected that by the morrow this number would be increased to fully ten thousand.

The next morning, while passing down one of the boulevards, I met Clothilde Beyresen going to a photographer's, and I accompanied her. She desired to find a picture of a beautiful child face, out of the ordinary type, to serve as a model for a painting, but was unable to procure one that pleased her.

"Possibly," said I, "I can furnish what you wish. I have the photograph of a little girl about six years of age which I think will suit you. If you will permit me I will send it to you, or if you can wait till evening I will bring it."

"I can wait," she replied, "and shall be very much pleased to see you."

So that evening I took my photograph and gave it to her. Clothilde looked at it long and intently. Finally she said: "Mr. Herbert, this is an unusual picture; the face and dress are peculiar, and evidently foreign; it interests me very much, and I am sure has a history."

"Yes," I replied, "it is a Spanish face, and its original was one of the sweetest, most attractive little persons that I ever met."

"Do you remember her so well?" she inquired, and then, looking at the back of the photograph, she exclaimed: "Why, Mr. Maxwell, this picture is eighteen years old!"

"I do remember her," I answered. "I remember the little girl distinctly, and I think very few who ever saw her would forget her; I am sure I never shall. The picture does not do her justice. She was far more beautiful and attractive than you could imagine from it."

"You interest me, Mr. Maxwell," she said. "You have kept the picture so long and are so enthusiastic over it. Who was the child, may I ask?"

"I will try and tell you," I said, "even at the risk of appearing somewhat ridiculous. That little girl was my first sweetheart. She was a little Spanish maiden of the name of Stephanie, the Princess Stephanie, for she was connected some way, I have forgotten how, for I was only a boy of twelve, with the royal family of Spain. She stayed with my mother for some weeks, and she was playmate and sweetheart to me in my boyish fancy."

"You seem, Mr. Maxwell, to have been unusually true to her memory; you have preserved her picture for so many years."   .   .

'Yes," I replied, "and I must confess I do not like— I would not talk about her to a stranger—for, child as she was, she took a very strong hold on my imagination."

"Did you never see her again—after she grew up?"

"No, Miss Clothilde, I never did. I have often wondered whether she was alive yet and what manner of person she became. I assure you she was very remarkable, but I left home at an early age, and I don't knew whether my little friend lived or died."

"Have you ever tried to find out?" she inquired, I thought a little mischievously.

"Pray be merciful when I have been so frank in confession," I replied. "I have tried many times."

"And you cannot find her, Mr. Maxwell? Well, I advise your lordship to keep on trying, and very likely success will eventually crown your efforts. Meanwhile, if you will let me have your treasure of a picture, I will promise you to take good care of it."

Events were now fast crowding upon each other. On the 23d of November the Parliament passed a resolution inviting the governors of the several states of the Union to appoint commissioners to visit the Nationality, to the intent that by personal inspection of its labor system, and the condition of the people living for the last twenty years under it, they might be able to judge of its merits, and be satisfied of the republican character of its government, and the loyalty of its officers and people.

The resolution assured the governors that every fa-

cility would be granted the commissioners for making
this inquiry, and they were earnestly requested, in view
of the condition of affairs in the United States, to take as
speedy action in the matter as possible.

The legislature of the states of Texas, Missouri, Arkansas, and Oklahoma were now in session and were
earnestly discussing the question of joining the Nationality, and a majority of them seemed in favor of doing so.

It cannot be doubted that the Money Power, fully
realizing that two systems of labor and distribution so
diverse could not long exist together, and that their own
must inevitably soon fall to pieces unless a vital blow was
given to the other, had determined to prevent such a
union at all hazards, and was largely responsible for the
warlike attitude and precipitancy of the general government.

On the 23d of November, 1935, the labor directors
having concluded their deliberations, adjourned. On
the evening of that day I called upon Clothilde and was
received joyfully.

"I was wishing you would come," she said. "I have
been shut up all day and I wanted some one to talk with,
or, better, some one to walk with."

In five minutes we were on our way. The evening
was pleasant, and it was just dusk.

"I have been out so little of late," she continued,
"that it is a pleasure to feel the evening air. Besides, I
have many questions to ask you about your eastern trip."

"I will answer all your questions, Clothilde," I replied, "but when you get through I have just one to ask
you to-night. Will you answer it?"

"I do not know what it is, Mr. Maxwell," she replied evasively.

"No, I suppose not," I said. "Let us sit down here

in this little park a few moments. There, now, we can rest. Do you remember the night of our boat ride, Clothilde? Do you not remember that I had permission to ask you a question again?"

"Mr. Maxwell!" she exclaimed quickly, "you said just now you would answer all my questions, and ask me none till I get through."

"Well," I answered, "I have no objections, but I want you to promise me to answer mine in exact accordance with the truth, when I do ask it."

"There is to be but one?" she replied inquiringly.

"There may be as many as two," I said.

"No!" she exclaimed, "there ought to be but one. I will answer one with the exactness you desire, but you must promise to first answer mine truthfully."

"Of course, I will," I replied, "but how many?"

"Well," she continued, "I shall want more than you, because I do not understand putting my questions as directly as you, but I think three will do me."

"Very well," I replied, "I will answer three."

"Another thing, you will promise not to be offended if I am not fully satisfied with the correctness of your replies, and tell you so plainly?"

"I cannot conceive of my being offended," I answered.

"But you will promise?"

"I will promise at least not to show any such feeling."

"Very well, then," she continued, "I have been looking at the picture you gave me, and thinking over what you told me in regard to it. You did not imagine I could forget it, did you?"

"No, I did not suppose you or anyone else could forget what I said so shortly before," I replied. "I have now answered the first of your questions, Clothilde," I added.

"Oh!" she exclaimed, "I did not intend that for a question. However, let it go. I have your promise to answer two more, and I think they will be enough for my purpose. Mr. Maxwell," she continued, looking at me very seriously, "you told me that the girl represented in that picture was very remarkable, and made a strong impression on your imagination. Was that impression so strong as to continue with you after the age of maturity; I mean after the age of twenty-one?"

The question was so unexpected, and put so directly, that I was confused and hesitated. But my interlocutor never wavered, nor removed her sparkling eyes from their straightforward look into my face.

"Answer, yes or no, please," she said in a calm, firm voice.

"Yes, it did," I replied, "but——"

"That will do," she interrupted; "now for my other question. Have you, Mr. Maxwell, ever again met this girl?"

"No," I declared promptly, "I have not."

"Mr. Maxwell," she said in an uncertain manner, "I suppose you consider you have answered my questions."

"And satisfactorily, I hope," I returned.

"No," she said quietly, "I do not believe you answered the last question truthfully. In fact, I am well assured, and believe that you have met this person later."

"I know I have not," I said positively. "I have never seen her nor spoken to her since the time of which I have told you."

"You must show no annoyance, Mr. Maxwell.

Please do not pursue the subject further. I am ready now to answer your question."

"I do not think I shall ask my question just now, Clothilde. I may ask it any time to-night, I believe."

"And I will answer it any time to-night," she said gravely.

We sat a few moments in silence.

"Let us walk on up the boulevard," she said.

We rose, she took my arm, and we resumed our way. She seemed much affected, and as for me I cannot describe my feelings. I was determined, however, to show no annoyance. We reached the Administration Square.

"Do you remember when we were here before?" she asked.

"Yes," I answered, "the night we sat on the portico of the University Building. Shall we go up there now?"

"No," she said, "do not let us go there to-night."

"Where shall we go?" I asked.

"Let us go home," she answered.

So we turned, and began to retrace our steps. She shivered.

"You are cold," I said.

"No," she returned, "it was only an involuntary movement; I am warm enough."

I caught her hand. It was really quite warm. We reached the house.

"Won't you come in?" she said.

"I will, Clothilde," I replied, "and I will ask my question," and I followed her in. "I will write it, and you may keep it, no matter how you answer." I picked up a sheet of note paper, and wrote: "Will you promise to be my wife?"—signed my name to it, and gave it to her.

She was quite pale, but she read it, and then, seating

herself, after a moment wrote her answer on the paper and, folding it up, brought it to me.

"I have replied to your question in writing also, and give up the paper to you so that you may do with it what you choose. Please do not read it now."

I arose to go, and she came with me to the door.

"I do not know what is in your note, nor what is in your heart, Clothilde, but I know what is in mine, and there is nothing to reproach myself with, and nothing but love for you."

Some distance up the street, by the aid of an electric light, I read what she had written, which ran thus: "I cannot, until you either find that girl or admit your mistake in answering my second question. You ought to know me better.—Clothilde."

I returned to my room, but sleep did not visit my couch for long hours. I could not understand Clothilde's answer to my question. At first I feared that I had been maligned, but the absurdity of the thought was manifest; no one was aware of an unusual interest between Clothilde and myself, and, besides, I thought I knew her well enough to be assured that any defamer of my character would be summarily rebuked. Again I thought it a mere caprice, but her earnest and agitated manner showed that she had a genuine motive. Her implication of untruthfulness was so extraordinary and so positive, that though aware that it was groundless, yet I felt that she believed it.

The hopelessness of undeceiving her was apparent, and so thinking the matter over, it grew more and more perplexing as I dwelt upon it, but finally I fell asleep.

CHAPTER XXVII.

I awoke early the following morning, and when I went out on the street I saw groups of men conversing earnestly, a thing unusual at that hour. After reaching the restaurant I discovered the cause. The President had issued his call upon the various state executives, and the country generally, for troops to assist the regular army in enforcing the laws, and the mandates of the courts, in the state of Nebraska.

As soon as I could I read the call, which, with the comments of leading public men, was published in the morning journals.

It was no half-way measure. It was an arraignment of the leaders of the Nationality as law breakers, and aiders and abettors of the insurrection. It insisted that the people in the states composing that body were deluded, and asserted that law and order must be maintained. It admitted that the ordinary force of the government was inadequate for this purpose, and ended by calling for five hundred thousand men of the National Guard, a certain number to be furnished within thirty days from each state, and also for volunteers.

Its publication had evidently been determined upon some time previous, for arrangements had been made for opening recruiting stations in certain large cities that very morning, and the locations of camps of preliminary instruction and organization were designated.

The effect in Neuropolis was very remarkable. In

315

the early morning, placards were posted giving information that the labor directors were called together again at
10 o'clock, and also that meetings of the citizens would be
held in various places, and men discussed the situation
gravely and solemnly, at their homes, and upon the
streets.

As the day wore on, and telegraphic announcements
were made on the bulletin boards that recruiting was
going on actively in various cities; that certain officers of
the army had been put in charge of certain camps; and
that the governors of some of the Eastern states had assured the President of their support, the temper of the
people changed from that of quiet, reflective solemnity
to patriotic manifestations and determination.

Later in the day the excitement became greater and
numbers of men filled the streets, arm in arm, on their
way to the various places where they expected to be addressed by certain of their leaders. There was, however,
no boisterousness, no loud noises, and, of course, no
drunkenness.

I attended several of these meetings and was impressed with the wisdom of the speakers, who, while ad-
mitting that the action of the President meant speedy
warfare, yet advised moderation, and assured the citizens
that ample preparation had been made for any present
emergency, and that further provision would follow to
meet any that might thereafter arise.

The feeling, though subdued, was, I could see, intense and universal and likely, as soon as the extreme
gravity and solemnity of the occasion wore a little away,
to result in an outbreak of patriotic feeling seldom witnessed.

The time had fallen on a Sunday, and services were
held in all the churches of the city, at which special men-

tion of the President's call, its character and conse-
squences, had been made; and a deep religious, patriotic
feeling had been evoked. Ministers had spoken at the
public meetings after their own services, and exhorted to
patience, moderation, firmness, and readiness. This was
the temper of the leaders and the people at the close of
the day.

In the meantime, in his room in another part of the
city, an obscure poet, fired by the occasion and permeated
by the intense feeling around him, was preparing a song,
which, with the music written by himself, was destined
to be a potent factor in the struggle at hand.

About midnight, thousands of printed copies of this
song were distributed among the labor directors, still assembled in deliberative session, and so readily did it express the prevailing sentiment among them that, for over
an hour before final adjournment, its words and notes
sung by these men filled the great hall they occupied.

I had not seen Clothilde, but on my return to my
rooms at night found a note awaiting me which had been
brought late by a messenger. It read as follows:

"I have not seen nor heard from you all this exciting
day, which is not to be wondered at, for you have had
doubtless many things to engage your attention; but if
you can find time to call to-morrow I shall be very glad.
There is nothing special, only in times such as these one
wishes to see friends oftener than at others.—Clothilde."

On the following morning, the 25th, I was astir
early. In the Eastern papers I read confirmation of the
news of the preceding day, and fresh assurance that the
President would be supported. In those of Neuropolis
it was announced that the business sessions of the labor
directors having ended, they would return to their homes,
but that before so doing another meeting would be held

at 2 p. m. at their hall in the Administration Building, and that some public demonstration would be made at that place.

Thinking that Clothilde would probably desire to see this, I sent a note informing her that I would call for her at 1 o'clock. I found her anxious, but animated by patriotic resolution, and we were soon on our way toward the Administration Square.

The streets about it were kept clear, but the throng was already so great on the sidewalks and boulevards leading to it that it was with much difficulty we could obtain standing room.

"I see no other way than to get to our old place on the porch of the University Building," I said.

So we were soon comfortably settled on the high porch, which no one had as yet discovered as a point of observation.

The great eastern entrance to the Administration Building was before us. Into it hundreds of labor directors were passing. They wore cocked hats and white sashes, which they seemed to have adopted as insignia for the occasion. These men were from all parts of the Nationality; they were the representative men of their localities. They had direct charge of the labor element of their communities; they were the captains of hundreds of other men, engaged usually in peaceful labor. In a day or so they would all be at their homes and with their commands, engaged in what? No one could now tell, but it was evident there was no need here for calls for volunteers, and but little for camps of instruction.

I turned to my companion, who seemed disturbed and wearied.

"Do you know what all this means?" I said, gently.

"I do," she answered. "I can see it all. I have seen it all."

"You have never seen war!" I exclaimed.

"Yes, I have," said she.

"Impossible!" I cried. "Where have you seen it?"

"In my dreams," she answered smiling sadly.

I said no more, for I saw she was thinking of other things, or possibly engaged then in dreaming.

Time wore on and the crowd below still increased.

Thousands of men now filled all the avenues and approaches to the Administration Square and the sidewalks round it, and the women occupied the houses and public buildings wherever a view could be obtained, every one curious, and anxious, and expectant.

A large platform, capable of holding several hundred persons, had been erected a little higher than the street on the eastern side of the Administration Square next us, and this was filled with seats as yet unoccupied.

It was now nearly 2 p. m., and the eyes of all were directed toward the entrance to the Administration Building. At a quarter before the hour a body of men, numbering about two hundred, issued from it, and walked arm in arm down to this platform and took seats upon it, facing the street. They were the members of the parliament of the Nationality, its chief dignitaries and officials. They were preceded by General Canley, who was dressed in the full uniform of a general of the United States, except that he, too, wore a white sash. There were a number of other officers in uniform, who also wore white sashes, among whom I recognized General Knox, St. John, and others. These gentlemen all preserved a decorous silence. There was no conversation and no movement, after seats were taken, and a deep solemnity at once fell upon the audience.

The great clock in the building now struck the hour of two, and immediately the body of labor directors within began to move out from the entrance. They bore white wands in their hands, and marched in ranks of fifties with the precision of military order. The column moved diagonally down the broad stone walk leading to the southeast corner of the Square; then, turning to the left, marched northward along the eastern boulevard, about two hundred feet past the center of the Square, and, facing toward the west and the Administration Building, halted in close order.

In a few moments the space in front of the platform for four hundred feet in length was occupied by fully ten thousand labor directors. They preserved perfect silence, and strict military attitude and attention.

As soon as they had taken their position the exercises began. The Right Reverend Matthew Kirkwood, one of the most eminent clergymen of the day, besought the Divine guidance and protection in these troublous times, in a prayer of great fervor and feeling, in which the entire audience, numbering now probably three hundred thousand persons, with bowed heads joined.

In the adjacent houses and public buildings, I was afterward informed, many knelt in supplication, so powerful was the feeling. We had risen to our feet and were standing together, and as the prayer began Clothilde's hand met mine, and with clasped hands we remained to the conclusion of the exercises.

The tall figure of General Canly moved to the front of the platform.

He said a few words inaudible to us, and then raised his right hand.

Immediately from the ranks before him ten thousand hands were raised toward heaven, and a solemn oath of fealty to the principles of the Nationality, to its system of labor, to its service to the death, and to obedience to its officers, was taken by those ten thousand men, themselves leaders of men.

Then ensued a scene which was not in the regular order of exercises, but which for intense feeling exceeded all others I ever witnessed.

A young man broke through the crowd, and sprang upon the platform to the place which General Canly had just quitted. He was hatless, pale, and excited, and was clothed in a black suit which accentuated his wild appearance.

He bore in his hand a white wand which he had snatched from one of the labor directors, and he began at once, beating the time with his improvised baton, to sing in a loud, clear tenor voice the song of which I have before spoken.

Immediately the whole body of the labor directors, most of them trained musicians, joined in by common impulse, and the great volume of sound swelled out over the vast space, thrilling the spectators as nothing else but song can do.

At first all eyes were fixed upon the leader, but the words and air being familiar from the preceding night's practice, he was lost sight of in the increasing excitement, and the directors flourished their white wands above their heads, and kept time to the music with their feet, while their voices in increasing volume rang out in the words and music of

The Hymn of the Nationality.

1. Hail! all hail! An arm-y here we stand, With weapons bright, in strength and might, To con - se - crate this no - ble land, This soil on which we tread, Rich in its pa-triot dead, By pro-cla-ma-tion long and loud, By cannon's peal and clash of steel, To man, to freedom and to God;

By cannon's peal, and clash of steel, To Man, to Freedom and to God.

2.

Hear! O hear! ye blessed Trinity,
These mountains strong, in ranges long,
Meet homes for men both brave and free;
These rivers deep and broad, endued with power from God,
To bless the thirsty land anew;
These plains as vast as ages past,
We dedicate all these to You.

3.

Sound, trumpets, sound! To all on earth proclaim,
That Freedom's laws and mankind's cause,
Till now so oft an idle name,
Shall here find royal home, and quickly overcome
All love of power and selfish pride;
And God's own right, not man's mere might,
Shall be this people's rule and guide.

4.

Call! loud call! the nations to the war;
Let kingdoms shake, and despots quake,
Let all their vassals from afar,
Summoned in cunning haste, men's lives and souls to waste,
Meet in God's own appointed place,
His power to learn, in combat stern,
'Twixt Freemen and the tyrant race.

5.

Smite, sword, smite! and spare not thou to slay;
Let cannon speak, and bullet shriek,
In this the Lord's own chosen day,

Avenge His people's wrong, which they have suffered long,
And let the oppressor's hireling band,
Stern foemen meet, and find defeat,
And no more foothold in the land.

6.

Hail! all hail! Sweet Freedom's glorious reign,
The battle past, in peace at last,
We rest beneath her shield again,
An army nobly grand, with might and keen-edged brand,
Quick to do battle at her word,
From powers of sin, the day to win,
For Man, for Freedom and for God.

When the third verse was reached the excitement
grew greater, and became still more intense with the
singing of the remaining ones. Men in the audience
waved their hats and gesticulated wildly, and embraced
each other while tears ran down their checks.

I looked at Clothilde, my attention being drawn to
her by the tightened clasp of her hand. She seemed unconscious of my presence; her eyes were flashing and
her face was glowing; the martial spirit had evidently full
possession of her, as it had indeed of every one in all that
great audience.

The hymn was no sooner finished than it was again
begun, and repeated with still greater effect. As, however, it neared its termination the second time, St. John,
who had from the platform been intently watching the
proceedings, threw himself at the head of the column, and
gave the order to quarter face and to march, and the
whole column was in a moment in motion down the
boulevard, from whence they moved through the city
toward the passenger station, still singing the song which

the action of that day was destined to render immortal.

Two months later it was sung in every town, village, and hamlet of the Nationality, and soon it had reached every portion of the United States, and proved its power by rousing like enthusiasm everywhere.

The young man who had led in the singing of it was unknown, and though inquired after could never be positively identified. It was supposed by some that he was the author of the song, and by others that he was simply a person acquainted with the words and the music, who in a moment of patriotic excitement had performed an act which might have immortalized him had his name been discovered.

From this scene Clothilde and I wended our way back slowly and almost silently to her father's house. In fact, much conversation or rapid movement was out of the question that day. The main streets were crowded, and groups of men stood discussing events, or still listening to the distant voices of the labor directors, who were yet moving in a circuitous route toward the railway station.

At last, however, we reached the house, and Clothilde asked me in. She was evidently much agitated, and excused herself from the room, and when she returned some little time after I could see traces of tears plainly visible in her dark eyes.

CHAPTER XXVIII.

For a few days succeeding the departure of the labor directors there was constant excitement in Neuropolis, and from the newspaper reports it was evident that this was not confined to the citizens of the Nationality. Full accounts of the proceedings of the 25th were published in the Eastern papers, and it was obvious that the power and unanimity displayed, and the intensity of the loyalty of the people of the Nationality to their principles had created a deep impression.

The governors of the Pacific coast states, of some of the Southern states, and those of Iowa, Minnesota, and Wisconsin, had already, in accordance with the request of the Parliament of the Nationality, appointed commissioners to visit its territory at an early day. In the Eastern states the feeling was abroad that such an appointment would recognize an organization which had no validity, and the invitation was almost universally disregarded.

Two great military camps, each containing now about one hundred thousand men, were established within the borders of the Nationality, one which I had seen in Nebraska, near the Missouri River, and the other at Neuropolis, on the western bank of the great canal. The smaller one, formerly spoken of, near its head, now contained twenty-five thousand men. In forty-eight hours troops from these camps could be concentrated on any point liable to attack, and at any time after the 30th of

November they could have been quickly and largely re-enforced from other portions of the Nationality. Such was the advantage of its labor and railroad systems, which converted the entire able-bodied population into one great army capable of unparalleled mobilization.

On the great inland rivers the government deemed itself supreme. Besides the gunboats I had seen at Cincinnati and St. Louis, it had fully twenty others on these waters, many of them carrying powerful guns. It had also a large number of vessels of smaller draft in process of construction, designed to ascend the Upper Missouri River and control, or destroy, if necessary, the head gates of the great canal, and compel submission by depriving the Nationality of its principal supply of water.

Shortly after the President's call for troops I had, however, been informed that six gunboats, composed of the white metal, were nearly completed at Bilboa, and would be launched on the Upper Missouri, and be amply able to defend it.

It was now the 8th of December, and I had been twice at Mr. Beyresen's since the final meeting of the labor directors; my other and increasing engagements having prevented me from more frequent calls. On neither of these occasions had I opportunty to speak for any length of time with Clothilde, though I wished to do so, for she was evidently much agitated and disturbed by the approaching troubles.

On the afternoon of that day I received a note from her asking me if I could spend an hour, or so, with her that evening. The note went on to say the next day would answer if more convenient, that she hoped she was not giving me unnecessary trouble, but she wished to see me as soon as possible.

In the evening I presented myself at Mr. Beyresen's,

and found Clothilde waiting for me. She shook hands with me, though in a somewhat embarrassed way, and after seeing me seated, moved about the room, arranging articles I thought a little uselessly and nervously. There was a saddened look in her large hazel eyes that I had noticed frequently of late, and which had caused me some anxiety.

At last she sat down near me and said in a tone of quiet badinage: "I am obliged to you for coming, Mr. Herbert. I wanted to see you, and have a good talk with you. Do you remember I once told you I might some time show you my own particular habitation? I wanted your opinion of it. That was when you were plain Mr. Maxwell, but since you have become a lord I do not know whether to do so or not."

I thought I saw what she desired, and answered: "I should very much like to see your room; I can leave my lordship outside if you wish, Clothilde."

"Indeed I do," she replied, earnestly. "I want only yourself, your best self. Will you come now, Mr. Herbert?" she continued, rising and moving toward a door in the south side of the room.

I followed her along a short hall, through another door, into a large and beautiful apartment. A tiled fireplace, in which glowed a clear fire, occupied the center of one side, above which rose a broad low marble mantel; stained glass windows occupied the space on each side of it, and a superb grand piano stood across part of the west end of the room, a doorway with a heavy silken portiere occupying the remaining space. The walls on the north and east sides, as well as the space above the piano were hung with fine paintings and engravings, the work of the best artists. The tapestries and hangings were of the most delicate shades; the floor was covered with Turkish and Persian rugs, and an elegant tiger skin was spread before the fire place. Several busts of composers stood on pedestals; a large ivory table exquisitely carved was placed near the center of the room, and smaller ones of rare and costly woods occupied places by walls and in corners. An ottoman was drawn up on one side the fire place, and an easy-chair on the other. A few other chairs superbly carved were scattered about the room, and a full length mirror set in frosted silver occupied a portion of the wall on the east side.

The apartment presented a tout ensemble, unique, delicate, and elegant, that called forth my admiration.

"This," said Clothilde, "is my sitting-room, and I pray, you, sir, be seated."

"Pardon me," I replied, "but I really want to look at the room," and I began to examine the paintings and the various bric-a-brac, etagerie, and other objects scattered about.

I observed two very rare vases of the choicest European manufacture, and many articles of gold and silver, and others ornamented with these metals. In fact, every object showed taste and elegance, without care for cost.

For some time Clothilde followed me, explaining things, but at last she grew impatient and exclaimed: "Won't you take the large arm-chair by the fire, Mr. Maxwell? That is Mr. Beyresen's chair; he is the only other gentleman visitor I have ever admitted here. Now tell me what you think of my room."

She was standing by the corner of the mantel, resting her right elbow upon it, and there was still the same expression of sadness on her face.

"Won't you sit down?" I inquired.

"No," she replied, "if you will excuse me I will stand.

I have been sitting all day. You can talk to me from where you are."

"I have not examined your room and its rare contents as carefully as they merit," I answered. "I could not tell what masters painted the pictures upon its walls, or in what city of Europe those delicate hangings were made; nor from what Oriental mart the rugs on the floors came; but I can say that, in its beauty and its grace and loveliness, the room seems to me a fit dwelling-place for its mistress."

"Mr. Maxwell," she said, starting forward, "I did not bring you here that you might compliment me." She hesitated. "Our conversation has gone wrong," she continued, "though for that I have myself to blame. I asked you here that I might explain, that I might beg a favor of you, and I hardly know how to begin."

She was very earnest, and she had approached nearer to me, in fact was standing beside the arm of my chair, resting her right hand on it and looking down upon me.

"Surely you are not afraid," I replied. "Surely you know, Clothilde, that I would do anything I could for you."

"I believe that," she said, "otherwise I could not ask you. I have hesitated to explain; I thought likely you might find out yourself, but you did not."

"Clothilde!" I cried, "what is there to explain?"

"Mr. Maxwell," she said, "there is no cause for apprehension, not the least, but, please, look at me closely, for in a moment you will know me no longer as Clothilde Beyresen, but by another name."

I looked up in her face astonished, and she returned my gaze in silence for a few seconds, and then in a low, plaintive voice added: "I am John Harvey's daughter."

It was a revelation, a surprise.

"Clothilde!" I rather gasped than spoke.

"Yes, Clothilde," she said in the same plaintive tone. "1 am Clothilde still, but not Clothilde Beyresen; I am Clothilde Harvey."

She paused and we were both silent, I thinking over the past, she of the present.

She spoke again: "Do you know me, Mr. Herbert? Shall I ask my favor of you?"

"Know you!" I cried. "Could I ever forget you by any name? Stay Clothilde, if you would but change your name once more."

A faint color came into her cheek. "By no means," she said. "I am proud of my own name. That was not the favor I had to ask."

"It is the favor that I ask, Clothilde," I said, "that I have been asking, that I shall always ask; that you will grant me some time, dear?"

"Hush!" she said gently, "this is no time to talk in that way. We may be very near friends; we may need each other; we may help each other in the trials which seem about to come; we must not talk of more now. I have a very great favor to ask of you, Mr. Herbert, one that I know a man like you will grant to a girl like me. It may involve you in difficulty; it may be followed by danger, and I have hesitated, my friend, on this account to ask my favor, because I thought of these things, not because I feared refusal. It will be necessary first to tell you more of my father's history before I ask my favor."

I saw that she was very much agitated and I begged her to sit down.

"No," she said, "I would rather stand by you; I want you to stand by me afterward," and her voice was tearful. "I will make the story short; I could not bear to make it long.

"My father, John Harvey, gave me all these things you see around, and many more. He was the noblest, kindest, and tenderest of fathers. He did not die at sea, Mr. Herbert, as is generally supposed. He died here in this city, and I, his daughter, was with him until within a few hours of his death. My father died heartbroken, in the prime of his life, within a year after that awful battle in the English Channel of which you yourself told me . in the other room. He was a proud man; when he returned home he found himself almost an alien. At first the advantage of his act to his own country was acknowledged, but a demand was privately made upon him by his government for two things: the first was for the booty he had taken; you saw a part of it in the treasury vault; I showed it to you, Mr. Herbert, very foolishly, because you had spoken so harshly of my father.

"This booty he would have given to his government, but they asked one thing more, and that my father would not grant. They demanded of him the secret of the fearful explosive with which he wrought such havoc among the English ships. This he would not reveal, and they then branded him as an outlaw, and threatened if he would not yield to take possession of all he had by force. My father was a wise man, and saw the result. He could not treat his own countrymen as he had their enemies; he was too loyal for that, and such a course would have made him indeed an outlaw. He could not let them have his secret; they might use it unwisely; it was the Money Power then, as now, that governed the country. Besides, he had determined that that secret should thereafter be used only to prevent war.

"My father bitterly repented his act in the British Channel. I was then a girl of eighteen, but I was much like him, and he confided in me, and told me all these things. He kept his own counsel and temporized with the government. He quietly removed his treasure from his vessel and brought it here. He brought me here also, and because it was unsafe to be known I was represented as the eldest daughter of Councilor Beyrésen, and have been so considered except by a few who know my history, and they called me princess, a title soon adopted by the rest.

"My father went back to New York with a few men in whom he could rely. He hired a companion vessel and secretly put to sea. Out in the ocean he scuttled the Albatross, entered the other vessel, and returned by way of Corpus Christi to the Nationality. He was a changed, heartbroken man. He was in his own country, but it knew him not; he was among his own people, but unknown to them. I cheered him what I could, but he lived only a year. He made all preparations for his burial, and for the disposition of his property. He gave all that he had, which was many millions, to the Nationality, except his last acquired treasure, and that he left to me, to be kept in my own vault in the treasury, to which I was to have access at any time by day or night. It was to be used at my discretion, for myself if I sorely needed it, or for the Nationality.

"My father was buried in the crypt of the Administration Building, and the secret of his terrible explosive is contained within his tomb, to be exhumed if at any time the life of the Nationality be imperiled by outside enemies.

"Four persons named by my father, and I myself, were present at his burial. My father gave me the key to open the tomb. I am, if living, to choose one of the four to do it. I must give the key to that person there, and after using it he must return it to me. The same five persons who were present at his burial, are, if alive, to be present when the tomb is opened. If any of them die, I, if living, am to choose another, two of the other three agreeing in my choice. If I am gone they fill my place.

"It has been decided that the preservation of the Nationality demands that the secret should be disentombed.

"This is the story, Mr. Herbert. Can you imagine the favor I have to ask of you? One of these four persons is dead, and I have chosen you to take his place and stand by me, and open the tomb, and recover the secret. I wanted you by me, but I hesitated to ask you to connect yourself with this fearful explosive. If you do, I understand it is proposed to appoint you to conduct the experiments necessarily attending it and to have charge of it thereafter."

"Clothilde," I said, "do you doubt my willingness? I would stand by you in any emergency. And if I am afterward to have control of this destructive agent I can direct its use wisely so as to secure peace."

"You cannot imagine," she said, "the service you do me. I think I realize how few would be willing to share this duty with me."

"I will do it most willingly," I said.

"And I thank you for it most earnestly," she replied.

For a few moments there was silence between us. "Then," she continued, "at 10 o'clock on the night of the 11th, you, I and three others, will meet at Mr. Beyresen's room; there we shall receive further instruction. Do not please come to see me again before this is over. I'll bid you good-night now; we have talked a good while and it is very late."

"One word more, Clothilde," I said. "Have you a portrait of your father; one that I could carry home with me?"

She went into the next room and soon returned with an ivory-type, and gave it to me. I looked at it, and at her.

"There is a great resemblance," I said. "You are very like; I have been blind not to have seen it. I thought you resembled some one I had met; your face always seemed strangely familiar; I ought to have known you."

I could see that she was pleased, for her tired expression changed.

"But you did not," she said. "Remember me now, please, as Clothilde Harvey, though I am Clothilde Beyresen in public. I have had to remember you as Lord Dudley really, but as Mr. Herbert Maxwell in public. It has been a strange comedy of errors, and it is not ended; I wish it were. I will go with you to the door, Mr. Herbert, and I thank you again for your great kindness."

I departed, pondering deeply over the story so simply and yet so earnestly told. This was the girl, who as the daughter of John Beyresen, I supposed had lived a quiet and comparatively uneventful life. She had told me nothing of herself, but I knew well now that hers had been a strange and tragical story.

She had stood by the deathbed of her father, one of the most commanding figures of the century; she had seen him die unknown and almost unwept. She had lived under an assumed name in an unaccustomed sphere. She had taken up and performed her new duties, and won for herself the love and respect of all around her. She had in fact been impoverished and orphaned for the good of this people, and yet she had been always loyal to them.

I was astonished at her great-heartedness, her magnanimity, her strength of character. I wondered at her unselfishness, her vivacity, her uniform cheerfulness. And as I reflected on her conduct to me a stranger, I was yet more astonished. Almost at our first acquaintance I had spoken harshly of a father whom she loved most dearly, yet though very angry, she had not discarded me. She seemed to know me thoroughly, and to trust me. She had been very fearless in her conduct, and yet not repellent; and, finally, she had disclosed to me the secrets of the Nationality and her family, and asked me confidently to do that which few persons would have cared to ask of any one except a lifelong friend.

I knew that she had committed no error in her choice. I knew that I would sooner die than reveal one iota of that with which she had trusted me, but how did it happen that this girl, who had so constantly refused to ally herself to me by dearer ties, had revealed such momentous secrets and asked me to perform such duties?

After I arrived at home I examined the picture carefully. It was John Harvey at the age of forty, in his mature and yet younger days, and I could see Clothilde's resemblance to her father in a hundred ways, modified, yet very evident. The night of the ball on the Albatross rushed into my memory, and with it came the image of a girl with whom I had then talked and danced, who gave me a foreign name as her own, and who was full of piquancy, mirth, and wit. She was the same girl to whom the next morning, as she sat by the open porthole, I gave my warning message, which care for her safety had principally incited.

I had not told Clothilde all about this girl. I had indeed been so much attracted by her that I had made many efforts to discover her, almost as many as I had to find my little love of six years old.

A thought flashed upon me; could it be possible that this girl was John Harvey's daughter; was Clothilde herself? I recalled her unguarded statement about the message, and how adroitly she had lulled my suspicions of her knowledge; and I was almost satisfied that she and the young girl were the same. I will find out, thought I, but I, too, will be adroit and strategic. I will have some sort of promise out of this discovery, if possible; at all events I will get at the truth of this matter.

And thus pondering, and by turns pitying my ladylove with a great compassion, and then forming plans to circumvent and surprise her, I fell asleep, and she held chief place in my dreams.

CHAPTER XXIX.

THE TOMB.

Strange changes are often wrought in our feelings and actions by the lapse of time, and influence of unforeseen circumstances.

I had accepted the responsibility of participating in the resurrection of that terrible secret which some years before had proven the destruction of the proud ship on which I held command. But this was no time for hesitation, and I was not one to give a half-hearted allegiance to a cause I deemed just. The government would use the latest improved weapons, and the most powerful explosives known to modern warfare, in dealing with its subjects; that much could be said in palliation of the intended procedure of the Nationality.

I had little knowledge of the manner in which John Harvey's secret was to be recovered, but I was aware from the way Clothilde had spoken that it was an ordeal she dreaded.

At 10 o'clock on the night of the 11th I knocked at the door of Mr. Beyresen's chambers in the Administration Building, and was admitted and shown into an inner room. I found there four persons—John Paul, who had been hastily summoned from Washington for this occasion; Clothilde, and Mr. Beyresen, and to my surprise St. John, whom I should never have suspected of being trusted with so important a secret.

Clothilde was very nervous and evidently only kept her feelings in check by a strong effort of will. She smiled appreciatively at me, as if to thank me, but spoke little. She was dressed in white, which made a striking contrast with the black suits worn by the gentlemen.

A few minutes after I entered, Senator Paul rose and said: "The time passes, and we will proceed at once to the pérformance of the duty imposed upon us. Marshal St. John, will you attend the princess, and follow me? And you, Lord Dudley, and Councilor Beyresen, please walk together, and come after."

We proceeded in the order he had named from Mr. Beyresen's room to the treasury department, and from thence, by the same passage which Clothilde and I had followed, until we reached the outside door of the vault we had visited. This the senator opened in the same manner, and with the same precautions Clothilde had employed, and we stood in the ante-chamber. There were two closed doors in it; the one by which Clothilde and I had formerly entered, and another which Senator Paul now unlocked, disclosing a vault about the length, but somewhat wider than the one I had previously seen.

The senator proceeded, without delay, and in silence, toward a polished granite shaft nearly four feet in height, which stood in the center of the vault. A small box was placed upon it, made of the black metal, and of about the same dimensions as the one I had before vainly attempted to lift.

Senator Paul took his place by the side of the shaft, and we grouped ourselves around it, and he, Clothilde and St. John, each produced a key, which they fitted into corresponding holes on different sides of the box, and on turning them it was unlocked and was easily opened, its top sliding backward in a groove. Within it there were two very flat keys made of the black metal. These Senator Paul took out, the box was then closed, and we departed from the vault in the same order in which we had entered.

We passed under the great arch of the dome to the eastern side of the building, and down a narrow corridor, until Senator Paul stopped before a panel in the marble wall, and after a short search found a small aperture into which he inserted one of the flat keys. This panel, which was made of the white metal, opened inwardly; we all passed through quickly and the door, or panel, was as quickly closed behind us.

We were left for a moment in darkness, but on touching a button, electric lights sprang into glow. We were in a hall, probably twenty feet long and six feet broad, closed in on all sides by stone walls. At its farther end a flight of stone steps descended, and we now proceeded down these toward the foundation of the building. When we had descended twenty-four steps, we reached a square landing, from which the stairway turned at right angles to its former course. When we had gone down twenty-four steps farther, a similar landing was reached and a similar turn repeated, and I soon found that the steps were built around a square of masonry about twenty-four feet in diameter.

The descent was long and fatiguing, but when we had passed down one hundred and twenty of these steps, and were, as I calculated, at least sixty feet below the level at which we had started, the stairway ceased, being barred by what seemed a solid wall of masonry.

After some little search, however, Senator Paul found an aperture into which he inserted the second key, and another door of the white metal opened.

We entered, the door was closed, and we stood in a room about eighteen feet square, furnished with chairs, and a table of white metal near which, on a granite pedestal, like that in the vault above, was a similar box of the black metal. The room was lighted by electricity, but had no visible opening, even the one through which we had entered being now indistinguishable.

We sat down together near the table, Senator Paul close by it, and all rested in silence for a few moments. Then the Senator arose and spoke as follows: "This room was opened last when five years ago we consigned to the tomb the mortal remains of a great man, who lived a noble and useful life, and died misunderstood and wilfully misjudged, but whose memory is held dear in the hearts of his friends, and who will yet be honored by his countrymen as the greatest hero and philanthropist of modern times.

"A few nights before John Harvey died he committed to his daughter, and to four of his nearest friends, who knew his history, certain trusts pertaining to the Nationality he had founded, accompanied with precise directions how to use them if necessity demanded, and bound them by a solemn oath to the performance of these trusts.

"Of the five persons who were then present I see but four here now, and it is well known to us that the fifth one has been recently removed by Almighty God from earth.

"In such a contingency, foreseen as very possible, certain provisions were made by John Harvey for the appointment and qualification of a successor, that the number might be kept complete, and it is now necessary for me to ascertain whether these provisions have thus far been properly complied with. Will you all, therefore, please rise? It becomes my duty, Lord Dudley, to ask you formally whether you are present here by invitation for the purpose of filling the vacancy thus occasioned, and whether you are willing so to do?"

I answered both of these questions affirmatively.

"Then," said Senator Paul, "I must ask these other persons present to state by whose invitation Lord Dudley is here?"

"By mine," said Clothilde in a low voice.

"What others vouch for him?" continued the Senator.

"I do," said Mr. Beyresen. "And I, also," said the Senator, and turned to St. John.

"I know little of Lord Dudley," said the latter, "but I can trust the worthiness of the nominee of John Harvey's daughter, and the endorsement of the others."

"Then," said the Senator, "it now only remains for me, before we proceed further, to administer for the first time to Lord Dudley, better known among us as Mr. Herbert Maxwell, the oath of secrecy and loyalty, which the rest of us will also repeat, as a reminder of former oaths to the same purpose taken.

"Will you all, therefore, join with me as I read from this manual one of the most solemn oaths ever taken by man, pledging ourselves to the utmost secrecy in regard to all that has happened, or may hereafter happen in this room, or at the tomb of John Harvey, or in regard to anything we may have learned, or may hereafter learn touching his death, his will, his sayings, his writings, and the intentions expressed therein, not now generally known to the public, and also to the utmost loyalty to the cause and the principles which he advocated and cherished, made publicly known and practically expressed, in the organization called the Nationality, and to the utmost zeal in the defense and preservation of those principles and that organization, even unto the death. Are you ready so to join me, comrades?"

We all signified our willingness. He then read from

a small manual, we joining him, an oath in character such as he had indicated, and at its conclusion asked heaven to register the vows thus taken.

There was a moment's silence, and then the Senator continued: "A few nights before John Harvey died he gave to us, his friends, full working plans and models of the vessel called the Albatross, and of its armament, from which the same might readily be reconstructed. He also enjoined upon us to sepulchre his body, with solemn ceremonies, in a tomb prepared by him, not to be visited save as directed in the will which he then committed to our care.

"He informed us, on that night, that the secret of the explosive used upon the Albatross was hidden in a portion of his tomb, to be exhumed and used if the Nationality should be threatened by outside enemies and powers with invasion or destruction. He charged us and those succeeding us to destroy this secret after the lapse of thirty years, by certain means which would hereafter be made known to us.

"He left to these five persons and their successors the prerogative of judgment when such emergency had come.

"Some time ago we four remaining thought that it had fully come. But we ask your judgment, also, Mr. Herbert Maxwell, as to whether the danger threatening us at present corresponds with that John Harvey feared."

I answered that my opinion coincided with the others, that such emergency existed.

Then the Senator proceeded: "Some nights before John Harvey died he gave to each of us his friends a key and to his daughter two, three of them to open the black box contained within the vault above, in which box, after his burial, we placed the keys you saw me use in coming

hither. The other three are likewise to be used in opening the box before us, in which, he stated, would be found
some other keys, and full directions how to proceed in
obtaining his dread secret. This box we shall now open."

The Senator, Mr. Beyresen, and Clothilde, then each
produced a key, and unlocked the box in like manner as
they had the one above.

On the bottom of the box reposed a small leather-
covered book, on which lay three keys, two of them similar to those with which the doors above had been unlocked; the other, made of the same material, was somewhat larger and its handle was in shape of a cross. A
small gold chain, attached at each end to the arms of the
cross, formed a loop about six inches in length.

At a gesture from the Senator, Clothilde took the
chain and key, and he the other keys and the small book,
and opening the latter, turned some pages and read solemnly and reverently from it thus:

"The hand of death lies heavy on me. His cold
fingers will soon close my eyes and still my pulses.

"I have given to the Nationality which I have founded, and for which I have a parent's love, all my riches, my
blessing, and my secrets save one only, so direful and so
awful in its character that I had thought to let it die
with me.

"But wherefore, when I see already foes arising,
cunning and powerful, and dangers coming, from which
that secret wisely used could save my people and my land.

"So until this people and this land have time to gather
strength, I will give that also into your custody and
guardianship, my friends, and that of your successors
whoever they may be, charging you solemnly that you
use this secret only for defense in times of gravest peril

from outside foes, and never for offense, or in internal trouble.

"I charge you also that you use it wisely, for procuring peace, and not for domination.

"And I charge you also that on the first day of the year A. D. 1960 you destroy this secret in manner as I have written for your instruction in this book.

"I, John Harvey, charge you now again to do this righteously, and in the spirit of my wishes, as you would answer before God.

"Let my daughter, if she be alive, or her successor, take the key herein contained, suspending it around her wrist by the golden chain. Let him who is your leader take the other keys. The latter are for doors now open, which will close after my obsequies, and must be passed to reach my sepulchre. Approach my tomb between the hours of eleven and midnight. Let no word be spoken after you leave this chamber until you return.

"Pass quickly, three upon the left, and two, my daughter being second, upon the right side of the figure lying on the tomb. Let my daughter, before she leaves this room, appoint some one to pass before her on the right side of the figure, and use the key which she will give him only after all have taken places.

"Let all take places and remain upon the white tiles on the floor, with their faces toward the tomb; the person designated by my daughter on the right of the figure nearest its head, my daughter next him; the others on the other side indifferently.

"When there is perfect silence, and not before, let my daughter give the key to him who stands beside her. Let all remain exactly in their places save him alone. Let him move forward to the figure, and, turning the third button above the right arm easily around, remove it, taking it in his left hand. Let him insert the key into the opening from whence the button was removed, and turn it gently round.

"An aperture will appear below the key, and a paper will be pushed forward. Let him take this paper also in his left hand. Let him reverse the key, withdraw it, put the button back into the opening and turn it round again, step back upon his place, and return the key into my daughter's hand.

"Let those upon the left side pass on out, my daughter follow, and the person with the paper last. Ascend the stairs in silence to this chamber, closing doors behind you. Let the paper there be given unopened to your leader. On the morrow meet, and consider well how you will use the secret, oh, my friends, in whose judgment I so much confide, and when the peril is well past destroy the paper.

"Three times, and three times only, will my tomb give up my secret."

Senator Paul ceased and closed the book. The faces of all, even that of St. John, showed intense emotion.

"Clothilde," said the Senator, calling her thus for the first time, "the hour has come; make your appointment."

"Mr. Maxwell," she said almost inaudibly.

"Let us understand each other fully, and our respective places in this solemn duty," said the Senator, and he repeated the instruction. "As leader I will precede you, Mr. Beyresen, and St. John will follow. We pass up the left side. You will attend the princess," he said to me, "preceding her up the right side."

He then unlocked another hidden door in the corner of the room, diagonal to that by which we had entered, and we passed through. The stairway was continued, winding downward as before. The door was closed behind us, and immediately the voices of a large chorus of singers, accompanied by the notes and swells of a powerful organ, reached us. These were at first distant and indistinct, but became louder and clearer as we moved down the stair and approached the level from whence they seemed to come. Finally the full chorus of the singers and the voices of men, women and children could be heard. It was a song of sadness, a long drawn and funereal dirge.

We were all, even thus upon the stairway, deeply moved. Clothilde looked once toward me; she was deathly pale and evidently summoning all her fortitude for the occasion.

We descended eighty steps; I counted them, and then the stairway ceased, but the dirge continued, evidently coming from a room to which Senator Paul was now trying to discover the entrance. He succeeded, unlocked the door, opened it, and the voices and music ceased at once.

We stood at the western end of a large chamber, probably twenty feet wide, and quite long; the funereal blackness of floor, walls, and ceiling rendering it difficult to determine its dimensions with much accuracy.

A cluster of four electric lamps dependent from the ceiling, near the center of the chamber, furnished the only light in it. The metal work of these lamps was gold, and their light shone through the media of ground glass, only dimly illuminating the farther portions of the room, but falling upon the figure of a man, recumbent upon a black catafalque, raised probably eighteen inches above the floor. On his right side and about three feet removed from the catafalque, were what seemed to be two white tiles set in the floor, and on his left I observed three others at a similar distance. In the glossy, purplish black of the catafalque and its draperies, as well as on the sides, floor, and ceiling of the room, I recognized at once the presence of the black metal.

Already pervaded with a feeling of awe by the strange surroundings, we moved forward to take our designated places. As we did so the figure, which in the distance had been dimly outlined, became so distinct and life-like that I am free to confess I was startled, and almost terrified.

It was the figure of the dead, a tall, powerful man; the hair and eyebrows perfect and black as night; the eyes closed; the hands crossed naturally on the chest; the feet shoeless, but stockinged; stretched at full length upon his back on the black catafalque. The hands, limbs and every outline were perfect; the face full of expression.

It was the face and figure of John Harvey. He wore a black coat, a white necktie, vest and trousers, and was in full dress except for the shoeless feet.

The light from the arcs above fell full upon this figure, and there was about it, taken with the funereal surroundings, an awful, fear-inspiring, majestic, unearthly aspect.

I glanced at Clothilde; her face was as colorless and almost as white as the dress she wore, but I saw that the excitement of the occasion would sustain her, and indeed I knew not what to do should she give way.

We took our places on the white tiles, and turned toward the figure as we had been directed, when immediately the organ and the choir again began in a low chant, seemingly remote, but growing louder and nearer, and I recognized that a solemn service for the dead had begun. The words and even the music I had heard before on the occasion of the interment of a German emperor.

As the chant proceeded, and we all stood awe-stricken

facing toward the figure, it seemed as if strange spirits were around us in the dusky air, and as if the supernatural had overcome the natural, and that those sealed eyelids might unclose, those hands might unclasp, the dead might arise, and speak to us.

Clothilde's gaze was riveted upon the figure; Mr. Beyresen's eyes were downcast, and his face showed perturbation as did that of Senator Paul, and St. John even was visibly affected.

The chant continued, distinct, slow and deliberate, and with awful solemnity, and we listened hoping that the ordeal might soon be past. The organ pealed, perfect in every tone; the words came clear and distinct, apparently from the darkness veiling the east end of the room; yet we saw no one. For fully fifteen minutes it continued, and then slowly died away on the heavy, oppressive air which filled the room.

It was gone and there was perfect silence. I remembered my instructions and reached toward Clothilde. Mechanically she unfastened the chain which she had looped round her left wrist, and handed me the key. I took it, stepped two paces toward the figure, and saw above the right arm, where it crossed the body, three black buttons. I knelt and took the third within my fingers, turned it round till it resisted, and then withdrew it. It was very heavy for so small an object; a fact I noticed even in my trepidation. I placed it in my left hand; a square hole was visible. In this I put the key and turned it also. Looking below it, I observed a sealed packet which had been pushed outward.

I drew this gently forth, again turned the key, withdrew it, put the button in its place and moved it round. I passed the key to Clothilde, and we started to leave the place. Immediately the strange choir began again to sing. We reached the stairway, closed the door, but heard them still as we ascended. Clothilde took my proffered arm and leaned wearily upon it. We entered the room above, and I gave the packet to the Senator.

After a few moments' rest the keys and the book were returned to the black box, it was relocked, and with faces yet pallid we began the final ascent, resting occasionally on the landing.

After some time we gained the top, passed out through the door we had entered, and again reached the vault of the treasury building, Senator Paul leading as before. There the first box was reopened; the keys placed in it and it was relocked, and for the first time we looked freely in each other's faces.

It was 2 o'clock in the morning. For four hours we had been engaged in this arduous work, with nerves wrought to the highest tension.

A carriage waited for us. Mr. Beyresen entered it, and then Clothilde and myself. There was little talk between us. At parting Mr. Beyresen asked me to meet him on the morrow at his room.

I sought sleep, but found it not. The image of John Harvey, the sounds of weird music, the voices of unseen singers drove rest from my pillow, and about 9 o'clock I rose, and at the appointed time reached Mr. Beyresen's room.

I found the members of the party all assembled, save Clothilde, who was unable to be present. It was decided that the packet might be opened in her absence, and Senator Paul broke the seal and drew forth this writing, which he read to us:

"For once only, my friends, I have broken faith with you, and I crave your pardon. When I talked with you some nights ago, I was determined and had made all preparations to leave my secret with you. But the portals of eternity have opened now before me, and I am forbidden. I cannot even for you, my brethren, disclose the nature of that secret. It must die with me.

"Your cause here on earth, my cause also whither I go, must be furthered by faith, and love, and charity—not by the means I thought to employ.

"In all things you must be wise as serpents, and in respect to offense you must be harmless as doves.

"If defense be needed, prepare yourselves with what is necessary. So much is lawful. Remember no one can enter a strong man's house, and spoil his goods, unless he first bind the strong man.

"Be at one with another, oh, my friends. Be exemplars to those who live around you. But protect your firesides, your homes, the country which God gave you in his divine way first, and I in my human way last. You have my full permission to use for this purpose all the means I have already left you. But these must now suffice you. It is better so. Equality of weapons will keep you humble and preserve you from aggression. It will engender care for good men's opinion, and the Christian virtues which secure divine approval.

"I can say but little more. I have thought it all out as I lay upon my bed, and I cannot leave my secret. I will tread my weary way to my place of sepulchre again to-night, and I will destroy it with my own hands. You will find this packet only in its place. I have made this resolution, and I am at peace. I shall soon depart this life, but I will still watch over you.

"I can only add this: The Lord has at last shown me as I pray He will show you, also, 'What is good, and what He requireth of us, to do justly, and to love mercy, and to walk humbly with our God.'

"John Harvey."

There was silence in the chamber for some moments. The Senator reverently folded up the paper and placed it in the packet. His eyes, and those of the two others who had been John Harvey's personal friends, were suffused with tears. Finally he remarked:

"I understand now the sudden aggravation of John Harvey's illness, which rendered him delirious and caused his death twenty-four hours later. Our departed friend has acted wisely. The employment of this agent would, I fear, have robbed us of moral support. We must modify our plans, and be content to use the weapons left us. We have John Harvey's black-mouthed guns as yet.

I am directed, Mr. Maxwell, by General Canly, to give you this commission, which entrusts you with the molding of these cannon at Bilboa, and the preparation of the missiles to be used. Please report to the General for further orders. Let us now depart, remembering our oaths of secrecy and common service in a common cause."

CHAPTER XXX.

Shortly after leaving Mr. Beyresen's rooms, I went to General Canly's headquarters, and received full instructions from him in regard to my duties at Bilboa.

He desired me to proceed with all dispatch to that city, and I promised him that I would do so on the ensuing morning.

In the evening I called to see Clothilde, and learned that she had been confined to her room all day by an attack of nervous fever. I left a note for her expressing sympathy, and telling her that it was imperatively necessary for me to leave in the morning, and asking her to write to me as soon as she was sufficiently recovered.

On my arrival at Bilboa I found that the six gunboats had been completed, and would be ready for shipment and launching on the Missouri River as soon as their armament was prepared, each vessel being designed to carry a single gun of the black metal.

The casting of these guns, and of others to be mounted on railroad cars for land service, and the preparation of missiles for them, fully occupied my time for some succeeding weeks.

I heard daily of Clothilde, but it was many days before she herself was able to write to me. She did so candidly, trustingly, and confidentially, and yet without a a word that might not have been written to a brother.

I could not understand this reserve when my own feelings were manifest in my every epistle. But I hoped much from the quiet, affectionate manner she so naturally assumed toward me, and I believed that she felt far more deeply than she cared to let me know. I was also satisfied that she was better acquainted with my history than she had ever chosen to reveal to me, and confident that she was the young girl I had met on the Albatross.

I longed to see her again and put this matter to the test, but I could not intrude thus upon her until she was restored in health.

In the latter part of December I received an urgent invitation from Mr. Beyresen to spend New Year's day with his family, but was obliged to send word that I could not come until the 3d. On that day I reached Neuropolis, and went at once to Mr. Beyresen's house.

All greeted me most cordially, but there was something in Clothilde's manner, and a sparkle in her eye which she could not conceal, that I thought augured well for my most sanguine hopes.

Our conversation at the dinner-table and in the family circle was commonplace to others, but the simplest words between us two were freighted with the extraordinary.

After the dinner I missed Clothilde for awhile, and on her return fancied I saw traces of tears in her eyes, and her buoyant and gladsome manner seemed somewhat assumed.

One by one the others dropped out of the room, and she and I alone remained.

"Miss Clothilde," I said, "you once promised to show me your library, and I should be very much gratified if I might be permitted to look into it this evening."

She seemed somewhat confused by my request, but replied: "Certainly," and led the way to her drawing-room.

She left me there, and went into the apartment adjoining, where she was evidently engaged in arranging something, but came out presently, and said to me: "I fear you will find the library in a little confusion; but if you will be so good as to come in, I shall be pleased to show it to you."

I sat still, and replied: "I am afraid I am intruding and giving you trouble. I wanted a little talk with you rather than to see your library. I would not annoy you for the world."

She had resumed her old position by the mantel.

"Annoy me," she said; "I hardly see how you could. You have been so kind and considerate, so careful and thoughtful of my interests and feelings, that I could not think anything you might do an annoyance. You have stood by me as a true friend. You are doing for me and my people now what few persons would care to do. You must not think that I underestimate your services; you must not think I do not know how to value them, Mr. Maxwell."

There were tears in her eyes as she spoke, and she sat down in a chair near me.

"You are very earnest and panegyrical, Clothilde," I said, "but you know very well that that is not what I long for. Have you no other words for me? Can you make no hopeful reply to the question I asked you some months past, when I told you I loved you?"

"Oh, Mr. Maxwell!" she exclaimed, "I promised to answer that question after you had answered mine truly, or found the person of whom you spoke."

"And is that to be all?" I said. "Is there to be no word of love from you to me? Are we to live on thus, divided by an impassable barrier which you have created; why, I cannot imagine. Could you not be happy with me, Clothilde? If you could not, why have you trusted me so much? I have been very candid with you; I have revealed my inmost soul to you. I have had but few loves, and those have been sacred. Do you condemn me for them, when I had not as yet met you?"

"No," she replied quickly, "I do not; I condemn no one. As you have told me of one love, Mr. Herbert, you might tell me of the others," she added.

"I will accept your challenge," I said eagerly, "though I hardly know the spirit in which it is made. But you must come nearer, Clothilde, if I am to reveal secrets which have never yet been told to anyone."

She placed herself on a low footstool still closer to me, with every appearance of interest.

"It is a strange thing, Clothilde," I continued, "for a woman to ask a man suing for her heart to reveal his former loves to her."

"It is indeed," she replied. "I should like to hear the history of my predecessors, but I will not persist if it is painful. I hope you are not offended at the inquiry."

"No, I am not," I said, "and I will go on. I will tell the woman I love the story of my other loves, and it will not be long. I have already informed you that as a boy of twelve I fell in love with a little girl visiting for a short time with my mother. Her name was Stephanie. It was a childish love, Clothilde, and yet it was no transient one. Its memory followed me for years, and I have often found myself wondering if she had grown to be the glorious woman her childhood promised."

"I remember," broke in Clothilde. "You told me, too, you had never seen her since."

"I did and spoke the truth."

"Well," said she, after a slight pause, "was there another?"

"There was," I answered. "You may remember I told you of my breach of discipline in visiting the Albatross the night of the ball, and of a letter of warning I afterward gave to a young girl sitting at an open porthole of the vessel?"

"Yes," she answered, "I do remember."

"I did not tell you all, however, for you interrupted me. At the ball I had danced and talked with the young lady, and strange to say, though I only saw her that one evening she was so bright, so joyous, so beautiful, and so charming, that she made a powerful impression on me. It was for her sake more than all the rest that the next day I gave the warning. The few hours I spent with her were so delightful that I long remembered them, and I believe, Clothilde, that the memory of my child love and my girl love has done more to keep me from temptation than all other things. Would you destroy their memory, Clothilde? Do you think they would render me less capable of loving you, or have you no love to give me, which I can hardly believe?"

"No," she replied hesitatingly, "I would not rob you of your memories. But," she added blushingly, "I would be sure they are only memories. Did I understand that you had never seen this other person since?" she asked.

"I believe now I have," I said, watching her narrowly.

She started and made a movement to withdraw the hand which I had taken, but I detained it, though only for a moment, for she withdrew it.

"How did she conform to your expectations?" she inquired.

"I think I have already told her; I believe that young lady was your own self, dear."

There was a pause and then she said: "How long have you believed this, Mr. Herbert?"

"Only for a few weeks. But I believe it, and I think ₁you knew it all the time, Clothilde; is this not true?"

"I certainly was on the Albatross at the time of which you speak," she said gravely, but with increasing color.

"You have hardly treated me fairly, Clothilde!" I exclaimed, "but you are great enough, and good and lovely enough, to make amends."

"I do not know about that, sir,' she said. "I am only two of your loves. There is the first and most important one."

"Oh, you objector!" attempting to seize her, which she evaded, "are not two enough?"

"No," she said, "I think not. "Besides," returning near me to her place on the footstool, "there are other difficulties."

"What are they?" I inquired.

"You and I," she said solemnly, "are hereditary foes."

"What!" I cried.

"Your ancestors and mine," she continued, "have fought each other on a hundred battlefields."

I looked at her wonderingly.

"It is true," she went on. "I am of the blood royal. It is true, as is everything I have ever told you."

She looked intently at me, and I at her. "Do you not know me, Herbert?" she said.

"What is your full name, Clothilde?" I cried hoarsely, bending forward.

"Clothilde Stephanie Harvey," she almost sobbed.

I put my arm about her, and in another moment she sat beside me, while I stilled her tears with kisses.

"And you will be my wife, Stephanie?" I said at last.

"I will not tell you again," she replied, with returning coquetry; "I promised that eighteen years ago."

"And," I exclaimed, "neither of us, it seems, has ever forgotten it!"

"I knew you all the time," she continued. "I knew you on the Albatross, by the scar on the side of your temple, made when you fell from the tree at your father's house. I thought I knew you when you threw me the flowers, and I was sure of it when I first met you afterward. Do you think I would have trusted you as I did, sir, if I had not known you? I wanted you to remember me, and I gave you many hints, but you never took them, and I supposed you had forgotten Stephanie till you told me about her. My mother, you know, or ought to know, was the Princess Stephanie, sister to King Alphonse of Spain. Come into the library and I will show you her picture."

We went at once. The picture was turned to the wall. Clothilde put it right.

"I turned it," she continued, "lest you should recognize me from it; I look much like my mother. I wanted you to remember me yourself. I supposed you would come into the library after what you said, and I did not know how to prevent you."

"I saw you did not want me there, Clothilde, and I did not come," I answered.

"You are so kind and considerate, Herbert," and she smiled up into my face. "I remember it as a trait of yours long ago."

"God help me to be so always with you, Clothilde, my love," I responded fervently.

We parted for the night, and I walked to my rooms with a step light as air, and a heart full to bursting. My child love, my girl love, my only love was mine, and royal in her beauty, charming in her manner, sunny in her disposition, and mine, mine only, in her heart.

CHAPTER XXXI.

THE MARCH OF THE THREE HUNDRED THOUSAND.

I remained in Neuropolis only till the evening of the next day, but I saw many changes. The encampment on the west bank of the great canal now held one hundred and fifty thousand men, and the city itself, containing a population of over a half million, could furnish one hundred thousand more.

The military spirit had infected the entire people, and though the pursuits of industry were not neglected, every moment hitherto given to recreation, or pleasure, was now devoted to warlike attainments.

The armament of the vessels at Bilboa had been completed, as had also the mounting of several guns of the black metal in turrets on railroad cars made ball-proof by the use of the white metal.

I intended beginning in February the erection of buildings and stocks for the launching of the gunboats, which I designed protecting by a few shore batteries placed on the Missouri River.

Though many of the states had not responded with their quotas of troops yet so great was the severity of the times that the government had obtained the five hundred thousand volunteers called for.

But already a change had occurred in the attitude of the people in the Eastern states. Suffering had nearly reached its limit; patient endurance had almost been exhausted; and wise and able leaders had arisen, who frowned down the suicidal attempts of anarchists and other enemies of law and order, which for years had furnished excuses for continued oppression; leaders who were not afraid to speak the truth, and claimed openly and boldly the right to hold public meetings; to denounce wrongs, and to demand their redress.

The people were awaking from their apathy, and in all the great cities meetings were held, public addresses were made, and the Hymn of the Nationality was sung by marching thousands on the streets.

Conflicts with the authorities had already occurred in several cities, where the right of free and open assemblage and discussion had been challenged, which, though bloodless, had excited bitter feelings, and keener sense of long-endured wrongs.

It was the opinion of the councilors and public men of the Nationality that the government would soon make some aggressive movement against it, if for no other reason than to divert the public mind from the dangerous broodings which were engrossing it.

About the 15th of January, 1936, the commissioners appointed by the governors of Texas, Louisiana, Missouri, Arkansas, Oregon, California, Washington, Idaho, Montana, North Dakota, Wisconsin, Minnesota, Iowa, Kentucky, Tennessee, Mississippi, Alabama, Georgia and the Carolinas, in all over a hundred persons, arrived in Neuropolis.

From three to eight commissioners had been sent from each state, generally from among its most distinguished citizens and in two instances, those of California and Iowa, the governors themselves were of the number.

On the 20th of January these commissioners, in charge of a committee of the parliament, left Neuropolis on two special trains for a tour of observation of the Nationality.

They were given full opportunity for forming a correct judgment of the condition of its people and its power and resources, both from an industrial and military point of view.

They were taken into many of its principal cities in the mountains and on the plains, and among the people in the smaller towns and villages.

They visited the encampment at Neuropolis before leaving, and later the one in the disputed townships, and were invited to mingle freely with the men that they might judge of their intelligence and their patriotism.

The journey was intended to continue two weeks and to terminate on their return to Neuropolis. At its very beginning the commissioners were evidently much impressed with what they saw of the prosperity and strength of the Nationality.

During this season the rural population had much leisure, and were now employing it in military training under their labor directors. As the commissioners passed through, or stopped at the towns and villages, they saw regiments of men zealously engaged in drill, and they frequently met these same men in the evening at their homes, or in some assemblage, and found them loyal to their land, ready to entertain strangers hospitably if they came as friends, and equally ready to meet them otherwise if they came as foes.

When a few days had been spent in this manner, many of the commissioners began correspondence with the governors and other officers of their states, the nature of which could be inferred from expressions which sometimes escaped them.

Said a Georgian: "Your country is already a great military camp."

"I marvel at your population, and your prosperity," declared a Minnesota commissioner.

"No power can subjugate such a people," tersely remarked a Mississippian.

Understanding that the commissioners would return to Neuropolis about the 5th of February, I arranged to leave Bilboa for a few days, and started for Neuropolis on the evening of the fourth. We had stopped at a small station about ten miles from the city, when the conductor handed me a telegram which had reached Bilboa after my departure, and had been forwarded me on the train. I opened it and read: "Report to me at Neuropolis at once. The President has ordered an advance in force, and his troops are in rapid movement to cross the Missouri." It was signed by General Canly.

"Ah, then," thought I, "the moment of action has come. Alas, for human greed, passion, and shortsightedness, which precipitate so many calamities upon the people."

We arrived very soon at Neuropolis, and I repaired at once to General Canly's headquarters. I saw him but a moment; he was very busy.

"How many cannon," inquired he, "have you at Bilboa, ready to move to-morrow or the next day?"

I replied that I had eight, mounted on railway cars, and trained men ready to use them.

"Then," said he, "till 10 o'clock to-night your time is at your own disposal. We have information that two days ago all available troops were ordered to cross the river at Omaha, and take possession of the disputed townships, and that they are now concentrating for that purpose. By 10 o'clock to-night we shall have more definite news. I will see you then with other officers in council."

I left the General and as soon as possible went to

Mr. Beyresen's house. Mrs. Beyresen received me gravely but very kindly, and after a little conversation withdrew. Clothilde came a moment later, met me, and burst
into tears. She had heard the news and understood my
errand. We went into her drawing-room, and I tried to
comfort her.

"Oh, Herbert!" she cried, "I am afraid for your sake
of this coming struggle. If I had never known you you
would have been safe, but now you will be in constant
peril. And yet I would not keep you if I could, for the
cause is holy. But oh, be careful of yourself. I have
lost my father, and if I lose the lover I have just found I
shall be desolate indeed. Oh, the suffering and misery I
have seen wrought by war!"

"You were in the Albatross, Clothilde," I said.

"I was," she answered. "I would not leave my father. The other women went ashore; I would not leave
him, and he let me stay. I saw nothing of the battle till
all was over. I heard the firing and felt the concussion
of the balls upon the vessel, and I knew no fear; but when
I looked out over the sea, which was strewn with wrecks
and had swallowed up men who had been alive but an
hour before, I realized that war was awful. I thought
of you, and I was anxious till I knew that you were safe.
But I could have lost you then, Herbert, and recovered.
I cannot now, dear, since I have known you better."

For a long time we talked together, and I left her
somewhat reassured, and went to meet the Commander-
in-chief. Many other officers were with him, and I learned
the latest intelligence.

The Governmental troops were concentrating rapidly about twenty miles east from Omaha. A large number were already assembled, which would be greatly in-

creased in a few hours, when the passage would probably be attempted.

Only a show of force entirely overwhelming could change the purpose of the government. Realizing this, General Canly had determined on an immediate concentration of the Nationalistic forces at a station called Oberon, ten miles inland from Omaha.

The railway officials whose lines led from Neuropolis eastward were instructed to keep their tracks clear for the passage of trains loaded with men from the camp near the city, who were already on their way to Oberon.

The troops in the disputed townships had orders to begin their march in the morning to that place, distant from them about forty miles. A great number of well-drilled men were ordered in from the mountain districts, and would be hurried to the front as soon as practicable. I was required to be ready at an hour's notice to proceed to Oberon with my Harvey guns.

I reached my lodgings late that night. It was after 1 o'clock when I retired, and nearly eight next morning when I breakfasted.

A great change had come upon the city. The streets were filled with regiments marching to their allotted cantonments, and with wagons conveying stores to trains. The arsenals were open, and boxes of arms were being sent to the encampment west of the city. Fresh tents, pitched at various points there, showed arrivals of large bodies of troops during the night.

I repaired to headquarters and was informed that the government had already concentrated two hundred and fifty thousand men, and it was expected that a movement would soon be made to seize the bridge crossing the Missouri at Omaha. I was ordered to transport my guns to Neuropolis at once. This I did, and they arrived and were safely housed that evening. All day long troops were arriving from the mountain districts, and going into camp to be fully equipped and armed before proceeding onward.

About 2 p. m. the trains conveying the commissioners reached Neuropolis. They had heard the news that day, and returned as rapidly as possible. They had left a peaceful city; they found a martial camp. Anxiety and distress were visible on their countenances as they saw the warlike preparations and the constant embarkation of men hurrying to the front.

They were met at the station, escorted to hotels, and treated with every courtesy. At first they doubted the authenticity of the reputed order of the President, and it was not until they had received telegrams from their own states that they fully admitted it. Then they held hurried meetings; then they realized that they were in the midst of the wildest storm cloud of war that the Continent had ever seen.

From room to room, all night long, these men consulted with each other, and telegraphed to their friends and superiors.

I visited Clothilde in the evening. She had recovered her fortitude and was again herself. Her depression was gone, and though anxious, the brave spirit of her ancestors was manifest in her bearing.

The morning of the 7th came, and the city awoke if it had been at all asleep. Many of the commissioners desired to return home that day. They were informed that the roads were now blocked by trains filled with troops, and advised to wait till the 9th, when a sufficient number of men having been sent forward for present defense, special trains would be provided for them. They inquired if they were at liberty to go where they wished, and were assured the freedom of the city, and of the camps, was theirs.

They took full advantage of the privileges accorded them. They visited the camps, the stations, and all parts of the city, in carriages, in cars, and on foot, in couples, in groups, or singly. They conversed; they telegraphed; they interchanged views without observation, or annoyance.

It was announced that at 2 o'clock there would be a grand review of the mountain men as they marched past the Administration Square to the southern depot for embarkation, and the commissioners were invited to be present.

These troops consisted of twelve corps of twenty-five thousand men each, and would be the last sent forward at present from Neuropoïis.

By 1 o'clock a large platform had been erected on the east side of the square, at the place where the labor directors had formerly assembled. At an early hour an immense throng, eager to witness the spectacle, filled the streets and sidewalks.

I was sent by General Canly to bring Clothilde. "It is fitting," he said, "that John Harvey's daughter, though as yet known to but a few, should be recognized, and should occupy the place of honor on this day when the troops pass by to defend the land he loved. I have invited her, and informed the officers and men of her identity, and you can tell her this from me, that the standards which these troops carry, bear by order of our Parliament the figure of a woman, and that figure represents John Harvey's daughter."

I told Clothilde this, and she accompanied me, a princess in her every attitude and movement. She took her seat by the General, among his staff, on the platform

where the commissioners, councilors, and others were
assembled.

A little before 2 o'clock the advancing column of
the mountain men wheeled into view from the Northwest
Boulevard, and passing along the Northern Avenue,
turned southward down the eastern side of the Administration Square.

As they reached it their arms were brought to a present, and carried thus past the platform on which we were,
and along the whole eastern side of the square. The
sight as the column wheeled and moved down upon us
was most impressive.

The men marched in companies, at a rapid, swing-
ing pace and with great precision, filling the wide avenue
from side to side. They were full grown, mature men,
robust and strong, and their determined faces showed
that they knew full well their mission. They looked
neither to the right nor left, but straight ahead, with true
soldierly bearing. Their weapons were repeating rifles
of the latest pattern; their uniforms were blue, with shako
helmets, and a white sash about the waist, with short ends
dependent. The colors which they carried were those of
the United States; the flag staffs bore the figure of a
woman in a flowing Grecian robe. These colors were
presented as they passed the platform, all upon it rising,
the commissioners with the rest.

The column marched in silence, until the middle
of the first corps of twenty-five thousand men was opposite us, when suddenly at a word their drums beat a
charge, and immediately the voices of the entire corps
burst forth, clear and strong, in the Hymn of the Nationality, which had been sung upon the same spot by the
labor directors.

"Hail! all hail! We march, an army grand,
With weapons bright, in strength and might,
To consecrate this noble land,
This soil on which we tread, rich in its patriot dead,
By proclamation stern and loud,
By cannon's peal and clash of steel,
To Man, to Freedom, and to God."

The effect was electrical and grand in the extreme.
No one on that platform doubted that, when the word
was given, those men would charge, singing that same
hymn, upon any foe before them. I looked at Clothilde,
who was standing in the front. Her eyes were flashing,
and her dark cheek was glowing with patriotic fervor.

The second corps marched by in perfect silence, but
the third, at the same point as the first, broke forth in the
words and music of the song, and this was repeated by
every alternate corps as they passed on.

For four long hours the men filed by, while we remained standing upon the platform. About 6 o'clock
the rear of the column passed, and the review was over.

Governor Brooks of Iowa, from amidst the commissioners, mounted on a chair, and gave notice that
they were requested to meet at 7 p. m. in the academy
of music, and turning to General Canly asked him if he
would attend the meeting for a few moments as soon as
they had organized.

The General replied that he would be in his office
at that hour, and would await their pleasure.

The great crowd melted rapidly away, and I escorted Clothilde to her carriage and went with her to her
home.

By General Canly's request I was at his office at 7
o'clock, and very shortly he was informed by a committee from the commissioners of their organization. He

desired General Knox and myself to attend him, and we
proceeded at once to the academy, where the commissioners were in waiting.

Governor Brooks presided, and we were escorted to
the platform, where General Knox and I took seats,
General Canly and the Governor remaining standing.

"We desire, General," said the latter, "in the interests of certain action which we intend to take at once, to
ask you a few questions. Will you please inform us how
many men you have at Oberon?"

General Canly replied: "By to-morrow night, sir,
six hundred thousand well-armed men, such as you have
seen to-day, will be camped around that place. Within
twelve hours I can reinforce them by two hundred thousand more, and in a week I could double the entire number."

"Then, General," said Governor Brooks, "if you be
at liberty to tell us, we wish to know what will occur if
the President persist in his attempt to cross the river with
his troops. Will he be permitted to do so?"

"I desire to be courteous with you, gentlemen," said
General Canly, with the light of battle shining in his face.
"I think you are met here in the interests of peace, and
in those interests I will reply to your question frankly,
hoping that my answer will not be considered an idle
boast, but a solemn warning. The President was yesterday informed by telegram from me that the crossing of
the river would be considered a hostile action. He may
cross that river with three hundred thousand, or five
hundred thousand men, but he will never recross it.
Within three days thereafter his forces will either have
surrendered or been annihilated."

There was a pause for a moment in the questioning,
and then Governor Brooks resumed: "Suppose the

President halts his men upon or near the east bank of the river, what will be your action?"

"That," replied General Canly, "I cannot tell. I can only say in my opinion his security in such event depends upon my further orders. The men you saw to-day, gentlemen," he added, turning to the commissioners, "are no holiday soldiers. They are used to finishing a business without unnecessary delay. Is that all, gentlemen?" he inquired, after a moment's pause.

"It is," said Governor Brooks. "We are obliged to you, General."

We departed, and on returning to headquarters I received orders to start by midnight with my guns for Oberon.

I sent word to Clothilde that I wished to meet her at eleven, and hastened to give the necessary instruction to my aides, and to see that everything was in readiness for movement. Then I visited my betrothed. I found her anxious, but brave, and I told her of my orders.

"Oh!" she cried, "this solemn day presaged a solemn ending, and yet it shall not be sad. You are my soldier, and you will return to me with duty well performed. The General is right; a lesson must be taught; this land must be protected, for it is the hope of the world. I will not detain you, Herbert, but oh! be careful of yourself, and let me hear daily from you. If you want me I will come to you at once."

I took her in my arms and embraced her tenderly, and then departed for the stern duties which I thought awaited me.

I saw General Canly a few moments and received further orders, and he informed me that he expected to leave Neuropolis to take active command on the day following.

We were soon on our way, passing during the night, and part of the next morning, through the fields and villages of the Nationality, and reached Oberon by noon.

A great army of six hundred thousand men was assembled there ready for onward movement. Constant dispatches from Omaha kept us informed of the enemy's position. His troops, numbering fully four hundred thousand men, still lay twenty miles east of Omaha, but had made no forward movement.

Nor was any ever made. Events occurred that stopped aggression, and settled all disputes between the Government and the Nationality, and ended finally in that reign of peace which has since been so glorious among us.

On the night I left Neuropolis, the following telegrams were sent to the President:

"For God's sake, and the country's, halt your troops at once. If you cross the river, your army will be ground to powder. Six hundred thousand well-armed, well-drilled men await your coming; a million will confront you a few days later."

This telegram was signed by all the commissioners. Another and more private one, from the two governors, read:

"Remove your troops to a safe distance. Their very presence on the border provokes this people, and may bring about hostilities. There must be no war; the governor of Iowa and the governor of California say so. There is no cause for war; this matter must be settled differently. We leave the city to-morrow evening. We respectfully request an immediate reply as to your intentions."

No answer was received, however, and the governors of the two states, before departing, advised General Canly and the councilors of their action.

CHAPTER XXXII.

By the 20th of February the reports of most of the commissioners who had visited the Nationality were made public.

They all admitted that great prosperity and contentment existed, and that the people were united, and attached to their form of government. They asserted that the two labor systems existing in the country were antagonistic, and that the question of which should prevail was one to be determined by the people.

Prior to this time the President had called authoritatively upon the governors of the states which were delinquent for their quotas of troops, and his demands were in many cases submitted to the various state legislatures then in session.

The action taken by these bodies was such that the governors of the Pacific Coast states, and those lying westward of the Nationality, and of several of the Southern states, refused absolutely to furnish men, or money, alleging that the cause was morally insufficient to warrant the government in a resort to force.

The states of Texas, Missouri, Arkansas and Oklahoma, which had formally decided to join the Nationality, made no answer. The basis of union had already been determined upon, and the necessary laws were passed by their legislatures, notwithstanding that all means, some of very doubtful character, had been used to prevent such action.

373

The plan of union showed the care with which the admission of new citizens was guarded by the Nationality.

Skilled appraisers had classified, and valued all productive property within each state. They had also scheduled the indebtedness of the state, and of her citizens, to foreigners, and to each other, and all credits, and other resources.

The undertaking of the Nationality was to assume the indebtedness of the states, and to succeed to all their property and resources.

The citizens, men, women and children, had been enrolled with name, age, occupation, and pecuniary condition. Boards of examiners were appointed to inquire into the qualifications of all who applied for admission into the Nationality, and if passed they were divided into two classes.

First—Persons under the age of forty-five years, who came in, partially at least, under the labor system.

Second—Those entering after that age and by virtue of payment of money or property.

Of the first class, each person admitted past the age of citizenship, was required to bring into the Nationality money, or property, at appraised valuation, as follows: Two hundred and fifty dollars for each year lost up to the age of twenty-four, the marriageable age encouraged by the Nationality. After the age of twenty-four and to the age of thirty, three hundred dollars for each year lost between these ages. After the age of thirty and to the age of forty, an additional sum of four hundred dollars for each year lost between these ages. If the applicant were married the payment of these sums admitted not only himself to citizenship and allowance, but his wife, and also his children born to him after the age of twenty-four.

A person then of the age of thirty must pay in three thousand three hundred dollars; of the age of forty, seven thousand three hundred dollars. All these citizens were also required to labor till the age of forty-five.

Each person admitted after the age of forty and up to forty-five must pay the sum of five hundred dollars additional for each year lost between those ages, but neither wife, nor children, were admitted by this payment.

Persons of the second class were admitted on the payment of ten thousand dollars at the age of forty-five, and increasing sums at increasing ages, and this payment did not make their families citizens.

There were in these states persons, otherwise well qualified, who had not property sufficient to enable them to enter the Nationality. These might be admitted by a system of indirect payment, its amount being the same as that required of others of the same age. They could be credited with a portion of the surplus paid by the wealthier over what was necessary for their own admission. The latter were allowed to designate, among those approved by the examiners, the parties to whom such credit should be given.

No one was compelled to join the Nationality, and yet the laws passed by the legislatures of these states, to take effect concurrently with their admission to the Nationality, made it to the interest of all qualified persons to become members speedily.

These laws abolished descents and distributions, wills and testaments, probate courts, etc., and provided for the escheating of all property to the state at the owner's death. They also provided for the merger of one judicial district into another, and the reduction of the number of civil courts and judges as the people of the district joined the Nationality, and also for similar merger of many other offices. The expenses of these courts and offices were hereafter to be paid by litigants, and persons doing business with them.

Similar laws were also passed for the merger of the criminal courts, and it was provided that in cases of offense against private property the cost of the proceedings should be paid by the owners.

Laws were passed in regard to the support of other public officers and of prisons, reformatories, etc., and in regard to the poor and those incapable of labor, not being citizens of the Nationality, dividing the charges for all these things equitably between the Nationality and those who yet desired to remain under the old system.

These laws were drawn with the utmost fearlessness and impartiality, casting upon each class all the burdens imposed by their system, and dividing mutual ones equitably between them.

Within a few years after the union, almost the entire population of these states became citizens of the Nationality, and their people were very soon as homogeneous and as prosperous as any portion of it.

There was another feature, to which I must refer as being a matter of compromise having much to do in bringing about this wonderful change. The city of St. Louis had been opposed to it, and her interests were so great that a promise was made to conserve them by the erection of extensive works of a public nature within her limits. The assurance was also given that she should be the directing city of the labor interests of a large part of the Mississippi states, if the latter should join the Nationality, and she was thus started well forward in the race for becoming the great governmental city of the Union.

All these preliminaries had been settled and agreed

upon by the 20th of March, 1936, and on that day the legislatures of the four states passed an ordinance declaring that they desired admission to the Nationality, and that all of their people thereafter becoming citizens thereof should be governed by its principles and regulations, and be entitled to its benefits.

A month later this ordinance was approved by the people of the Nationality, and these four great states became part and parcel of its organization, increasing its population to an aggregate of thirteen million persons.

CHAPTER XXXIII.

I now return to the history of the forces left confronting each other on the banks of the Missouri, and to the narration of occurrences in the Eastern states which speedily gave other employment than that intended, to the army of invasion.

The condition of the people of those states had become heart-rending. Though the late levies of troops had been taken largely from among the ranks of the unemployed, thousands of that class yet remained in the great cities, and were daily becoming more vicious, and ready to take by force what they were denied the right to acquire by labor.

On the 23d of February a riot of alarming proportions broke out in the City of New York, which was quickly followed by similar disturbances in many other places.

The authorities appealed to their state governments for aid, and they called upon their militia, but so universal had become the contempt for the rotten administration of both municipal and state affairs that assistance was stolidly refused. The authorities therefore invoked the aid of the General Government, and in self-preservation it was necessitated to respond at once.

By the 1st of March the army lately assembled near the Missouri had been divided to meet these demands, and one hundred and fifty thousand of its troops preserved a semblance of order in New York City, and one hundred thousand more scarcely kept the peace in Chicago. A large force was also required in each of the cities of Philadelphia and Cincinnati, and other detachments were employed in various places guarding railroads and private property.

As the government troops were thus recalled, the forces of the Nationality were disbanded, leaving only a few thousand men in the disputed townships to meet any renewed attempt upon them.

On the 11th of March a meeting of the governors of many of the eastern, middle and southern states was held at the City of Buffalo, ostensibly for devising some plan for the relief of the people, and the restoration of law and order. The project was there broached of forming a new nation, whose western boundary should be the Mississippi and Missouri Rivers, leaving the Nationality and the Pacific Coast states to their own devices.

This plan met with the disapproval of the representatives present from the southern states; but after their departure, those of the remaining states, seventeen in number, entered into an alliance for forming an independent government among themselves.

The scheme was that of the Money Power. Knowing itself defeated in its attack on the Nationality, it endeavored to perpetuate the system upon which its existence depended, by its usual tactics of dividing its enemies, and creating dissension among them.

On the 15th of March, John Paul and Philip Oram introduced into the respective houses of which they were members concurrent bills providing for the submission of certain constitutional amendments to the legislatures of the several states and the enactment of a law regulating immigration.

The amendments contemplated were three in number and were as follows:

"First—That the right of any state, or aggregation of states, to adopt any system of ownership of property, and of labor, and government of the same, and especially the system now known as the Nationalistic System, shall not be denied or abridged; provided that the citizens of such state, or aggregation of states, who conform to such system, have the right to select the directors, or managers, of property owned under, and officers engaged in conducting it; and provided further, that no person, without his consent thereto, be deprived of property during his life by the adoption of such system.

"Second—That the right of any state, or states, to ally themselves together, or to join other states, for the purpose of peaceably promoting and extending such system of ownership, and of labor and the government thereof, shall not be denied by the United States; nor shall the intendment that persons joining such system of ownership, labor and government, and their families participating in the benefits resulting therefrom, shall be bound by the laws, rules and regulations thereof, be denied by the United States; nor shall Congress make any laws in contravention thereof.

"Third—That the right of any state, or aggregation of states, to abolish or change the laws in regard to descents and distributions, wills and testaments, and to pass laws causing all property at the death of the owner to escheat to the state, and also to pass laws distributing the burdens of government, and of the care and protection of property, equitably, as the same may be occasioned by diverse systems, among the citizens living under the system by which the same is wholly, or chiefly, or in part incurred, shall not be denied by the United States, nor shall Congress pass any law abridging, or interfering, with said rights."

The bill relating to foreign immigration read as follows:

"That a Bureau of Immigration be established to have full control of that department, and to be in constant correspondence with foreign bureaus, as well as those within the United States, and to make known to them the laws, rules and regulations in regard to immigration.

"That twelve ports of entry be designated, at which alone immigrants shall be allowed to land, to wit: Boston, New York, Philadelphia, Baltimore, Charleston, New Orleans, Corpus Christi, San Francisco, Tacoma, Seattle, Duluth and Chicago.

"That a board of not less than three, nor more than six examiners shall be appointed at each of said ports, who shall receive, care for, and examine immigrants applying for admission into the United States, noting carefully:

"First—The applicant's name, age and nationality, and if married that of each member of his family.

"Second—His moral character, to be certified by not less than three reliable and trustworthy persons who have known him for at least five years previous to his coming to this country.

"Third—His intelligence and health, to be judged of by the examiners and their attendant physicians.

"The applicant must be of, or over, the age of eighteen, if male, and fifteen if female, of good moral character, able to read and write fluently, and in reasonable health, and shall be required to state the occupation in which he desires to engage, the particular portion of the United States where he intends to locate, and the bureau of immigration, or the officers of the labor system, with whom he has been in correspondence, or if there be none such, then some reliable, responsible citizen in that locality, with whom he has corresponded. He must also have sufficient pecuniary means to reach his intended destination, and have remaining a sum equal to that now required of citizens of the states of Texas, Missouri, Arkansas, and Oklahoma, of the same age as himself, upon joining the Nationality.

"If the applicant fail in any of these particulars, he shall at once be returned to the foreign port from whence he came, at the cost of the transportation company bringing him hither. If competent for admission, he shall pay the sum before mentioned into a United States depository, and the examiners shall telegraph all particulars in regard to him to the officer, agent or person with whom he stated he had been in correspondence, inquiring if such correspondence has been had, and if such officer, agent, or person desire to receive him.

"Upon an affirmative reply, the examiners shall send such immigrant and his family, if such there be, to such officer, agent or person, transmitting at the same time the certificate of deposit of his money, to be paid to him on his arrival, or to be credited as an entrance fee if he be sent to any officer of the Nationalistic labor system."

The bill further provided that this act, and the constitutional amendments, if adopted, should go into effect on the fourth day of July, 1936.

The introduction of these bills was followed by such a storm of opposition in both houses as had never before been witnessed. All the influence of the Money Power was employed against them. They were declared anti-republican, revolutionary, and dangerous. Including the representatives from the Nationalistic states, they had the support of a respectable minority in both houses, but it was soon evident that they could not pass the present Congress.

Meanwhile the condition of affairs throughout the country had been rapidly growing worse, and was now almost intolerable. Business was entirely disorganized, finance and credit wrecked, and the poor were unable in many cases to earn their bread. Deaths from starvation among men, women and children were so frequent as to pass almost unnoticed, and the number of suicides became appalling. The whole country was like a vast fever ward, ill regulated and unclean, whose patients were suffering and dying from want of proper nourishment and care.

The situation of the governments of the nation, and of the states, outside those composing the Nationality, was deplorable.

A spirit of disobedience to laws and regulations, affirmed with reason to be made only in the interests of the rich and powerful, was abroad among the masses.

In the city of Pittsburg a mob of great proportions had for some weeks held possession of a suburb, had fortified it and appropriated goods by car loads, and a reign of terror was inaugurated.

The new levies by which the army had been recruited were unreliable, nearly one-half of them having already deserted. In fact, toward the end of April, 1936, the governments of these states, and of the nation, were on the verge of dissolution.

On this spectacle all right-minded citizens looked with pity and indignation, and compared it with the happiness and plenty they had seen, or been assured was existent, in the Nationality; and many of the rich even sought refuge within its borders from the distresses and calamities of the times.

In the latter part of March, the Money Power had broached their project of division of the country, and now pushed it in congress, and among the state legislatures, with the desperation of gamblers staking all upon a single card. They declared the interests of the country had grown too diverse to be managed by a single government, and division to be the only means of securing peace between antagonistic systems.

They advocated it in public speeches; they filled the press with references to dangers and distresses, and promises of deliverance and reform; they procured support for it by appeals to personal cupidity, lust of power, and other base and selfish motives. So successful were their efforts that toward the end of April the first steps in the project seemed assured, and a majority of both houses of congress looked favorably on it.

But a power, hitherto unreckoned, was about to interfere, and unsettle all these plans. The labor organizations, long discordant, had for months been silently engaged in federation and in preparation, and were now united in one great union with a common purpose, which found expression in its motto: "Justice, Equality, and Fraternity."

This union was about to show its strength, as irresistible as the tides of ocean.

On April 24th it made proclamation, that on the 26th organized labor would cease throughout the land, warning all persons to supply themselves with necessaries, and informing the poor where thereafter they could be provided with them; forbidding the sale of intoxicants on peril of confiscation, or destruction of such goods; and robbery, rioting and incendiarism on pain of instant death,

This proclamation was published throughout the United States, except within the Nationality, and its authoritative and determined tone commanded universal attention, and excited much apprehension.

On the morning of the 26th labor ceased throughout this vast extent of territory.

Trains reached the cities and their conductors and employes left them; the mails remained unopened; newspaper offices were tenantless; workshops were deserted; manufactories were silent; stores were destitute of salesmen; all business stopped, and a more than Sabbath stillness descended on the land.

In the cities armed patrols, wearing white sashes, occupied the streets, and enforced such orders as were issued by the leaders of the union.

Any concourse of the populace was at once dispersed; public buildings were thrown open for the shelter of the poor and needy, and they were supplied with necessaries taken for the purpose, due bills of the union being given for them.

As the day wore on, the stillness and the apprehension grew oppressive. Employers sought their employes to learn from them the cause of this strange action, but learned nothing; transportation companies sent out agents to hire other men to man their boats and run their trains, but found none willing. Civic authorities consulted with each other as to the meaning of this strange intrusion on established rights, but were none the wiser; and in the face of armed patrols upon the streets, and the awful might of those who put them there dared make no struggle.

The day passed slowly by in silence and conjecture, and the night came on, and the white-sashed guards were doubled. In the city of New York two hundred thousand men patrolled the streets, and in other cities overpowering numbers, and peace unusual reigned.

, The next day came in still greater quiet. Vessels lay idly at their moorings, or by their unfrequented wharves; motors rested supinely in their stables; men walked who used to ride in crowded trains to business, and found no business.

The factories were noiseless, their useless fires were dying in their ashes; the very streets were silent and deserted; for, as with one accord, the members of the union kept within their homes, and others did so also, dreading some disaster.

There was no rioting, nor disturbance; stern men dispersed all crowds; the occupation of police and troops was gone, and both lay idly in their quarters, for the folly of their interference was apparent.

The day dragged slowly by; night came; the guards were doubled; another morning dawned, with the same unvarying stillness.

Apprehension took on deeper shades, for want was imminent. Supplies were failing, even water, light and heat, which the laborers still furnished, were dependent on the stock of fuel, and this was scant.

The value of a man rose in the market. Employers sought their employes and begged them to return to service, and offered higher wages, but received no answer. Officials telegraphed the Government, but there was no power competent to drive ten million men to labor; in all their providence the Money Power had passed no statute for that purpose.

Fear seized upon the dwellers in the cities who were strangers to this movement; fear not for property alone, but life itself.

And so the day wore by; another dawned upon the

land; and still the awful quiet reigned supreme. Men waited for the hour when the workmen would resume their labors, but they gave no sign.

Self-imagined kings of the earth met secretly, and whispered to each other: "The world must suffer; we ourselves must suffer, want, or die, if the laborers refuse to work; if this strange apathy continue; can the government do nothing?"

They telegraphed to Washington, to Albany, and like centers, but uselessly; all officers were terrified, and nerveless. The rulers of the land found no one now so poor to do them reverence.

The horses of the sun had ceased to draw its chariot, and it now moved only by its own momentum.

The vital forces of the body politic had left it, and now hung in threatening thunder clouds above it.

Vesuvian fires burned beneath this awful quiet, and must result in earthquakes and convulsions.

Forebodings filled the souls of men lately in power, who imagined chaos would follow if their rule were ended.

Night came on; again the guards were doubled. The morning dawned; trains were reported moving through the land toward the great cities. But they were directed by some strange power that refused conveyance to all but its own subjects; and these were men—most of them sons of toil, and heavy-handed. They reached their destination and were shown to lodgings; in armories, in theaters, and other public places. They came in overwhelming numbers; and alarm increased, for these were alien to the cities, and were men of will and might, whose designs were hidden, but whose strength already had been felt.

That day passed by in quiet, but the next, the first of May, looked down on something terrible.

In every town and city of the land, great bands of

men, wearing white sashes, were assembling; their faces
stern; their words but few; their purposes unknown, save
to themselves.

The scene was most imposing in the greatest cities; I
shall attempt description of that witnessed in New York.

It was 10 o'clock a. m., and the streets were quiet;
for one hundred thousand guards patrolled them, and allowed no idle concourse of the populace.

Down on the Battery, and on all the streets around
the Bay, great multitudes of men, wearing white sashes,
were forming into column. All carried knapsacks and
blankets, as do soldiers on the march, and many, who
moved in companies to their places, bore weapons in their
hands.

An hour later that column began its movement up
Broadway. A hundred thousand armed men marched in
front, filling the street from side to side completely, and
other hundred thousands followed after, wheeling into
line from out the crowded side streets round the Battery.

Save the sound of marching feet the column moved
in silence till its armed head had reached the City Hall,
when the solemn booming of minute guns shook the surrounding buildings, and then the voices of its first division broke forth in the well-known, oft-repeated Hymn of
the Nationality:

> "Hail! all hail! We march an army grand,
> With weapons bright, in strength and might,
> To consecrate this noble land,
> This soil on which we tread, rich in its patriot dead;
> By proclamation stern and loud,
> By cannon's peal, and clash of steel,
> To Man, to Freedom and to God."

On up to Madison Square the mighty column passed,
and wheeled with rapid tread into Fifth Avenue; each suc-

ceeding division repeating the Hymn after the preceding one had finished it, while the heavy boom of cannon, from the lower portion of the city, gave the words a terrible accentuation.

It was an awe-inspiring, fearsome sight, in that proud metropolis. For a hundred years Mammon had controlled it, and human life, and brawn, and labor, had been cheaply bought and sold. But to-day the city and its treasures lay at the mercy of the class whose souls and bodies had been traded in; whose toil, and sweat, and blood, had made its wealth, and palaces, and splendor, possible.

Without a battle a mighty army had possession, whose movements were mysterious, whose purposes were hidden, but whose power was supreme.

Alarm showed in the faces of the dwellers in the city, and great fear fell on those who had garnered in injustice the harvests sown by other men.

Along the palatial avenue the mighty column moved, still unfolding its sinuous length from the precincts of the Battery, until its glittering head had passed the Fifty-ninth street entrance into Central Park, while its body formed of nine hundred thousand white-sashed men stretched throughout the city to the Bay.

In the Park the column halted, its divisions as they reached it massing in close order, and by 5 o'clock, when the rear guard entered, an army greater than any living man had seen, was gathered there.

Then the message, which I give below, was read and ordered sent at once to Washington:

"To the Senators and Representatives of the United States, in General Congress Assembled:

"One million working men, who to-day marched through the streets of New York City, and to-night will camp in Central Park, demand of you, their servants, the immediate passage of the bills providing for the submission of the constitutional amendments to the legislatures of the states, and for regulating foreign immigration."

The army speedily broke ranks and bivouacked for the night on ground hitherto reserved for recreation and enjoyment, but now made memorable by the assembly of these sons of toil, met to redeem the land from grinding monopoly and selfish greed.

On that solemn first of May, the Congress of the United States held a protracted session. All that afternoon they listened with blanched faces to messages such as I have quoted; from five hundred thousand men met in Chicago; from thrice that number camped in Boston, Philadelphia, Baltimore, Pittsburg, New Orleans and Cincinnati, and from many million more in a hundred other places.

They felt the land shake with the tread of those who had given it strength and prosperity, who held its riches and its honors in the hollow of their hands, and claimed a portion of them as their right, and demanded unwonted haste in restitution.

All through the night the session lasted, made more earnest by constant inquiries from the leaders of the union, and from citizens of beleaguered cities as to progress; and lo; when morning came, Congress had passed the bills and the President had signed them.

The news was published in the encampments of the workmen, and at the orders of their leaders, their armies melted quietly away, and with stern satisfaction the men resumed their various employments. The smoke of factories, the throb of engines, and the whir of wheels, again arose; and the cities breathed in safety. But that day, when the voice of the people was as the voice of God, will never be forgotten, for from it is dated the emancipation of the masses, and their united and rapid progress in true freedom and civilization.

The toilers were no longer slaves, but freemen; accorded consideration, and respect, commensurate with the strength and dignity of the union they had formed.

The legislatures of the states discussed the amendments so earnestly and effectively that by the 5th of June they were duly ratified. Nothing now remained but the official proclamation of the President as to the result, and he announced this would be issued on the morning of the 4th day of July. Many other events happened over which I must pass quickly.

The history of the Nationality, its labor system, and everything concerning it, engrossed the attention of 1 people determined on reform. It was taken as the model on which to found the civilization of the future. The truth about John Harvey's life and labors, his death and burial, was made known, and he was recognized as a great and philanthropic leader.

Clothilde's parentage, her disguise as Councilor Beyresen's daughter, were disclosed, her recognition by the officers and soldiers of the Nationalistic army was recounted, and the romantic story caught the public heart and fancy, and she became the heroine of the people. My history was given, and our engagement was mentioned in the public prints.

Letters full of love and inquiry came to her from Spain, rejoicing that she whom they thought dead was yet alive, and others reached me from my people full of congratulations and pleasant messages.

The authorities of the Nationality had some time since begun their preparations for commemorating the adoption of the amendments by a magnificent celebration in Neuropolis on the 4th, and now besought us to fix on that day for our marriage, and to make the ceremony a semi-public one. They urged this with so much earnestness and with such good and patriotic reasons that at last we both consented.

It was, therefore, settled that our marriage should take place on the evening of the 4th, in the great hall of the Administration Building, in the presence of the councilors, and representatives, and other dignitaries of the Nationality, and should be the closing event of the celebration.

CHAPTER XXXIV.

The morning of July the fourth came quickly, and with it the President's proclamation, that the amendments to the constitution having been duly ratified by the legislatures of three-fourths of the states, were now a part of the organic law of the land, and entitled to like respect and observance with other portions of it.

In the general rejoicing with which this announcement was hailed by the people throughout the United States, the original cause of the dispute, the payment of the judgment claim against the Nationality, was forgotten; and though some years after, lawyers of the ancient school talked learnedly concerning it, holding that the General Government was still liable for its non-collection, yet I have no knowledge of what was finally done about it.

The morning broke in glory in Neuropolis. Great preparations had been made for the celebration.

Garlands of evergreens, with flowers interwoven, and electric lights interspersed among them, formed canopies over the boulevards around the Administration Square. Great archways composed of similar materials were thrown across the points of intersection of the Administration boulevards, with the others, and far down the latter these archways were continued by a multitude of globes, of varied coloring, hung across them at a height of many feet.

All the public buildings were decorated tastefully, and strung with chains of delicately colored lamps; the fountains were in full play; the great vases near the Administration Building and all the parks were gay with evergreens and flowers; bands discoursed sweet music; and the universal effect was a most exquisite and surprising harmony of music, light and coloring.

A multitude of visitors had arrived from all portions of the Union, and from foreign countries; many of them distinguished men and women; governors of states and other rulers; scientific men, and men of letters; all gathered here to see and enjoy the celebration in this the fairest and happiest city of the globe.

The officials of the Nationality and its invited guests assembled in the eastern portico of the Administration Building; and upon the grounds and the broad boulevards around it seats were provided for the people.

At the hour set for the commencement of the exercises a great audience, variously estimated at from three hundred to four hundred thousand persons, was assembled.

The National Hymn, America, was first in order; a prayer followed, and short speeches from various distinguished orators. Then the Hymn of the Nationality, dedicating the land to Man, to Freedom and to God, was reverently sung by the assembled thousands; and when its final stanza welcoming the return of peace was finished, Philip Oram came forward and was greeted with such manifestations of respect, love and admiration, as few men have ever received.

When the ovation ceased, he began his address, stating his subject to be, "Certain Eventful Fourths of July."

I venture at the risk of being considered tedious to give some extracts from this speech.

He called attention to the work set before the pilgrim fathers, which he defined to be "The reclaiming of a continent from primitive barbarism, and the founding therein of a government upon principles of justice, morality and equality inherent in the race."

He then spoke of the first notable Fourth of July, and graphically described it thus:

"On the fourth of July, 1776, these people took the first decisive step toward the accomplishment of these objects.

"On that day their delegates signed that great charter of universal liberty, the Declaration of American Independence; a document far transcending in its clear and distinct enunciation of the inherent nobility and equal rights of man, the famous Magna Charta of England, forced by her lords from King John at the point of the sword on the memorable field of Runnymede.

"In that immortal document, Thomas Jefferson, a name never to be forgotten, declared in language brief and sententious, as became the occasion, yet elegant, keen, and polished as a Damascan blade, these axioms as fundamental principles of all true government: 'That all men are created equal, endowed by their Creator with certain inalienable rights, among which are life, liberty and the pursuit of happiness; that to secure these rights governments are instituted among men, deriving their just powers from the consent of the governed; that whenever any form of government becomes destructive of these ends it is the right of the people to alter or abolish it.'

"In the Declaration, Jefferson but formulated the sentiments of the people, evolved by long years of upward growth; sentiments for whose free expression they had sought these western wilds, by which they had been cheered and encouraged amid the difficulties and dangers of a frontier life, and through the realization of which alone they expected to secure the blessings of liberty to themselves and their posterity. His was the task, the mighty task, to shape these glorious ideas, to embody in living language such as they should recognize, these aspirations of the masses; theirs it was to accept and defend them with their best blood and their best treasure."

He then spoke of the apparent uncertainty of the result of the conflict with the Mother Country, "whose troops then mustered in every clime, and whose fleets swept proudly and victoriously over every ocean under heaven.

"But there were prophets in those days when it seemed hard to prophesy. Hearken to the voice of John Adams, the old man eloquent, on all occasions, among the people and in the halls of congress, the earnest advocate and able defender of the Declaration. Permeated with the faith of a believer in an overruling Providence which would give victory to a just cause, he thus pledged his support to the Declaration, and expressed his conviction that it would ultimately prevail: 'I am well aware of the toil and blood and treasure that it will cost to maintain this Declaration, and support and defend these states, yet through all the gloom of the present I can see the rays of ravishing light and glory. I can see that the end is worth more than all the means, and that posterity will triumph in this day's transaction.'

"The oracle which thus spoke was inspired by the Genius of Liberty, and its utterance was divine.

"The issue was in fact no longer doubtful. England, with all her strength, her savage allies, and her wealth of resources, was no match for arms nerved and breasts mailed by principles such as these.

"The sympathies of the world were with the people, and the people of that day were true to themselves, true to their leaders and true to the Declaration.

"God grant that in all future ages; in all eventful

crises; in all questions of public duty, principle and honor, the people of these United States may stand as stood their fathers, steadfastly true to the doctrines of that Declaration, which is the noblest expression of the fundamental principles of civil right, civil equality, and civil government, ever vouchsafed to any people." . . . . . .

"The conflict was over; the victory was won and the new nation took its place among the powers of the earth.

"Fifty years more had passed, and the summer's sun of the fourth of July, 1826, looked down on a changed people and a changed land. Population had increased, and prosperity smiled upon all. A number of new states had added fresh stars to the lately arisen constellation; and the free institutions which the wise forethought of our revolutionary ancestors had provided had made America already the bourne to which the eyes of the oppressed and downtrodden of all nations involuntarily turned as to a sweet and long desired haven of rest.

"Peace spread her angel wings over this broad domain, and the ravages of war had long since been obliterated by her busy hands. The battle field, once bristling with armed men, was now covered with the serried ranks of the yielding grain; the soil, once trampled by the hurrying feet of the pursuer and the pursued, now grew green under the easy tread of the quiet cattle, and the village bell, whose peal had often called the citizens to arms, now summoned them weekly to peaceful prayers, and on other days was answered by the glad voices of children on their way to school.

"Trade flourished, and the ocean's wide expanse was no longer reddened by the murderous broadsides of contending ships; but instead, over its restless bosom sped a multitude of white-winged merchant vessels, laden with the rich products of the new world, and bearing them to the busy marts and populous cities of the old, in safety and security.

"A generation, too, had passed away, and been succeeded by another. The heroes of revolutionary conflicts, the masters of the sword and pen, were mostly gone; and their children, and their children's children filled the land. Washington was dead; Henry was dead; Franklin was numbered with his fathers. Jefferson, the author, and Adams, the defender of the Declaration, alone remained, old men and full of honors.

"And now on this day, this fiftieth anniversary of its publication, in the divine fitness of things, came to both of them, that call appointed once to all mankind, the call to die.

"In His wisdom, God had chosen upon that day to take into His guardian keeping the spirits of those two grand old patriots, so intimately connected with its earliest history. And He sent the summons to them, not in loneliness and exile, not amid civil strife and commotion, but quietly and peacefully at home surrounded by friends and dear ones.

"Not unto Washington was this boon granted. Like David of old he had been a man of blood; he had borne the sword and was not permitted to share in this further dedication of the day to Liberty. To Jefferson and to Adams alone, this immortality was fitly given.

"And the summons found them ready. Life to them had been a busy scene; full of cares, of trials and responsibilities. In a tremendous conflict they had borne the heat and burden of the day; in a great and patriotic purpose they had been successful beyond their highest anticipations. Their best years and their best strength had been spent in the service of their fellow men; and in that service they had gained the brightest laurels ever won, the respect, the reverence and gratitude of all mankind, and they were ready now to close the scene, leaving behind them their actions, and their memories, as the best legacy they could bequeath to posterity.

"And so on this, the fiftieth anniversary of their glorious and long-cherished work, these patriots breathed their last; while all around them the annual rejoicings of a free and ransomed people swelled on every breeze, and were borne like glad music to their dying chambers, and soothed their fading senses to their last repose.

"Glorious consummation! Blessed privilege! to behold so great a work so well accomplished; and then in ripe old age, on such a day, to yield back calmly a wellspent life to the source from whence it came.

"Thus again was the day ennobled; thus again was the date engraven on the pages of our National History.

"Thirty-seven years more had passed, and the Nation had grown to manhood. It boasted proudly of its intelligence, of its prosperity, of its strength, and of its liberty; but, alas! it had not walked in the straight path of rectitude.

"The principle of equality, and the inalienable right to life, liberty, and the pursuit of happiness, affirmed in its great bill of rights as belonging to all men, had been denied to certain classes of its people; and an attempt had been made to extend, perpetuate and legalize this wrong.

"High Heaven in its wise counsels determined to purify the Nation and restore it to the paths of truth and right by awful and well-remembered punishment.

For three long years, the chastisement of Almighty God had fallen upon it; and compelled it finally to confess its sin against these eternal principles of justice, and promise reparation.

"But that covenant could be sealed only in blood; and

the sword of Omnipotence and Atonement smote fiercely
and effectually over all the land, on that fourth day of
July, 1863.

"In the East, upon that day, a blood-stained, stricken
field of fight—the field of Gettysburg—lifted its hecatomb
of human sacrifice to heaven in mute appeal for mercy;
while throughout the wide land was heard the voice of
lamentation, Rachel again mourning for her children, and
refusing to be comforted because they were not.

"In the West, upon that day, the Mississippi was un·
fettered, and the Confederacy, founded on human slavery,
was cleft in twain, and received a mortal wound.

"Thus, once more in the far-reaching dispensation
of Providence, was this day dedicated to Freedom's holy
cause.".............. ....

"It has been customary on this anniversary to boast-
fully recount the advancement in material prosperity
among us; to point with pride, as evidence of our National greatness, to this mighty continent we have reclaimed; in whose vast extent Europe could be hidden,
in whose abundant wealth the Orient finds a rival; and to
the countless cities, towns and villages dotted all over it,
bound together in action by the sinews of steel that stretch
along the ground, and connected in thought by the
nerves of iron that hang above their track.

"We forget that these but constitute the circumstances, the abodes, and dwelling places of the people;
and that mere outward power, increase in wealth, and vast
extent of territory, are not sufficient grounds on which to
predicate the true greatness, permanence and happiness of
a nation; but that these must have their sure founda-
tions in the intelligence, virtue, good sense and sound
morality of the people themselves."................

"Only the assertion of some great right, only the

triumph of some grand principle, or some special act of Providence emphasizing and approving such, have immortalized the sacred anniversaries just mentioned.

"Seventy-three years more have passed since that last great struggle for freedom reached its culmination on the fields of Gettysburg and Vicksburg, and to-day we stand in the sunlight of an anniversary which we have reason to believe will be as memorable as any of the others.

"I thank God that to-day we are as a nation constitutionally guaranteed in all the rights spoken of in the Declaration.

"I thank Him that all men have in fact, from this day onward, an equal opportunity to enjoy life, liberty, and happiness, under a broader and a truer exposition of these rights than has hitherto been accorded them.

"I thank Him that the slavery of poor and rich; the former to the latter, and the latter to mammon, has to-day been done away with; that hereafter intelligence, energy and skill will find approval, and brainless ostentation and pretension will have no followers; that the talent of the land will be employed, hereafter, not in pursuit of riches or of fame, but of that higher honor, gained in the service of humanity and its common brotherhood.

"I realize, my Fellow Citizens, that toil, thought, patience and prayerful earnestness must have their day before we reach the full fruition of those principles which our fathers planted in this soil, and which we, for the first time have fully recognized; but I see with the patriot Adams, 'that the end is worth more than all the means and that posterity will triumph in this day's transaction.'

"The proclamation just made will have an influence on mankind second only to the words of Holy Writ.

"Throughout the civilized world, the principles it legalizes will sink deep down in every human heart, giving to each man ready syllable for emotions that have often swelled within his bosom, and kindling fires that can never be extinguished; but which will spread and speedily be felt, either as the peaceful element which cheers and warms and comforts, or as the devouring flame which consumes and burns, until that time shall come when every man throughout the globe shall in fact have equal opportunity afforded him to enjoy life, liberty and happiness, and to become a member of the universal brotherhood of man.

"My Fellow Citizens, we have glanced at the early history of the Declaration; we have traced our present advancement largely to the adoption of its truths; we have dwelt upon their wonderful expansion recognized to-day. We have tried to estimate our own responsibilities; it remains now only for us in conclusion, and by way of benediction, to give utterance to that hope for the future which springs unbidden to the lips of every true American on this, the nation's birthday.

"May, then, our population swell; may our enterprise increase; may our knowledge extend. May the future be even brighter than the present; may Freedom ever be a dweller in our borders; may the principles of the Declaration ever be cherished in American hearts; and may the glad Angel of Peace never more flee affrighted from our land.

"May the Latin motto of one of our oldest states, 'Qui transtulit, sustinet' He who transplanted will sustain, ever be true; may our national domain and greatness be hereafter bounded only by the confines and resources of this vast and fertile continent; and may our course in the future and our progress among the nations be like that of yon bright sun as it moves to its place in the zenith; the herald of increasing light, and joy, and beauty; the harbinger of peace, and plenty, and prosperity; no lurid, fitful, and quick-fading meteor, rendering darkness more appalling by its transient splendor; but a glorious and day-bringing luminary, governed by established and enduring laws, attracting, vivifying and enriching all by the golden rays of heavenly effulgence which it sheds upon them."

The speech was ended, the public exercises were over, and the great crowds of people slowly and thoughtfully dispersed; while hundreds of workmen cleared the grounds of obstacles, and prepared them for the beauties of the night's display.

All the afternoon the voices of the rejoicing people were heard throughout the city; and processions of men and women, themselves singing, or headed by bands of music, passed through the streets.

All the parks were filled with people making merry over their lunches, and with children singing songs, or playing upon the greensward.

Rudeness, or inebriety, were nowhere to be seen; but everywhere a contented, happy and joyous people; glad that the threatened evils of war had passed away, and that their victory had been won, not by the sword, but by the universal concord of public opinion.

I returned to my lodgings and thought upon the ceremonial of the evening, in which Clothilde and myself were to be the chief actors; by which we two, such firm friends in childhood, and in after years so strangely met and made known to one another, were to be united in the indissoluble bond of holy matrimony.

The great dome of the Administration Building swung grandly in the air, and as I sat musing at my window, I saw again upon its summit the figure of John Harvey, resting upon his sword and gazing intently to the eastward.

His had been a strange history. The discoverer of boundless wealth and wonderful secrets in Nature; the creator of a new world of life, hope, and enterprise; the arbiter of the destinies of millions of his fellow men; the imperious commander who resented a hostile shot by the destruction of his most formidable adversaries; he had at last fallen a victim to the ambition, the greed, and selfishness of the Money Power, then omnipotent in the world.

Could he have lived till to-day, and have seen that Power receive its death wound in the legalization of the principles he had maintained; could he have moved among the people whom he loved and observed their prosperity, what good cause for righteous exaltation, what happiness and peace would justly have been his.

Could he have seen his daughter honored as his child; could he have been by her as she stood before the altar and placed her hand in mine, knowing that I, too, had done service for the land he cherished, and judging me worthy of the boon he gave me, how great would have been his joy and how inexpressible the delight to us. But this happiness was denied us.

His story would be read by millions; it was now well known; immortality would crown his name; it was now on many lips; but his body lay in the weird, awful tomb in the crypt below that mighty dome, and his soul was with his Creator, who alone knew the thoughts that to-day moved its hidden depths.

Another, her chosen godfather, would this evening stand beside that daughter, while she plighted her troth and gave her heart to me, her childhood's lover.

Though the eyes of an admiring concourse would be on her; though a great people would reverence her; yet no father's or mother's, no sister's or brother's care would attend her at this momentous hour.

A tempest of such thoughts rushed through my mind. I recognized the lonely sublimity of her position, and in the silence of my room I registered a vow to heaven, which I have ever kept, that to life's end I would be worthy of the confidence reposed in me; that I would be to her, lover, husband, brother, friend, from this time onward, aye through the silent ages of eternity in which we should dwell together.

Evening came on apace, and Clothilde and I met in the great hall of the Parliament. It was beautifully decorated, and filled with a distinguished and brilliant gathering.

The councilors were there in session; governors, and senators and ambassadors and their wives and daughters were present. All the beauty, grace and manhood of the capital, all the glory and intelligence of the nation were represented.

The high ceremonies of the solemn compact followed; and through it all I had but one thought, and that was love for the queenly woman at my side, and tender solicitude for her future welfare and happiness.

And she, with her radiant beauty, seemed in every movement and in every word and glance to think but of me, and to rejoice in publicly attesting her devotion.

The ceremony was over, and for an hour we received our friends in the assembly hall. It was a joyous day, and all felt joyous. Good wishes were showered on us; short, graceful speeches were made to us by distinguished persons; young girls presented flowers; and when we left to take our carriage, we walked beneath overhanging arches, and past mossy banks, which prevented us from seeing the full wonders of the night's display.

When we reached the street, we looked around; and all the Administration Square was hung with evergreens and choicest flowers, their perfumes breathing out sweetly on the balmy air.

The boulevards were bathed in a flood of light of various colors delicately shaded into one another; music pervaded the atmosphere, and numerous birds concealed in cages, and awakened by the light, lent their voices to the enchantment. The waters of the fountains shone with a thousand changing colors; sparkling like diamonds, then ruddy as rubies, or yellow like gold, or green like emerald.

The Administration Building had a beauty all its own; millions of tiny lamps, strung together like pearls and shedding a silvery light, covered it from foundation to summit; all the doorways, windows, arches, cornices, pillars, entablatures and sculptured figures were thus plainly outlined.

We looked upward toward its dome and in a halo of light on its summit, saw the statue of John Harvey; the face and lineaments plainly revealed in the flood of golden radiance enveloping the whole figure as with an aureole.

Clothilde's eyes as she turned to me were filled with tears, but they were happy tears; the child rejoiced in the honor done by a grateful people to a father's memory.

We made our way toward our home amid a multitude who welcomed us on every hand with demonstrations of respect, gratitude, and affection.

Our separate histories were finished, and our life union was begun.

So also was it with our country; its separate interests were united, and its history of joint effort had commenced.

State by state took advantage of the privileges afforded by the amendments and joined the Nationalistic system; until to-day it is the only one known throughout the

Union; and peace, prosperity, and happiness have universally attended its adoption.

Clothilde and I lived quietly and joyfully within Neuropolis, which had been the scene of our meeting, courtship and marriage.

Other cities came into prominence; the Government of the United Nationalistic System was established in another; but none seemed to us so fair, so joyous, and so homelike, as that associated with our early memories.

Twenty-four years later, Clothilde and myself, with John Paul, St. John, and Philip Oram, Mr. Beyresen having gone to his long home and the latter having been selected in his place, stood again before the tomb of John Harvey; our errand being to perform his bidding, and destroy whatever he had not destroyed, and to do honor to his memory while we had the opportunity.

Again the solemn music heralded our approach; again the dread mystery of the dead in his sepulchral chamber fell upon us; again I stood by Clothilde's side, she more womanly and more beautiful than ever; again I took the key from her hand and turned the fateful lock; but this time when the aperture opened no evidence appeared of any writing hidden there.

Then I closed it, and we left the chamber, while weird music for the last time sounded from the choir, seeming to tell us, as the doors shut silently behind us, that John Harvey's tomb was not accessible again to mortal man.

The End.